Fractured

To Amanda,

Great to meet you at
the State Library of WA.

Fractured

DAWN BARKER

Dawn Barker
Oct '14 x.

hachette
AUSTRALIA

To Will – for never doubting

Fractured has been written with the encouragement of Queensland Writers Centre (QWC). Dawn Barker participated in the 2010 QWC/Hachette Australia Manuscript Development Program, which received funding from the Queensland Government through Arts Queensland.

Published in Australia and New Zealand in 2013
by Hachette Australia
(an imprint of Hachette Australia Pty Limited)
Level 17, 207 Kent Street, Sydney NSW 2000
www.hachette.com.au

10 9 8 7 6 5 4 3 2 1

National Library of Australia
Cataloguing-in-Publication data:

Barker, Dawn
Fractured / Dawn Barker

978 0 7336 2985 3 (pbk.)

A823.4

Cover design by Christabella Designs
Cover image reproduced with permission from Getty Images
Author photo copyright © David Phillips
Text design by Bookhouse, Sydney
Typeset in 12.25/15.5 pt Adobe Garamond Pro
Printed and bound in Australia by Griffin Press, Adelaide, an Accredited ISO AS/NZS 14001:2009 Environmental Management System printer

MIX
Paper from
responsible sources
FSC® C009448
www.fsc.org

The paper this book is printed on is certified against the Forest Stewardship Council® Standards. Griffin Press holds FSC chain of custody certification SGS-COC-005088. FSC promotes environmentally responsible, socially beneficial and economically viable management of the world's forests.

PROLOGUE

The room is bare except for a metal-framed bed and a mustard-coloured plastic chair. She lies still. Her skin itches under the stiff sheets and the coarse blue blanket. Her pillow is too high, too firm, and she can feel the holes picked out of the foam by the others who have lain here before her. The mattress groans as she turns to ease the ache in her hip. Through the grimy window to her right she sees the concrete courtyard, empty except for a cracked terracotta pot holding a thin, twiggy plant mulched in cigarette butts.

It's getting dark. She glances at her left wrist. Her gold watch, an anniversary present, is missing. She looks at her wedding ring, loose on her finger, and instinctively makes a fist, her uncut nails digging into her palm. No one has told her why she is here in this lonely room.

She is too afraid to ask.

CHAPTER ONE

That day

Monday, 14 September 2009
8.40 A.M.

Tony's footsteps echoed as he hurried across the underground car park and into the lift. Inside, he repeatedly pressed the button for the top floor of the building until the doors slid closed, then looked at his watch. He hated being late, but today there was nothing he could do about it. His stomach lurched as the lift started to move. As soon as the doors began to open, he squeezed though the gap, ran out onto the landing and through the glass doors of the office.

'Morning, Tony,' said Julie from behind the reception desk.

'Morning. Have they started yet?'

'Not yet. They're waiting for you.'

'Great, thanks,' he said over his shoulder. He was already halfway down the carpeted corridor, and could see through the glass walls of the conference room that his team and the clients were already inside, chatting and eating pastries and croissants from a platter on the table. He took a deep breath then pushed open the door.

'Sorry,' he said, smiling. 'Traffic was terrible.'

There was a general murmur of understanding as he took off his suit jacket and hung it on the back of the black leather chair at the head of the table. As he sat down he noticed the crumpled creases between the buttons on his shirt that he had forgotten to iron that morning. He smoothed down the material with his hand and tucked it tighter into his waistband, then leaned over to pour himself some coffee from the plunger on the table. Everyone seemed

happy to keep chatting as he took a few more deep breaths to settle
his nerves. He tried to tell himself it was just the presentation that
was making him anxious, but he knew that wasn't the real reason.

Danielle, one of the copywriters, pushed the milk and sugar
closer to him and smiled. 'You getting any sleep yet?'

He smiled back and pointed at his eyes. 'Not much . . . Can't
you tell?'

She wrinkled up her face and put her hands on her pregnant
belly. 'I've got all that to look forward to.'

'It's all worth it – or so they keep telling me.' He unzipped
his laptop bag. As he started to take out his computer, his phone
rang. He sighed, wishing he'd switched it off. He put his bag back
on the table then took his phone out of his pocket and glanced
at the screen. It was his mum. He groaned. Why was she calling?
She should be at the house by now. He hesitated for a moment,
then stood up and walked towards the door. 'Sorry, I need to get
this. I'll be right back.'

He stepped outside and let the door swing closed behind him,
then answered the call. 'Mum? What's wrong?'

'Hi. Don't worry, nothing's wrong. Sorry to call you at work,
but I've just arrived and Anna's not home. The door's locked. Was
she going out?'

His heart began to beat faster. 'Out? No. She was still in bed
when I left. She knew you were coming round.'

'That's OK. I'm a bit late. She probably waited then went to
the shops.'

'Is her car there?'

'Hold on . . . No, I can't see it. Maybe she forgot I was coming.'

'Have you called her mobile?'

'Yes, but it's ringing out. She'll have gone to get milk or something. She won't be long, I'm sure. Don't worry, I'll wait for a bit.'

He paused. What his mum said made perfect sense, and on
any other day he'd agree with her, but something told him that he
should be worried. He was standing only a few metres away from
the small office kitchen where three people were talking while the

kettle boiled. He walked back along the corridor, past the reception desk and out of the office. He paced around the landing near the lifts and started to talk again, quieter this time. 'They should be there. Something's not right . . .'

'What do you mean? Is it Jack?'

Tony was hot, and his chest felt tight. He pulled at the neck of his shirt. 'I don't know.' He cleared his throat; he needed some water. 'I just don't understand why they're not there, that's all. Jack was sleeping when I left, and Anna was still in bed.'

He ran his left hand through his thick, dark hair then rubbed the back of his neck. He looked towards the conference room. Everyone was waiting for him. They'd been preparing for this meeting for weeks; he needed to get back in there. He felt a surge of irritation. Anna hadn't left the house all weekend. Why would she go out now?

'Anthony?'

He realised the phone was trembling in his hand. He looked down at the polished black leather of his shoes. He could hear the muffled laughter and chatter coming from behind the glass doors, and the faint buzz on the end of the phone as his mum waited for him to explain.

'Sorry, it's just that Anna hasn't been getting much sleep, she's been really tired. And Jack – he's been difficult.'

He closed his eyes and pictured Anna lying in bed this morning, exhausted. She had asked him to stay with her, but he couldn't. Was that why she'd gone out, to show him that she'd been serious about not wanting his mum to come over? He took a step back towards the meeting, then stopped and shook his head. Anna wasn't like that. There was something else going on; he had to go home.

'Mum, stay there. I'll be back as soon as I can.'

'No, don't be silly, there's no need —'

'I'm leaving now. I won't be long.' He ended the call before she could argue and hurried back to the conference room.

Danielle's eyes widened as he grabbed his bag and jacket. 'What are you doing?' she whispered, leaning towards him.

'I have to go – something's come up. I'm sorry.'

'But —'

'You can handle it. The presentation's all ready to go.' He looked up: everyone was watching him. He knew his workmates were alarmed; he rarely missed a day of work and would never walk out without a good reason. The clients deserved an explanation but he didn't know what to say. He didn't really understand it himself; something just told him that he had to find Anna. He cleared his throat, looked around the room again, then turned and quickly walked out.

The lift wasn't waiting when he reached the lobby, so he wrenched open the heavy fire door and clattered down endless flights of concrete stairs to the car park. He ran towards his silver four-wheel drive, opened the door and climbed in. When he turned the key in the ignition the CD he had been listening to on the way to work roared around him. He hit the volume button to turn it off; he had to concentrate. His mind was flitting around, thinking of all the possibilities, but he told himself to take it one step at a time.

Put your seatbelt on, put the car into gear, release the handbrake, press the pedal, drive. Slowly.

*   *   *

When Tony pulled up at his house, its familiarity reassured him. The semi-detached bungalow stood where it always had, pressing against its neighbour for support. He and Anna had bought it a few years ago, just after their engagement. Their half was painted creamy white; the neighbour's half was beige. Birds of paradise flowers nodded their heads at him over the fence. The lemon tree they had planted in the front garden when they moved in was covered in waxy white flowers, and the passionfruit vine clung to the green trellis around the front door with thin, curly fingers. A few months ago Anna had ceremoniously picked the only passionfruit that had ever grown on it and served it with vanilla bean ice-cream; they had agreed that it was the best dessert they had ever eaten.

He stepped out of the car and looked up and down the street. Cars still drove past, builders still hammered at the house opposite, and the neighbour's retriever still barked at the birds pecking the patchy grass verge. He shook his head and his heart rate began to settle. He was being silly: there was no doubt a simple explanation for Anna and Jack not being here.

His mum, Ursula, waved from the driver's seat of her blue station wagon, where she sat reading the paper with the door open to let in the early spring breeze. She took off her reading glasses and let them dangle from the cord around her neck, folded the paper and placed it on the passenger seat, then picked up her black handbag.

'I couldn't find a key,' she said, as she stepped out and locked the car door.

'Sorry, it's round the back.'

'I'm sure everything's fine, Anthony. One thing I learned from raising you and your sister is that there's always a simple explanation for things – it's never as bad as you think.'

'You're right, I know . . .'

'Well, come on then.'

He took a deep breath and walked up the path to the front door. Turning his key in the lock, he pushed open the door, jumping at the jingle of the string of bells hanging on the back of it. Anna's best friend Emily had bought them for her as a present from some yoga retreat in India. The heels of Tony's work shoes made the same hollow noise they always did on the blackbutt floorboards, before being muffled by the runner that stretched down the length of the narrow hallway. The bedrooms were off to the left, but he headed straight for the kitchen and living area at the back of the house.

'Anna?' He stood in the kitchen and looked across the living room and through the French doors to the small back garden. Their Staffordshire terrier, Jessie, gazed hopefully through the glass, her tongue lolling and tail wagging.

'She must have gone out, Anthony,' Ursula said, walking up behind him. 'I've checked the bedrooms – she's not here.'

'But she knew you were coming round.' He rubbed his face, trying to think clearly. It didn't add up.

'Well, maybe she's gone to the shops to get something. Is this hers?' Ursula picked up a mobile phone from the kitchen counter.

He nodded, staring at it. 'She never goes out without her phone.' He looked at his mum, silently pleading with her to keep reassuring him.

'It's only a phone, it doesn't mean anything. Has she taken her bag?'

Tony glanced around the kitchen, then went into the living area, lifted up the sofa cushions and bent down to check under the coffee table, even though he could see that it wasn't there. 'Looks like it.' If she had her bag, then she had her purse; his mum was right, she must have gone to the shops.

'We'll just wait a bit. I'll put the kettle on.' Ursula filled the kettle, then opened the cupboard. She rummaged around for a moment before looking at the dishwasher. 'Did you put this on before you went to work?'

He tried to remember, but there were so many other memories from that morning crowding his thoughts. 'Um . . . I don't think so.'

'Well, she hasn't been gone long then – it's still running.' Ursula opened the door. The rush of water paused as she reached through the steam and took out two mugs.

He stood still as he watched her take them to the sink to rinse. Where the hell was Anna? She definitely hadn't said she was going out; she hadn't said much at all. That didn't mean anything though, did it? She was an adult, she didn't have to tell him insignificant details. She must have gone to the shops but forgotten her phone and so couldn't tell Ursula. But she wouldn't go far; Jack must be due for another feed soon and Anna didn't like breastfeeding in public.

While Ursula made the tea, he walked back down the hall to Jack's room. It looked the same as it had this morning, except that Jack was no longer lying asleep in his cot. The blinds were still drawn and his blankets were ruffled. He left and went into his and Anna's bedroom. Anna had tidied up before she left: the bed was made and the dirty laundry was gone from the floor. That was a good sign. But then he noticed the cup of tea he'd made her this morning sitting untouched on the bedside table, the slick sheen of congealed milk floating on top. It was still full; she hadn't even taken a sip. His eyes filled with tears. Why hadn't she drunk the tea?

He glanced down at the bedside table to the silver photo frame that held their wedding picture. They looked so young: was it really only two years ago? He remembered Anna's smile when she walked down the aisle towards him, her knuckles white as she gripped her bouquet of pink lilies. She had looked like a princess. He had tried to hide his own tears as they exchanged vows, but later, when they sneaked away from the dancing for some time together, she had teased him for crying. They had been happy.

Tony admonished himself for thinking in the past tense. They were *still* happy.

He picked up the frame. In the corner, Anna had wedged a photo taken on the day they brought Jack home from the hospital, less than six weeks ago. Tony had his arm around her and, between them, she held Jack, wrapped up in a white cotton blanket, fast asleep. They were smiling, but it was different from the grins of excitement and anticipation of the newlyweds in the main photo. These were the smiles of brand-new parents, full of pride but tinged with uncertainty. He blinked several times, put the frame back down. There was nothing in here to tell him where she was. He walked quickly back to the front door and opened it again; the pram was gone from the porch.

Closing the door, he stood inside with his hands in his pockets. He thought back to that morning. He had lifted Jack out of bed, given him a bottle of breast milk, then put him down again. He'd made Anna some tea and left it on the bedside table next to her. He *had* told Anna that his mum was coming over; she hadn't been happy about it but she definitely knew. And she also knew that Tony would be back in a few hours. So where had she gone?

Everything looked exactly as it should. But Anna and Jack weren't here.

CHAPTER TWO

That day

11 A.M.

Ursula finished reading the newspaper for the second time, then rummaged through the pile of magazines on the shelf under the coffee table. She picked up a surfing magazine and flicked through it, watching Tony from the corner of her eye. He sat on a stool at the kitchen bench with his computer open, tapping the mouse pad every so often. He picked up his phone, checked it was still connected to the charger, then put it down next to the laptop.

She tossed the magazine onto the table and stretched her arms above her head. She yawned loudly, then stood up. 'I might go and get us some lunch,' she said.

Her words seemed to break Tony's trance. He closed his laptop, then scraped the metal legs of his stool back along the floor as he stood up. He reached for his car keys. 'Don't get me anything. I'm going to go and look for them.'

'Where will you go? They could be anywhere.'

'I don't know, but I can't just sit here and wait any more. Can you stay here in case Anna comes back? I won't be long. I'm just going to have a drive around.'

Ursula nodded. She was getting worried now too. 'OK. I'll call you if I hear anything.'

She watched Tony leave. As soon as the sound of his car faded, she called Jim. 'Hi, love, not interrupting anything, am I?'

'No, it's fine, just having a cuppa. One of the apprentices didn't bother showing up today so it's been a bloody nightmare, but I'm back in the office now. What's going on?'

She filled him in.

'That doesn't sound like Anna,' Jim said.

'I know, it's strange.' She gazed at the grinning monkeys and giraffes on the fabric of the bouncer chair in the corner of the living room. It had been her and Jim's gift at the baby shower; Anna had squealed when she saw it, as excited as any expectant mother. She had been surprised at Tony's comment today that Anna had been finding Jack difficult; he always seemed so settled, and Anna was so capable. She looked away. 'I wouldn't be so worried, but Anthony's really stressed. It's like there's something he's not telling me.'

'She wouldn't have left him, would she?'

'No, of course not! She wouldn't just walk out; you know how good they are together.' Ursula paused and looked out of the window. 'Though God knows it's hard with a new baby. I told him he should have taken some time off instead of going back to work the minute she got out of hospital.'

'Don't go on at him again about that.'

'I'm not!'

'She'll be fine; they've probably just had a fight about something.'

She sighed. Sometimes she wished Jim would take things more seriously. He always made light of even the worst situation. Ursula knew that this was one of the ways they balanced each other, but carrying the burden of worry for the entire family sometimes wore her down. 'I'll let you get back to work. I'm sure it's nothing. I'll call Lisa, just in case Anna pops into her shop or something. She's been dying to see Jack again – maybe . . . Anyway, I'll call you later.'

Ursula put the phone down. She switched on the television, but couldn't concentrate. She remembered the first time that Tony had taken Anna home to meet them. It was Lisa's twenty-first birthday, almost six years ago now. They had met at the races a few months earlier; Tony had been at a work function, while Anna was celebrating the end of her teacher training with friends. Ursula had watched them together at the party and known that night that they would marry. No, Anna wouldn't walk out on Tony.

Besides, if she wasn't coming back, she would have taken clothes and toiletries for her and Jack, but she hadn't. No, there must be another explanation.

She stood up and walked into the kitchen. She rechecked the room: no bag, no keys. She opened the drawers and the cupboards but everything looked the same as it always did. She switched the kettle on again and opened the fridge to find the milk. As she went to close the door, she hesitated. On the top shelf, four baby bottles full of milk lay in a row, their teats covered with clear plastic lids. She reached out and picked one up. She curled her palm around it, then opened the lid and squeezed some of the milk onto her wrist: it wasn't chilled yet. Anna had made these bottles up this morning, before she went out. They were for Jack.

Anna would be back soon.

*   *   *

Tony felt better once he was out of the house. Pretending not to notice his mum as she pretended not to watch him had made him even more restless. He drove along the streets around the house, then turned onto the main road that ran down to the beach. It was a while since he'd been at home on a weekday; he was surprised at how quiet the traffic was. The midday sun was high above him, and even though it wasn't really swimming weather, backpackers and tourists were baking themselves on multicoloured towels along the beach. Anna hated the sun: it seared her fair skin and gave her freckles. She wouldn't be on the beach.

He indicated right, towards the city, then flicked the indicator off again. Anna never drove to the city: she always caught the train so she wouldn't have to find somewhere to park. He kept driving straight ahead, scanning the roads for Anna's car. Every time he saw a black hatchback he held his breath, then deflated when he realised that it wasn't hers.

Parking at the local shops, he walked towards Anna's favourite bookshop. She used to spend hours in there; perhaps she had lost track of time? She was probably sitting at one of the tables with a coffee reading some huge novel while Jack slept in the pram next to her. She'd laugh at Tony for being so worried. He paused at the doorway, giving himself another moment of hope. If they weren't inside, it would be another victory to the choking, viscous fear that was rising in his chest, his throat, his mouth. He breathed in: the air was fresh. He swallowed, told himself not to be so silly, then walked into the store. But Anna and Jack weren't at any of the small tables, or among the shelves, or in the children's section at the back.

They weren't here.

Back out on the street, he walked faster, methodically checking every shop and cafe, trying to ignore the uneasiness that became stronger with each step. He headed across the road to the beach-front and marched through the playground in the park, glancing involuntarily in every pram, listening carefully for Anna's laugh or Jack's cry. Crossing back to the shops, he began to jog. Perhaps she was walking and they were going round the same circuit, constantly missing each other. If he sped up, he'd catch her. He passed the same row of shops again, faster, frantic now, his feet starting to swell and rub against his work shoes. But there was still no sign of them.

He ended up back at the bookshop. He wiped the sweat from his forehead and forced himself to sit down and have a coffee, to think, to be logical. It wasn't like him to panic; it wouldn't help. He checked his phone again: there were no missed calls and it hadn't run out of power. He tried to swallow down the gnarled twist of anxiety rising in his chest.

Anna and Jack had disappeared.

He stared at the swirls on top of his coffee, which he supposed were meant to look like some sort of leaf. He ripped open a brown paper sachet of raw sugar and dumped it into the centre of the cup, watching the crystals slowly sink, then finally collapse and submerge, leaving a gaping hole in the middle of the intricate pattern. Blinking hard, he picked up the teaspoon and began to stir. He already had a headache, so the caffeine probably wasn't a good idea, but fatigue and a sense of inevitability were starting to weigh him down. Shaking his head, he dropped his spoon on the table with a clang. He couldn't slow down. He had to find them.

He looked at his phone again but there were still no messages. He scrolled through his numbers until he found Emily's. Emily and Anna spoke almost every day, they had grown up together, and until Anna went on maternity leave they had worked together. If Anna had been planning anything, Emily would know. He dialled the number, annoyed with himself; he should have called her sooner.

She answered on the third ring with a cheery, 'Hi Tony!'

'Hey, Emily. Sorry to bother you at work. Can you talk?'

'Yeah, of course. I'm just walking to the staffroom – thank God it's lunchtime, the kids have been a nightmare today. There's only so many hours I can spend teaching five-year-olds about the letter M. How are you?'

He felt some of the tension in his shoulders slacken as he listened to Emily's chirpy voice. His relief only lasted a few moments, though, as he realised that he hadn't heard Anna speak like that for weeks. She used to sound like Emily did now – bright, excited, enthusiastic – but lately she'd been so quiet and distracted. He took a deep breath.

'I'm good, thanks. Um . . . it's probably nothing, but have you heard from Anna today?'

'No, I haven't spoken to her since last week. Why?'

'I'm sure everything's fine. It's just that Mum was coming round to see her and Jack this morning, but she's not here, and I can't find her. They've disappeared.'

'She's probably just taken Jack for a walk. She must have lost track of time.'

Tony nodded, eager to be reassured. Emily was right. She didn't sound worried at all, and she was probably the only person who knew Anna as well as he did. In the background he could hear schoolchildren chattering and squealing, and the trample of little footsteps running down a corridor. It all sounded so normal, and that meant there had to be a reasonable explanation for this. 'Yeah, you're right. Thanks. Will you let me know if she gets in touch with you?'

'Of course . . . Tony, is everything all right?'

'Yes, yes. It's just not like her, that's all.'

'I know, she never forgets anything, does she? God, remember that spreadsheet of jobs she gave me for your wedding?' Emily laughed. 'But I've read about new mums and baby brain – it's the hormones. When I last spoke to her, she said she was exhausted. I'm sure that's all it is. She was going to call me this week and arrange to bring Jack into work for a visit. The kids can't wait to meet him.'

'Good. Well, if you happen to hear anything . . .'

'I'll tell her to call you straightaway. Don't worry, Tony, she'll be fine!'

He sighed. 'Thanks, I better go. I'll talk to you later.'

He put the phone down on the table and stared at it. What Emily said made perfect sense. Anna was tired; she had just forgotten. She was organising a visit to work to show Jack off to everyone. She wouldn't have said that if she hadn't meant it; Anna always stuck to her commitments. Tony repeated these facts to himself, hoping that if he said them enough times, he would start to believe them.

*   *   *

As he was driving home, a young guy in a sports car pulled out in front of him. Tony swore and slammed the heel of his hand onto the steering wheel to blare his horn. Anger bubbled over.

Why the hell hadn't Anna taken her phone? Then he could call her, she could tell him where she and Jack were, and everything would be OK. Maybe Jack was sick and she'd had to take him to the doctor. But then she would have called him, surely? They would have let her use the phone at the GP's rooms. Maybe her car had broken down and she was stuck somewhere. He should call the hospitals, just in case. Was he being ridiculous? He drove slowly, giving her one last chance to appear before he arrived back home again.

He walked into the house, hoping to hear Anna and his mum chatting. The television was on but only Ursula was there. She looked at him and shook her head. Anna had been gone for over four hours now: he could no longer kid himself that she'd just gone to the shops or for a walk. Without a word to his mum, he opened his laptop, still on the kitchen bench, and searched for the number he wanted. He typed it into his phone, then dialled.

'Yes, hello. My name is Anthony Patton. I need to make a report.' He paused and gulped. 'My wife and baby are missing.'

He heard his mum walk towards him and knew she was trying to catch his eye. He turned his back to her and walked into his bedroom as he answered the operator's questions. What was his name? His date of birth? Anna's full name and date of birth? When had he last seen her? He answered in an even voice, hoping that he was overreacting, hoping that before he'd finished making the report, Anna would walk into the house and ask him what he was doing.

The operator continued, 'Have you checked with her family and friends? Often people turn up —'

'Yes, of course I have!' He clenched his fist around the phone. Did the police think he was stupid? He bowed his head and wiped his eyes with the back of his thumb.

'Are you still there?' the operator said.

Tony cleared his throat. He needed to stay calm. 'Look, she hasn't been well . . . The doctor gave her tablets . . .' He glanced towards the open door, where Ursula stood frowning. He looked away. 'She's taken the car, and the pram, and her bag, but it's just not like her to go out without leaving word. I wouldn't call if I didn't think there was something very wrong.'

The questions kept coming. The operator asked for a description of Jack. He hesitated: how could he describe Jack? He was a tiny baby. Tony tried to picture him, but could only see him as a little bundle in Anna's arms; that was where he always was. When the operator asked what Anna was wearing, he admitted that he hadn't seen her in anything but baggy old pyjamas for days.

His heart pounded, but he forced himself to concentrate on the questions. He could barely hear them over the ringing in his ears, louder and louder as the voice on the end of the phone droned on and on until he was sure his head was going to split open.

'For God's sake, just do something!' he burst out. 'Please find them!' He threw the phone down on the bed and covered his burning face with his hands, trying to catch his breath. Where the hell were they?

'Anthony!' Ursula said from the doorway.

He looked up, shaking. 'They're useless! So many fucking questions! They need to get out there and help me look for them —'

'Anthony, what's going on? What tablets? Why didn't you tell me any of this?'

He fell back onto the bed and looked up at the ceiling, blinking hard. He had tried to rationalise it, tried to find a logical answer, but he couldn't pretend any more. He turned his head to the side and looked at Ursula.

'Something's really wrong, Mum. I know it.'

* * *

Ursula busied herself in the kitchen making cheese on toast even though Tony said he wasn't hungry. She didn't know what else to do or say: her reassurances sounded fake, even to herself. Dread had begun to creep through her, but she couldn't let him see her apprehension. She longed to call Jim again, but she didn't want Tony to know she was worried. And it wasn't fair of her to want support from her husband, when Tony was going through this alone. She had called Lisa again, and Anna's mum, Wendy, but neither of them had heard from Anna. She glanced over at the couch, where Tony now sat in front of the television. The one o'clock news was on, but he wasn't watching it: he held his head in his hands and stared at the floor.

Tony's phone rang and Ursula jumped. He grabbed it from the arm of the couch before it could ring a second time. Ursula held her breath and put her hand to her throat, placing it over the gold crucifix hanging around her neck. Her other hand paused in midair, holding the knife with which she'd been slicing the cheese. Tony hesitated before he spoke and, for a moment, Ursula saw her little boy standing at the top of the skateboarding ramp in front of all his friends, just before he took a deep breath and stepped off the edge.

'Hello?'

Ursula could hear the low tones of a male voice at the other end of the phone. The dread crept in a bit further.

'Yes, this is Anthony Patton.' Tony's forehead knotted. His eyes closed for a moment; his nostrils flared. 'I'm leaving now. I'll be there as soon as I can.'

He disconnected the call and grabbed his keys. His eyes were wild. Ursula put the knife down and stepped towards him. 'Anthony, what's happening? Who was it?'

He was already running down the hallway. 'They found her, they're taking her to hospital. I've got to go.'

Ursula turned off the grill, grabbed her bag and rushed after him. 'The hospital? My God . . . What about Jack? Is he OK?'

She watched as her frightened little boy looked back over his shoulder at her. He paused, then looked down at the floor, blinking hard. He took a deep breath. 'Anna's on her own – they haven't found Jack. She was at some cliffs, at the beach. They don't know where he is . . . I'm scared, Mum.'

Ursula closed her eyes. Dear God, what was going on? She opened her eyes again, and looked at Tony's trembling hands. 'I'll drive. Get in the car.'

She took the keys from Tony, then followed him outside and slammed the door behind her.

CHAPTER THREE

That day
2 P.M.

As they turned in to the hospital forecourt Tony reached for the door handle, opening it as soon as Ursula stopped the car in an ambulance bay outside the emergency department. A group of ashen-faced patients attached to drips milled around in a cloud of smoke, sucking on cigarettes. He jumped out of the car, and didn't look back as his mum drove off to park. The automatic glass doors opened and he ran towards the reception desk directly opposite them. The receptionist tapped at the computer behind a glass window while he stood there, waiting. He cleared his throat, but she continued to look at her screen.

'My wife . . .' he said finally. 'The police told me to come here. Her name's Anna Patton.'

'I'll be with you in just a moment.'

He shook his head, and looked around the waiting room for someone else who might be able to help him. This was a hospital, for God's sake; was this woman's typing more important than people dying? Didn't she understand that Anna was lying hurt somewhere in there, waiting for him? He turned back to the desk and put his hands on the counter.

'Excuse me!' he shouted. 'My wife's been in an accident – I need to see her now!'

The receptionist still didn't look up, but she briefly stopped typing. 'Have a seat, sir. I'll let the doctors know you're here.'

He walked back towards the rows of chairs in the waiting room, too agitated to sit down. There were only two other people there: an elderly man with a rattling cough and a young man in paint-speckled clothes clutching his elbow. They both stared at the television mounted on the wall, showing some American chat show. He paced back and forth. The receptionist would have rushed him through if Anna had been seriously hurt, wouldn't she? Did she even know who Anna was or did she just enjoy acting as gatekeeper? He watched people come and go through the plastic swing door to the emergency ward; it slapped open and closed, teasing him with glimpses of what lay beyond. What were they doing to Anna through there? Every minute that passed was a minute that Jack was still missing; he needed to see Anna now. At the thought of Jack still being out there somewhere, on his own, his legs began to shake and he had to reach out to steady himself on the back of a chair. The whole situation was so absurd, so unreal. Things like this didn't happen to people like them – they were just a normal family. Acid burned in his throat and he coughed. Suddenly filled with resolve, he looked around; no one was watching him. He put his head down, strode towards the plastic door and pushed it open.

No one seemed to notice him inside either. In front of him was a long bench covered with piles of yellow folders, phones perching precariously on top of them. A herd of staff in baggy blue and green outfits hovered over it. Around the outside of the room, patients lay on trolleys and beds. Some had flimsy curtains drawn around them; others had nothing else to do but watch the activity in the centre of the room.

He approached the end of the bench closest to him, where a man with a stethoscope around his neck sat on a stool scribbling in a file.

'Excuse me, I need to see Anna Patton – I was told she was here.'

'Sorry, not my patient,' the doctor said, barely looking up.

His cheeks flushed. He didn't know whether to cry or scream. 'For God's sake! The police called me to say my wife's here, and my baby's missing. Does anyone in this place care?' His voice cracked.

The doctor closed the file and looked up. 'Oh, that lady.'

'What?'

'Wait here for a minute. I'll find out who you need to talk to.'

He couldn't keep the sarcasm out of his voice. 'Thank you.'

The doctor approached a tall, thin young man in green scrubs. They spoke quietly and the younger man nodded, put down his pen and walked towards him, holding out one hand. Tony shook it, noticing the beetling veins in his forearms. The other doctors and nurses skulked away.

'Mr Patton, I'm Dr Hall, the registrar looking after your wife. Sorry to keep you waiting.'

'Where is she? Is she all right? The police said —'

Dr Hall held out his hands, palms facing him, and spoke slowly. 'First of all, she's OK. She was pretty cold and shocked when the ambulance picked her up, but she seems stable, physically.'

'Thank God . . .' He let out a big breath, then swallowed, trying to force the panic down again. 'She was with my baby, Jack, but the police said he wasn't there. He's not even six weeks old . . .'

Dr Hall cleared his throat and looked down. 'Yes, the police told us that.'

'They still haven't found him?' The room began to reel. He closed his eyes, but that made it worse, so he forced them back open.

'I don't know. I haven't heard anything, but I'm sure they'll contact you the moment they have news. All I know is that your wife was lying on some rocks just over the edge of a cliff. We're assuming she fell.' Dr Hall paused and looked at Tony. He didn't want to think about the implications of that look.

'But Jack was with her. I don't understand . . .' How could they still not have found him? Jack couldn't walk, he had to be where Anna had left him; why hadn't she told anyone where he was?

'Mr Patton, I know the police are doing everything they can to find him.'

Dr Hall's deliberately calm, slow voice petrified him. They must teach student doctors at medical school how to speak like that in order to tell people they have only two weeks to live. He breathed deeply and forced himself to concentrate. 'Can I see her?'

Dr Hall nodded. 'It would be great if you could try to talk to her. Anna hasn't said anything to us yet.'

His eyes widened. 'What do you mean she hasn't said anything? You said she was OK!'

'She is OK physically, apart from some cuts and bruises. My consultant's going to come and have a look at her too, and we'll order some tests. But she isn't responding to questions. We just don't know what's going on at this stage.'

The room began to spin once more; he looked for a wall to steady himself against. Dr Hall put his hand on his shoulder and guided him to a chair. He sat, no longer sure that he could stand. What did he mean, Anna wasn't responding to questions? What was happening? There must have been a mistake – Anna had dropped Jack off somewhere, probably somewhere really obvious. Think, think, think: where would she have taken him?

'It's a lot to take in, I know,' Dr Hall said. 'We need to know a bit about her medical history. Does she have any illnesses?'

'No, no, she's always been healthy.'

'Has she been well recently?'

He hesitated. Could he honestly say she'd been well? He had convinced himself that she was, but he wasn't sure he could trust his judgement. 'Well, yeah, I suppose so. She's been tired, you know, a bit down, with the new baby . . . but she's been well, I mean —'

'How about any medications – is she taking anything that you know of?'

He nodded. 'She saw the GP a couple of weeks ago. She got some tablets to help her sleep.'

'Can you remember what they're called?'

'I don't know . . . Do you think this is something to do with the tablets? I've heard about people sleepwalking, driving cars while they're still asleep, that could explain why she was there . . . ?'

Dr Hall shrugged. 'At the moment we need to look into everything. I'll give her GP a call. I'll need to get some more information from you, but that can wait.'

He struggled to his feet again. He could barely hold up his head. 'Can I see her?'

Dr Hall glanced over Tony's shoulder. 'Of course.'

He was relieved. When he saw her, this would all make sense. Maybe Anna wouldn't talk to the police and the doctors, but of course she would talk to him. Anna had always told him everything. She would explain everything. She had to.

*   *   *

He followed Dr Hall past the patient bays to the door of a small room that he hadn't noticed before. Dr Hall seemed to pause for a second, then pushed open the door. He held it for Tony, nodded at him, then left.

From the doorway, he could see the familiar shape of Anna, curled up in a bed with her back towards him. The noise behind him seemed to fade. All he could hear was her heavy breathing, and the beeps of the monitors attached to her.

'Anna?'

Tony walked forward, letting the door swing closed behind him, then put his hand gently on her shoulder, which had escaped from the shroud of the thin sheet.

'Anna?'

Her muscles tensed under his hand. He increased the pressure, shaking her slightly. 'Anna, it's me, Tony. Are you OK?'

He slowly removed his hand and walked around to the other side of the bed. When he saw her face, he gasped. 'Oh, Anna . . .'

The woman lying there was barely recognisable to him. She lay on her right side, curled up tightly like an injured dog. Her eyes were open, her eyelids peeled back to stare at the wall. He turned his head and followed her line of vision, sure he would see some horror etched there, but it was just a blank wall. Strands of her hair had escaped from the rubber band that tied it back and were frozen in disarray, matted stiff with salt water and sand. Her pale lips blended almost perfectly into her pallid face, though he could see them moving slightly. He leaned towards her, but couldn't catch any of the words she whispered. Her cheek and forehead were scribbled with dirty scratches and on her chest a bruise was already forming around a deep cut.

'Oh Jesus,' he said. What had happened to her? 'Anna, Anna, it's me.' He shook her now, harder, and his voice grew louder. Her eyes flickered towards him, and for a moment he saw his wife peering at him. His Anna, who laughed every time he tried to do a French accent; his Anna, who pretended that she didn't let the dog sleep on the bed when he was away; his Anna, who strapped Jack to her chest when he was upset and walked around with him for hours so that he could feel her heartbeat. For just a moment he saw her, and knew how frightened she was, but before he could tell her that everything was all right, she disappeared again.

He spoke again, but more softly so he wouldn't scare her. 'Anna, where's Jack? Where's the baby?'

Why wouldn't she answer? Couldn't she hear him? Didn't she understand that they had to find Jack?

'Anna? Please! This is important!'

He reeled back and sat down on a grey plastic chair in the corner. He held his head in his hands for a few moments. Nothing made sense. He looked at Anna again, but she hadn't moved. He considered shouting louder, slapping her cheek, but he knew it would be useless. He couldn't bear feeling so helpless. In the past he'd always known what to do if something was wrong, how to fix it, but now, when it was the most important thing in the world, he had no idea.

The door creaked open behind him. He lifted his head and saw Dr Hall.

'I heard a noise,' the doctor said. 'Are you OK?'

He shook his head at such an idiotic question: of course he wasn't. He opened his mouth to answer, but had no words. What was the point? He stood up and moved towards the door, but before he walked out, he remembered that the woman lying in the bed was Anna. She was hurt; it wasn't her fault. He turned back and kissed her forehead. She didn't seem to notice; she just kept staring at the wall. He turned away from her again and went through the door Dr Hall held open for him.

They walked back to the bench, and both sat down.

'I don't understand,' Tony began. 'What's wrong with her?'

'Mr Patton, we're not sure what's going on at the moment, but we have a few things we want to do. At the moment we're monitoring her and ordering some tests. I'm organising a CT scan to rule out any significant head injuries, though there's no neurological signs to suggest that's the case —'

Tony leaned forward, frowning. 'Have you seen her? Obviously something's wrong with her! She wasn't like that this morning . . .' He stopped as the reality of the situation struck him afresh. Jack. He could see him, gazing up into his eyes as he guzzled down the bottle of milk this morning before he left for work. He gripped the arms of the chair to stop himself crumpling in a heap. 'Oh God. Where's the baby? Where's Jack?'

'I'm sure the police are doing everything they can.'

'I need to go. If she's like this . . .' His breath quickened. 'What the hell has happened? I have to go.'

Without waiting for a reply, he ran back towards reception, oblivious to everything around him. He pushed through the opaque plastic doors and saw his mum standing near the main entrance with her back to him. Ursula's arms were crossed, and she looked up at a uniformed police officer.

Tony stopped, froze, then took a deep breath. It wasn't what he thought: if it was bad news the police would have told him first, not his mum. They would have asked the doctors where he was, or called his phone. The police officer was writing something in a small black notebook. He strode forward.

'Mum,' he said, over her shoulder.

Ursula spun around, startled. 'Anthony! What's happening? Is Anna all right?'

He shook his head. 'No . . . I don't know. What about Jack? Have you heard anything?'

Ursula moved her head a little, not looking him in the eyes. 'This is Constable Pagonis.'

He shook the hand offered to him, feeling the coarse hairs on the back of the policeman's fingers. 'What's going on?'

'I was just explaining to your mum, we've alerted all of our units and have several teams out looking for . . . the child.'

'Jack,' Tony said, narrowing his eyes. Was Jack so unimportant, so routine, that the police officer couldn't even remember his name? 'His name is Jack.'

'Is there anyone your wife could have left him with?'

'I went through this on the phone already! No! Her mum lives in Western Australia, her best mate was at work. The only other person she'd leave him with is Mum, but obviously that's not the case . . .' He took a sharp breath as his mind scrabbled for something to cling to. 'Maybe she left him at your place, Mum? She got there and you were gone so she left Jack with the neighbour or something. Let's —'

'I thought of that, Anthony. I've called your dad and Lisa, and they're checking again, but I don't think . . .' Ursula's voice quivered and trailed off. He stared at her. His mum never got upset about things. She never cried. Her voice never faltered.

'Mum.' He hunched over slightly and put his hands on her shoulders, looking into her eyes. If she gave up, then that was it. 'It's like you said, there's a simple explanation for this, something so simple we've missed it.'

Ursula nodded at him. 'I know, I know, Anthony.' Her voice was quiet, unconvincing.

He rubbed his face and forced himself to think. Suddenly he knew what it was they'd missed. 'Her car! Where's her car? Jack must still be in the baby capsule!'

'Mr Patton.' Constable Pagonis put his hand out towards him.

'Have you found it?'

'I'm not sure . . .'

'It must have been stolen. That's why she's like this, she's in shock, she's been attacked.' He took a step towards the door.

'Jack – they've got him, he was in the capsule. They would have abandoned it when they realised he was in it. It's a black Corolla, put out a message on your radio . . .'

The dragging dread in his guts was replaced by a surge of purpose. He knew what he had to do: he needed to find Anna's car and everything would be all right. Anna was safe now, and soon Jack would be too.

CHAPTER FOUR

That day

2.30 P.M.

Wendy leaned her elbows on the old wooden kitchen table. She held a cigarette in her right hand and, in between drags, bit the nails on her left hand.

She'd been at work, picking up wet towels from the bathroom floor of a hotel guest who was perfectly capable of picking them up himself, when Ursula called and spoke the words that she would never forget: *Anna and Jack are missing.* She'd shrieked. It was the type of call she had been expecting her entire life, not because Anna was flawed in any way, just the opposite: she had always known that her good luck in having a daughter as perfect as Anna couldn't possibly last, and something was bound to go wrong one day. It was the way things worked in her life.

She quickly finished up, then sped along the winding road home, wiping away burning tears. She needed to get back to the house in case Anna had called. But when she unlocked the door of her fibro cottage and ran down to the kitchen in the old lean-to, there were no messages on the answering machine.

She stubbed out her cigarette in the overflowing ashtray, swearing as the ash crumbled over the edge of the frosted glass onto the scratched jarrah table. Suddenly the phone rang; she jumped and let out a breath.

She was already anticipating the sound of Anna's cheerful laugh as she explained where she'd been, as she picked up the phone. 'Hello?'

'Wendy, it's Tony.'

Her stomach dropped. 'Oh. Hi, I thought —'

'I know,' Tony said and sighed. 'Listen, I'm sorry I didn't call sooner, but I'm just leaving the hospital.'

'The hospital? Oh Jesus, I knew it!' She clenched her hand around the receiver to hold it steady. 'What's wrong? What's happened?'

'I don't know . . . Anna's there, in the hospital. They found her near the edge of a cliff. She's got some cuts and bruises, she's in shock or something. She won't say anything. But . . .'

Wendy held her breath. *But?*

'Jack's still missing. They can't find him.'

She froze as she heard the terror in Tony's voice; her body and her thoughts stopped, and the world around her seemed to fall away.

'What?' she said faintly.

'They can't find him.' Tony's voice broke. 'I just – just don't understand what's happened. I'm going to look for him now. We're thinking maybe someone's stolen the car, and didn't realise he was in it . . .'

She couldn't speak. She had never felt further away from her daughter's life than she did right now. What could she do from the other side of the country? She might as well be in Africa as Western Australia. She should never have listened to Anna, she should have gone to Sydney as soon as Jack was born. Anna had said to wait until Jack was older and more interactive before she spent her money on flying over, and she hadn't wanted to intrude, but now look what had happened.

'Oh God,' she said. Her thoughts jostled and scrambled. There was only one thing she could do: go to Sydney. 'I'll book a flight now. I'll be there as soon as I can.'

'Let me know when you'll get in. Sorry, but I have to go. Mum's driving, I've got to make some calls.'

She nodded, not trusting herself to speak, then heard the drone of the dial tone as Tony hung up. She dropped the receiver, laid her clammy palms flat on the table and inhaled deeply. She couldn't let herself think about the worst-case scenario. She couldn't let it overwhelm her; she had to take everything one step at a time and stay calm.

A moment later, she leapt to her feet, knocking her rickety chair onto the kitchen tiles with a clatter, and ran to her bedroom to start packing.

*   *   *

Wendy drove north, concentrating on keeping the car at exactly the speed limit. She didn't want to be pulled over, not today.

The last time she'd flown to Sydney was for Anna and Tony's wedding. She had driven up this same road with her dad in the passenger seat. He'd been like an excited child: he'd never been on an aeroplane before. He had beamed with pride, his eyes watering, when he walked Anna down the aisle. Wendy had been so relieved that he had stepped into the role of Anna's father that day, a role that had been empty since Anna was a toddler. Wendy realised now that she hadn't called him; that could wait.

She lifted her mobile into her lap, put it on loudspeaker, then called Pam. She hated having to ask her sister for help. Pam was one of those people who seemed to succeed at everything: she had a great house, a great job, a great husband. She had managed to escape to the city long ago, as soon as she'd finished school. When Mum died, eight years ago, it was assumed that Wendy would look after Dad. After all, Anna was at university in Sydney by then, so what else did she have to do? She clearly didn't have any dreams of her own. The only thing she had ever done better than her sister was having Anna. Pam didn't have any children. She'd never asked why.

'Hi Pam, it's me.'

'Hi there, how's things?'

'Oh, I don't know where to start.' She wiped her eyes. 'Something terrible's happened. Anna's in hospital, and they don't know where Jack is.' She heard Pam gasp. 'I've managed to get a ticket on the first flight to Sydney tomorrow morning. I'm on my way to Perth now, but I'm still a few hours away. Can I stay at yours tonight?'

Pam paused, as if trying to take in what Wendy had said, but quickly recovered. 'Of course you can. Are you right to drive, though? I can come and pick you up.'

'No, no, I'm fine.' She could hear the hysterical edge in her own voice and knew that she wasn't really safe to drive. But she had to keep going; stopping wasn't an option. She needed to feel that she was doing something.

'All right. But Wendy . . . drive carefully, OK?'

'Yes. I'll see you in a while.'

After hanging up, she checked the phone for messages in case she'd missed a call, but there were none. She wished she'd asked Tony for more information; at the time, she'd been too shocked. She didn't want to bother him again. Gripping the steering wheel tighter to control the shaking in her hands, she looked straight ahead and concentrated on the road.

CHAPTER FIVE

That day
3 P.M.

While Ursula drove south towards the cliffs where Anna had been found, Tony sat forward in the passenger seat and scanned the unfamiliar streets. His vision had never been more focused, his hearing never clearer. It was a primal, animal instinct for survival that sharpened every sense. He'd done everything he could think of: Wendy was flying over, Emily was ringing their friends, and his dad and Lisa were contacting family then meeting them at the cliffs.

He peered out of the window. They'd been driving for half an hour now. It would be dark in a few hours. He had to find Jack before night fell. Otherwise, whoever had stolen him would have more chance of getting away; worse still, they might just leave him somewhere, cold and hungry. At the thought of Jack scared and alone, he bit the inside of his cheek until he tasted the metallic tang of blood. The physical pain stopped his thoughts running away. He needed to concentrate, think, plan. There was no time right now for emotion.

Anna had never believed that he didn't feel anxious about little things the way she did, but it was true. It wasn't that he didn't feel the buzz of adrenalin that hummed through him when things started to move out of his control but, unlike her, he thrived on it. Anna had told him that it wasn't healthy to enjoy stress, that he needed to relax more and not work so hard. Maybe he should have listened to her. Maybe then he wouldn't have gone to work this morning.

That was what it came down to: he should have listened to her.

The blood trickling inside his mouth brought his thoughts back to the problem that he needed to fix. The answer was simple: he had to find Anna's car and, to do that, he had to see where Anna had been found. Then he could work out where Jack might be.

'Slow down, Mum,' he said, squinting into the distance.

Ursula slammed on the brakes. 'What is it?'

'There's a church.' As they crawled past, he started shaking his head. 'I just thought . . . You hear about people leaving babies on the doorsteps. Whoever did this, if they hadn't known Jack was in the car when they stole it, they might have found a place to leave him.'

'Good thinking.' Ursula turned her head towards him, then looked back at the road. 'Someone will have him, Anthony. I know it. He'll be OK.'

His eyes stung. He had to believe that. Surely car thieves weren't interested in harming children. 'I know. Let's just go to the beach now.'

Ursula nodded, then indicated and turned onto the main road. He sank back in his seat and continued staring out of the window. His stomach churned and he realised he hadn't eaten since breakfast. He wondered again if Jack was hungry. Even the most awful people in the world, the type of people who would steal a car from a mother, would know that you have to feed babies, wouldn't they? They would have enough sense to buy some milk, or even just some water. Wouldn't they?

Up ahead, he saw a police car stopped at the turn-off from the main road to the car park. Ursula slowed down and pushed the button to open the driver's window. He leaned across her and gave his name to the policeman, who waved them through.

The road to the car park was rough, and the stringy trees on either side leaned forward to clutch at the car. The sun was starting to dip in the sky, but within the shade of the trees it was twilight already. Occasionally a fallen limb allowed the light to push through the gloom. What the hell had Anna been doing here? They had only been here a couple of times before: he'd surfed in the bay while Anna lay under an umbrella, reading. She'd never been here alone, and he couldn't see why she would have driven all this way with Jack just to go for a bushwalk along the track above the beach. It proved that he was right: someone else must have been involved. His tears welled up again. He closed his eyes briefly and swallowed hard. He needed to get himself under control.

Reaching the car park they emerged into the afternoon light. There was only one access road, the one they'd taken. A wooden board pinned with laminated maps of walking trails stood on their left, and behind it was a track leading through the bush to a path along the cliffs. At the other end of the carpark was a wooden fence and a set of steep, worn stairs down to the beach below. Ahead, Tony saw an ambulance. His stomach clenched. Two paramedics stood at the back of the van, one with her arms folded, the other scuffing his foot in the sand that covered the tarmac. They were laughing at something. Just then, the female paramedic looked up, saw their car and stopped laughing. She nodded her head at them. Tony forced himself to exhale: they were waiting, just in case. It must be standard procedure; it didn't mean anything.

There were two more police cars parked beside the ambulance; both were empty. And at the far end of the car park, near the stairs to the beach, there was another vehicle. Tony could only see part of the bonnet, but he knew it immediately. It was Anna's car.

He looked away, not wanting to believe that it had been here all along. Finding the car had been his last hope, and clearly Jack wasn't in it or the police would have found him. Could he dare to hope that the authorities had missed something so obvious, and maybe Jack was still strapped in his capsule?

Ursula pulled on the handbrake and switched off the engine. 'Come on,' she said.

He undid his seatbelt and opened his door. He swung his legs out, forced himself to stand, then took a tentative step. He needed to get out of the car, but somehow it was also the last thing that he wanted to do.

*　　*　　*

Ursula watched Tony walk slowly around his car. She noticed for the first time how his thick dark hair was flecked with grey behind his ears. He was only thirty, but he walked like an old man, and Ursula quickly looked away in case he caught her staring at him. She longed to be able to make it all better, to tell him that she would take care of it, that he could leave and go back to his life. But he wasn't her little boy any more: he was a man, a husband, a father.

She turned as she heard a car crunch along the road behind them, then smiled in relief as she saw Jim's ute. 'It's Dad, and Lisa.'

Tony looked up and nodded. Jim and Lisa jumped out of the car and ran over to hug Tony, then her.

'You OK, love?' Jim whispered in her ear while he embraced her. Ursula looked up at her husband. His receding hair was grey and coarse now, the way Tony's would be in years to come, but his eyes were the same deep brown as the day they'd met. Jack had the same eyes. Beautiful, big, bright eyes. She clung tighter to Jim, feeling the lean knots of his muscles through his thick flannel shirt, still hard from years of manual work. She blinked back her tears.

'I'm all right. We just have to stay strong.'

She glanced over to Tony and Lisa. Lisa's long dark hair was loose, blowing in the breeze that swirled the sand around her grey peep-toe sandals and flared the skirt of her pink chiffon shift dress. She always looked so pretty in her own designs. Her dark eye make-up was smudged, though, and she dabbed at her nose with a tissue. Now she looked up at her big brother, who was at least a foot taller than her, and years older, and put her slender arm around his waist. Tony and Lisa had never been particularly close as kids – the five-year gap left them with little in common – but as adults they were good mates. Lisa had always treated Anna like an older sister; Ursula, too, had thought of Anna as family. But did she really know Anna as well as she'd thought? Ursula reached in her bag for her handkerchief. There was no time to think like that, not now.

A policeman walked towards them from the bush track. 'G'day. I'm Constable Brad Dixon, from Sutherland Police.'

Tony stepped forward and offered his hand. 'Tony Patton.' His voice was strong and she felt a surge of pride. 'This is my mum and dad, Ursula and Jim, and my sister, Lisa.'

Constable Dixon shook hands with each of them. Her palms were clammy against his strong, cool grip. She stared at the freckles on his nose as he began to give them a run-down of the search. He was in his early twenties, even younger than Lisa; it didn't seem right that such young kids had to deal with things like this.

Tony interrupted him. 'The car.' He pointed towards it without looking. 'Was Jack . . . ? He wasn't . . . ?'

She blinked hard and focused again on the conversation. She knew what Constable Dixon was going to say. She was sure Tony did too.

'No. It was empty. There was no sign of damage, or a struggle, but of course we're getting Forensics out to examine it. I'm sorry, but there was nothing to explain what happened.'

Her last sliver of hope was snatched away by the salty wind. She closed her eyes, then dared to open them and look at Tony. He was pale. She clutched Lisa's hand; her daughter was trembling.

'I need to see it,' Tony said, his voice firm.

'Yes.' Jim put his arm around Tony's shoulders. 'Let's have a look. We might see something that isn't obvious to the police.'

Tony nodded. 'I'm sure there'll be something, something to prove . . . To find whoever did this.'

Dixon furrowed his brow. He opened his mouth as if to say something, then closed it again and nodded before walking towards the car. They all followed him.

Tony peered through the windows of the Corolla, ducking to see inside from every angle. She came up behind him and put her hand on his shoulder. At that, he stopped moving.

'Jack's not there,' he said in a flat voice.

'I know, love.' She squeezed his shoulder to keep her own hand from shaking, and looked through the back window too. On the floor on the left-hand side, just beneath the baby capsule, was a big black bag. It was the nappy bag, the one Anna always kept stocked up with everything Jack would need. She gently steered Tony away from the car. 'Come on, love. Let's go. We'll be more help back over there.'

Tony nodded. Ursula led him towards his family.

*   *   *

He couldn't stand it any more. The light was fading. They had scoured the beach and the path and the bush, but found nothing. A helicopter was on its way to help search the craggy rocks and caves that lined the ancient sandstone cliff wall, only visible from the churning air above the ocean. The police had stopped reassuring him that they would find Jack; now they only said they were doing everything they could. Their glances were drenched with pity. They wouldn't look directly at him, or allow themselves to be engaged in conversation. He knew they were giving up.

But Tony knew that Jack wasn't here. He couldn't be. Jack was somewhere else, somewhere safe. He had to be.

He stood at the top of the cliff, swaying with the wind, and wondered what it would feel like to fall, and whether he would survive. What had Anna been doing here? Was she running, afraid? He squeezed his fists tightly then stepped back onto the path. He was losing his mind; Anna and Jack needed him to take charge here, to help them. He crouched down and put his head in his hands again, trying to concentrate, then heard himself let out a moan. He looked up, shocked, then noticed his parents and sister behind him. His dad held out his hand to help Tony to his feet. Ursula hugged him.

'Mum, where is he?' The words forced their way out of him raggedly.

Ursula took a deep breath, then shook her head. 'I wish I could answer that.' He heard the tremor in her voice.

'We need more people! He could be anywhere! Time's running out.'

'We'll find him,' Jim said, stepping towards him. 'We will, Tony.'

Lisa covered her face and muttered something before hurrying away. He could hear her stifled cries.

He suddenly thought of something. 'We need to get it on the news, now! Everyone in Sydney needs to get out there and look – he could be anywhere, he could be on a plane by now. I don't know what to do! I feel like I'm doing nothing, and every minute . . .' He couldn't finish the sentence. He'd never felt so helpless before. 'Where the hell is he?' He swiped at a tear. He couldn't let himself think like the policemen, couldn't give up on Jack. 'Take me back to the hospital. Anna knows where he is – she has to. I'll try again, she might be better now, she has to talk to me, she's the only one who knows what happened!'

Ursula put her hand on his arm. 'Please, calm down, the police said they're doing everything they can —'

'It's not enough! We need to do more!' He clenched his fist then punched the trunk of the gnarled gum tree behind him.

'Tony! Stop!' Jim grabbed his wrist.

He tried to wrestle his arm away, but his dad's grip was too strong and he gave up, letting himself go limp. Jim put his arm around Tony's slack shoulders. He couldn't look at his father. All his life, Jim had quietly trusted him to do the right thing; he had never pressured him into anything. As a kid, he'd sometimes wished that his dad would be more involved in his life: yelling at him from the rugby pitch sidelines like the other dads instead of just telling him he'd done a good job, or clipping him round the ear when he staggered home drunk. Now, like then, he knew that Jim wouldn't blame him, or believe that he'd been wrong to leave Anna and Jack this morning; he'd say that Tony had done his best. That was what he wanted to hear but, on the other hand, he was terrified that he might, for once, have let his father down. Let his own son down.

Ursula glanced at Jim, then took Tony's elbow. 'Go back to the car. I'll just check on Lisa, then we'll call the hospital and see if there's any change. If not, we'll go back to the house in case there's any messages, or something we missed.'

He nodded and tramped wearily back to the car, his head down. Ursula arrived a few minutes later. He slumped back in his seat and let her call the emergency ward. He couldn't think any more; he'd run out of possible explanations. He closed his eyes and turned his head away from his mum. He didn't say another word, not even when Ursula pulled up at the house. Like an infant roused from sleep, he was aware of his surroundings but didn't want to wake up. He longed to be young again, to be carried into bed and tucked in, to fall into the long, deep sleep of a child.

'Anthony? Anthony, we're here.'

He opened his eyes and looked around, then emerged into reality. Nothing had changed. He rubbed his face then got out of the car, walked up to the door, and unlocked it. Behind him he heard his mum lock the car.

Inside, he went straight into the bedroom with a new-found sense of purpose. He needed to be methodical about this. He would start with Anna's diary and notebooks, which she kept by the bed, then he would read every email, every document on her computer and every message in her phone, until he found . . . what? He opened the drawer of her bedside table and began raking through it. As he lifted up a book, he stopped suddenly and his heart raced. He picked up Anna's box of medication and slid out the foil strip of tablets: there were only two missing. He closed his eyes and shook his head. This was all wrong; she had started these about two weeks ago. Why hadn't she been taking them? He put the box back, trying to think clearly, and closed the drawer. Just then he heard the front door open, and smelled grease and garlic. It made him want to throw up. He heard his dad's voice, the clang of plates, the oven door opening, the tap running.

And then he heard his phone.

The ring was like a scream.

The tap stopped running, the murmurs ceased and the house seemed to hold its breath. Without even thinking about it, and before it had a chance to scream again, Tony raced down to the hall table, picked up the phone and answered it.

* * *

Ursula froze. Her right arm was raised, ready to put the pizza box into the oven to warm. Jim and Lisa also stopped mid-action, as though they were all playing some bizarre game of statues.

Tony said his name. Then he said nothing. Finally, 'I understand. I'll be there as soon as I can.'

She breathed out, then put the box on the kitchen bench. She looked at her husband and daughter. Lisa had tears running down her face; Jim was slowly shaking his head. She swallowed, then she walked out of the kitchen and down the hallway towards her son. Tony was standing still, staring at the phone in his hand as if he'd never seen anything like it before. His mouth was slightly open but he didn't appear to be breathing. Ursula was afraid that if she spoke he'd shatter into a thousand brittle pieces.

'Anthony? Who was it?' She was practically whispering.

Tony didn't move; he just stared at the phone.

'Anthony?'

It seemed like an age before he lifted his gaze and turned towards her. His face was pale grey and waxy.

'The police.'

She gasped involuntarily, then clasped her hand to her mouth.

'I have to go back to the hospital straightaway.'

Until then she'd never believed that a person's heart could actually stop for a moment, but she had no doubt that her own did as Tony covered his face with his hands.

'Why? What's wrong? Is Anna . . .' She stopped as Tony shook his head. He took his hands away from his face and held them in front of him, recoiling as if they were stained with blood.

'They've found him.' His voice broke into a wail and he looked up at her. 'I'm too late, Mum, it's too late . . .'

Somehow she managed to reach Tony without collapsing, then she put her arms around his broad back and cradled her sobbing son to her chest.

There was nothing she could say.

CHAPTER SIX

Six weeks before

Tuesday, 4 August 2009

Anna had assumed that it would happen naturally. Her contractions would start in the middle of the night and, just like in the movies, she would shake Tony's shoulder and he'd jump up with his dark brown hair all ruffled from sleep. She'd kiss him and whisper, 'The baby's coming.' Tony would grin, rush out of bed, dress quickly, help her to the car, then drive them to the hospital.

They were on their way to the hospital now, but there was no rush. There was no panic, no speeding, no weaving through the traffic. The road was quiet as they drove against the dregs of the Sydney evening peak hour. She was nine long and heavy days overdue. She had tried everything to start labour: long walks, raspberry leaf tea, curries, even sex, despite feeling huge and unattractive. But none of it had worked. She was being admitted tonight, and her labour would be induced tomorrow.

She touched Tony's left arm. 'I'm sorry, sweetheart,' she said, staring straight ahead.

Tony turned to look at her, frowning, then looked back at the road as he indicated left, towards the hospital. 'Sorry? What for?'

She shrugged. 'I didn't want it to be like this. It feels so unnatural.'

'Babe, don't be silly, please.' He placed his hand on top of hers and squeezed it. 'It's just the way it is. Tomorrow, this'll all be over and we'll have our baby.'

She nodded. He was right, of course he was. There was nothing she could have done differently. She busied herself with changing the radio station as the hospital building appeared in front of them.

They parked the car easily on the ground level of the nearly empty multistorey car park. Opening the door, she swung her legs out and eased herself onto her feet. She put her right hand under her swollen belly, and closed the door with her left hand. The thud echoed and bounced around her, as did the high-pitched bleep as Tony locked the car. She looked around at the grey concrete walls, shining in the sallow fluorescent light, and shivered.

'Ready?' Tony said.

She nodded again.

He picked up the two bags at his feet and they walked out into the twilight. They crossed the quiet hospital grounds. A few smartly dressed people walked quickly, looking at pagers or talking on phones. An elderly lady held a bunch of yellow tulips as she stared at a board with a map of the hospital on it. A quiver of excitement pierced her disappointment: no, this wouldn't be the natural labour that she'd wanted, but her baby would finally be here tomorrow. She smiled and walked forward to push open the heavy glass door into the maternity building.

They checked in at the reception desk then took the lift to the tenth floor. The doors slid smoothly open and they walked out into the ward. The smell of fresh paint made her giddy. The soft, grey carpet was springy, and muffled the sounds around them. A nurse showed them to a room, asked Anna some questions then left them to settle in.

She looked around her. The room was tiny, the single bed taking up most of the space. On one side of the bed was a tall locker with a faux-wooden laminate, and on the other was a bedside cabinet with a beige plastic phone on top of it. A sliding door led to a small ensuite bathroom.

'Ooh, a chocolate!' She picked up the foil-wrapped square on the pillow. 'Only one, though. Do you want it?'

Tony laughed. 'No, you can have it. I think you'll need the energy.' He put the bags down at the foot of the bed, and looked out of the window over the hospital grounds, towards the lights of the city. 'You're easily pleased. Just like a hotel, eh?'

'Well, kind of. All we need is a bottle of wine and the overpriced Toblerone and we can imagine we're on holiday.' Noticing the oxygen tubes and plastic mask on the wall near the bed, she turned away. She opened the bar fridge door and laughed as she took out the two bottles of water. 'This will have to do us for tonight!'

Tony winked. 'I wonder if they'd notice if I stuck a six-pack in there for later?'

'They'll probably let us off if we have some champagne ready on ice.'

As soon as she mentioned champagne, her joy drained away, replaced with a jolt of dread. They didn't have a cause for celebration yet. She couldn't ignore the nagging feeling that something was wrong. But at least things were moving now, she told herself. There was no reason to feel so apprehensive.

While Tony fiddled with the television she started to unpack her bag. She refolded her clothes and placed them in the drawers under the window seat that converted into a small bed for Tony. She kept the smaller bag aside to take with them to the delivery suite in the morning, and handed Tony a t-shirt and boxer shorts to change into later.

He raised his eyebrows and smiled. 'You thought of everything.' He kissed her forehead and smoothed her fair hair back off her face.

'You know me,' she said. 'You don't have to stay here tonight if you don't want to, you know. They won't be doing much – nothing will happen until tomorrow. I don't mind if you want to go home, have a good night's sleep and come back in the morning?'

'No, I want to be here with you. You need to stop worrying and try to get some rest.'

She smiled in relief. Of course she didn't want Tony to go home. She wanted him right here with her, and their baby. She looked over at him and reminded herself how lucky she was. Realising she was staring, she turned back to her bags and took out a new novel.

She hadn't finished the first chapter when the nurse returned with the gel to start the induction. She laughed at Tony's alarmed face; he went to wait outside while the nurse put on a pair of gloves.

She lay down on the bed and prepared herself, closing her eyes and imagining she was somewhere else.

She thought of their honeymoon in Margaret River. She and Tony had sat at a small candlelit table at the edge of a wooden deck, from where she could make out the lean limbs of grapevines stretching into the night. She could taste the sweet fizz of cold champagne and the tang of salty olives, and feel her excitement when Tony agreed to start trying for a baby. Then, like now, she had imagined that it would be easy, that it would all happen the way it was meant to. She had stopped taking her contraceptive pill straightaway and there began the monthly cycle of hope, followed by tears of dismay and an overwhelming sense of failure when her period started.

When the nurse finished and told her she could get dressed again, Anna shrugged off the memories. They didn't matter any more. Eventually, she had become pregnant and her baby would soon be in her arms.

She and Tony had a cup of tea and shared the chocolate, then he kissed her and they got into their respective beds. Tony laughed as his feet poked over the edge. 'I feel like I'm sleeping in a kid's bed.'

Smiling, she switched off the light. Soon, Tony was snoring gently while she lay awake. She watched the numbers on the digital clock change and counted down the hours until morning, willing her mind to rest while her body started to work.

CHAPTER SEVEN

That day

7 P.M.

The hospital, so alien to Tony only hours before, was now horribly familiar. The paediatric emergency department was a Lilliputian version of the area in which Anna still lay. The walls were covered with paintings of brightly coloured butterflies and spaceships, but it couldn't conceal that this was a place of tears and grief.

Tony couldn't cry any more, though.

He had listened in silence as the doctor said in hushed tones that there was nothing anyone could have done. But he knew that wasn't true: the police could have organised a helicopter immediately. Then they would have seen Jack where he'd been the whole time, so close to them, hidden by a rocky crag further down the cliff.

Or he could have stayed home that morning.

Outside the hospital, he leaned back against the rough brick wall and slid down until he was sitting on the cold concrete with his knees bent up in front of him. He held his head in his hands. He felt numb. Something inside him had shut down when they took him in there to see Jack.

Words swirled in and out of his memory. *Tragedy. Police. Coroner. Autopsy.* His head throbbed. He prayed that this was all a dream. If only he could wake up, Anna would be with him and she'd tell him it wasn't real.

Anna. She was still lying in that bed, in that room. He now knew why she couldn't speak; she was as broken as he was. Whatever they'd given her to knock her out, it couldn't anaesthetise her as much as this pain did. Something terrible had happened to her and Jack. The pram was still in the car; she hadn't gone to those cliffs for a stroll. Something terrible had happened, and she'd been running. Perhaps she'd seen Jack fall and knew that she was too late, she couldn't reach him. No wonder she was silent.

Some things were unspeakable.

He gripped his hair in his hands, then rubbed his burning eyes with the heels of his palms. He sensed someone sit down beside him and knew it was his dad. For a moment he imagined he was a kid again, sitting with Jim on the beach with their fishing rods wedged in the wet sand, silent except for the occasional comment about the flathead biting. They had never needed to say anything. Tony would sleep soundly on those nights with the smell of salt and fish in his dreams.

They didn't need to say anything to each other now, either.

He raised his head and looked over at Jim, whose eyes were bloodshot and glistening. He'd never seen his dad cry before. He looked old, gaunt; his hair was greyer than Tony remembered. There were tiny flakes of tissue paper stuck in the silver stubble on his upper lip.

'You OK, Dad?' he said.

Jim let out a sound that was at once a laugh and a deep moan. 'Bloody hell, don't ask if I'm OK! I just . . .' He shook his head. 'I'm just so, so sorry. I don't know what to say.'

'Where's Mum?' he croaked, before his own tears had a chance to start.

'She's with Lisa – they went to make some calls. They won't be long.'

'How are they?'

'Don't worry about them. They're all right. We're all here for you, whatever we can do . . .' Jim's voice cracked and he looked away.

Tony dropped his head too. Every night when he was a kid his mum had hugged and kissed him and told him she loved him, the same way Anna did with Jack. His dad had always been more reserved. But Tony knew there was another way to show you loved someone; you just needed to be there. He looked up again.

'Take Mum and Lisa home, Dad. There's nothing you can do tonight.'

'I know, but we want to be with you.'

'Please.' He wiped his eyes. 'I just need to be here with Anna, get my head around this —'

'Tony, you don't need to be here on your own.'

'I want to, Dad. I just can't . . . can't talk or think for now. Please. Go home with Mum, come back in the morning.'

Jim raised his voice and Tony could hear the pleading in it. 'Come home with us.'

'No.' Although he wished he could, Tony shook his head. 'I need to be here when Anna wakes up. But thanks. Thanks for everything.'

Jim put his arm around Tony and pulled him close. 'If you won't come home, then we're staying. We won't get in your way, we'll leave you alone, but we'll be here if you need us.'

He nodded, relieved. He struggled to his feet, then held out a hand to Jim to help him up. They looked at each other for a moment, then Jim clapped him on the back. Tony turned around and headed back into the hospital.

*　　*　　*

He didn't need help to find Anna this time. He walked into the emergency room he'd been in earlier – was it only that afternoon? – and the chatter stopped. He shrugged off the sympathetic looks and kept walking, towards Anna's room. The door was propped open by a chair, and on that chair sat Constable Pagonis, who he'd met earlier.

The policeman stood up and offered his hand to Tony. 'Mr Patton. I'm so sorry for your loss.'

Tony stared at him, saying nothing. A police guard? What the hell were they thinking? But as soon as he thought it, he knew exactly what they were thinking. A searing heat burned away his fatigue.

'What are you doing here?' he asked, pulling his hand away from
Pagonis's. This man wasn't a colleague or a friend; he was accusing
his wife of . . . of what? He couldn't let himself finish the thought.

'Sir, this is standard procedure. Until we can interview your
wife —'

'Interview her? You're kidding!' His voice rose, and his hands
began to shake. 'You can't . . . Look at her! Jesus, she can't even
talk, they're doing scans on her . . .'

The room had gone quiet except for the rhythmic beeps and
hisses of machines. He didn't need to look behind him to know
that everyone was watching them. Anna had always hated a scene;
he felt a fleeting sense of relief that she couldn't see this, that she
didn't know what was going on around her. Well, let everyone listen,
then they could go home and gossip to their partners. Anna had
done nothing wrong; they had nothing to hide.

Staring at the policeman, he spoke slowly and loudly. 'I don't
know what you're thinking happened, but you're wrong.' He stepped
forward until he was only centimetres from Pagonis's face. 'You will
not talk to her. I am her next of kin, and I will decide when you
can interview her.'

Pagonis's jaw bulged, but Tony held his stare until the policeman
sat down again. 'I understand. I'm just here to make sure she's
safe tonight. The detectives will talk to you some more and take
it from there.'

Tony nodded, no energy left to even think of a reply. He took
a step past the chair, then heard someone clear their throat behind
him, a false, high-pitched noise. He wanted to ignore it, but instead
turned around to see a young female nurse.

'Mr Patton, I just wanted to warn you . . .' She looked at the floor.

'What?' he said, unable to keep the weariness from his voice.

'Anna was pretty restless earlier, quite agitated. The doctors gave
her something to help calm her down. So she's sleepy now, and you
might not get much out of her.'

'Agitated? When I saw her earlier, she was barely moving!'

'We needed to take some blood from her, she got very distressed . . .'

'Did she say anything? Anything about what happened? Or my baby?'

The nurse bit her lip and shook her head. 'Sorry. No, she didn't. She was just . . . screaming.'

Tony looked into the room again. Screaming? Anna had the most self-control of anyone he had ever met. She was mortified if they had any sort of row in public, or if she started crying. What the hell had happened to her? What had happened to his Anna, to make her scream so loudly that the doctors had to knock her out? He waved the nurse away with his hand, then walked into Anna's room. Pagonis had the sense to move his chair and Tony closed the door on the bustle behind him.

*   *   *

Anna was asleep. He stared at her peaceful face, and finally let himself weep quietly. He held her limp hand, then dropped it. He silently willed her to wake up, hoping that somehow she could hear his thoughts. *Wake up, talk to me*. Anna didn't move. The next instant, he wanted to shake her, hit her, make her tell him what was going on. Could she have done this? The police obviously thought so. He was immediately ashamed to have even thought it: Anna would never hurt Jack. It was impossible. What had she seen?

He suddenly realised how incredibly tired he was. He wanted to get into the narrow bed beside his wife and hold her, feel her warmth and her heartbeat and her breath. They would cry for Jack together.

He hated to think of her waking up alone earlier; she would have been so confused, so terrified. That was why she'd been agitated, it was the trauma of everything: the police, the tests, whatever she had witnessed today. It was possible that she didn't even know that Jack was dead. A shudder ran through him. How could he tell her?

His phone vibrated in his pocket. He lifted it out and saw his mother's mobile number displayed. He disconnected the call, switched the phone off, then put it back in his pocket.

Some time later, someone brought in a styrofoam cup of watery tea, which he let go cold. Someone else told him that his dad was outside, but he shook his head; he wanted to be alone. Faceless nurses padded in and out of the room, checking Anna's temperature, her pulse, her blood pressure. She didn't wake up. He shivered. There was a chill in the room, and he noticed through the small window that the doctors and nurses had put cardigans and jumpers over their scrubs. He pulled Anna's blanket up to her neck and tucked it around her body. He moved his chair closer and laid his head down on the bed so it was touching her arm. When she woke up, he wanted her to know that she wasn't alone.

CHAPTER EIGHT

Six weeks before

Wednesday, 5 August 2009

Anna watched the grey light from outside begin to creep into the hospital room, softly edging its way through the gaps in the blinds. It draped itself over the bed; she rolled away from it so it couldn't reach her. She was sure she had only fallen asleep a few minutes earlier. She blinked, yawned, then reached for the glass of water on the bedside table.

Tony sprang up. 'Is everything OK?'

She looked at him and smiled. 'Yes, I'm fine, babe.'

He yawned, then rubbed at the dark stubble on his face. 'How do you feel?'

'Tired. I don't think I slept at all.'

'Me neither,' he said.

'Yes, you did! You were snoring all night.' She got up, and went to sit next to Tony. She leaned into him and ran her fingers through his hair. He lifted his head onto her stomach, kissed it, then whispered to the baby that it was time to come out now.

Closing her eyes, she savoured the peacefulness of that moment, knowing it would be the last time they would be a couple. Soon, they would be a family.

* * *

She screwed her eyes closed and pursed her lips, panting, as the force of a contraction powered through her body.

'Just do your breathing, babe,' Tony said, holding her hand. 'Remember, they said in the classes not to hyperventilate, you need to slow down.'

'Yes, I remember!' She shook off his hand and moaned, looking up at the high window that let some daylight in to counter the harsh white fluorescent light of the delivery room. The contraction started to ease.

'Is it going away?'

She nodded. Her mouth was so dry; she licked her lips. 'Can you get me a drink from the bag?'

Tony stood up from the chair beside her and went to the black daypack at the end of the bed. The bag had sat inside the front door of their house for weeks, decorated with bright pink sticky notes to remind her of last-minute items to add before they left for the hospital. Tony rummaged in the bag and found the drink. He unscrewed it for her, and she took a sip.

'Thanks.' She turned to the midwife, who was sitting at a small workstation with her back to them, looking as though she was so absorbed in her work that she couldn't hear everything that was going on. 'Debbie?' she said. 'Can we turn down the air conditioning in here? I'm a bit cold.'

Debbie turned and smiled. She was in her fifties, with bleached-blonde hair tied back with a fluffy black hairband. She spun the squeaking chair around with her toes, jumped down and walked over to the bed. She picked up the remote control for the air conditioner and changed the temperature. 'Do you want another blanket?'

'No, thanks.'

'OK. I'll leave this remote here for you.' She padded back to her desk.

Anna looked at her watch; was it really only 10 a.m.? So much had happened since they came down from the ward. None of it was in her written birth plan, which she'd given to Debbie when they arrived. There was nothing in there about having needles in the back of her hand and medications to start contractions. There was nothing about having her membranes ruptured by something resembling a large crochet hook, or about the gush of hot liquid that pulsed and poured from her straight afterwards. She hated that Tony had seen her like that.

Another contraction was building. She put the drink down and closed her eyes, bracing herself. As it strengthened, she swung her legs over the end of the bed and bent forward, moaning. Tony rubbed her back; she swept his hand away. 'Don't!'

Tony stepped away. 'Sorry.'

She wanted to apologise, but didn't have the energy.

Debbie turned around again from her station at the desk. 'The anaesthetist is in the ward – have you considered an epidural?'

Anna shook her head. It was in her birth plan that she didn't want to be offered pain relief; if she wanted it, she'd ask for it. Why had she bothered?

'Why don't you try it, babe?' Tony said.

She glared at him. He knew how much she wanted to do this naturally. 'I'm OK.'

'No, you're not,' he said. 'It's hard to see you in such pain. You don't need —'

'I said I'm fine!'

Debbie came over and looked at the screen of the machine attached to the leads on Anna's belly. 'Well, it's entirely your decision. But it's early days yet. I'm going to turn up the drip soon to get these contractions going a bit, and things might get pretty intense quite quickly. Once the anaesthetist is in theatre, I can't guarantee that he can come straight away when you need him; it could take an hour or so . . .'

'An hour?' Anna looked over at Tony again. What if she couldn't cope for an hour?

'Just get it now, babe,' he urged her. 'You're going to be tired enough, don't make this harder than it needs to be.'

'It's your choice, Anna,' Debbie said, turning back to her desk.

She looked from Debbie back to Tony. It was obvious that they both wanted her to accept defeat. It didn't feel like she had any choice at all.

She'd embraced every part of her pregnancy, good and bad. Even in the early weeks when she was tortured by nausea and pounding headaches, when she retched and vomited every day, she never complained. It was all part of the experience that she had wanted for so long; it was her body's way of bonding her with the life growing in her womb. She knew then that she would do anything for her baby, and she had wanted to experience every moment of labour, too, to know that she had done the best for her child.

Another contraction was hovering, about to grip her. She held her breath and braced herself, then closed her eyes as it rose to a crescendo. Every muscle in her body clenched until she was sure her bones would break. She felt light-headed and wanted to scream. Maybe they were right; maybe she couldn't do it on her own after all.

'OK, call the anaesthetist. Let's do it now,' she said, gasping, then turned onto her side and drew her knees towards her chest. Her eyes filled with tears.

Debbie picked up the phone and spoke calmly. 'I have another epidural here for you.'

Anna heard herself being reduced to just another nameless patient, just a procedure. As she felt her self slipping away, she couldn't shake the feeling that she had failed.

*　　*　　*

Once the epidural was in, she rested on her back on the bed. She was amazed at how quickly it had worked and how much stronger she felt without the pain, though she wouldn't admit it out loud. Her abdomen and legs were numb; she could hardly move. She rested her hands on her belly to feel it tightening, reassuring herself that her body was still doing what it should. She watched the machine beside her churn out a long strip of paper graphing the peaks and troughs of her contractions. It didn't seem as though it was connected to her belly, to her baby.

Tony was sitting in the corner, playing with something on his phone. He looked up.

'Are you all right?' he said.

She nodded.

'Why don't you close your eyes, try to have a nap?'

'I'm OK, I'm just resting.'

As Tony turned his attention back to his phone, she watched the clock on the wall, willing it to go faster, imagining that it was going slow on purpose.

Debbie came over and uncurled the strip of paper, frowning as she scanned it. She wrote something down, then turned up the drip again.

'Debbie?' she asked. 'Can you turn it up, the volume, just so I can hear . . . the baby?'

'Of course.' The midwife fiddled with a button, then rearranged one of the monitors strapped to her, and there it was. *Ba boom, ba boom.* Her baby was still there.

'I just need to do an internal examination, Anna.' Debbie pulled on a pair of rubber gloves.

She nodded. Debbie lifted up her numb legs. She looked away while she was poked and pushed.

'All done. Hope that wasn't too uncomfortable.' Debbie snapped her plastic gloves off.

'No, it was OK. What's happening?'

Debbie raised her eyebrows. 'Well, that cervix isn't behaving – it's just not where I'd expect it to be.'

She wondered why medical staff were trained to talk to patients as though they were children. She felt her jaw tighten. She wasn't just irritated with Debbie, she was irritated with herself, her body. She knew that didn't make sense, but if Debbie reckoned that her cervix could misbehave, she had every right to be angry with it. She had a sudden surge of energy and pushed down on the mattress with her hands to hoist herself up in the bed.

'So what are we going to do then?'

Debbie turned back to the drip stand and pressed the black button again. 'We'll just keep going. I'll check you again in two hours.'

Two hours? She could have cried. She wanted to get out of bed and walk around, to use the bathroom instead of having a catheter in her bladder. She wanted to have a shower or sit on the fit ball as she had planned. She tried to breathe deeply as a horrible sense of suffocating claustrophobia settled on her. She felt as though she was stuck on a long flight, with no way to stretch out without touching someone, no way of protecting her own space. But she could no more get up from this bed than open the door of an aeroplane and step out.

She felt Tony watching her. She turned away from his gaze and closed her eyes. Tony pulled his chair across the floor towards her; the grating noise drilled through her. He took her clammy hand and stroked it with his thumb. She was too warm now; he was making her hotter. She knew he was only trying to help, but she just wanted to be left alone. She forced a smile, then pulled her hand away.

But he stayed by her side.

CHAPTER NINE

The day after

Tuesday, 15 September 2009

As the sun started to rise, a cleaner arrived and began mopping the floor around Tony. Soon afterwards the full lights came on to indicate that a new day had started. The next shift of nurses breezed in, bright and chatty, sipping coffee from cardboard cups with plastic lids. He watched them huddle around the desk and make notes as a senior nurse worked her way through a pile of patient files, talking and gesticulating. She spoke too softly for him to hear clearly, but he knew when she was describing Anna's case by the way the nurses all glanced over at him. The door to Anna's room was propped open again, but a new policeman was on the chair. Tony stroked Anna's hand; her eyes were still closed.

Laying his head back down on the bed he tried to sleep. Some time later, he saw a group moving from bed to bed in the main area. He recognised the tall, thin frame of Dr Hall, the registrar he'd spoken to yesterday. Maybe they had some test results now, some explanation for Anna's condition. He stood up and waited just outside the door where they couldn't miss him as they walked towards Anna's room. Dr Hall nodded in his direction but said nothing as the group crowded into her room and stood with their backs to Tony. He hovered, trying to see what they were doing, but there was no room for him, so he watched through the small window as they examined her. Their voices were low, and he couldn't hear what they were saying. He didn't have the energy to push his way in, to ask them to speak up. The doctors finished and filed out, darting off to the next bed like a frightened school of fish. Dr Hall, however, paused beside Tony with an older, balding man, who held out his hand.

'Mr Patton, I'm Dr Cooper, the consultant here in Emergency. Come with us, please, so we can have a quick talk.'

Tony nodded, suddenly feeling intimidated. He followed them down a passageway to a small, windowless room with two sofas crammed into it. Dusty yellow silk flowers drooped from a vase on a small white formica coffee table against the wall. Dr Cooper and Dr Hall sat on one sofa; he sat on the other. He rearranged the cushions to make more room, but his knees still practically touched Dr Hall's.

Dr Cooper asked the same questions Dr Hall had yesterday and he wearily repeated the same answers. There was nothing more he could tell them.

'Mr Patton —'

'Tony.'

'Tony, as you know, we've monitored Anna overnight, and we've been waiting for the test results. The good news is that we can't find anything medically wrong with her. Her head CT is normal, her temperature is good now, her blood tests are all normal.'

'Oh.' While he was relieved, part of him was disappointed. It would be easier if the doctors had found something wrong with Anna, something tangible, something with a name.

'The next thing we have to rule out is any psychiatric condition,' Dr Cooper went on.

His head snapped up. 'But what about shock or something? You know, if someone's attacked her or taken Jack from her. That would explain the way she reacted.'

The consultant nodded. 'If that was the case – and I don't think it is – then the psychiatrist is still the best person to help us. There's no physical reason for her to be so unresponsive, and we haven't found any evidence that she's been assaulted —'

'But she's covered in bruises and cuts!'

'Yes, but they don't look like they were done by a person or a weapon. I think they're just from the rocks.'

He rubbed his forehead. He felt as though he was losing, running out of ways to make this man understand. 'Then maybe they just snatched the baby and she fell or something . . .'

Dr Cooper took a deep breath. 'Tony, you're right, that could have happened; the police will be looking into all possibilities. But you've told us that she hadn't been sleeping, that she'd seen her GP who gave her tablets – we must rule out significant mental illness.' He looked at Dr Hall, then back to Tony. 'The police have probably asked you this already, but did you ever worry that Anna could be a danger to herself . . . or to Jack?'

He looked at each of the doctors in turn. Did they really believe that she was capable of hurting her son? 'No! Never! She'd never hurt him – or herself – in a million years. Jesus, I can't —'

'OK.' Dr Cooper held up his hands as if they could deflect Tony's incredulity. 'I'm sorry, it's a standard question when people have been very depressed.'

Weren't they listening? 'But she hasn't been very depressed, I've told you.'

Dr Cooper's pager beeped rudely. Tony wondered if he'd set it off deliberately so that he had an excuse to leave. He couldn't imagine doctors enjoyed this sort of conversation; it must be much easier to hand someone a prescription or give them an injection. Regardless, he was glad of the few seconds it gave him to breathe, to think.

Dr Cooper looked up from his pager. 'I'm sorry, Tony, but I have to go. Do you have any final questions?'

He was silent for a moment. His head was full of questions but Dr Cooper wasn't going to answer them. He shook his head.

'Just wait here. Dr Hall will page the psychiatry team – they'll come straight away.'

He blinked, then held out his hand. 'Thank you, doctor.'

*   *   *

Tony waited in that small, windowless room. He rubbed at the grainy silk petals of the fake plant to clean some of the dust from them. He turned his phone back on and listened to his voicemail. The police, his parents, Wendy, a few teary messages from friends and family who'd heard what had happened. He deleted them all, then called his parents' number. His mum answered on the first ring.

'Anthony! Are you all right?'

'Yeah, yeah. I'm still at the hospital. I'm sorry about last night, I just couldn't face seeing anyone.'

'For God's sake, don't worry about that. We waited a few hours, but they told us you'd fallen asleep so we went home to freshen up – we wanted to let you rest. How's Anna this morning? Any change?'

'Oh Mum, I don't know what's going on. They say she's physically OK. I'm waiting to see a psychiatrist. The doctors seem to think that she could have done this deliberately.' He spoke in a monotone; the idea of Anna harming Jack was so ridiculous that he couldn't find any anger. Let them do their assessment, and soon enough they'd find out they were wrong.

'Has she said something? Is that why they think that?'

'She hasn't said anything. They knocked her out with some drugs last night, they said she was screaming. And then they wonder why she can't talk or wake up from this. They don't get it! I can't keep up with it all.' He swallowed hard and rubbed his face as his voice cracked. 'Sorry . . . it's just . . .'

'What can we do? I'll come straight away —'

'No. I need to stay here, I just need to sort this out. She hasn't woken yet. It'll kill her, Mum, when she realises . . .' He heard Ursula take a sharp breath in, but she let him carry on. 'Some detective left a message – they want to go to the house and have a look around. Can you go and let them in? The spare key —'

'Of course. I know where it is now.'

'And Wendy's getting in at about midday – can someone pick her up? I don't know when I'll be done here.'

'Yes, yes, of course, don't worry, we'll sort it out . . .'

He heard footsteps approaching. 'Thanks, Mum. I think the psychiatrist is here now, I'd better go. I'll call you soon.'

'OK. And Anthony . . . we're just so very, very sorry.'

Tony closed his eyes and bit his bottom lip to stop tears from starting. Crying wasn't going to help; there was too much to sort out. He managed to say goodbye, then put his phone back in his pocket as two men entered the room.

The taller of the two wore dark grey chinos and a checked blue business shirt, open at the neck. 'Mr Patton, I'm Dr Paul Murray. I'm one of the psychiatry doctors, and this is one of our senior psychiatric nurses, Eamon Byrne.'

Tony nodded at the man standing just behind the doctor then turned his attention back to Dr Murray as the two men sat on the couch opposite him.

'We're the psychiatry team working in the main hospital here,' Dr Murray went on. 'We see patients when the medical team is worried that there may be a mental health issue affecting their physical health.'

'They told me. But, look, I've been through this. You just have to take one look at her. She looks awful, she's covered in cuts and bruises, she can't talk. She's not making this up, this isn't all in her head.'

Dr Murray looked at him steadily. 'No one is saying that your wife is making this up, not at all. We know that physical and mental health are closely linked: physical problems can cause emotional problems, and vice versa. We're just here to see if we can help the medical team untangle the issues a bit.' He paused. 'I've also heard about your son. I can't imagine how difficult this is for you.'

Tony sat forward, suddenly furious. No one really wanted to help Anna; they just wanted to blame her. 'That's why you're here, isn't it? The police, that doctor, everyone thinks she did this. I'm telling you now, you're wrong! There's just, just no . . .' As quickly as it had come, his fury burned out, leaving smouldering disbelief.

Dr Murray leaned back on the sofa. 'Please, calm down. That's not the reason we're here. This is a complex and difficult situation and that just needs a few different perspectives. What the police do is their issue: I'm here from a medical point of view. I have nothing to do with the police.'

Tony rubbed his face. 'Look, I just want . . .' He faltered. 'I just want to know what happened to my baby . . . and I want Anna to be OK.' He realised immediately that he'd spoken about Anna as an afterthought.

'I do too.' Dr Murray said nothing for a few moments while Tony composed himself, then started again, gently. 'Does Anna have any history of mental health problems?' At that, the nurse opened a pad of paper and clicked his pen.

Tony's fists tightened and he clenched his teeth. 'No! My God, I've been through this so many times, don't you people talk to each other? No! Anna has never been depressed, she was not depressed, she was just tired and couldn't sleep. She saw her GP two weeks ago, and she said Anna was fine. So no, this is not depression!' He rested his head back on the sofa, exhausted. The doctor and nurse glanced at each other. Tony knew what they were thinking: they thought he was naive, that they knew Anna better than he – her own husband – did. And he knew that by being defensive, he was only convincing them in their belief that there was something wrong with her. 'Look, I'm sorry, it's just been . . . It's been a long twenty-four hours.'

Dr Murray spoke calmly. 'I understand, Tony. I know this is really hard for you. What we might do is go and see Anna now, see what we think, and come back and talk to you soon, OK?'

He nodded, but couldn't look at them. He focused on a piece of lint on the arm of the sofa until they had left the room, then he closed his eyes.

When they returned fifteen minutes later, the nurse, Byrne, was holding papers in his hand. 'Sorry to keep you waiting,' he said as he and Dr Murray sat down.

'That's fine,' he replied, trying to read the words on the paperwork.

Dr Murray cleared his throat. 'From the history that we have, and from what we can see, I am worried that Anna is very, very unwell. We need to get her out of the emergency department and admit her to the ward for more specialised care.' He hesitated.

Tony knew what was coming next; there was no point fighting it. Suddenly, every muscle in his body ached and he could barely hold his head up.

Dr Murray continued, 'And the most appropriate place is our psychiatry unit. Anna can't make that decision for herself at the moment, so I'm going to admit her under the Mental Health Act.'

'What?' He had no idea what that meant. He felt like he was under attack, with a new assault being hurled at him every minute.

'It means that I am making the decision for her, and if she were to try to leave, then I would have to stop her. I can do that because I believe she is suffering from a severe mental illness, and that mental illness means she is a danger to herself and others. Does that make sense?'

Tony pressed his fingertips into his temples and knew he owed it to Anna to at least try to protest. 'She's not dangerous. And look at her, she's not going anywhere – she can barely move.'

Dr Murray continued as if he hadn't heard. 'On the ward, another psychiatrist will see her. And if they agree with me, Anna will stay there under the Mental Health Act until we make further decisions about her treatment.'

Byrne handed Tony the bundle of paperwork. 'This explains everything in writing.'

He took it, then dropped it on the sofa next to him without looking at it. The decision had clearly already been made. 'What about the police? They said something about an interview.'

'I know,' Dr Murray said. 'Don't worry, they can't interview her until she's better. She'll be under our care and supervision until she's well enough.'

He thought about the policeman guarding Anna's door, the police at the beach, the police who might be going through his house at this very moment. They were hovering around, waiting to pounce. He hadn't managed to keep Jack safe; he needed to try harder to protect Anna. Perhaps committing her to a psychiatric ward was the only way of keeping the police from her.

'Do what you need to do,' he said at last.

'Great. We'll just organise the bed and someone to take her up there.' Dr Murray looked at Byrne, who nodded, leaning forward.

'Tony, we'll give you a call later when she's settled in. Why don't you go home and have a shower, something to eat, then come back and see her on the ward?'

Tony nodded slowly, realising he was still in his work clothes. He looked at his suit pants, and couldn't believe that it was only yesterday that he'd kissed Jack goodbye and gone to work. Jack's face flashed in front of him; suddenly he no longer cared what happened to Anna. He felt sick. 'I think I will go now, for a little while. I'm sorry . . . I've got so many things to do.'

Dr Murray spoke softly. 'Anna will be all right, Mr Patton, try not to worry. And I really am sorry about your son.'

The doctor and nurse stood up. Both of them shook Tony's hand, then walked out. He pushed himself up from the couch to follow them. He left the room and closed the door behind him, but they had already disappeared.

CHAPTER TEN

The day after

Tuesday, 15 September 2009

Anna lay still; her shoulder ached when she moved. She opened her eyes, just a little, just enough to tell her that she was in the same bare room. She kept her head steady but moved her eyes to the right and saw that the uneven pavers in the courtyard outside the window were illuminated by sunlight, although the high brick wall threw down a wedge of shadow. It must be the middle of the day. Was it the same day? She'd pretended to be asleep when they had wheeled her in here earlier. Someone had tried to give her some food, but she couldn't risk eating anything; she didn't know if she was safe. Could they be drugging her? Tony had been there, he'd held her hand, but that seemed a long time ago. Where was he now?

That policeman was still at the door, pretending to read the newspaper. He must know – must be a part of it. She heard a snap and jumped; the policeman had shaken the paper to straighten it, and was now folding it up on his lap. Footsteps were approaching, getting louder: someone was coming. She closed her eyes again and tried to breathe slowly. She silently pleaded with her limbs to stop shaking.

It was impossible to lie completely still when the voices were almost constant now, taunting her, jeering. Anna wanted to cry, but she had to be strong; it was the only way. There was another voice too, a woman's, closer, clearer than the others. She opened her eyes, and through the slits of her eyelids saw in the doorway a small woman not much older than herself. She had long brown hair loosely tied in a knot at the nape of her neck and wore glasses with dark frames. She looked down at the seated policeman, and then her heels began to clip across the vinyl. As the woman put her large tan handbag down on the floor near the wall, Anna saw the yellow fluorescent light glinting in her red nail polish. Her heart raced. She quickly closed her eyes again, wishing everyone would just leave her alone.

'Good morning, Anna. Do you remember meeting me?'

She didn't move. This woman was lying: they'd never met before. What was she trying to do?

'I'm Dr Morgan, the psychiatrist looking after you.'

A psychiatrist? She started to breathe more quickly, anxiety flooding through her. Why had they sent a psychiatrist? Hadn't they done enough? What were they planning?

'I'm a medical doctor who specialises in looking after people who have had problems with their mood or feelings. Does that make sense?'

Her chin twitched involuntarily and she held her breath. Had the psychiatrist seen her move? Did this Dr Morgan know she was pretending to be asleep? She squeezed her eyelids tightly shut to stop the tears that were pooling behind them from spilling out.

'Anna, do you understand?'

She felt the warm tickle of a tear run down her cheek, follow her jaw back towards her ear, then drip onto her collarbone. She couldn't pretend any more; maybe it was safer to cooperate, maybe then they'd stay away from Tony and Jack. She heard the hollow sound of something dropping onto the bedside table next to her, and opened her eyes slowly, blinking as they adjusted to the light. Dr Morgan slid a box of tissues towards her. She didn't reach for one.

Dr Morgan looked over at the policeman by the door and asked him to wait outside. When he had skulked away she went over and closed the door behind him. Anna's heart pounded; this doctor must be in charge. While she was glad that the policeman had gone, it meant that they were alone now, without any witnesses.

She blinked to clear the tears from her vision; she needed to see what was coming.

Dr Morgan pulled the policeman's chair to the side of her bed, sat down and then nestled back as if it were a comfortable armchair. Anna forced herself to ignore the mumbles behind her and focus.

'Anna, do you know why you're here?' the doctor asked.

Anna shook her head, certain that if she opened her mouth she'd scream.

Dr Morgan's voice became soothing, soft. 'Do you know where you are at the moment?'

If she spoke, things would just get worse.

'You're in hospital, in the psychiatric ward.'

Anna felt faint as panic rushed through her. She wanted to explain, to tell Dr Morgan that she had tried to make it right. She didn't know what had happened, she had tried to do what they said, but obviously something had gone wrong.

Dr Morgan continued, 'Do you know what day it is?'

The murmuring in the room behind her kept going, on and on, louder and louder, laughing and mocking. What did it matter what day it was? Anna needed the noise to stop, but Dr Morgan went on, just adding to the babble and confusion.

'What about the time of day? Is it morning, afternoon, evening? Who is the prime minister?'

Anna's body began to rock, and she couldn't stop it. Her hands were tingling. Were Tony and Jack OK? They didn't deserve this: it was all her fault. She wasn't good enough for them, it was true, they were better off without her in their lives. Anna's eyes filled with tears again and she turned her head away.

Dr Morgan urged her back. 'Anna, it's all right, there's plenty of time. You've been very unwell. I'm going to see you every day and we'll see how we go. If you need to talk in between times, let the nurses know and they can page me. Even if I'm not here, they can call me and I'll talk to you by phone.'

Anna blinked hard. She wanted to believe that she could trust Dr Morgan, but she couldn't. She didn't have any choice but to play along, though, so she nodded slightly, flinching from the pain in her shoulder. There was nothing she could do.

Dr Morgan picked up her bag and left the room. Anna breathed out in relief and started to tremble. She thought about trying to stand up, to run, but then the policeman came back and took up his post by the door. She whimpered and curled up on her side.

She tried to count slowly in her head, and concentrated on tensing and relaxing each muscle as she had learned to do in yoga when she was pregnant. It used to work. She had loved those Saturday morning classes, feeling her baby prod and wriggle in her belly as she relaxed. Now, that seemed like someone else's life; maybe it was.

Breathe in for two counts, out for four.

Her eyes stung. She begged sleep to take her away from this. What had happened to Tony? Where was Jack? Had they got to them after all?

Things were getting foggy, blurry in front of her eyes, but something sharp and persistent darted around at the edges. As the fog thickened, Anna listened to the noises around her: alarms beeping, the policeman sighing, the birds outside screeching. They blended into a horrible lullaby. No one could possibly hear her scream over that cacophony. No one was coming to rescue her. She was alone.

CHAPTER ELEVEN

The day after

Tuesday, 15 September 2009

Wendy hesitated at the top of the stairs, oblivious to the crowd tutting and muttering as they squeezed around her to reach the escalator down to the baggage collection area. The flight had been long. She had sat next to two burly blokes heading home to Sydney after a month on the mines. Small talk was difficult for her at the best of times, but this had been torture. They had asked why she was going to Sydney; she had told them that she was visiting her daughter. She was desperate to blurt out the truth in the hope that telling someone else would make it hurt less. And it did hurt, physically, in the depth of her chest, her head, her back. But she hadn't said anything; she had put her headphones on as soon as they took off, and stared intently at the seatback television as the tiny plane on the screen made its way inch by inch across the Nullarbor to the east coast.

She walked forward onto the escalator. A young woman behind her stumbled and swore, but it barely registered. At the bottom, Wendy scanned the throng but couldn't see Tony, so she stood still, unsure of what to do. She should have known this would happen; she should have made a plan, just in case. She wanted a cigarette. Her eyes filled with tears. Where was he?

Then she heard someone shout her name; her shoulders dropped in relief as Jim strode towards her, with Ursula following. Wendy's lip started to quiver, and she dabbed at her eyes with her sleeve as they approached.

'Hi,' was all she managed to utter before her face crumpled. She opened her arms and clutched Ursula. 'I promised myself I wouldn't cry . . . I'm so, so sorry.' She reached into her bag for some tissues, but could only find used ones, dried and clumped together. Ursula handed her a clean one.

Wendy took it with a nod. Ursula was crying too, though she made no noise. Wendy blew her nose. 'Is there any more news?'

Ursula looked down. 'No. Not since this morning.'

Jim cleared his throat and put his arm around her, steering her towards the baggage carousel. 'Come on, let's go get your bags. How was the flight?'

'Long, horrible, the usual. We sat on the tarmac for about an hour before taking off.' She managed to smile at Jim, grateful to him for asking a question that she knew how to answer. She liked him; Anna often said how lovely he was to her. That meant a lot to Wendy, who had always worried that not knowing her father might have damaged Anna in some way. There was no evidence of this, of course; Anna had done so well in her life and seemed to know exactly what she wanted. At the thought of her daughter, lying alone in hospital, her eyes filled again with tears.

'You must be exhausted,' Ursula said. 'Travelling such a long way, on top of . . . this.'

Wendy shook her head. 'I'm sure we all are.'

They had arrived at the carousel; the shrill alarm sounded as the conveyer belt began to move. Falling silent, all three of them stared at the luggage snaking past them. At last, she saw her suitcases and pointed them out. Jim took one in each hand.

'Come on,' he said. 'Let's get out of here.' He started to walk towards the exit while she and Ursula walked side-by-side behind him.

Wendy bit her lip. 'My sister Pam's calling a friend who lives in Sydney, to see if I can stay with her. I'm sorry, I just haven't had time . . .'

Looking relieved to have something practical to discuss, Ursula spoke firmly. 'Don't worry, we're sorting it out. Lisa's spoken to

Emily; she's going to stay at her boyfriend's for a while and you can stay in her apartment. She's cleaning it up at the moment, so you'll come back to ours for now and we'll take you over later. We thought you'd like your own space rather than cramming in with us.'

Wendy nodded, grateful. She had known Emily since she and Anna were small, and she'd be much more comfortable there than with Ursula and Jim. Ursula had always intimidated her. She seemed so capable and Wendy worried that Anna compared the two of them and was disappointed in her own lot. Even today, when she must have been up all night, Ursula had managed to style her short dark hair and put on the burgundy lipstick she always wore. She wasn't a thin woman, but she carried her weight well, unlike Wendy, who could never seem to hide the kilos that had crept on over the years. She was suddenly aware of how she must look after the flight: she should have put on some make-up, brushed her hair instead of scraping it back with her fingers into a ponytail. She had been meaning to book into the hairdresser to get her roots done for ages. Then she remembered the picture of Jack hanging on her wall at home. It didn't matter what she looked like.

'Great, thanks. I'm sorry, I don't mean to put anyone out —'

'It's no problem. It's the least of our worries. I just didn't want to ask Tony – he probably needs his space. He might not even want to stay there now. I don't know, it's all so . . .' Ursula turned away. Jim had stopped up ahead at the parking ticket machine. 'Jim! Don't use your credit card, I've got change.' She turned back to Wendy and frowned. 'He never uses coins, just leaves them in drawers or in his car. Then he complains when he needs them.' She sped up, already taking her purse out of her handbag.

Wendy opened her own bag. 'I've got money, here . . . You don't need to pay after driving out here to get me.' But it was too late. Ursula was feeding coins into the machine.

She watched them squabble. It felt like she was intruding on something intimate, so she hung back until Ursula beckoned to her to follow them to the car.

* * *

Tony opened his front door, stepping quickly inside, then closed it behind him. He hoped none of the neighbours had seen him. They would have seen the police car this morning, discussed it over breakfast, then gossiped outside the school gates when they dropped off their kids. He had no doubt that they would have heard about Jack, but he wasn't ready to face them. He peered out of the frosted glass panel in the front door, but the street was empty. After locking the door he turned around. He wasn't sure what he expected to see – black whorls of fingerprint dust or yellow crime scene tape, maybe – but, cruelly, everything looked the same as it had yesterday, as it did every day. As it had when Jack was here.

He saw a piece of notepaper on the hall table and recognised his mum's handwriting: *Fed Jessie. Police been and gone, they want to talk to you. Call me. I love you, Mum.*

He left the note where it was and looked down the hallway. The door to Jack's room was closed. He took a deep breath and hurried past it into the bathroom. He stripped off his clothes and kicked them into the corner then had a quick shower. In the bedroom he put on some clean underwear; opening the wardrobe, he tried not to look at Anna's clothes hanging politely next to his. He closed it again and put on some shorts and a polo shirt from his drawer. For a moment he looked at the bed, still made, and Anna's cold cup of tea. He longed to crawl in and hide under the blankets. The last time he had slept in it, two nights ago, Anna had been with him. He needed her; he wasn't good on his own, he was only good with her. He knew he needed to leave this room; there were too many intimate memories. After closing the bedroom door carefully behind him, he went into the living area.

The kitchen bench was tidy, with no signs of the pizzas his dad had brought over the night before. His mum would have tidied up when she let the police in. In a way, he wished she hadn't. Anna had struggled to keep on top of the housework since Jack had been born, but he hadn't cared. He'd liked to see the toys littering the floor and the nappy bags piled outside the front door. Clean, it was as if she'd wiped away some of the spirit of Jack. And Anna. He opened the patio doors and Jessie came running in, wagging her tail. He crouched down and scratched her ears, then took his bag and laptop over to the coffee table and sat on the couch. His secretary, Donna, had left a message on his phone and he had some emails that he needed to sort out. Jessie jumped up next to him; for once, he let her stay. He felt better when he opened his computer and it started up. Work was comfortingly familiar, and Tony wanted to grab onto something in his life that was still the same, where he knew his purpose and his role.

The screen flickered in front of his eyes, then settled. The desktop background was a picture of the three of them, the same one that Anna had printed out and kept by their bed, taken just before they walked out of the hospital to bring Jack home for the first time, six weeks ago.

He had woken early that morning. He'd slept at the hospital for the first four nights, lifting Jack up when he woke and handing him to Anna to feed in bed, changing his tiny nappy so that Anna could rest. But on that last night, Anna had insisted that he stay at home and get a good night's sleep. He had slept well, but woke at 5 a.m., excited that his son was coming home. He tidied the house, put some washing on, and changed the sheets on the bed. He had dressed, then walked Jessie to the shops and bought some flowers and blue balloons. Back home, he rechecked the baby capsule in the car; it looked so big for such a little baby. When he was sure it was secure, he'd driven to the hospital where Anna was dressed and ready for him. They had loaded up a trolley with all the flowers and gifts, then asked the nurse to take this photo of their family.

How could it all go so wrong so quickly? What had happened? Tony rubbed his clammy face and blinked hard. He pushed the thoughts away and forced himself to breathe slowly. He would sort out work first, then he could move onto the more difficult things. He opened up his email program and scanned through the messages. He hadn't yet told work what had happened. Donna had assumed he was still unwell and had cancelled his meetings for the day. She wanted to know if he'd be back soon. Tony didn't know what he was going to do tomorrow. Or next week or next month.

Seconds passed, maybe minutes. The laptop went into sleep mode and the screen went dark; he shook his head quickly to banish his thoughts and sent a brief reply to Donna saying he'd be away for at least a week. That was the best he could do for now.

His phone, on silent, vibrated in his pocket. Without looking at the screen, he rejected the call and turned it off. He couldn't talk to anyone yet. He reached across and picked up his bag from the coffee table; balancing it horizontally on his knee, he opened it to find some paperwork. As he did so, several documents slid out and fell onto the floor.

'Shit,' he said, and bent down to pick them up: an A4 notebook, a printout of his presentation, and some unopened mail. He shuffled them back into a pile, then stopped. On the top of the pile was an envelope with his name handwritten on it. He had never seen it before but he recognised Anna's handwriting.

His hands started to shake as he turned the envelope over, lifted the unsealed flap, then pulled out a single folded sheet of plain white A4 paper. He didn't want to read it. He knew that he'd be better off ripping it up and pretending he hadn't seen it. But before he could stop himself, he was unfolding the paper and scanning the messy handwriting. The tremor in his hands increased; he had to put them down on his lap to stop the letter flapping about in front of his eyes. He smoothed it out, leaving patches of sweat from his fingers on the paper. He read it, then read it again, disbelieving. Was this a joke? Some cruel trick intended to torture him some more? He began to hyperventilate and tears filled his eyes, dropping onto the letter, soaking into the paper. The ink spread and the words blurred. He threw the letter down next to him. He lifted the front of his shirt and covered his face with it as he sobbed.

Suddenly, Jessie raised her head and her ears pricked up. He jumped, expecting someone to walk through the door at any second.

He sniffed and wiped his face, then quickly refolded the letter, stuffed it back in the envelope and shoved it back into his bag.

No one walked in, but he left the letter where it was. He didn't want to look at it again. He closed his eyes and let his heart rate settle, but the words taunted him. What did it mean? He kept his eyes shut, wishing he hadn't just seen what he had. But it was too late; he would never forget.

*   *   *

Later that afternoon, Tony stopped his car just around the corner from his parents' house with the engine idling. He didn't want to be here; he wanted to stay at home, lock the doors and turn out the lights, but he had responsibilities. A car slowed, then drove around him. Tony watched the driver, an ordinary man going home after an ordinary day at work, probably to his wife and kids. Lucky bastard.

He put the car into drive and turned left into his parents' cul-de-sac. The nature strip was littered with purple petals from a big jacaranda tree. The sound of a television blared out of the open window of the Soutars' house next door. He drove up onto the verge and parked the car on an angle, then got out before he could change his mind and reverse back onto the road. He wasn't even halfway up the path to his parents' front door when it opened.

'Anthony, love, we were worried,' Ursula said, holding the door wide open.

'Sorry, I had some work to do.'

'Work?' Ursula frowned, then held her arms out as he stepped into the house. He didn't hug her; she dropped her arms by her side. 'Anyway, how are you?'

Tony shrugged, and took off his shoes, leaving them side-by-side on the shoe rack in the hallway. 'I'm all right. Did you pick up Wendy earlier?'

'She's here now. We'll take her to Emily's place later. Come in, come in, can I get you something?'

He closed the door behind him. 'A beer. Thanks.' He walked into the living room while his mum went into the kitchen. Jim and

Wendy were sitting on the cream leather couch. They both stood up. Wendy hurried towards him.

'Tony,' she said, starting to cry. 'I'm so, so sorry . . .'

'Thanks,' he said, as he hugged her. He gently extricated himself. 'Thanks for coming . . .'

'Oh, of course . . . I just wish . . . You know, I wanted to come over when he was born, but I wanted to give you space, and she said, she said not to. And now . . . I never even got to meet him!'

Tony felt his own tears threatening to escape as Wendy covered her face with her hands and sobbed. He cleared his throat and looked over at his dad, who stared at the floor. Just then, Ursula walked into the room and handed Tony a beer. He gripped the foam stubby holder and took a gulp.

'Wendy, can I get you another glass of wine?' Ursula said, putting her hand on Wendy's shoulder. Wendy took a deep breath, nodded, and picked up her empty glass from the floor beside the couch. Ursula walked over to the half-empty bottle of wine on the walnut sideboard and poured two glasses.

Jim raised his own bottle of beer as if he was going to propose a toast, then let it drop again. 'It's been a long couple of days.'

Everyone nodded, then Wendy looked up at Tony. 'How's Anna?'

He shook his head. How could he explain it? If he hadn't seen her for himself, he'd never have believed it. 'Not good. She was still sleeping when I left this morning, conked out on some medication they gave her. I haven't been able to speak to her.' He closed his eyes for a moment. 'They moved her to the . . . psychiatry ward.' He waited for Wendy to protest, to gasp in horror, but she just nodded. Was he the only one who thought she shouldn't be there?

'I heard. I called the hospital earlier but they said I couldn't visit until after her rest time.' Wendy wiped tears from her eyes. 'I'm sure the doctors know what they're doing.'

He nodded, but his face started to flush as he thought of the letter in his bag.

'Does she know about Jack?' Wendy asked, almost whispering.

He shook his head. He was too tired to piece everything together, and he wasn't sure he really wanted to try. 'I don't know. I have no idea what she knows.'

'Dear God,' said Ursula, under her breath. 'Well, we need to go and see her. They can't keep her family away. Wendy, Tony can take you.'

He picked at the label on his beer bottle, avoiding his mum's gaze. 'They have rules, Mum. She's in the locked ward.'

Ursula frowned. 'The locked ward?'

'I'm sure that doesn't mean anything, love,' Jim said.

'Why is she locked up?'

'Mum, surely you can work it out.' He slammed his beer bottle down on the coffee table. 'They think she's dangerous.' He let out a laugh that was close to a cry.

Ursula opened her mouth to speak, but Jim caught her eye and shook his head. She closed it again and looked at Wendy, who was sitting forward with her hands over her face.

'She'll need some clothes,' he said quietly, looking at Wendy.

Wendy sniffed and wiped her cheeks. 'Of course. Where —'

'I've got a bag in the car. Just a few things, her toothbrush and shampoo. She hates the stuff they give you in hotels – I can't imagine the hospital having anything she likes. And some expensive soap that she uses when she wants a treat.'

'That sounds great, Tony.'

'And a book – you know what she's like, always reading . . .'

'Well, let me just wash my face and we can go now.'

He looked at Wendy. 'I can't.'

'Can't what?' Ursula said.

'I can't visit her. Not now. I'm just . . .' He stood up. He didn't want to explain. He needed to sort things out in his own head before he could see Anna. He didn't know what to say to her, what to ask her. This morning, he'd been so certain that he knew what had happened, but now nothing made any sense. 'I just want to be on my own for a while.'

Jim stood up and put his hand on Tony's shoulder. 'Fair enough, Tony. It's only been a day since . . . well, you know. She'll still be there in the morning.' He looked at Wendy. 'I'll take you to the hospital to see her, Wendy, and you can let Tony know if there's any change.'

'Of course. I'll just be a couple of minutes.' Wendy stood up and walked out of the room.

'Thanks, Dad.'

Jim nodded. 'Give me your car keys. I'll go and get Anna's bag and put it in my car.'

Ursula began clearing up the glasses and bottles. He held out the keys for his dad and whispered, to no one in particular, 'I'm sorry.'

*   *   *

When Jim and Wendy had left for the hospital, and Tony had gone home, Ursula made herself a piece of warm, buttery toast. She wiped crumbs from her lips as she leaned on the kitchen bench. Her back ached, and her jaw felt stiff and frozen as she chewed. She forced herself to swallow, then picked up the plate and dropped the second half of the toast in the bin. She opened the dishwasher and started to stack it with the dirty dishes scattered all over the kitchen. Why couldn't people put things straight in there instead of leaving them in the sink? It just created extra work for her. She screwed up her face as she poured the dregs of Wendy's wine away, then noticed the pink lipstick stain on the glass. She sighed; she'd have to wash that off by hand.

Half an hour later, she heard Jim's ute pull up. She realised that she was still standing by the sink, staring at the mess. She closed her eyes, enjoying the last moment of solitude before he trudged into the kitchen.

'Did they let Wendy in to see Anna?' she asked when he came in and perched on a stool. She noticed the dark shadows under his eyes.

'Yeah. No problem. I was going to wait, but Emily called

her. She's going to meet her at the hospital, then go back to her apartment tonight. They'll pick up her stuff on the way.'

'Good.'

Jim raised his eyebrows. Ursula continued stacking the dishwasher. 'Are you OK?' he said.

'As well as can be expected.' She closed the dishwasher door while the drawers were still pulled out; the dishes crashed against each other. She knew Jim hadn't done anything wrong, but she had no energy left to be polite.

Jim slid off his stool and started to help. 'Don't worry about cleaning up now, love, sit down. You must be exhausted.'

She spun around. 'Yes, I *am* exhausted! We've been running around after everyone, worrying about Wendy and Anna, and being all nice and supportive. But who's supporting us? We've lost our grandson, our son has lost his son, and everyone seems to have forgotten that!'

'Hey!' Jim moved towards her. He put his arms around her shoulders and rubbed her back, but she shrugged him off.

'Everyone's forgetting about him, Jim.' She dropped her head to her chest. 'Poor little baby. Poor little Jack.' She clenched her eyes shut, wiping away a tear. 'I just have this horrible feeling about it.'

'What do you mean?'

'Well, what if she *did* do it?'

'Do what? We have no idea —'

'You know what I'm saying – don't be so naive. She's locked up in a psychiatric hospital for God's sake. They must think she —'

'Don't say that! We don't know what happened. Like Tony said, she could have been mugged, attacked. We just don't know.'

She let herself cry. She wanted to agree with Jim. But no matter how much she prayed that Anna had had nothing to do with Jack's death, she couldn't ignore the gnawing feeling that she could have done it. It wasn't impossible.

She bit her lip. 'Jim, what if she *did*? Jack was just a tiny baby! Poor Anthony, how's he ever going to get over this?'

'Love —'

'Well, I'm telling you, if it was her fault, she shouldn't just get away with it. I don't care if she's sick.'

'Ursula, stop!' Jim reached out and hugged her, firmly this time. 'We're all worn out, we're all grieving. Let's just wait and see. We're a family – we're all in this together.'

She relaxed a little in Jim's embrace, but she couldn't let it go. 'Well, we can't just sit around pretending it didn't happen. There are things to be done, a funeral to organise . . .' She started to crumple. 'I'm so worried about Anthony.'

'Oh love, give him time. He'll get there.'

'There is no time!' she said. 'There are so many things to do. The police, the doctors, they won't wait! It feels like I'm the one having to deal with it all. It's hard for me too . . .'

Jim pulled her closer. For a moment she tensed and started to protest, then gave in and clung to him. Jim kissed the top of her head. 'And you're doing a brilliant job, love. Tony knows that. Everyone deals with things differently.'

She brushed at her cheeks again. 'I know, I know . . . But I don't want to see Anna. Not yet. Not until we know a bit more.'

'That's fine, no one's asking you to. Go and wash your face. I'll finish up in here. We'll get through this.'

She nodded and walked towards the bathroom. Jim was right: they would get through this. It was her job as a mother to make sure Tony did too.

*   *   *

Tony balanced a carton of beer on his knee and pressed the intercom button for Sean's apartment.

'Hello?' said a voice.

He looked straight at the camera. 'Hi, mate.'

'Tony! Come up.'

Lifting the carton onto his shoulder he pushed the gate with his hip as he balanced a half-bottle of vodka under the other arm. He struggled up the stairs to the third floor, and walked through the open door. The news blared from the television, and Sean was perched on the edge of the couch eating a burger and chips. His work shirt was untucked, and his red hair was dishevelled.

He looked up, licking the salt off his fingers. 'Come in, mate. What's up? Don't usually see you on a school night.'

'Want a drink?' Tony wrenched open the top of the cardboard box and pulled out a six-pack. He cracked the lids off two bottles with the bottle opener on his key ring and handed one to Sean. After taking a long swig of his beer, he opened a cupboard and found two glasses. 'Vodka?' he offered.

Sean laughed. 'Bit much for me, mate, I'll stick with the beer. Got work in the morning. As do you.' He wrapped what was left of his food in the paper bag it had come in and stood up to put it in the bin. 'You OK?'

Tony rummaged in the fridge. 'You got any juice?'

'Nah. Should be a can of Coke in there somewhere, though.'

'Doesn't matter.' He closed the fridge door, then twisted the top off the vodka bottle and half-filled one of the glasses. He took a big gulp, then coughed.

'Tony! What's going on?' Sean said, frowning.

He finished the glass and coughed again. He pulled out one of the kitchen stools and sat down with his beer. Shaking his head, he looked up at Sean. 'I don't know where to start.' His voice cracked. He really didn't know how to say it. 'Anna's in hospital.'

Sean's eyes widened. 'Oh shit. What happened? Is she all right?'

He shook his head again. 'She's in the psychiatric ward.'

Sean raised his eyebrows. 'I'm sorry to hear that, mate.'

'And Jack . . .' Tony couldn't continue.

'What? What about Jack?'

He bit his lip; he had to say it out loud. 'Jack's gone.'

'Gone? What do you mean, gone?'

'Gone.'

Sean's face froze. 'Gone as in missing, or . . . ?'

Tony rubbed at a spot on the kitchen bench with his thumb. 'The second option.'

Sean's mouth opened, then closed again. His face leached of colour. 'He died? Is that what you mean?' He gasped. 'Jesus. What happened?'

Tony's eyes filled with tears. 'I don't know. I just can't understand it. Yesterday morning everything was fine. I went to work, then my mum went over to the house but they were gone and we couldn't find them, then they found her, but Jack's —'

'Shit. Mate, I . . . But how? Was Jack sick? I didn't know —'

'No, he wasn't sick.' He stared at Sean. 'He was perfect.'

Sean was pale. He shook his head slowly. 'I can't believe it. I'm so sorry. But I don't understand . . .'

Tony cleared his throat; the whole length of his gullet burned from the alcohol. He couldn't let himself think about Jack in any detail, to picture his face or his smile or his cry; he had to just stick to the facts, to what he knew for certain. 'I don't know what happened. They were found at the beach – looks like they fell down a cliff. Anna's covered in bruises, and she's in some kind of . . . trance, she won't say anything. And Jack . . . There'll be an autopsy. Mate, I looked everywhere for them! But I was too late.' He stared at the wall across from him.

'Jesus. I don't know what to say. How's Anna?'

'Not good. I don't know, they've done tests and scans and they say she's not hurt but if you saw her . . . She's just lying there, not saying anything. It's like I'm not even there.' Tony felt his cheeks start to redden with guilt at the thought of Anna lying in that hospital bed, wondering where he was, when he was here, drinking. He should be with her. But he couldn't be. Not tonight. Besides, Wendy was there.

He lowered his head. 'The police are involved.'

'Why? What do you mean?'

'Well, that's what I mean, it's ridiculous! She just wouldn't have done that —'

'Wait.' Sean held his right hand up, palm open. 'What are you talking about? Done what?'

It was such a relief to hear the shock in Sean's voice; it proved to him that he wasn't crazy for believing in his wife. 'Get this: they all seem to think that maybe she did it deliberately, like she went there with a plan to kill him – I have no idea what they're thinking. Everyone keeps asking me if she'd ever tried to hurt him, or herself, and if she'd been depressed, and was she on tablets. They've locked her in this mental ward, and she even has a fucking policeman guarding her!'

'Oh mate, there's no way . . .'

'I know! Jesus, she wanted to have a baby so bad, and she was so happy. You saw her when Jack was born – at the hospital, remember? – she couldn't stop smiling or staring at him.'

'Tony, come and sit down over here.' Sean put his arm around his friend, guiding him to the sofa. He picked up the remote and switched off the television. 'Think I will have that vodka with you, after all.' He walked back over to the kitchen area and reached up into the cupboard for a glass. He poured himself a nip of vodka, then opened two more beers as Tony kept talking, staring at his lap.

'Maybe, I don't know, someone stole Jack or something. People do that, you know, you hear about it all the time. She could have been trying to save him. Or she was carjacked, and she's in shock . . .'

'Slow down.' Sean handed Tony another beer and sat down beside him. 'Of course Anna wouldn't do this. They'll work that out. Jesus, I can't think . . . Mate, I'm so sorry about Jack.'

Tony covered his face with his hands and sobbed.

Sean was quiet for a moment. 'I just can't believe it, I can't believe we're having this conversation.'

Tony took his hands away from his face and wiped his nose with his arm. 'She's locked up. Like a criminal. God, what she must have gone through.'

'Where's your folks, and her mum?' Sean asked. 'Do they know you're here?'

'Her mum flew in this morning, she's gone to the hospital. I just couldn't . . . face it, you know?'

'Of course not, mate.'

Tony stood up again. 'Look, do you mind if we don't talk about this any more? I don't want to think about it any more.'

Sean nodded. 'Sure. Stay here, I'll run down to the DVD shop and get us a movie or something.'

As Sean grabbed his wallet and keys, Tony slumped back on the couch. He closed his eyes; the room was spinning. He kept his eyes closed, not sure if he could prevent himself from vomiting. Some time later, he heard the door open and close again as Sean returned. He tried to sit up, then shook his head, lay back again and closed his eyes; it could all stay away for just a few minutes longer.

CHAPTER TWELVE

Two days after

Wednesday, 16 September 2009

Wendy rubbed her gritty eyes as the taxi approached the hospital grounds; she may as well have been grinding grains of sand into them. Her eyes watered and she wiped them with the back of her hand. Seeing Anna for the first time yesterday, just lying in the hospital bed, had been overwhelming. She understood why Tony had stayed away. By the time she had made it back to Emily's flat last night she was worn out, but she'd still barely slept. Her mind had churned everything over and over. She had even found herself thinking back to the sight of Jim and Ursula squabbling over the ticket machine. She missed the intimacy of having a partner, even the bickering. She wished she had someone to talk to right now, someone to share the pain with.

As she stepped out of the taxi, she smelled the damp, dusty odour of rain steaming from roads that had been dry for weeks. It was just a drizzle now, but she pulled her jacket closed at the neck and folded the top of the plastic bag in her hand to stop the magazines inside getting wet. She walked down the path towards the mental health building – less intimidating in the daylight than it had been the night before – stepping over small puddles that shimmered in the sunlight that was breaking through the clouds. Inside the reception area, she signed the visitors book then sat and waited. Seeing her reflection in the glass door, she smoothed down the tendrils of her hair that had sprouted like shoots in the rain. She looked at her brown leather boots, reached down and rubbed at the scuffed toes.

'Mrs Shafer?'

Wendy jumped and looked up to see a young woman in a grey fitted dress with dark-framed glasses. 'Yes, hi.' She stood up, snatching her handbag and the plastic bag from the floor.

'I'm Dr Morgan. Thanks for coming. Come through, please.'

The doctor held the door open for her, and Wendy walked through, then paused in the corridor beyond. Dr Morgan closed the door behind them; Wendy heard the clunk as the lock fell into place and her stomach lurched. She followed the psychiatrist down a corridor to their left, past several closed doors and into a small room that was empty except for four chairs. She hesitated, then chose the seat nearest the door. Dr Morgan pulled one of the other chairs from the corner of the room closer to Wendy, sat down and crossed her legs. Wendy noticed her shiny black patent heels, and tucked her own feet under her chair.

'Sorry about the decor,' Dr Morgan said, smiling.

'I've seen worse,' Wendy said. 'I tried to get hold of Tony, but his phone was off, and his mum couldn't reach him either.' She was painfully aware of his absence, terrified as to what it might mean.

'That's a shame. I'm sure he'll be in touch soon. I can't imagine how he's feeling.'

'No.' Wendy shifted back in her seat slightly. 'I saw him yesterday, before I came in last night, he was . . . Well, you know.'

Dr Morgan nodded. 'The nurses told me that you came in to see Anna.'

'Yeah, but I don't think she even noticed. She barely opened her eyes, and when she did, she didn't seem to know what was going on at all.' Wendy sniffed and reached into her handbag for a tissue. It had been the hardest moment in her life. Nothing could compare to seeing your child in such anguish, being unable to reach her or do anything to make it better. 'Sorry.'

'Don't apologise – it's fine.' Dr Morgan looked away while she blew her nose and dabbed at her eyes, then continued, 'I've been to see her this morning, and there's not much change. The nurses tell me she hasn't said much, and she's barely moved. I'm also worried that she hasn't been eating or drinking since she got to hospital. We've been giving her fluids through the drip, but . . .'

Wendy shook her head. 'I've never seen her like this.'

'It must be very hard for you.'

'Tony might know more. Anna hasn't lived at home since she left for university.' She looked up and smiled. 'Did you know she'd gone to university? Here, in Sydney? She's always done so well.' She realised how proud she was of Anna; she wondered if Anna knew that. Had she ever told her?

Dr Morgan wrote something on her notepad, then tapped her pen on the paper. 'I don't know much about her at all. That's why I'm glad you've come today. I do need to ask you about her background, her childhood, the family history, things like that.'

Wendy nodded. 'Anything.' She was glad there was something she could do to help. Wendy had thought about Anna's childhood a lot over the years. Wendy was young when she'd become pregnant, only eighteen. She'd thought she was in love with Anna's father, that they'd raise their child together, but three years later he was gone. Those three years had been hard. Anna was a delight, but he drank, and when he drank, he became belligerent. She'd told herself that Anna was too young to understand the violence she witnessed, too young to be affected, but now, she wasn't so sure. Or, maybe having a father in her life would have prevented Anna from ending up here. Anyway, Anna had stopped asking about him years ago, and Wendy was happy to leave it that way.

She turned her attention back to the psychiatrist.

'One other thing we do need to discuss urgently today is Anna's treatment.' Dr Morgan leaned forward and Wendy held her breath. 'I'm very worried about her mental health – and her physical health if she continues to refuse to eat. I'm going to start her on some medications, but I'm worried they'll take too long to work. That is, if she'll even take them. What I want to discuss with you – and Tony – is giving her electroconvulsive therapy: ECT.'

Wendy closed her eyes; suddenly she had a pounding headache in her temples. Lights flashed on her eyelids, and she could feel her teeth grinding together and her limbs flailing. As soon as the sensation started, it stopped again. She opened her eyes again and rubbed them. She wished that she was surprised, even horrified, at the suggestion, but she wasn't. She looked up at Dr Morgan, who was waiting for her to respond, and she nodded.

*   *   *

'Shock treatment? Do they still do that?'

Tony held the phone away from his ear as his mum's voice pierced through his aching head. The light from the window in Sean's flat was hot on the side of his face, so he lay back on the couch in the shade. He had woken at 10 a.m. and switched on his phone to face four messages. Surprisingly, only one was from his mother. Wendy called a few minutes later. After talking to her, he'd rung Ursula back.

'Well, they must do, Mum, that's what Wendy said. I don't know the details – she had just finished with the doctor when she called.'

'Haven't you spoken to the doctor? You'd be her next of kin, not Wendy.'

'Not yet. I will, in a bit.' He could almost hear his mum forcing herself to bite her tongue. 'I don't want to talk about this on the phone. I'll go and get Wendy, then we'll come over. I just need to run home and get changed.'

'Home? Where are you?'

'I'm at Sean's.'

Ursula sighed. 'Anthony, I know this is difficult, but —'

'Mum! Leave it, please.' He threw the blanket back and sat up, running his fingers through his hair.

'Wendy might not feel like coming over,' she went on. 'She must be exhausted. She probably doesn't want to have to talk to all of us.'

'What do you mean? I'm sure she needs the company.' He walked over to the kitchen and turned on the tap, holding his hand under the water until it ran cold. Cradling the phone between his shoulder and ear, he filled a glass. 'What is it, Mum? I can tell you're dying to say something.' He took a big gulp of water.

'Sorry, Anthony. I don't know if I'm up to talking to anyone today.'

'What else am I supposed to do? She's here on her own, I can't just leave her.'

'Anthony, it's not your job to look after her, you've got enough on your plate. Just let her deal with Anna and the doctors and shock treatment. You deal with . . . Jack.'

He put the glass in the sink, which was piled with dirty plates and mugs. 'I *am* dealing with Jack, and that also means dealing with Anna. She's my wife! I don't understand —'

Ursula took a big breath. 'I've been thinking about this all night, and talking to your dad. If she did do this, even if she is depressed —'

'What?' Tony's head pounded. Was his mum really about to say this? 'Do what?'

'Anthony . . .'

He closed his eyes. He could see that envelope falling out of his bag in slow motion, floating down like a feather, swaying from side to side. In his mind, he saw himself catching it before it hit the ground. How long had it been in there? If his mum hadn't called him at work to say Anna was missing, would he have noticed it when he took his papers out of his bag for the presentation? He would still have been too late. If the traffic had been faster would it have made any difference? He opened his eyes again. He felt nauseous; a cold sweat trickled over him. The letter proved nothing. And he didn't need his own mother making judgements when no one knew what had happened that day yet.

'You're as bad as the police! Number one, we don't know what happened. And number two, she's not just a bit depressed, she's really sick. Jesus, Mum.'

'OK, OK, I'm sorry.'

His voice broke. 'Wendy feels the same as you, the same as all of us. He's her grandson too. This isn't her fault. I'm going to get her from Emily's and we'll come over.'

'You're right. I'm sorry. It's just . . .'

'I know. Look, I'll see you soon.'

Before his mum had a chance to say anything else, he hung up. He didn't need accusations and assumptions flying around from his own family. That wasn't going to help. If the police even suspected that Ursula had her doubts – or, worse still, that he had a tiny sliver of uncertainty – they would pounce on Anna. He put both hands on the kitchen bench and tried to breathe deeply, but he retched at the smell of alcohol evaporating from his pores. He straightened slowly, found his car keys, then headed outside.

*   *   *

Tony usually loved driving over the bridge, but today the view of the harbour made his stomach churn. He looked straight ahead, concentrating on spotting the turn-off towards Emily's apartment. A few minutes later, he drove into the car park of a towering white building and looked up. The sight of the wavy edges of the balconies interlaced above him made his head reel, so he looked away again towards the glass doors of the apartment block. He got out of the car, pressed the buzzer, and stared at the small video camera. Wendy answered and said she'd be right down.

He waited in the car with the door closed and the air conditioning on full. It wasn't hot outside, but he still felt clammy.

A couple of minutes later, Wendy opened the passenger door and leaned in. 'Hi, you haven't been waiting long, have you? I just thought I'd sit down for a second and —'

He clenched the steering wheel. 'No, only the two minutes since I buzzed your apartment.' He heard the sarcasm in his voice and regretted it instantly. It wasn't her fault; why had he let his mother rattle him so much? 'Sorry, Wendy. How are you?'

She hoisted herself up into the passenger seat of Tony's four-wheel drive and closed the door. 'OK, thanks . . . How are you?'

He glanced at her. In the bright midday light she looked so much older than he remembered. Her eyes were bruised with fatigue. Her lips were thin, dry. Just like Anna's were in the hospital. The chemical smell of her perfume filled the car; Tony turned his head towards the air vent to stop himself from gagging. 'It was good of you to see her this morning . . . I —'

'You don't need to explain.'

He clicked on his seat belt and began to drive out of the car park.

'I had a call from the police just then,' Wendy said quietly. 'They want to talk to me.'

Tony looked straight ahead. 'Me too. I had a message on my phone. What do they want from you, though? You haven't been here, I don't know what you can tell them. I wish they'd give us some space.'

Wendy shrugged. 'I don't know . . .' He could just see her in his peripheral vision; she was biting her lip. Anna did that too when she was worried. 'I suppose they just need to find out everything they can. Tony, was there anything that made you think . . . Well, you know, anything that made you worry about her?'

'No, of course not.' He knew he'd answered too quickly.

'Oh, I didn't mean that, that came out all wrong . . .' She leaned her head back on the headrest. They were driving back over the bridge now, and she turned away from Tony to look out of the window.

Tony realised he was in the wrong lane. Without checking in his mirror, he pulled hard to the right and crossed two lanes. A car horn blared behind him. He clenched his hand into a fist and hit the horn, then uncurled his middle finger and held it up in front of the rear-view mirror. Wendy grabbed onto the handle above the passenger door; Tony pretended he hadn't noticed.

'I know it looks bad, the way she is, and what's happened,' he said. 'But the police need to do their investigations properly. They should be out there doing something, not harassing you and me. Everyone just assumes they know what happened, that she —'

'No, they don't.'

'Yes, they do. The police didn't take me seriously when I called them to say Anna was missing, or that they needed to find the car. After they found Anna, the car was in the car park the whole time and they didn't even tell me! They didn't want to listen to me then, and now they want to talk so they expect me to drop everything. Why aren't they out there looking for whoever did this?'

'Tony —'

'There's no doubt she was struggling.' He turned to Wendy. 'But you know Anna as well as I do: there's no way she'd do this, no way! Something must have happened, something that made her like this.'

He realised he was out of breath. They were approaching the tunnel to the eastern suburbs now, stuck in the middle of a knot of traffic lanes. He looked to his left, then sped up to get in front of a car that was trying to merge into his lane. He carried on talking, louder and faster, to make sure that his words got through to her. 'You hear of people being in shock, don't you, when something horrible happens to them? Someone's done this to them —'

'Tony! Stop.' Wendy put her hands up, palms facing him, as if she was trying to deflect his words. 'I'm sure the police have thought of that.' She shook her head and blinked back tears. 'But the way Anna was this morning . . . She's just so very sick – it's no one's fault.'

'God, what if the guy who did this to them is still out there. Or it could be a woman, you hear about women stealing babies —'

'Please, stop this.' Wendy wiped the tears from her face. 'We don't know what happened . . . but, yes, it's a possibility, Tony. Maybe she . . .' Her voice trailed off and she shook her head. 'My God, I'd swap places with her in an instant if it meant that everything could go back to normal.'

He pressed the brake pedal and came to a stop at some traffic lights. Even Anna's own mother thought she could have done this; his shoulders slumped. Was he the fool here? He turned to face Wendy. 'I just don't know if I can do this.'

Wendy put her hand on his shoulder and squeezed it. 'Yes, you can. We have to, for Anna. And for Jack.'

He nodded slowly. When the lights changed to green he turned off towards his parents' house. Neither of them spoke again for the rest of the car trip.

There was nothing left to say.

*   *   *

The four of them – Tony, Wendy, Ursula and Jim – sat on the couches in Jim and Ursula's living room, just as they had the previous afternoon. Tony could tell that his mum had made an effort by the furrows on the carpet from the vacuum cleaner and the smell of furniture polish. He wasn't sure if she'd felt guilty after their conversation earlier, or whether she had tidied up because she didn't know what else to do. He looked down at his white china cup and saucer; they usually only came out at Christmas. His fingers didn't fit through the handle, so he clasped his hand around it to drink the black coffee. A plate of shortbread sat untouched on the glass coffee table in the middle of the room. It seemed absurd to be sitting around, pretending they were at a morning tea, when everything around them was falling to pieces.

'We all meet again . . .' he said sarcastically, then regretted his tone.

Ursula glared at him; Jim reached for a biscuit and dipped it in his tea; Wendy matched Tony's wry smile, then blinked back tears.

'Wendy, Tony told me you'd been to the hospital this morning to see Anna,' Ursula said.

Wendy nodded. 'Yes. I went last night too, but she was asleep. She was better today, she seemed more awake, but she's not good. I don't even know if she recognised me. Well, I think she did at first, but then . . . It was horrible, I've never seen her like that.'

'Sounds like there's not much change, eh Tony?' Jim said.

Tony shook his head. 'No. That's what she was like yesterday morning.' He felt disorientated, unsure whether he had really seen her only one day ago or whether the past day or two had even happened. The room began to spin; he rested his head carefully against the back of the couch. Why did he feel as though even his own family was trying to trick him into saying what they all thought? 'But she wasn't like that at home. I would never have left her if she was.'

'Of course you wouldn't have, Anthony, no one thinks that,' said Ursula. She turned back to Wendy. 'So, Anthony told me they want to give her electric shock treatment, is that true?'

Wendy nodded again. 'I spoke to the psychiatrist, Dr Morgan, this morning.'

'Have you spoken to this doctor, Anthony?' Ursula asked.

'I'll call her later,' he said tersely. She knew he hadn't. He clunked his cup and saucer down on the coffee table.

Wendy glanced at Tony, then Ursula. 'Anyway, they want to start it this week.'

'This week? What's the rush?' Ursula slid a coaster across the table to Tony.

Wendy gazed out the window for a second, then shook her head slightly as if flicking away a memory. 'She won't eat or drink, so she's on a drip. She's very ill.' She faltered. 'Dr Morgan said it's a lot better than it used to be, it's not like in the movies. They do it in the operating theatre under anaesthetic.'

'It seems very sudden – she's only been in hospital five minutes,' Ursula said.

Jim put his hand on Ursula's arm. 'Just let Wendy talk. Wendy, did the psychiatrist say what they think is wrong?'

Wendy nodded. 'They think she's psychotic. Apparently you can get it after having a baby, sometimes after being depressed.' She looked up at Tony. 'The doctor said that it comes on really quickly, sometimes too quickly to know what's happening.'

Tony couldn't meet Wendy's eye. He wished everyone would stop trying to reassure him that it wasn't his fault: it made him suspect that maybe it was. He put his hand to his throat; the coffee was giving him heartburn.

Wendy drained her tea and put the cup and saucer down on the carpet at her feet. 'Anyway, to do the ECT they need to have a legal hearing, because Anna's too sick to give consent. It's tomorrow, at the hospital. I'm going, but obviously they'd like you there too, Tony.'

'What do you think, love?' Ursula said, looking at Tony.

'I don't know. I don't know much about it.' He leaned forward and held his head in his hands. 'Sounds like it's a done deal anyway.'

Wendy shook her head. 'No, Dr Morgan said —'

'It sounds pretty brutal to me,' Ursula said sharply. Wendy shrank back. Ursula turned to Tony. 'Anthony, you need to talk to this psychiatrist.'

Jim frowned at Ursula before looking back at Wendy. 'What do you think? You're her mum.'

'I think she should have it. The doctors know best, and to see her like that . . .' She looked down at the floor and spoke quietly. 'I know that ECT works.'

Jim kept looking at Wendy as if he expected her to continue; she sat back and shook her head slightly.

'I agree,' he said at last. 'The doctors know what they're doing. If that's what they recommend, then that's what we do.' Wendy smiled a little at Jim. 'Tony? What do you think, mate?'

What did he think? Tony didn't think anything. He couldn't think. 'I don't know! I'll go and see her, OK?'

'Anyone for more coffee?' Ursula picked up the plunger pot and began to pour without waiting for an answer. She took a deep breath, and spoke quietly without looking at anyone. 'Did Dr Morgan say anything about Jack?'

Tony's eyes immediately filled with tears; he closed them. He had been trying not to think about Jack. It was easier to think about Anna: at least there was something tangible he could do.

Wendy shook her head. 'No. Well, she said how sorry she was. But she said Anna hasn't mentioned him. Tony, she might respond to you, when you go.'

'I said I'll go! I've just got so much . . .' He picked up his cup, now half-full of thick grainy black coffee again, and gulped it down. 'I can't . . . I can't get my head around this. The psychiatrist, the police, the coroner —'

'Oh Tony! I'm sorry!' Wendy covered her face with her hands, crying.

Tony's ears began to ring and the room swirled around him. It was as if everything was shrinking and spinning away while he sat still, unchanged. He stood up and staggered towards the door. 'I can't talk about this any more.'

Before anyone could reply, he walked out and slammed the front door behind him. He got into his car and locked the doors, but he knew that no matter how far he drove, he couldn't avoid the reality that this was his life now. Distance wouldn't help him escape. Nothing would.

*   *   *

Ursula stood on the porch and watched Jim's ute drive away with Wendy in the passenger seat. Stepping back inside she closed the front door and turned the latch to lock it. She was relieved Wendy hadn't wanted to stay all afternoon; Ursula needed to be alone without having to entertain someone. Tony hadn't returned after storming out earlier, so the house was empty. She went into the bedroom, took her shoes off and put on her slippers, then unbuttoned her pants at the waist. After getting a tray from the kitchen she walked back into the living room and collected all the cups and saucers. She ate a piece of shortbread as she walked, then another when she got back into the kitchen. It was easier than making something for lunch. Leaving the tray on the kitchen bench, she walked into her bedroom, closed the door, and drew the curtains.

She lay down on the bed next to their ginger tabby, who was curled up as usual on her pillow. She was so tired. She closed her eyes, but all she could see was the look in Tony's eyes after he had answered that call two days ago. The memory was as vivid as a film; Ursula could almost touch him. She opened her eyes again and let the image fade. It wasn't a good idea to nap in the afternoon anyway; it would make it even more difficult to sleep tonight. She picked up a library book from her bedside table, and tried to concentrate on the letters in the words on the page; anything but the horror on Tony's face.

*   *   *

Tony pulled his car into a bay marked POLICE VEHICLES ONLY, switched off the engine, then sat still for a moment. He leaned to the side, taking the folded envelope from the back pocket of his jeans. He slipped out the letter, unfolded it, then read it again, even though he knew it by heart. Should he show someone, or burn the damn thing? He didn't want to make things worse, but was he really making things better by hiding it? Refolding it along the same two creases, he put it back in the envelope, then put it in the glove box, hiding it under the car manual. He clenched his hands in an attempt to stop them shaking, wiped sweat from his upper lip, then looked at the police station. It was an ugly concrete box of a building that lurked among the swanky cafes and expensive shops in the street.

He watched a couple saunter past along the footpath and heard the woman shrieking with laughter. They both carried white paper bags and plastic bottles of juice; their lunch. How long had it been since he'd eaten? He didn't feel hungry, but he had the distinct feeling that his body was shutting down, cell by cell. He wished he'd brushed his teeth again; he could taste bitter coffee mixed with stale alcohol. He almost smiled at the thought that he was about to walk into a police station and was probably still over the limit. The sun came out from behind a cloud and shone through the windscreen. Opening the car door, he breathed in the cool breeze, then walked briskly up to the front door of the station and went inside.

'Tony Patton. I've got an appointment with Detective Inspector David Hill.'

The police officer sitting behind the reinforced glass picked up a telephone. 'Have a seat. I'll let him know you're here.'

There were four low chairs against the wall. He sat on the edge of one, avoiding the brown stain on the pilled fabric. A skinny guy, probably not out of his teens, stared at Tony through a bruised, swollen eye. Tony tried to smile, then picked up a magazine and flicked through the pages. There was a distinct smell – maybe not a smell, more of a taste – that he remembered from the one and only other time he'd been in a police station, when he'd been caught driving home from a party at Sean's house after a couple of beers while still on his P-plates. The cops had shoved him in the back of a paddy wagon and taken him to the cells for a few hours until his mum and dad picked him up. They hadn't said a word to him on the long drive home.

Tony heard a buzz and a click from the door to the left of the reception desk. He looked up to see a muscular, balding man holding open the heavy door. He stood up, wiped his sweaty hands on his jeans, then walked forward. Detective Hill's handshake was strong as he introduced himself; Tony fought the urge to squeeze back even harder.

A door slammed somewhere behind him, and a shrill phone rang unanswered as he followed the detective along the empty corridor. As they walked, Tony saw a photocopied poster hanging by one corner on a crumbling cork noticeboard, advertising last year's Christmas party. A drawing pin was still stuck where the other corner should be, but now it held only a torn shred of paper.

They entered a small room with a plain faux-wood desk and three grey plastic chairs scattered around it. Hill pulled one over to one side of the desk, indicating for Tony to sit. He left the room without comment; Tony sat down and looked around. A camera stared down from the corner of the room, and an old air conditioner grunted on the wall. There was a small window but the view was blocked by dingy venetian blinds that clattered in the draft from the open door. He tried to sit still on the chair, flexing and rotating his ankles and toes. He even sat on his hands to prevent himself from wringing them.

Hill returned with another, younger detective, and they sat down opposite Tony without a word. Hill pushed a red button on the tape recorder on the desk. It began to hiss faintly. The younger one put a paper cup of water in front of Tony. Hill began, 'This is the interview of Mr Anthony William Patton. Today is the sixteenth of September 2009, and the time is 12.20 p.m. Mr Patton, for the tape, can you confirm your name, and the date and time from the clock behind me on the wall?'

Tony looked up at the clock, then cleared his throat and repeated the information. His mouth felt dry. He took a sip of tepid water from the paper cup in front of him, then put it down on the table.

'My name is Detective Inspector David Hill. Also present is Detective Senior Sergeant Stephen Kaminsky.'

Kaminsky could have been Hill's younger brother. He was a few inches taller but had that same solid physique that would soon become stocky if left unchecked. Kaminsky wasn't completely bald yet; his dark hair was shaved close to his scalp and Tony could see the shiny skin on his forehead and crown.

'Mr Patton, can you tell us when you last saw your wife on the morning of the fourteenth of September?' asked Hill.

Tony took a deep breath. He reminded himself that he wasn't in trouble, and if he stayed calm, neither would Anna be. 'Yes. When I left for work, at about eight.'

'And what can you tell us about that morning?'

'I woke up when the alarm went off at 6.30 a.m. I left Anna sleeping, fed Jack, made Anna some breakfast, then I went to work.'

'Had you noticed any change in your wife recently?'

They already knew that she hadn't been herself; he had to be consistent. 'Well, she was a bit quieter than normal; she was tired. Jack wasn't sleeping much, and she was up every couple of hours to feed him. But she was breastfeeding, you see, so there wasn't much I could do to help her at night.'

Hill leaned forward and put his elbows on the table. 'When you say "quieter than normal", what do you mean?'

'Nothing really, she just wasn't as lively. She was tired. She had a new baby, you know?'

He saw Kaminsky glance at Hill, and felt a jolt of anger shoot through him. 'What was that look for? Have you got kids? She was just tired! She hasn't done anything wrong.' Tony swallowed hard as the tears started. He reached over and grabbed some tissues from a cardboard box on the table and wiped his eyes. 'I'm sorry.

I just don't know why we're sitting here talking rather than finding whoever did this.'

Hill nodded slightly. 'Mr Patton —'

'Tony.' He wanted them to use his first name, to remember that he was a husband, a father, not a suspect. He screwed up the tissue and stuffed it in his pocket.

'Tony – our job is to gather as much information as possible. I can assure you that we're doing everything we can to find out what happened.'

Panic tightened in Tony's chest and he began to hyperventilate. The police sounded so impassive, but they needed to listen to him; he had to convince them. 'I'm not stupid, I know you think it was her! Jesus, there's no way she would have done this. No way in the world. You don't understand —'

Hill continued, unaffected. 'We're not making any assumptions, we're just trying to find out what happened to your son. Was there a reason you had asked your mum to go round to the house that day?'

Tony forced himself to exhale. 'I asked her to go round to help out. As I've already said, Anna was exhausted. She wasn't getting any sleep. I thought Mum would be able to help her with the baby, make her some lunch, tidy up, just to give her a break.'

'And you called us that afternoon to report Anna missing.'

'Yes.'

'Can you tell us more about that, about when you realised she was missing?'

'She wasn't at home when Mum got there. She hadn't told me she was going out, and she knew Mum was coming, so it was unusual. I went looking for her, I called her friend, I did everything I could think of. I couldn't find them.'

'And why did you call the police?'

'Because I was worried! I didn't know what else to do.'

'What were you worried about? What did you think might have happened?'

'Not this!' Tony slammed his hands down on the table. They were trying to make him say it, but he wasn't going to. 'I thought she might have had an accident or something, that she had fallen asleep at the wheel and crashed the car, or got lost. Or maybe she'd gone out because something was wrong with Jack.'

'Tony, I have to ask you a difficult question. Had Anna said anything to you about hurting Jack, or herself?'

'No! Of course not! Why does everyone keep asking me that?' He folded his arms. 'Jesus, she would never have done this. She adored Jack, she wanted him so much. There's just no way . . .' Tony's voice trailed off and he shook his head. 'Look, Anna did not do this to Jack. I can tell you that now. You're missing something! Check her car, do some DNA tests or whatever. Something happened to her, to make her like this. There's more to this, there must be.'

'Tony, we're looking into every possibility at this stage,' Hill said. 'Forensics are involved, we've looked through the house – I assure you that we're not going to miss anything.'

The detective's smug, patronising tone made Tony narrow his eyes. They were so sure of themselves, so convinced they knew what had happened, but they didn't. 'And you didn't find a note, did you?'

As soon as he'd said it, he regretted it. He kept his face neutral. Why had he brought that up?

Hill frowned and spun a pen between his thumb and fingers. 'A note? No. But that doesn't mean anything.'

'And she left milk! Don't you see – Jack was breastfed. I used the last of it from the freezer in the morning, so she must have made up bottles of formula. That proves she didn't . . . didn't do this to him. Why would she bother doing that if she was going to kill him, for God's sake?' Tony leaned back with his arms folded.

'But what worries us, Tony, is that it suggests she wasn't planning on coming back. It doesn't make me think there's been an accident or a third party involved.'

Tony uncrossed his arms and rubbed at the stubble on his chin. His hands shook. He didn't know what to say, what to believe. They were backing him into a corner, and he knew he was trapped, flailing. He glanced at Hill, then Kaminsky, who seemed to be hiding a smirk.

'We're not criminals, you know. We're just ordinary people.' He tried not to start crying again. Anna couldn't have done this. He pleaded with himself to calm down, yet his mind was racing. He thought he knew Anna, but did he really? Everyone – the police, even her mum – seemed to accept that she was so ill, so deranged, that she had killed her own baby. Was he the idiot? Was he as bad as her?

'I'm sorry, can we stop for now?' Tony felt his mouth fill with saliva. He had to get out of here before he vomited.

Hill glanced at Kaminsky, who nodded. 'Interview terminated at 12.45 p.m.,' Hill said, then clicked off the tape recorder.

He stood up and held out his hand to Tony, who also stood and shook it without making eye contact. 'Call us if you need to. Otherwise we'll be in touch soon.'

Hill paused then spoke more softly. 'You know how to contact me if you need to, OK? Don't hesitate.'

Hill was the last person he would call if he needed help. He followed the detectives out of the room and then made his way out of the building. Standing in the middle of the car park, he breathed slowly, deeply, willing the nausea away. Life went on around him: two teenage boys crossing the road; a truck reversing with shrill beeps; the wind tumbling rubbish in the gutter. Then he slowly walked to his car and got in. He turned the radio on, found a station playing some pop song, turned up the volume, and pretended it was the most normal thing in the world to drive away from a police station after your wife had been implicated in murdering your child.

There was nothing normal about his life any more.

*   *   *

Ursula heard Jim's ute pull into the driveway and jumped up from the bed, reaching onto the bedside table for her glasses. She looked at the bright red numbers on the radio alarm clock. It was after 4 p.m.; she must have fallen asleep after all. She hurried to the door and opened it as Jim walked up the path. He kissed her.

'Come on, love, let's get inside,' he said.

'Everything OK?'

'Yeah. I told Wendy we'd call her later – she looked exhausted. I popped into work, just to check on everything. Did you manage to have a nap?'

'A little one.' She pulled away from him and closed the door.

Jim sighed. 'Any word from Tony?'

'No. I don't know if he'll come back here or go home. I hate this, not knowing what's going on, but I can't keep calling him.'

'He'll call us when he's good and ready. Give him some space to work it all out. Come and sit down, I'll put the kettle on.'

She followed Jim into the kitchen and let him fill the kettle and put tea bags in the mugs. 'I just hope he hasn't gone off drinking again.'

'He'll do the right thing. Give him time.'

'I am!' She slumped forward with her elbows on the kitchen bench. 'I just want to help him, I can't imagine what he's going through.' She dropped her head into her hands.

Jim put a teaspoon of sugar into one of the mugs, and then slipped his arms around her from behind. He led her through to the living room and onto the couch, and they held each other.

'Why us, Jim?'

He shook his head, wiping his eyes. 'It could have happened to anyone. It's just bad, terrible luck.'

'No, it's not luck, it wasn't an accident. What the hell happened?'

'Don't do this, love. We just have to wait and see. I've been going over it too, but it doesn't help. Maybe she did, maybe she didn't. The police are looking into it, and Anna will tell us more when she's better.'

Ursula sneered. 'I doubt it!'

Jim pulled her head to his chest and they were both silent. She listened to his heartbeat through his chest. She could feel the ridges of his ribs and she realised how old they were getting, how frail and fallible they really were. She clung tighter to him.

After a while, Jim got up and finished making their tea, then brought it back into the living room. He switched on the television to watch the five o'clock news, then lay down on the couch beside her.

Just as the weather forecast was starting, they heard a car outside. She sprang out of Jim's arms and sat up straight. The front door opened, then banged as it slammed shut. She and Jim looked at each other without saying anything. After a moment, Ursula stood up and walked out into the hallway. Tony was leaning with his back against the door, staring at the ground.

'Anthony?' she said quietly.

'What, Mum?'

'Are you all right? Can I get you anything?'

'That's not what you want to ask, is it?' He lifted his head and stared at her, his eyes red.

'What?'

'You want to know where I've been, what I've been doing. Well, I've been interrogated by the police, who treated me like I'm covering for a murderer.'

'Oh, darling.'

Tony blinked and a tear fell down his cheek. 'What if she did it? What if she killed Jack?'

'Anthony . . .' Ursula stepped forward, but he shook his head and stepped away.

'Just leave me alone, OK?' He walked past her, into his old bedroom, and closed the door behind him.

Ursula stayed where she was, with one hand on the wall to prevent herself from falling. She wanted to follow him, but she couldn't. She closed her eyes, and when she heard his sobs, quietly moved back to the living room where Jim waited for her. She leaned into him, and let her own tears fall silently.

CHAPTER THIRTEEN

Six weeks before
Wednesday, 5 August 2009

Later, Anna's memories of the rest of her labour were hazy. She remembered her fear when the midwife said that her baby was distressed. She remembered the obstetrician rushing into the room and saying that the child needed to be born straightaway. She remembered her confusion when Tony disappeared as she was wheeled down the corridor into theatre. She remembered the terror as they pulled at her abdomen to get the baby out, and how her skin had itched all over and her body had shaken uncontrollably. And then she remembered the relief when her baby cried, and when they told her it was a boy, and he had all his fingers and toes, and a face that was crinkled and swollen but sweet and hers.

They named him Jack.

And now she was stuck on the bed in the operating theatre, fighting wave after wave of nausea and terror. They whipped Jack away from her and she couldn't see what they were doing. She turned her head as far as she could to see bodies in green hunched over a little trolley. A nurse came over and told her through a mask that the baby was fine, but he needed some oxygen to help him breathe. She started to cry. Tony stroked her head but she could see the fear in his eyes too. 'Go and see what they're doing,' she said, her voice rising.

'No, I'm staying with you.'

She began to sob. 'Tony, go and see what's happening with the baby, please.'

He shook his head and whispered, 'I can't. I'm too scared.'

She tried to calm her own tears so that she could listen for the baby's cries, but all she could hear was the whirring and pumping and hissing of the machines around her, and the murmurs of the doctors and nurses. Finally, she heard a whimper, a baby's whimper, and she started to cry again.

'I want to see him,' she said. 'Let me see him!' She jammed her arms into the mattress and tried to lift the dead weight of her abdomen and heavy, anaesthetised legs.

'Whoa, Anna,' said the obstetrician. 'Don't try to move, I'm still sewing things up down here.'

'Let me see my baby! What's happening?' she said, wrenching her neck to the side again, trying to see through the crowd of green.

The nurse came back over. She was still wearing a cap and mask, and Anna could only see her brown eyes. She placed a hand on Anna's shoulder. 'Your baby is OK, I promise you; he's just a bit stunned. We'll bring him to you as soon as we can.'

She looked up at Tony: he had tears streaming down his face. 'Tony, for God's sake, go over there and see him!' she shouted. She gnawed on her lip as Tony finally allowed the nurse to lead him over to the baby.

And then, at last, they wheeled the little trolley over to her bed, and she saw her son, all bundled up in a blue blanket. She reached out and stroked his tiny head. 'Thank God,' she said. 'Thank God.'

But they took Jack away from her again. He had to go to the nursery for monitoring. Tony stood between her and the baby and hesitated.

'Go,' Anna said. 'Go with him, see what they're doing, please. Make sure they look after him. He needs one of us with him.'

Tony leaned down and kissed her. She heard him sniff. 'I'll go with him, I won't leave him, I promise. I'll be back as soon as I can.'

'Let me know if anything changes. Please, don't keep things from me.'

'I promise.' He swallowed. 'Well done – I love you.' He walked out after the nurse with the baby.

She looked at the stool beside her bed where Tony had been sitting, and then at the table next to it. On it was his mobile phone, ready to call their parents, and the camera, fully charged with an empty memory card. They hadn't even taken a photo of Jack.

Anna closed her eyes and sobbed.

CHAPTER FOURTEEN

Four days after

Friday, 18 September 2009

There was muffled laughter far away, somewhere outside of the room. Her mouth was dry and tasted sour. She craned her stiff neck around to look for some water. She saw a scratched plastic jug on the trolley next to her bed but knew that she couldn't reach it, so she ran her rough tongue around her mouth instead. Her face felt sticky, grainy, and she rubbed at her smarting eyes. She heard footsteps approaching, then the door to her room creaking open. Simultaneously she heard the click of a light switch, the clunk of the power surging, and the humming of the fluorescent tube that flickered a few times then soaked everything in fulvous light. A shadow grew behind the beige curtain surrounding her bed. She jumped as the curtain whipped open with a metallic jangle.

'Good morning, Anna!'

She stared at the young woman smiling at her from the end of the bed. She looked younger than Anna, but the large bunch of keys hanging at her hip gave the impression of importance. Anna looked at her name badge hanging on a lanyard around her neck: RACHEL, REGISTERED NURSE. Her eyes widened as she saw a neon-yellow sticker of a smiley face over the space where the nurse's picture should be. People used to wear those stickers on their shirts at uni parties. Wasn't it something to do with ecstasy? Why would this woman, who claimed to be a nurse, put that sticker over her face? It meant something, Anna was sure, but she didn't know what. She bit the inside of her cheek, and stared at Rachel.

The nurse picked up the blue plastic chart from the bottom of the bed, opened it, and wrote in it with a red pen, which she then pushed through her ponytail. 'They're almost ready for you. I'll save your breakfast for when you come back.' She handed her a small paper cup with a single tablet in it; Anna put it into her mouth and swallowed it. She no longer cared if it was poisoned. With a smile, Rachel walked out.

The mattress creaked under her as she pushed herself up the bed. She pressed the button to raise the head of the bed, her pillow sliding down to the small of her back. She tried to move it up and wedge it behind her head as she leaned back, but that didn't work either. She grabbed it and threw it on the floor. It was disgusting anyway. How much saliva had soaked into it from other people's dribbling mouths? She pushed the buttons, up and down, up and down, but couldn't find a comfortable position. Giving up, she sat stiffly, folded sharply in the middle like a hollow cardboard tube, and waited for them to come and get her.

She didn't have to wait long before two huge men walked in, the type that Anna would normally have crossed the street to avoid. The man pushing the wheelchair had tattoos on both forearms and another creeping out from his collar. The other man carried a sheaf of papers. He was taller, but lither, and looked ready to spring on her if she tried to run. Both of them had the same edgy stare. She couldn't read their name badges, but it didn't matter anyway. They read out her name and date of birth, checked that it matched what was written on her wristband, and asked her if she could get in the wheelchair by herself.

The one with the tattoos pushed her. The taller man walked to her left, clutching his papers and a manila file in one hand, and pushing the drip stand that was connected to her arm via a plastic tube with the other. They trundled along the corridors, then through the main doors out of the building. She shut her eyes against the bright light until they reached a shaded walkway that ran around the perimeter of the car park towards the main hospital building. As she was jostled around, Anna gripped the arms of the wheelchair

and looked down at her lap, at her knees pointing through the thin
yellow hospital gown that seemed to float above her flaccid thighs.
Smoothing down the gown, she noticed the plastic ID band hanging
like a bracelet from her thin wrist. She blinked back a tear.

Inside the hospital building, they went into a lift, and her pulse
quickened. She looked around the small space, squeezed the arms
of the chair and looked up to the ceiling. She remembered. She'd
been here before; she had been frightened. She closed her eyes
and breathed deeply, but the air seemed to stick to her dry mouth
before it could reach her lungs. A bell chimed, and the doors slid
apart. She opened her eyes as she was pushed though some heavy
doors below a sign that read 'Operating Theatres'.

Anna looked around the large room. Six empty beds were
arranged around the edges with a silver metal trolley at the end of
each. There was a sweet, cloying, chemical smell; Anna had smelled
this on her skin before. Two people stood next to a small desk with
their backs to her, talking in low voices. She guessed from their
height that they were women, but it was difficult to tell with the
identical blue scrubs, elasticated paper hats and white clogs. They
had face masks hanging around their necks; the long white straps
hung down their backs. This room was quiet, but she could hear
hisses and beeps coming from behind another set of doors in front
of her. The last time she'd heard those sounds, she'd just given birth.
She had cried. Someone had offered her countless tissues that she'd
refused to take.

This time, she didn't cry. She waited until she was told to
stand up from the wheelchair and lie down on a bed. Someone
then pushed her through the doors into a small corridor, and into
'Theatre 1', according to the sign on the door. There were another
three people in here, wearing those same blue scrubs. They didn't
wear hats or masks. The bed stopped under a huge light that a
man with stubble switched on and moved until it pointed at her
right hand. He was smiling as he talked to her, but she didn't listen
to what he said. He was going to do whatever he wanted anyway.

She clenched her teeth and looked away as the man put a needle in the back of her right hand and fiddled around with tubes and tape. A woman attached a plastic clip to her left index finger and switched on another monitor. Her forehead stung as someone scrubbed it with small, square, cold alcohol wipes, then pushed hard to stick wires above her eyebrows and behind her ears. A strand of her hair was caught and pulled at her scalp, but she didn't bother saying anything.

Tired now, she wanted to close her eyes. Someone told her it would be over in five minutes, and something cold swept up her right hand into her arm. She had no energy to fight. She was dizzy, and felt as if she was swaying even though she was lying down. Something was being held over her face. She gasped, she couldn't breathe, her throat was closing. She tried to turn her head away, then to lift her arms to push it away, and to kick for the surface, but it was too late. It all went dark.

*　　*　　*

Her head pounded. Her mouth was dry, and she tasted metal. She moved her eyes to look around her; where was she? Her vision was blurry, and it was hard to focus on anything. Voices around her got louder and softer, louder and softer, and there was a ringing somewhere behind her. She tried to sit up; she couldn't breathe. Someone held her down.

'Where am I? Where's my baby? I need to see him.'

She felt bony fingers gripping her arms. She writhed and struggled, then fell back onto the bed. She remembered now and started to cry. They had taken Jack away from her, left her alone, unable to move, and taken him. Tony had left too. They had all walked out and left her.

She was alone.

Someone was leaning over her now, near her mouth. She wanted a toothbrush.

And then she was sitting up, back in her hospital room, and that nurse, Rachel, was there. Anna accepted a cup of lukewarm sweet tea and gulped it down. There were two pieces of thin white toast on the bedside table; she quickly ate them, even though they were cold. Reaching up she felt a sticky residue on her forehead, and a cold slime in her hair near her temple. She pulled some tissues from the box near her bed and wiped off as much as she could. Her hair felt greasy and limp. She looked towards the small bathroom, pushed back the sheets and tried to swing her legs out of the bed. Her head throbbed and a wave of dizziness flooded through her. She groaned, and the nurse was there, pulling the sheets over her again. Anna lay back, and heard the hum of the bed as it slid flat. She rolled over onto her side, curled up, then fell into a deep sleep.

CHAPTER FIFTEEN

Four days after
Friday, 18 September 2009

Tony waited in the hospital car park with the engine running. His left hand rested on the gearstick, threatening to push it into drive and head back home. He looked at the clock on the dashboard: it was 9.45 a.m., Anna would be back in the ward in fifteen minutes.

He'd woken at 4 a.m., and almost came straight to the hospital then so he could be with Anna when she went for her first ECT session, but he had lain in bed until he convinced himself that it was too late, or that he'd only get in the way. Anyway, he didn't know what he'd say or do when he saw her. He didn't really want to be here now either, but staying away would cause more problems, lead to more questions, more speculation. He knew that Anna needed him. And more importantly, he needed to talk to her.

Turning off the engine, he got out of the car before he could stop himself. He turned away from the psychiatric block and made his way towards the main hospital building.

There was a queue to order at the cafeteria. The two elderly women behind the counter bustled around while staff in white coats and blue scrubs looked at their pagers and mobile phones, and visitors sighed and shuffled their feet. When he reached the front, Tony took a copy of the *Herald* from the pile on the counter and ordered a flat white. He usually bought his morning coffee and paper from the stand at the bottom of his office building; it seemed important to keep up that routine. He paid, then sat down at a small round table near the counter to wait for his coffee. Out of habit, he spread the paper out, scanning the headlines. Suddenly, he stopped. His heart started pounding. He quickly looked around him, then back down at the paper, to the left-hand column of page five. There it was.

BABY DEAD. MOTHER IN PSYCHIATRIC HOSPITAL.

Underneath the bold headline were two short paragraphs, but he could no longer see properly to read them.

He screwed his eyes shut until the stinging stopped, then opened them and tried to focus on the print again. He couldn't believe it was in the paper, a story that thousands of people would be reading, people just like he was a week ago. They would read it aloud to their husbands or wives or workmates, then turn the page and forget about it. But this was his life, his wife, his baby. Who the hell wrote this stuff? What did they know about anything? Two bare paragraphs, as if what had happened to Jack was just another story. If they were going to print it, couldn't they at least try to explain what had happened? People would jump to conclusions now; how could they not with that headline? The pages of the paper rustled in his trembling hands. He looked up, expecting to see people watching him, but no one was. He closed the paper again, folded it in half then stood up. The old ladies were still busy. He put his head down and walked out, leaving the newspaper on the table.

Before he could change his mind, he followed the path through the grounds and around the car park to the psychiatric building. From the front it was a generic concrete block rendered grey, just like the rest of the hospital. As he got closer, he noticed a group of people standing near the front entrance smoking, but not talking to each other. One burly guy stood slightly apart from all the rest. He was less dishevelled and had a bunch of keys attached to his belt.

Tony held his breath and hurried past them all into the building. He introduced himself to the receptionist, then waited a few moments until the security door opened. A young female nurse greeted him and smiled. She wore jeans and a blue t-shirt, and had a black radio clipped to her waistband on one side, and a conspicuous alarm button on her other hip. She swaggered off in front of him. He followed her down the corridor, wishing he could turn around and walk straight back out.

The door to Anna's room was open. Tony stopped beside the nurse. He needed a moment to gather himself so he didn't break down. Then he turned and looked at his wife. Anna sat on a chair in the corner of the room hugging her knees while she gazed out of the window. She was in her pyjamas, but her feet were bare. Tony wanted to run over to her and put his hands on her toes to warm them. It was cold. Why didn't she have her slippers on? He'd put them in the bag. He held himself back. He needed to stay in control of himself.

She looked thin. The skin on her face sagged, as if all the moisture had been sucked out of her. Why hadn't he noticed that at home? A bag of clear fluid on the stand next to her dripped into a tube that was connected to her hand. He made himself walk forward into the room, but Anna didn't look up. She was watching a bird pecking at the pale grass sprouting up between the pavers in the courtyard. He took a step back again, then knocked on the open door. Anna started, looked at him, then smiled, just for a second. He tried to smile back but knew that he had hesitated too long. It was too late, she had seen through it. He saw the confusion in her eyes, and the flush in her cheeks. He opened his mouth to say something, but she turned back to the window. He knew he should go to her, hug her, but something stopped him. He tried hard not to cry.

He walked further into the room, then sat on the bed, just behind her chair.

'Hi,' he said. 'How are you?' It was a stupid question. Anna didn't reply. He raised his hand, and it hovered just behind her, then he let it drop back onto the bed. 'Anna. I need to talk to you.'

She turned back to face him again. Her eyes were wide and watery. He reached out and touched her face softly. It felt hot. She moved her head ever so slightly, breaking contact with his hand, then looked down, blinking hard.

Tony put his hand back in his lap then linked his fingers, hoping that they'd stop trembling. 'How are you feeling?'

She shook her head. 'I don't know.' Her voice was thin, hollow. 'I don't . . . don't understand.'

'Me neither.' He knew that she hadn't mentioned Jack to Wendy when she visited yesterday. Did she know? 'What don't you understand?' he asked carefully.

'I don't know.'

'Where do you think you are? What do you think has happened?'

'I don't know! I can't remember!' She was crying now.

He stopped himself from reaching for her. If he touched her, he didn't know whether he'd hold her or throttle her.

'You're sick, you've been sick, I know that and I'm so, so sorry. But why? Why did you do it? I can't stop thinking about it . . . Why? Why the hell didn't you listen to me?' He stood up and walked around in front of Anna's chair, then kneeled down before her. This wasn't what he'd planned to say. He stared at Anna: her eyes and nose were streaming but she made no effort to wipe them. 'Oh Anna, I told you to take it easy, I told you to see the doctor. Did you tell the doctor how you were feeling? Why didn't you tell me? I told you Mum was coming —'

'Stop, Tony! Please!' She dropped her chin to her chest and rested her forehead on her knees.

He put his hands on the back of her head as she started to rock forward and back. He stroked the nape of her neck until she stopped moving, then he tried to lift her head. She allowed him to do this, but kept her eyes closed. She was silent, still.

'Anna, tell me why!' Tears continued to roll down her cheeks, but no other part of her moved. Tony stood up and staggered: his legs tingled from crouching.

'Look at me!' He picked up the pillow from the bed and slammed it back down, as if the noise could startle her, focus her attention. 'Answer me! You could have told me, you could have stopped this!'

He heard a knock at the door and turned around to see the nurse standing there with her head tipped to the side and a concerned look. 'Is everything OK?' she said.

Tony shook his head and walked towards the door without a word. Of course it wasn't OK. He wanted to tell the nurse to leave them alone, to let him talk to his wife, but he didn't really know if he wanted to hear what Anna had to say. Part of him was glad for the excuse to walk out of this room and leave her.

As he went through the doorway, he thought he heard Anna call his name, very quietly. He looked back but she hadn't moved. He turned away and kept going, walking down the corridor towards the heavy locked door that he had entered by. A woman was standing there, smiling at him, and Tony moved faster so that she could unlock the door for him. She was wearing a black dress and heels. She kept smiling as he approached and Tony realised she was waiting for him. He put his head down, hoping she would take the hint and let him out.

'Mr Patton?' she said.

'Yes,' he said.

'I'm Dr Morgan, Anna's psychiatrist. I've been trying to get hold of you.'

Tony raised his eyebrows. Somehow he had expected that she would be older. 'Oh, Dr Morgan . . . I know, I'm sorry, I . . .'

'I'd really like to talk to you to get some information.' She was still smiling.

He sighed. He just wanted to get as far away from here as possible. 'Yeah, of course, I'm just —'

'How about now? It won't take long.' She was looking him straight in the eyes.

He sighed in resignation: he had managed to avoid the psychiatrist all week, but couldn't keep putting it off. 'I suppose . . .'

'Wait here,' she said. 'I'll just get my bag. Let's go outside and get some fresh air.'

*   *   *

Anna kept her eyes closed until she heard Tony's footsteps disappear down the corridor. Then she opened them again, wiped her nose with her sleeve, and slowly looked around, hoping that she had been mistaken and he would still be standing there. He wasn't. Someone else was coming back, but she knew the steps weren't his. It was the nurse.

'Anna,' she said quietly, standing at the door. 'Are you all right?'

Anna nodded. She couldn't look up; she didn't trust herself. She didn't want to talk to anyone. But the nurse came into the room and closed the door behind her. She pulled the other chair over from near the door to sit close to Anna, and she looked out the window too.

'Was that your husband?'

Anna nodded again.

'What did he say?'

She shook her head. Anna had never seen Tony so upset. What was he talking about? She didn't know what had happened, nothing made sense. Her head throbbed. 'What have I done?' She covered her face with her hands and sobbed.

The nurse didn't answer. She passed Anna a box of tissues then waited until she had started to calm down. 'I'll ask Dr Morgan to come and see you.'

Anna turned away and blew her nose. What was the point of talking to Dr Morgan? She couldn't concentrate, there were too many thoughts rushing around in her head. She felt light-headed, and shivered, even though she was so, so hot. There was an ache in her chest, so tight, so heavy. She didn't know what to believe, what was real, any more.

If her own husband couldn't stand to be around her then the voices were right and she was a terrible person after all.

*   *   *

Tony followed Dr Morgan outside, and around to the back of the psychiatric building. The sweet, green smell of grass swirled around his face as he inhaled, making his jaw and palate itch. There was an earthy, pungent odour too, fertiliser maybe. The path led them further away from the hospital to a grassy area with trees stretching out around the perimeter. Here, Tony could almost forget that the hospital existed.

'A few people come here to eat their lunch, but it's usually quiet.' Dr Morgan stopped at a wooden bench with a brass plaque on the back of it. 'It's nice to get out of the ward for a while.'

He sat down at one end of the bench, in the shade of a large fig tree. Dr Morgan sat at the other end and put her bag down on the ground. Tony was glad that she couldn't look directly at his face: he knew that it wouldn't take much for him to break down. He was scared; a psychiatrist should understand Anna, and that frightened him more than the intimidation of the police. What if she confirmed what he couldn't bear to believe, that Anna was capable of killing Jack? He pursed his lips and breathed out slowly.

'How are you feeling?' Dr Morgan asked.

He gave a wry smile. 'Not great.'

'I can only imagine how difficult this is for you.'

His eyes were burning again. He looked to his left, away from her.

'Tony, you don't have to talk to me about Anna, or Jack, if you don't feel ready.'

His hands began to tremble. He stared into the distance. 'It's like I'm stuck in a nightmare.' Dr Morgan waited. 'She always wanted to have kids. And now this happens . . . She – she loved him so much . . .'

Dr Morgan leaned forward. 'I wish I could say that I understood how you feel, but I don't think anyone can. It must be terrible, and very confusing for you.'

'I just don't understand what happened. One minute they were at home, and then . . . they're gone. Well, Jack's gone.'

'It probably feels like Anna's gone too.'

He nodded. He scratched the back of his neck. 'All I thought I'd have to worry about when we had kids was not being able to go out and get pissed on a Saturday night, or have a weekend at the snow.' He smiled sadly.

'Those sound like pretty normal concerns to me.'

Tony leaned back against the bench and looked up at the wavering tree canopy above them. 'She really did want a baby more than anything, you know. We both did. This . . . this isn't her. Getting pregnant was all she thought about for months and months.'

'What was that time like for you both?'

'She thought – we thought – that it would just happen, you know, the first time, but it didn't. She'd build herself up each month, telling me she felt a bit sick, or had a headache, so she must be pregnant, getting all excited. Then she'd take a pregnancy test, before it even said to on the packet, and it'd be negative. She'd say it was too early to test anyway. Then she'd get her period and come crashing down: thinking there was something wrong with her, or with me, or that she'd made a mistake with her charts and the timing.' He shook his head. 'It wasn't much fun in the end.'

'It sounds like having a baby was very important to her.'

'Yeah. She said there was no rush, that it would happen when we were both ready, but . . . once we got pregnant, she told me that she'd been doing all these things without telling me: taking her temperature, ovulation tests, herbal tablets, the lot.'

'Why do you think she didn't tell you?'

He started to pick at a splinter of wood on the arm of the bench. He thought back to those months: the bickering, Anna pretending that she hadn't been crying even though her eyes were red and swollen. 'Because I would have told her she was being silly, that maybe the reason she couldn't get pregnant was because she was too stressed, trying too hard. We were in the supermarket one day and she stood for ages in the aisle reading the backs of the little bottles of vitamins that claimed to be able to help with fertility. She picked one up, said that it was probably rubbish, so I nodded and said yes, it was a load of crap. That was it: she threw them on the floor, accused me of not wanting a baby, and burst into tears.'

Dr Morgan waited as a nurse walked past them towards the hospital, then turned to Tony again. 'Why do you think she said you didn't want a baby?'

'She knew I did, I just didn't feel there was any rush. She wanted me to go to the doctor after only six months, to get some tests too, but I didn't see the need.'

'Anna had already been to see her doctor about it?'

'She went to the GP without telling me. The doctor ordered some blood tests or something and told her that there wasn't any need to worry yet, that it can take a year. But she got so desperate, so obsessed with it all, so I went too. All my tests came back normal. The GP said we had to wait a few more months before she could refer us to a fertility doctor . . . So eventually we went, and the specialist couldn't find anything wrong either. He said that sometimes couples just weren't *compatible*.' He smiled sarcastically and turned towards Dr Morgan. 'Can you believe that? He meant the egg and sperm, but it was ironic – by that point, I was almost starting to have my doubts about us.'

Dr Morgan said nothing, but kept watching Tony. He blushed. 'No, I wasn't. I don't know why I said that. I knew from when I met her that she was the one.' His voice was cracking; he tried to cover it up by laughing. 'She wanted something to be wrong with me, so she could blame me.'

'It sounds like she was blaming herself.'

He stretched his legs out. 'Yeah.' He remembered how relieved he'd been when the test showed that the problem wasn't his fault. Had he blamed Anna, just a bit? Had he been a little smug in the knowledge that there was no problem with his fertility? He had tried to stay supportive and sympathetic, but had Anna seen through him? He pushed the thought away. 'Anyway, we didn't need any treatment in the end.'

'No?'

'No.' He smiled. 'We were ready to start IVF. Anna seemed to be back to her old self by then – you know, she had a plan, she said she knew it would work. She was more positive, less anxious. But then she felt weird when she was teaching one day; she stood up in the classroom and felt dizzy. I got home from work and found her asleep on the couch, then the next morning she came back through to the bedroom after her shower and held up a little plastic stick.' He smiled at the memory of Anna squealing and jumping all around the house. He'd realised then, when the test was positive, that he wanted a child as much as she did, that his life before that moment seemed empty and frivolous, and how much he looked forward to having his own family.

His face crumpled and he rubbed his eyes with the heels of his hands. He didn't want to take his hands away; for a few moments, he had been back with Anna and Jack, back in their life before all this had happened. Back with their excitement and dreams and anticipation.

It was all gone now.

He looked straight ahead, swallowed, then spoke. 'Does she understand what's happened? To Jack, I mean?'

Dr Morgan shook her head. A breeze had picked up and it blew her hair around her face; she tucked it behind her ears. 'Anna's still . . . she's still very unwell. I don't know that she'd be able to understand right now.'

'Has she mentioned him?'

'A few times. She's asked if he's OK, but then she moves on to something else. But that's not unusual in this situation, Tony. She's psychotic, her thoughts are very confused, and she's paranoid. I also think she's been hearing voices. We've noticed her muttering to herself, and she's talked about people telling her to do things.'

Tony bit his lip. He pictured her at home lying in bed, staring into the corner as if there were someone there, mumbling, then pushed the image away.

'Before she came into hospital, how was she?'

Tony wanted to tell the psychiatrist all of his doubts, every moment, every word that he'd gone over and over in his mind. How much was relevant? How much did Dr Morgan need to know? He couldn't help but feel that he was betraying Anna by talking about her. He reminded himself that Dr Morgan wasn't the police. She was there to help Anna, and that's what he wanted to do, too. Wasn't it?

'She wasn't good. I just thought she was tired, you know, she had a new baby, no sleep.' His voice got softer. 'To begin with I thought that maybe she was depressed. She'd be really down, then she'd be OK, then down again. I told her to go to the GP. I said that my mum could come over and help her. I didn't know . . . I didn't know it was serious. She'd gone to the doctor and she said she was fine.' His heart was racing now. He could see her, lying on that damn bed, saying nothing. He had walked out the door and left them. 'I didn't know this was going to happen!'

'Tony, Tony . . .' Dr Morgan held her hands out towards him. 'Please – it's not your fault. I'm just trying to find out whatever I can to help Anna.'

'Sorry —'

'Don't be silly, there's nothing to be sorry for.'

He wasn't so sure.

Just then, he heard the electronic chirping of a pager. Dr Morgan apologised and reached down to rummage through her bag. She took out a black plastic pager the size of her palm, pressed a button on the top to make the beeping stop, then another to read the message. She frowned, put it back in her bag and stood up. 'I'm sorry to cut this short, but that was the ward – I need to go back.'

'OK, I —'

Dr Morgan hesitated. 'It's Anna. The nurse is worried about her.'

'What? What's happened?' He stood up straightaway, his heart pounding. What else could possibly be wrong?

'We don't need to panic, it's just that she's got a bit of a temperature —'

'A temperature? She's sick! I knew it! I told them in Emergency – there's something physically wrong with her, they haven't looked properly. My God. She's just had ECT, but she was sick all along!' He shook his head. 'I should never have agreed to this.'

Dr Morgan took a step towards him and spoke calmly. 'It could be anything. It might just be a cold. Let's go back and see.'

He wanted to yell, to lash out. He had trusted the doctors, even though he hadn't wanted to, when they told him Anna was physically OK. He had trusted their judgement when they said she needed to be in a psychiatric hospital, that they'd make her better, but now she was getting worse. He had trusted them to care for her properly. Shame bolted through him like an electric shock – he had failed to look after her, too.

CHAPTER SIXTEEN

Five weeks before

Sunday, 9 August 2009

When Jack had finished feeding, Anna wrapped him up tightly in his blankets, then put him in the clear plastic cot in the corner of the hospital room. She hung the 'do not disturb' sign outside the door, then undressed and showered with the bathroom door open so she could hear him if he cried. She was glad she had brought her own shampoo. She wanted to make sure that she looked nice today, the day she took her baby home.

She dried herself with the thin hospital towel, wishing she'd brought her own – she would definitely remember to put that on her list for the next baby. She smiled at the thought of Tony's face if she told him she already wanted another one. She unfolded the pale green dress from her drawer, unrolled a tan belt, then dressed quickly before checking on Jack. He was fast asleep now, his mouth making little sucking motions. She resisted the urge to touch his soft cheek again, in case she woke him. He hadn't slept for most of the night; he needed some quiet time now. She towel-dried her hair, in case the hair dryer woke him, then combed it. With the bags packed beside her, she sat on the bed and flicked through a magazine until Tony opened the door ten minutes later.

'Your taxi is here!' He leaned over to kiss Jack, then her. 'Are you both ready?'

'Yes, *so* ready! We've just got to wait for all the paperwork. I told them you were coming at nine but of course it's still not here.' She rubbed at her eyes and stifled a yawn.

'How did the night go? You look tired.'

'You're lucky you went home. Jack was unsettled all night again; every time I thought he was falling asleep I put him down, and then he'd start crying again. The only way he'd settle was in my arms, but of course you're not allowed to cuddle them in bed.' She blinked back tears. 'Sorry, I'm being silly. That horrible night nurse was on again, the one who said I was breastfeeding all wrong. I don't know, I just felt intimidated by her. So stupid . . . She came in with her torch and shone it in my face and made me put him back in the cot, and then he woke up again.'

'Oh no, I'm sorry.'

'It's fine, I'm just so glad to be going home. Then I can do what I think is best.'

Tony took a step closer to her and put his arm around her shoulders. 'You should have called me. I told you to phone if you needed me.'

At one point last night she had held her mobile phone in her hand, urging herself to call Tony and tell him how lonely she was, and that she needed his help, but she had put the phone down again. He was tired too; it wouldn't have been fair. She looked at him now and smiled. 'Doesn't matter. I hope you enjoyed your good night's sleep – it's probably the last one for a while!'

He looked down at Jack again. 'I can't wait to have my little family at home. I'll go and get a trolley for all these flowers.' He squeezed her shoulder and walked out.

Anna rechecked all the cupboards and drawers. She couldn't wait to get out of here, away from the noise of nurses chattering and babies screaming, away from the constant stream of people in and out of her room, the lack of privacy. But at the same time it was strange knowing that she was going home to the place where she'd only ever lived as one half of a couple. And now they were three.

Within minutes, Tony was back, waving an envelope in one hand and pushing a metal trolley with the other. 'We are officially free to go!' he said in a mock deep voice. She laughed, carefully picked up Jack, and stood waiting for Tony to load the trolley. Just then, a cleaner came into the room. Anna asked her to take their picture, then stood next to Tony and smiled for the camera. Their first family photograph.

They left two of their eight bunches of flowers at the nurses' station for the ward staff, went down in the lift, then walked out of the hospital. Anna raised her head and breathed deeply. She hadn't been outside for five days.

'I'd forgotten how cold it was,' she said as she wrapped the white blanket tighter around Jack. 'It's like being in a bubble in there.'

When they got to the car, Anna strapped Jack into the capsule. 'Babe, do you think he's in right?'

Tony glanced over. 'Yeah, looks good.' He continued to load the boot with the bags and gifts.

'Can you check it for me?' Jack looked so tiny and vulnerable. He had no idea what was happening to him. She leaned down and kissed his head. Her eyes filled with tears as she whispered to him, 'We're taking you home now.'

*　　*　　*

Back at the house, Anna gasped and laughed when she saw the front door. It was covered with blue balloons. She was so lucky: she had a thoughtful, loving husband, and now a gorgeous son. She kissed Tony. 'Aw, that's very sweet, babe, thank you!'

'I was hoping they'd still be there when we got back – I didn't think about how to attach them, all I could find was sticky tape.'

'They're lovely. Let's get inside.'

Anna lifted the sleeping baby out of the capsule and cradled him in one arm. She looked around, hoping that one of the neighbours would be out in their garden so she could show him off, but the street was quiet. She followed Tony up the path to the door.

Inside, she gently laid Jack in his wicker bassinette next to their bed. Ursula had given it to her; it had been Tony's and Lisa's when they were babies. The white sheets with little yellow elephants embroidered in the corners were pulled tight across the mattress. The cot was all set up in the nursery, but he was too little for that

at the moment, and Anna wanted him to sleep next to them for a
few months. As she looked down at Jack, Tony put his arms around
her waist from behind and hugged her. 'He's beautiful,' he said.
'Well done, Anna.'

'I didn't do it on my own!' She leaned down, wincing from the
pain of her scar.

'I'll get him,' Tony said. 'You're not meant to lift, remember?'

He picked up the bassinette and they went into the living room.
She heard Jessie's claws clattering on the glass doors at the back
of the room, and looked up to see her leaping around in circles,
her tail in a frenzy. Anna laughed. 'Jessie!' She turned to Tony. 'I
think we should wait until she's calmed down a bit before we let
her in to meet Jack.'

'Good idea.' He put the bassinette on the kitchen bench that
separated the kitchen from the living area. He smiled. 'What now?'

'Yeah – weird isn't it?'

'Go and have a lie-down, babe. You must be tired. I'll bring
him through if he seems hungry.'

She slowly made her way back down the hall into their bedroom,
loosening her belt, and lay down, groaning with pleasure at being
back in her own bed. She rolled onto her side, still surprised that
her bump had gone, and fell fast asleep.

Jack's cries woke her from the middle of a dream and she jumped
up instinctively, then fell back down again from the tight, pulling
pain in her abdomen. 'Shit!'

Tony walked in with the baby. 'You OK?'

'Fine – just got up too quickly.'

'I think he's hungry.'

'Help me get some of these cushions right, will you?'

Tony put the baby down on the bed and helped Anna get settled
against the pillows. 'Good job you were organised and made all
those meals for the freezer. I've put some lasagne in the oven, and
I even bought some of that yucky rocket to make a little salad.
I might even have some too.'

'Thanks, babe. Just give me half an hour or so.'

When Tony left, Anna tried to remember what the midwives had told her about getting the baby to latch onto her to feed. Jack was crying. His little face was red, and his fists were clenched on the end of his rigid arms. 'Shhh, little one, I'm trying . . .'

She couldn't seem to get it right. She held Jack's weight in her left hand and forearm, trying to remember where to put her fingers, and with her right hand she moulded her breast into what she thought was the correct shape. She could see a blister on her nipple: it was going to hurt. She tensed her shoulders, then, when he opened his mouth to scream, she pushed Jack onto her breast. He started sucking straightaway. She squeezed her eyes shut as a burning pain shot through her. 'No, no, no . . .' She poked her finger into the side of Jack's mouth to break the suction and tried again, then again. 'What am I doing wrong?' she said aloud, her eyes smarting with tears. He was hungry, getting more and more worked up. Anna forced herself to relax and swapped him to her other breast. She gritted her teeth against the pain and tried to breathe deeply, telling herself that it would pass. The nurse had told her that it would be uncomfortable for a while. It was getting better now. She lay back on the pillow and closed her eyes.

*   *   *

The afternoon passed quickly. Jim and Ursula came over with a bottle of champagne, a chicken casserole and some gifts from the family, but left after a glass of bubbly. Anna was glad when they went home; she just wanted to be alone with Tony and Jack. By 8:30 p.m., she couldn't stop yawning.

'I might go to bed soon,' she said, thinking of her soft pillow and warm blankets.

'I'll hold him while you get ready,' said Tony. 'Go and get into bed. I'll be there in a minute.'

'It's OK, he'll need a feed soon anyway. I'll take him through with me and try and get him settled. You can sleep in the spare room.'

'No, I'll stay in with you, babe.'

'Don't be silly – I'll probably be up all night.' She couldn't help but feel excited. This was what she'd waited so long for: these long hours in the dim light, cuddling her newborn baby. She wanted to be part of that mothers' club, to complain about how little sleep she'd had; she looked forward to it. 'You have to work tomorrow, so get some sleep. There's not much you can do anyway during the night; he'll just need to be fed.'

'Are you sure?' Tony looked relieved. It made Anna smile. Other wives would make their husbands stay up with them, but she wanted to show Tony that she could cope on her own. He had to work; she would care for Jack. 'Well, only if you promise to come and get me if you need any help. Anything at all.'

'I promise.'

Tony carried the bassinette through to the bedroom. She hadn't noticed earlier that he'd put fresh linen on the bed. She smiled at the mismatched pillowcases and opened her mouth to mention it, but saw his serious face and closed it again. She loved that he had tried. He picked up the small table from the corner of the room and moved it next to the bed then lifted the bassinette onto it. He left and came back with a big glass of water that he put on the bedside table. After arranging the pillows around Anna, he handed Jack to her and kissed them both goodnight.

'I'll leave the door open so I can hear you, OK?'

'OK. Goodnight.'

'Promise you'll shout if you need me?'

'Yes! But I'll be fine!'

Anna prepared herself for the pain of Jack latching on again, then once he was feeding, turned out the bedside lamp. She nestled back into the pillows and let her eyes adjust to the dark, gazing at the little person in her arms. Jack looked just like Tony. Maybe his nose was a little like hers, but already she could see that his eyes were the same as his father's, the eyes that were now closed in concentration as his jaw pumped up and down to extract every last drop of milk from her. It burned. It would get better though, Anna was sure. She leaned down and smelled Jack's skin, all soapy and milky. That was the baby smell they talked about, the smell that mothers loved.

At that moment, she never wanted to let him go.

* * *

The following days and nights rushed by in a confusion of catnapping and crying. The books said to sleep when the baby did, but if Anna had done that, she wouldn't have had time to get out of her pyjamas. Jack seemed to know the minute she closed her eyes: that was when he would wail. There was so much else to do too: washing, tidying, shopping. The books said to leave the housework until things settled down, but then she was more agitated about the mess. The books also said to eat properly, but she was too tired to get out of bed and prepare some food. Jack seemed to be feeding so much; every two or three hours he'd cry, Anna would prepare herself for the pain as he started to feed, then she would change him and try to settle him, and an hour later it would start again. It was relentless.

As she fed Jack, she trawled the internet on her phone, trying to find out what she was doing wrong, but everything she read told her that this was normal. She couldn't see how it was possible: how could people survive this?

On the third night at home, Anna gave up hoping that she would sleep. She sat on the edge of her bed holding Jack, using her legs to bounce him up and down as she didn't have the energy to stand up any more. It was after 3 a.m.; Jack hadn't slept for longer than twenty minutes since they went to bed at nine. She had written it all down in her diary. She had fed him four times, but he wouldn't stop fussing. Her mind was racing. Was she making enough milk? Her breasts felt empty. He obviously needed something from her that she wasn't able to give him.

She started to cry. She needed some help. Couldn't Tony hear him crying? Hear her?

'Shh, Jack . . . Shh . . .'

But she was only making it worse; Jack screamed louder. It was as if he was in a trance. Anna knew that she was too tired and too upset to help him now. 'Stop crying, please!' She put Jack on the bed, covered her face with her hands and sobbed.

Tony heard that. He came through to the bedroom, rubbing his eyes and yawning. 'What's happening?'

She glared at him. How dare he yawn and look tired when he'd been fast asleep for hours? 'Can't you hear him? I haven't been to sleep yet, I've fed him again and again, I don't know what's wrong, he won't stop crying . . .'

Tony picked up Jack from the bed. 'Why didn't you come and get me?'

'What's the point? You can't feed him. I'm just so tired. Even an hour's sleep . . . It's been days and days and I haven't slept for more than an hour or two. I can't do it – I don't know what to do.'

'Oh, Anna. I'm sorry, babe. You get into bed, I'll take him through to the living room and just watch TV.'

'You can't have the TV on, it'll overstimulate him!'

'I'll keep it quiet.'

'It won't work, he needs to be fed!'

Tony patted Jack on the back with his right hand as he rocked him. 'Why don't we do what Mum suggested then and give him a bottle? It'll give you a break, help him sleep —'

'No! I want to breastfeed him. I'm not giving up already. I don't need a quick fix, Tony, I need . . .' She stopped as she saw Tony start to yawn. Adrenalin surged through her and she gritted her teeth. 'Don't worry about it. Just go back to bed, you have to work tomorrow.'

'Don't be like that.'

She saw the hurt in Tony's face, took a deep breath and made herself speak more gently. 'Look, thanks – thanks for trying. It's just that I want to breastfeed him. Mothers have done this for thousands of years, I'm not the only one. I just have to toughen up.'

Jack's cries were slowing down now. She looked at Tony holding him, and pushed away a feeling that she knew was jealousy. And rejection. Of course Jack would settle for Tony, she thought, make it look like she – his own mother – didn't know what she was doing. 'Do you want to try and put him down again?'

Tony nodded and laid him in the bassinette. Jack fussed a little, but didn't cry.

'I'll sleep in here with you tonight,' Tony said. 'Come on, get in.' He held back the covers while she crawled into bed. She put her head down on Tony's chest and cried. She didn't know if they were tears of relief or shame.

CHAPTER SEVENTEEN

Four days after

Friday, 18 September 2009

Wendy looked at the spines of Emily's cookbooks on the shelf above the fridge. She reached up and took down one by a chef she'd seen on TV, then carried it over to the suede couch and sank into the cushions. She looked out through the glass doors that opened onto a large balcony, facing south towards the city. Even though the sky was overcast, the harbour still sparkled. The bridge curved like a rainbow, and she could just make out the white sails of the Opera House. Toy ferries zipped across the water, and miniature boats bobbed about in their wake. She could see why Anna chose to live in Sydney. Wendy thought back to her own cramped house and for a moment felt ashamed, then admonished herself. She had tried her best; it wasn't easy raising a child on your own.

She kicked off her thongs and curled her legs under her, then started to flick through the cookbook. It was no wonder Anna wouldn't eat the hospital food – Wendy had seen the tray of lukewarm mashed-up meat casserole that they had brought her for dinner. It was awful to think of Anna being hungry: Wendy wanted to take her some home-cooked food. What did Anna eat these days? It was a long time since she'd cooked for her, and she suspected that Anna would have outgrown her macaroni cheese, made with a sachet of powdered cheese sauce. She needed to find a recipe for something nutritious; with some food in her, Anna was bound to feel better.

Wendy scanned the pages, then sighed. She could never make these fancy meals; she hadn't even heard of half the ingredients. She looked at her watch; it was already lunchtime. She had to go to the shops, buy everything she needed, make the food, and then get to the hospital by visiting time at three o'clock. Her heart sped up and she felt the familiar flurry in her belly. She didn't have time. Anna needed to eat something, she *had* to eat, otherwise . . . she closed her eyes and spread her fingers out wide. She could see Anna having her first proper meal as a baby, wearing a blue smock and a pink bib. She had pureed apples all over her face, and a gummy grin. Wendy's hands shook; she raised them up to her face as she cried. She let herself sob, really sob, for the first time. It didn't matter; there was no one here to hear her.

Her mobile phone rang from the bedroom. She ran across the soft carpet to the spare room. The sound was muffled; the phone was under the blankets somewhere on the unmade bed. It was Tony ringing.

'Hello?'

'Wendy?'

'Yes, sorry, I . . .' Wendy knew she sounded terrible.

'Are you all right?'

'Yes, I just . . . Bit of a cold. Is everything OK?'

Tony paused. 'I'm at the hospital. I was in seeing Anna, and talking to the psychiatrist.' Wendy held her breath. 'They think she's got an infection or something. She's not well, she's got a fever —'

'A fever? My God, what kind of infection? Is it bad?'

'I don't know. They're calling in a medical specialist to see her, and they're doing some blood tests.' Wendy heard Tony's voice break. 'It's just one thing after another. I told them that there was something else wrong, but they said they'd checked and that she was OK.'

'Is this why she's like this? Have they missed something?'

'Dr Morgan said she didn't know.'

'But they've started ECT – what if it's something else?'

'I know! It's like they just jumped to conclusions. I told them this wasn't her, she's never been like this before.'

Wendy screwed her eyes shut, then opened them. 'I'll come now. I was just going . . . to make her something to eat, but I realised I don't know what she likes any more.' The tears started again.

Wendy hung up, then called a cab. She quickly washed her face and pulled her hair back into a ponytail. Grabbing her bag, she put her thongs back on and went downstairs to wait for the taxi.

*   *   *

Tony leaned on the wall outside Anna's hospital room, next to the closed door. A doctor was in there looking at her. He'd noticed how the doctor had hesitated before going in, then hung back behind the nurse, as if he was frightened of Anna. Were medical staff scared of everyone in a psychiatric ward, or just his wife? Tony should have insisted on being in the room while Anna was examined, but he hadn't. Was fear to blame for that too? Was he any better than this doctor?

He heard Wendy's voice at the nurses' station and walked back along the corridor to meet her. Her face was swollen and blotchy. She saw him, then walked towards him and hugged him. He felt her tears drip onto his shirt. He pulled back.

'What's happening?' she asked.

'The doctor's in there now. Come on, we'll wait up there.'

Wendy nodded. 'God, I must look a state. I just left straightaway . . . I can't bear to think that on top of all this, she's sick too.'

'I know.'

'Not that she's not sick – I mean, clearly she's not well – but something else. I just don't know —'

Anna's door opened. 'He's finished. Come on.' He started walking down the corridor as the doctor came out.

'Doctor? I'm Anna's husband,' Tony said when he was a few metres away.

'Oh, hi.' The doctor shook Tony's hand.

'And I'm her mum, Wendy.'

'Good to meet you both. I'm Dr Nguyen.'

The nurse, Rachel, came out of Anna's room and closed the door behind her, then joined them.

'What's wrong with her, doctor?' Wendy asked shakily.

'She's got a high temperature, and she says she doesn't feel well, but it's hard to get a history from her.' Dr Nguyen clutched Anna's notes to his chest. 'There's a few things it could be. When someone has a high temperature after starting antipsychotic medication, we do have to rule out a serious reaction to them. But her blood tests don't seem to fit with that – they suggest that she's got an infection somewhere.'

'What kind of infection? They did head scans in Emergency,' Tony said.

Dr Nguyen shook his head. 'I don't think it's her brain – there was no sign of infection when she was admitted.' He dropped his gaze just a little. 'Mr Patton, Anna was breastfeeding, wasn't she?'

Tony nodded. 'Yes,' he said quietly. 'She was.'

'I think she has a condition called mastitis.' Dr Nguyen cleared his throat. 'Her left breast is red and quite engorged. When someone stops . . . breastfeeding suddenly, the ducts can get blocked and the breast can get infected.'

Tony heard a buzzing in his ears. He leaned back against the wall.

'How do you treat it?' Wendy said.

'She needs antibiotics, but the best thing to do is for her to express milk, to clear the blockage.'

'Express milk? We can't ask her to . . .' Tony looked at Wendy.

Dr Nguyen carried on as if Tony hadn't spoken. 'The risk is that this can turn into an abscess, and that's much harder to treat. We can use ultrasound to break down the blockage, or drain it surgically.'

Tony couldn't believe what he was hearing; shouldn't someone have thought of this already? 'How the hell can we explain that to her?'

Dr Nguyen's face went red and he looked at his feet. 'I'll talk to Dr Morgan and recommend some treatment, and I'll write it in the notes.' He cleared his throat again. 'Any other questions?'

Tony was stunned.

Dr Nguyen darted off with the file. Rachel squeezed Tony's arm. 'I'll just go and let Dr Morgan know.'

Tony looked at Wendy, 'We're going to have to tell her,' he said.

'We can't, we can't.' Wendy's voice shook. 'She's too sick, it's too soon . . .'

'We'll have to! How can we tell her that she has to have a pump on, or people prodding and draining her breast? She'll ask why! She needs to know.'

'We should ask Dr Morgan, see if —'

'It's not up to Dr Morgan! Jesus, Anna has to find out sometime; I want to get it over with. She keeps asking about Jack, and I don't know whether she genuinely doesn't know, or . . .' He ran his fingers through his hair. Or what? Did he think she was lying, pretending that she didn't remember? Or had she blocked it out? He needed to see her reaction; it might help him figure everything out.

He looked straight at Wendy. 'When Dr Morgan gets here, I'll do it. I'll tell Anna what happened to Jack.'

CHAPTER EIGHTEEN

Four days after

Friday, 18 September 2009

Anna watched Dr Morgan disconnect the tube attached to the cannula in the back of her hand, then reconnect a plastic syringe full of pale yellow liquid. It could be anything in that syringe, but she didn't care. As Dr Morgan squeezed the solution into her veins she felt nothing; it was as if it was someone else's arm. She shivered, even though she could feel sticky sweat under her arms.

Then she did feel something: an icy chill creeping up her hand and crawling up her forearm. She wanted to scratch it, but didn't move. Her arms were too heavy, and she could barely lift her head. She lay back on the pillows, and shivered again.

'Anna? That's the antibiotics in now – you'll feel better soon. Are you all right?'

She managed to nod.

Dr Morgan put the blue plastic kidney dish on the bed, then sat on the arm of the chair by the window. 'Anna, Tony and your mum are here and want to see you.'

Anna managed a smile. 'He came back . . .'

'He was with me when Rachel called about your temperature. He's been very worried.'

Anna thought about this carefully. Tony had been so angry with her, but if he was here then maybe he *did* still care for her. If he was really upset, then he would have left, wouldn't he? Did he understand after all?

'Anna, they want to talk to you about something, and Rachel and I would like to be part of that conversation too.'

Anna nodded, knowing she couldn't refuse. She wanted to talk to her mother and Tony too, but she didn't want an audience. She wanted it to just be her family, not these strangers. A wave of heat washed over her; she dabbed at her upper lip with her finger, then wiped it dry on the sheet. She had a sudden urge to jump out of the bed and run, far away from this conversation that everyone wanted to have. But there was nothing she could do. There had never been anything that she could have done, this whole time. She had never had a choice.

Dr Morgan went to the door of her room and held it open. Tony, Wendy and Rachel filed in. They looked so serious. Anna drew her knees up to her chest and wrapped her arms around them. Her mum sat on the end of the bed, and stroked Anna's bare foot like she used to when she was a child. She was torn between kicking out at her and wriggling closer. Tony dragged a chair to the head of the bed. It creaked when he sat down on the vinyl cushion, a coarse noise followed by a puff of air. She had to stifle a laugh. Tony didn't laugh: he looked like he'd been crying. Anna clasped her hands together to stop them shaking. Suddenly she didn't want to hear what they had to say.

She turned towards the sound of the door closing. Dr Morgan leaned against it; next to her, Rachel stood against the wall. This room was too small for them all. Anna couldn't get her chest to expand properly; there wasn't enough air in the room.

No one said anything; they seeemed to be waiting for something. She looked around at everyone. Was she meant to start?

She tried to make her voice sound bright. 'Tony? Mum?'

Wendy let out a sob and buried her face in her hands. 'Oh, darling.'

What was going on? The throb of her headache quickened. Everything was so strange, like she was here but she wasn't. 'Mum, it's OK.' She knew that, somehow, she was the cause of all this: the crying, the anger, the upset. She had never wanted to drag anyone else into this.

'I'm OK.' Wendy squeezed Anna's foot. 'I'm OK, don't worry about me.'

She had heard that before, too many times. It had always been like this: her mum would cry, Anna would worry, her mum would reassure her, and Anna would worry even more.

Tony cleared his throat. Anna stared at him, silently pleading with him; she didn't want him to say anything.

'Anna, you know you've had a fever and the doctors have been trying to find out what's wrong. Well, they think you've got an infection . . .'

She shook her head and let her tears drop. 'It's all right Tony, it's not true, I know it. I've worked it out.'

'What? It is true, what do you think —'

'I know where I am.'

'Where do you think you are?'

Anna looked away. 'You've locked me up. It's OK. It's the best place for me.'

'Anna, no. Jesus . . .' He sat forward and rubbed his face with his hands. 'Well, it is a psychiatric hospital, but you do have an infection. From breastfeeding.'

Anna froze. She glanced down at her chest and an image of a tiny baby nursing flashed before her eyes. She refused to see it. 'I'm not breastfeeding.'

'But you were – you were breastfeeding Jack,' Tony said softly.

Anna clenched her jaw and looked at the wall straight in front of her. 'Where is he?'

'Jack? Is that who you mean?'

'What have you done with him?'

Tony stood up. 'What have I done with him? I haven't done anything with him, Anna!'

She stared at the wall in front of her and focused on a black smudge. Was it a squashed bug, a mosquito maybe? Her head shook, and she tried to keep her eyes still, fixed on that little black spot.

'Anna!' Tony took a step towards her, but Wendy held out her arm and he stopped.

'Anna,' Wendy said. 'What Tony's trying to say is, there has been a horrible, horrible tragedy. I'm so sorry . . . but Jack's gone.'

The black smudge was getting bigger in front of her eyes; it was blurry now, and Anna couldn't keep her eyes on it. She looked away from the wall and stared at her mum. What had she said? Wendy looked pale, and thinner than ususal. Something wasn't right. She turned to Tony. He didn't look right either. Was it really them? He raised his face and Anna looked into his brown eyes; those *were* the eyes she knew. So what was going on? She felt so light that she thought she could almost float away off this bed, over all of them and out of the door. Tony was still staring. It was almost more than she could bear. What did he see when he looked at her?

'Tony,' she said quietly, not taking her eyes off him. 'Tell them all to go away, please.'

'Who?'

'Everyone! Let's make it just us, Tony, just us . . .'

He shook his head. 'It's just your mum, and the doctor and nurse.'

'I don't trust them,' she whispered. 'Please.'

Tony moved closer and took her hands. 'It's OK, babe. I trust them.'

How could she make him understand? He wasn't listening to her. 'Please . . .'

'Anna, did you hear what your mum said? Do you understand what we're saying?'

They were all looking at her. Anna squeezed Tony's hands; they were hot and damp. It couldn't be true. Jack had to be safe. That's all she had cared about, protecting him. 'Tony . . . where's Jack? Tell me, please.'

'Anna, we told you.'

She felt the panic clawing at her throat, strangling her words and stifling her breath. She breathed more quickly, trying to get some air in. She was dizzy; everything around her was spinning and spinning. 'Where is he? Give me my baby . . .'

'You know, Anna! Just stop!' Tony shook his head, then let go of her hands and covered his face. Her mum was still stroking her foot; her skin was burning and she pulled her knees in tighter to her chest, looking from Tony to her mum, and back again. Tears poured down Wendy's face. Anna began to wail. She could hear the noise she was making but somehow it didn't seem to be coming from her. Tony was going now, he was going to leave her here, alone, without her baby. She took a deep breath and screamed. The noise was alive, malevolent, and it echoed and amplified as it gathered up all the grief around it.

She swung her legs off the right-hand side of the bed. Wendy jumped up and ran around the foot of the bed towards her, but Tony didn't move. Would her legs hold her? She had to get out.

She pushed past her mum and lunged towards the door, not taking her eyes off the door handle. The drip stand clattered behind her as it fell and she felt the cannula rip out of her hand. From outside the room, she heard an alarm, shrill and piercing, becoming louder. Someone held her by the waist. Anna put her hands in her hair, grabbed it and pulled as hard as she could. She could hear the wailing still.

Then her knees buckled and she was down. Her head hit the floor; she lifted it up and banged it again and again.

'Tony!' she screamed. 'Tony, help me! Get me out of here!'

She looked around for him; he was there, looking down at her, his face red and wet and contorted. His mouth moved but Anna couldn't hear what he said. He stepped back out of her view and was gone.

She felt something pinning her limbs down and a sharp sting, and then the terror was leaving her, she was floating, and she didn't have to think any more, just breathe slowly and drift off to sleep.

See, she told herself, *it wasn't real. Just go back to sleep.*

CHAPTER NINETEEN

Four weeks before
Monday, 17 August 2009

Anna picked up her cup of tea. It had gone cold. She refilled the kettle, then put a fresh tea bag in another mug. She leaned on the kitchen bench and waited. Above the bubbling of the boiling water, she heard Jack cry. She looked at her watch and sighed. Right on cue: two hours since the last feed. She switched the kettle off. She would feed Jack, then try to get to the shops to buy something for dinner before Tony got home.

She picked Jack up and he snuggled into her. She closed her eyes and breathed him in; this made it all worth it. He was so warm, so little. She kissed his head then sat down on the couch to feed him.

Straightaway, her phone rang. She smiled when she saw Tony's work number on the screen; he must be leaving work early. She supported Jack in one hand; and leaned forward to pick it up.

'Hi, babe,' she said.

'Hi. What are you up to?'

'Oh, you know, just cooking a three-course meal, about to go for a 10K run, reading a novel . . .'

Tony laughed. 'Sitting on the couch?'

Anna looked down at her bare legs, unshaven, and the chipped red nail polish on her toes, left over from a trip to the day spa with Emily a few weeks ago. She had barely been able to see her toes over her stomach then. Maybe this weekend Tony would mind Jack between feeds so that she and Emily could go for a coffee and have their nails done. The thought of even an hour to herself was wonderful.

'Yeah, just feeding the baby – again. I worked out that I spend about ten hours a day just feeding him.'

'Shit, that's a lot of milk. He must be growing!'

She glanced down at Jack's serious face. He *was* growing; it was good to know that as hard as it was, she was providing for him, giving him what he needed.

'Are you leaving soon? It's not even four yet.'

'In about half an hour. I thought I'd invite Mum and Dad over for a drink.'

'Oh.' Anna looked around the room, saw the washing basket full of unfolded clothes on the floor near the patio doors, the day's dishes strewn over the kitchen bench behind her, and the coffee stains on the table. 'When? The house is in a state . . .'

'It doesn't matter about the house. They were going to come straight after Dad finishes work, so in an hour or something.'

'An hour? You've already organised it?' She looked down at her baggy dress, unbuttoned to the waist, and her unhooked maternity bra stained with milk. She must smell. 'But I need to have a shower, and tidy up. We haven't got anything in the house . . .'

'I'll stop by the shops on the way home, get some dips and beer.'

'Tony, some notice would have been good.'

'It's only Mum and Dad. They don't care what the place looks like, they just want to see us.'

She wished Tony would be a bit more thoughtful sometimes. The last thing she wanted was to have to make conversation. She just wanted him to bring home some dinner and then go to bed early, full of hope that maybe this was the night she would finally get some sleep. Now Jim and Ursula and Tony would have a few drinks and chat and say how wonderful Jack was, and they'd end up staying for dinner, and she wouldn't get to bed until late.

What was the point in arguing? Then she'd look like the bad one. 'Fine, but hurry home – make sure you're here before them.'

Jack's feeding was slowing down now. She sat forward and swapped him to the other breast. She gritted her teeth until the searing pain settled, then stood up and gingerly started to tidy up with her one free hand.

*   *   *

Ursula, Jim and Lisa waited at the door. Tony's car wasn't in the driveway; he must have been held up at work. Ursula rang the doorbell again, and heard it chime above the sound of a vacuum cleaner and the baby crying. She tried the door but it was locked. The afternoon drizzle was becoming steadier now and Ursula's glasses had a fine mist on them. She was going to get soaked. Lisa huddled under the front porch, while Jim – still in a fluorescent-yellow work vest – walked into the garden, stepped between some shrubs and knocked on the window. The vacuum stopped. Ursula heard a cupboard door creaking open and the clatter of the plastic hose of the vacuum cleaner being shoved in. The baby stopped crying, then the door opened.

Anna stood cradling Jack in her left arm. She smiled. Her hair was wet and combed straight, but she wore no make-up and Ursula could see the dark shadows under her eyes. 'Come in out of the rain! I'm sorry I didn't hear you. I was just having a shower.'

Ursula wiped her feet on the mat, then stepped into the house and kissed Anna's cheek. 'How are you, love? And how's my gorgeous boy doing?' She leaned down and kissed Jack's forehead, then moved aside to let Jim and Lisa in.

'Lisa!' Anna said. 'I didn't know you were coming. It's great to see you!'

Lisa hugged Anna. 'Mum called me. I can't stay long, I'm going round to a friend's place to work on some designs, but I thought I'd pop in and see my nephew first.' She looked down at Jack, whose eyes were closing now, and held out her arms towards him. 'Can I have a cuddle?'

Anna hesitated, opened her mouth to say something, then nodded and handed Jack over. Lisa rocked him in her arms and tickled his chin with her finger. Ursula watched her daughter talking softly to the baby: she was a natural. Realising she was staring,

Ursula looked away and handed Anna a bottle of pinot gris, then ushered Jim inside and closed the front door. Lisa and Anna were walking down the hallway and chattering. Jim put his hand in the small of Ursula's back and they followed them to the kitchen.

Anna looked into the pantry without taking anything out, then opened a cupboard and clattered the crockery around. She talked loudly; Ursula could hear a hysterical edge to her voice. 'I don't know where Tony is. He was meant to be home half an hour ago. He shouldn't be long. Jim, a beer?'

'Love one, Anna,' he said, perching on a kitchen stool. 'It's been a long day.'

'Work still busy?' Anna rummaged in the fridge. 'We've only got one beer – Tony's getting some more from the shops.'

'Great, thanks.' Jim took the bottle and twisted off the top.

'Now, wine. We should have something cold in here somewhere . . .'

'Open the one we brought, Anna, that's what it's for. Here, I'll do it. You sit down.' Ursula took the bottle from Anna's hands.

Anna took down two wine glasses and put them on the bench in front of Ursula. 'Sorry, I thought we had some chips in the cupboard, but we don't. I'll call Tony and ask him to get some on his way.'

'Doesn't matter, we don't need any.'

'No, that's OK. I'll call him.'

She went to the couch and picked up her phone, then walked to the back of the room and turned to face the corner, speaking in a shrill whisper. As she poured the wine Ursula watched Anna out of the corner of her eye but couldn't hear what she was saying.

Anna came back over, her cheeks red. 'Tony's been held up, he's only just leaving now, I'm sorry . . .'

'Doesn't matter. I don't need to see my brother, it's this little one I've come to see,' said Lisa, still cuddling Jack.

'Come and sit down,' Anna said. 'I'll put some music on.' She pushed the cushions on the black leather couch to the side, and Jim and Lisa sat down. Jim arranged some of the cushions under Lisa's elbow until she was comfortable. Anna took a box of laminated cork coasters from the shelf under the coffee table and laid them out. 'Sorry they're a bit ugly. Wedding present from someone at work; I think they were regifted.'

Lisa laughed. 'Australian native flowers, classy! I'll have the bottlebrush please.'

'You sit down, Anna. I'll get you a wine.' Ursula opened the cupboard to get another glass.

Anna shook her head. 'No, thanks. I'd love one, but I can't – breastfeeding.'

'Just a little one?'

'No thanks, Ursula.'

'You can have a little one, can't you? Won't hurt. In my day —'

'No,' Anna said, sharply. 'I don't want one, thank you.'

Ursula looked up: Anna's face was flushed and blotchy, like she was going to cry. Ursula nodded, then screwed the lid back on the bottle and put it in the fridge. Tony really should be here; it wasn't good enough that he was working so hard when Anna was on her own with a new baby.

'I'll get you a glass of water, Anna. Sit down.'

Anna took a step towards the kitchen, then stopped, walked back and sat on one of the two armchairs. Ursula let the tap run and filled a glass with water, then went over to join the others.

She could see that Anna was making an effort: she asked Lisa about her work, her latest boyfriend and her new flat, then asked Jim about his work, and whether or not he'd been fishing. But something wasn't quite right. Her laughter seemed hollow; her smile tense. Ursula sipped her wine and let the girls talk. She didn't hear much about Lisa's life these days, so it was nice to listen and feel involved. But as Ursula watched Anna's performance, she felt as though they were intruding on something. She glanced at her watch: where was Tony?

Then she heard the front door close and smiled in relief. Tony struggled into the room with a carton of beer on his shoulder and a plastic bag in his hand. 'Sorry everyone, sorry . . .' Jim stood up to help him.

'Busy day?' Ursula stood up to kiss him on the cheek as Jim took the carton from him.

'Oh yeah, it's a nightmare at the moment. We're trying to get this new account and we're under the pump.' Tony set down the plastic bag and stretched out his shoulders. 'Time for a beer, I think! Dad, another one?'

'Yeah, cheers.'

'Mum, another wine?'

'Maybe just half a glass, I'm driving . . .'

'I'll have another one!' Lisa waved her empty glass from where she sat on the couch.

'Oh Lisa, didn't see you down there. How are you?' Tony smiled.

'I'm great, ta. Just being aunty to this gorgeous boy.'

Ursula relaxed. The room felt warmer now. She glanced at Anna, who was still sitting in the armchair, with her legs curled under her. She laughed along with everyone else, but seemed to join in just a second too late.

Ursula rummaged in Tony's shopping bag. 'Anna, there's some lemon, lime and bitters here. Can I pour you some?'

'You don't want a wine?' Tony said, looking up at Anna as if he'd only just noticed her.

Ursula saw the tiny movement of Anna's jaw clenching. 'I've asked her already,' she put in quickly. 'I'll get her some soft drink. Go and sit down, Tony.'

Tony untucked his work shirt from his pants and went to sit next to Lisa. Jack was still asleep. 'He's sleeping now, eh?' He looked at Anna. 'He must like all the noise.'

Ursula passed Anna a glass. 'He's not sleeping well?'

Tony shook his head, opened some chips, then put the bag on the table. 'Anna's been having some bad nights.'

'Oh no,' Lisa said. 'That's what I don't think I could cope with, not getting any sleep. I'm bad enough if I have a night out . . .'

'You were like that, Tony,' Jim said. 'Your poor mother was exhausted.'

'I didn't think you noticed, Jim, you seemed to sleep through it all.' Ursula raised her eyebrows.

'I'm fine,' Anna said. 'He's just being a baby, it's nothing unusual.'

'But it's hard on you, babe.'

Anna swallowed, then nodded. 'A bit. But it's OK.'

'I can come round and help you, love, take him for a while so you can grab some sleep. I'm not doing anything else.'

Tony looked eagerly at Anna. 'See, I told you Mum could help.'

'Honestly, it's fine.'

Ursula watched Anna's face tighten as she broke eye contact with Tony. Then, forcing a smile, she turned to Ursula. 'Thanks Ursula. It's just that he seems to feed all the time, so there's not much anyone else can do. It's not worth trying to sleep, I'd only get half an hour. I think I'd feel worse. It'll settle down soon . . .'

Ursula heard the quaver in Anna's voice and saw that she was only just holding it together. She remembered the tiredness, the certainty that it would never end, that you'd never again get a full night's sleep. Tony was about to say something else, but Ursula spoke first. 'You're right, he will settle down soon. See how you go, but if you need help, just ask. Even if you want me to pick up some groceries for you or something.'

'Thanks, I'll keep it in mind. But we're OK, honestly.'

Ursula took the hint. She looked away from Anna. 'So Tony, what's going on at work? Why's it so busy at the moment?'

As Tony leaned back and started talking, Jack began to fuss. Anna jumped up as Lisa tried to shift him in her arms. Ursula stood up too and leaned over Tony, taking Jack from Lisa. Lisa looked relieved, stretching out her arms and reaching for her wine. Anna sat back down in her chair, but Ursula could see that she was ready to spring up again.

Ursula walked around the room, bouncing her arms and singing quietly to Jack. He looked just like Tony had as a baby. She loved the feeling of the tiny warm body against her chest. But he wouldn't settle. He shook his head from side to side with his mouth open, sucking at Ursula's shirt. She walked over to Anna's chair and spoke softly. 'Sorry, love, but I think he's hungry.'

Anna closed her eyes for a few moments and took a deep breath. She stood up without saying a word, took Jack and walked out of the room.

Ursula watched Anna as she left: she was holding Jack away from her body and wasn't looking at him. 'Is she OK, Anthony?'

Tony paused in his conversation with Jim. 'Yeah, she's fine. She'll just be feeding him, she'll be back soon.'

Ursula sat back down with her drink. She heard the baby cry from behind the bedroom door. It soon went quiet, but Anna didn't come back to join them.

*   *   *

Anna sat on the couch in her pyjamas, watching an American talk show, the only thing on television at 1 a.m. She tried not to look at the empty beer bottles and dirty wine glasses on the coffee table, or the plastic takeaway containers littering the kitchen bench. She was not going to tidy them up in the morning; Tony could do that. Jack was asleep in her arms, but she knew he would scream if she tried to put him down. It was easier to give in and stay awake. She could hear Tony snoring from their bedroom. She would do anything to swap places with him tonight, just for one night, just to get a stretch of sleep. Then she could handle anything. All she wanted was a bit of time to herself, to have a shower without Tony bringing Jack in because he wouldn't stop crying. Jack was his baby too; why did it always fall back on her?

She rubbed tears away from her eyes. Tony was trying his best, she knew that. He had to go to work during the day, and she had nothing else to do or worry about other than Jack. It wasn't fair of her to expect any more from him. Was it? She just had to cope. What other choice did she have?

The talk show was finishing. The host made some jokes, a live band in the studio sang some stupid song, and the audience roared with laughter. Tony liked these shows, but she remembered now why she didn't.

She turned the TV off with the remote and paused, waiting for Jack's reaction, but he didn't stir. She stood up, trying to keep her arms in exactly the same position, and tiptoed across the room. The bassinette was on the floor at the end of the couch. Anna crouched down. She curled her back and lowered Jack into the bassinette then waited with her arms underneath him: he was still asleep. She slowly withdrew one arm, then the other, her heart pounding. *Don't wake up, don't wake up*, she prayed to herself. And, for once, he didn't.

She tucked Jack's white blanket around him, then picked up the bassinette by its handle and walked towards their bedroom. Tony was still snoring. She put her hand on the door handle, then let go again and walked towards Jack's room. Maybe Tony was right: Jack might sleep better in his own room. He would tonight anyway: Tony always snored louder after he'd had a few drinks. Maybe Anna would sleep better this way too. Every time Jack whimpered or grunted, she opened her eyes and held her breath, instantly on alert. She had wanted to keep him in their room for six months, like the books she'd read recommended, but maybe this was worth a try, just for one night. She lifted the bassinette inside the cot, and checked that the baby monitor was on. She picked up the receiver and crept out, leaving the door ajar.

Two hours later, Anna lay in bed with her eyes wide open. Slices of light from the streetlights outside cut through the blinds, which weren't closed properly. She had never noticed before how noisy this bedroom was. Her ears rang with the hissing of traffic from streets away, and the grating of Tony's snores. If only it were quiet, she could sleep. She lay on her left side and held her hand over her right ear to muffle the sounds.

She started to relax.

Suddenly, Jack cried out, the noise amplified by the monitor next to the bed. She didn't move, trying not to let herself wake up fully in the hope that he would go back to sleep, but the noises continued. She rolled over towards Tony. His breathing was still heavy; he hadn't even flinched. How could he not hear the baby screaming? Was he ignoring it, assuming that she would deal with it as usual?

She threw back the blankets; Tony wriggled slightly, then fell asleep again. She picked up the monitor, wanting to hold it to Tony's ear until he took some notice, or hurl it at his back, but she didn't. Instead, she stumbled almost drunkenly through the dark to Jack's room.

She picked Jack up and sat in the rocking chair. She couldn't get comfortable, but eventually she found the right position and fed him. She was wide awake now, and wished she had taken a book from her bedroom to read. No one had told her how boring the hours and hours of feeding could be. She waited until Jack's sucking slowed and he had fallen asleep again, then put him gently back to bed.

Desperate to get some sleep, she crawled back into her own bed. She looked at the bright red numbers on the digital clock next to Tony and counted how many hours she had before Jack would wake again: two. She counted how many hours there were left until Tony's alarm would go off: three. Then it would all begin again, the tiredness, the tedium.

She pushed Tony's shoulder. 'Roll over. You're snoring,' she said, not bothering to whisper. He mumbled something then rolled over. The snoring stopped.

She wanted to shout at him. How could he lie there when he must know how exhausted she was? Why didn't he offer to help? But she didn't shout; she lay still. Tony wasn't sound asleep yet; he was waiting to see what she would do. He turned back over to face her; Anna immediately turned too so that all he could see was her back. His hand touched her waist; the warmth comforted her, the same way that Jack must feel comforted when she held him. A pang of guilt swept through her: this wasn't Tony's fault.

'Just relax,' he said.

She clenched her jaw, and her muscles tensed.

'Relax,' he said again. 'This way, neither of us is getting any sleep.'

Anna didn't move, didn't say anything, even though she wanted to scream. She felt her tears start. There was no way she could sleep now. Couldn't Tony understand how she felt? She knew he was waiting for her to respond, but she didn't. She froze in her position and fought against the discomfort in her neck, the itch on her leg, the cold air on her shoulders. Soon enough he started snoring again.

She didn't sleep. She fed Jack two hours later, settled him, then came back to bed. In no time, it was 6.30 a.m. and the radio alarm blasted into the room.

Tony rolled over and looked at her, worry creasing his brow. 'Bad night, huh?'

'No different to any other.' Anna's voice was rough and croaky. Why was he talking now? Now, when she had finally started dozing, when Jack was asleep; now that it was time for him to get up he decided he would show some concern?

'Why don't you have a lie-in today?'

She said nothing, afraid that if she started, she wouldn't stop. He just didn't get it. She sniffed quickly and blinked hard.

'Babe, just take it easy.'

She sat up and glared at him. 'I can't take it easy! Who's going to look after Jack?'

'He's still sleeping. When he wakes up, take him into bed with you for cuddles. He'd like that.'

How would he know what Jack liked? 'It doesn't matter what I do, he won't sleep. He'll wake up soon for a feed, and then that's it until tonight, when it starts again.' Her voice was getting higher. She took a deep breath before Tony could tell her to calm down. She didn't have the energy for a fight right now; she could tell she would lose. 'It's OK. Sorry. I'm just tired. I'll have a quick shower now if you can listen out for him. I'll be all right.'

She watched Tony open his mouth to say that he needed to get ready for work, but he closed it again. She rubbed her face with her hands while Tony took an unironed shirt out of the wardrobe and left the bedroom, taking the baby monitor with him.

CHAPTER TWENTY

Nine days after

Wednesday, 23 September 2009

Tony held Jessie's lead loosely in his hand and walked along the path past the beach. The sun was coming up, and the only people around were early morning surfers, and a few backpackers staggering back to their hostel after a night out. He headed north, past the golf course. Looking out to his right he saw swirls of pink appearing between the grey sky and the black ocean. It was going to be a beautiful day. How ironic. What weather would be appropriate for Jack's funeral? Pouring rain, a relentless drizzle, howling wind? As if the weather cared about him.

By the time he reached the cliff-side path, dabs of orange had spread along the horizon, and the sea was turning blue. Anna used to love this walk. She had always wanted to live in a house with a garden that pushed out into the cliff reserve, to be able to look out and see nothing but the ocean. Was that why she'd gone to those cliffs? Was she looking for that peace, that space? But why not here – why drive so far away?

He now knew she hadn't wanted to be found. Or had she? Once again he remembered the letter fluttering to the ground from his bag, and imagined himself grabbing it before it fell, before it hit the ground. Could he have caught Anna? When was the moment she'd drifted out of his reach?

Magpies chattered as they woke and gulls shrieked as they swooped down to the ocean for their breakfast. He stopped, dropped the dog's lead and stood on it. Jessie sat down and waited while Tony took off his hoodie and tied it around his waist. He could hear the sharp yells of a fitness instructor coming from one of the parks. A thin woman with a thick dark ponytail and an iPod strapped to her arm ran past him and smiled. He smiled back. He wished that, like her, he was simply out for some exercise before work.

He picked up Jessie's lead and kept walking. How long had it been since he'd slept properly? It was nine days since Jack had died. It was physically impossible to have gone that long without any sleep at all: his body would have shut down, he'd be hallucinating. He now understood why sleep deprivation was used as torture. He'd feel better if only his mind would rest, but every time he closed his eyes he castigated himself over and over with questions and accusations for which he had no answer. Was this how Anna had felt?

He reached the end of the path and sat down on the grass, looking out to sea. Jessie lay down beside him, panting. Those first nights at home with Jack, he'd heard him crying, but he'd rolled over and gone back to sleep. He'd been tired. What had he been thinking? Anna was exhausted, like he was now. He had been sleepy and too bloody comfortable to get up and help. It hadn't even crossed his mind that Anna couldn't handle it. He had been so stupid, so bloody selfish.

He swatted at a fly buzzing around his face, and missed. His hand was heavy and clumsy and it moved too slowly. Was this what Anna felt like before her mind collapsed in on itself? Last night, he'd been so close to falling asleep, finally, but then he heard a baby cry out from Jack's room, 'Dada'. He'd jumped out of bed, but it wasn't real.

Jack would never call for his dad.

The night before last, he'd felt Anna cuddle into his back and tickle the skin between his shoulder blades with her soft breath, then wiggle her cold toes into the warm crease behind his knees. He had reached a hand behind him to rest on her hip, but it fell . into cold, empty space. Of course she wasn't there. That was when he'd cried: he cried and cried until there was nothing left.

The sun was bright in the sky now. He shielded his eyes with his hand as he looked out at the ocean. It was really beautiful out here. He took a deep breath, then stood up. It was time to go back home.

It was time to say goodbye to Jack.

*   *   *

Ursula woke just as the sun was rising. She wondered what Tony was doing. She had tried to get him to stay with them, even just for a night or two until the funeral was over, but he had refused, just as he'd refused to have anyone stay at his house with him. She could hear the grunt of trucks on the highway and the hum of commuters' cars trying to beat the rush hour traffic into the city. When they had bought this house, when the kids were little, it was a quiet area, full of families. But the children had all grown up now and moved nearer the city; the city too had grown and stolen the space where kids used to play.

Jim was asleep, so she gently lifted the blankets and eased herself out of bed. She reached for her glasses from the bedside table, put them on, then shuffled her feet on the floor until she found her slippers. Ridiculous things, really, with pompoms on the toes, but Lisa had given them to her for her birthday. She took her robe from the back of the chair and put it on over her nightgown, then tiptoed out of the bedroom. The door creaked as she closed it.

The carpet in the hallway was still damp from being cleaned; she hoped it would dry by the time everyone arrived. She walked into the kitchen, poured out the water in the kettle and refilled it, then switched it on. She hated it when her tea tasted all tinny. Leaning on the sink, she ran through her mental list of things to do. She decided to allow herself twenty minutes to have her breakfast while it was quiet.

She was still sitting on the high stool at the kitchen bench when Jim walked in, yawning, his hair askew. Her cup of tea was untouched and lukewarm; cold toast peeked out of the toaster.

'You're up early,' he said.

'I couldn't sleep. Thought I may as well get up and start getting things ready.'

Jim pulled another stool close to her and sat down. 'Are you sure you're up to it, love? Having the wake here, it's a lot to ask. We can easily move it to the club – Chris said they'd give us the function room, rustle up some sandwiches. People won't care, they just want to be together for a few hours and have a drink.'

'We can't say goodbye to Jack in a pub!'

Jim raised his hands. 'OK, OK, I was just trying to help.'

She sighed, then put her hand on Jim's. 'I know, I'm sorry. It's going to be a horrible day no matter what. You go and have a shower, I'll get started here.'

Taking a deep breath, she jumped down off the chair and went back into the bedroom. She made the bed, then took out Jim's black suit and her own charcoal dress. Laid out on the bed, the clothes looked like shadows of her and Jim lying next to each other. Then she saw, on the left lapel of Jim's jacket, two little holes where he had pinned his carnation at the wedding. It had been such a fun day; he had led Anna out onto the dance floor in her long white gown, and they had danced to Elvis. 'Blue Suede Shoes', it had been. Anna had thrown her head back and laughed as Jim had twisted, gyrating his hips. She'd welcomed Anna into her family that day.

Ursula put her hand over her mouth and closed her eyes as tears prickled her eyelids. This wasn't the time to cry; she could do that later. She had to keep busy, get through it all. Tony needed her.

She returned to the kitchen, threw the cold toast away and poured her tepid tea down the sink. After wiping the kitchen benches down, she took out all the mugs, glasses, and wine glasses and arranged them in neat rows. She took the strawberry cheesecake and chocolate gateau out of the freezer to defrost.

She had made a start on polishing the glasses with an old soft tea towel when Jim walked back in. His skin was pink and smooth from the shower. She had an urge to nuzzle her face into his freshly shaved cheek.

'Don't bother polishing the glasses, no one will notice,' he said.

'It won't take a second.'

'It's not important.'

She gritted her teeth, squeezed her fist around the stem of the glass she was holding. Jim took a step back. She forced herself to relax her grip, and held the glass up to the light filtering in through the kitchen window. She slotted it back into its space next to the other identical glasses.

'I just want everything to go smoothly today. We don't need anything to go wrong on top of . . .' She blinked hard. 'Well, on top of the obvious wrongs of a day like today.'

Jim put his arms around her. He smelled clean, fresh. Ursula looked down at her old robe, then smoothed down her unruly hair. 'The kids will be here soon, and Wendy. I'd better go and get dressed.'

'What can I do to help?'

'Can you go and get a couple – no, get four loaves of bread for the sandwiches, and milk. Tony's bringing some beer and wine. Oh, ice – get some ice from the servo too. I think I got everything else yesterday.'

'OK love.' Jim kissed the top of her head and let go of her. 'You have a nice long shower, I won't be long.'

She started to walk out of the room. In the doorway she turned back to look at Jim. His elbows were on the kitchen bench and he was staring out the window. She felt a pang of guilt; she knew he was hurting too, he was keeping his grief private.

'Jim,' she said. He looked over. 'I love you.' He tilted his head to the side and smiled at her.

She turned around, glad to have her family close.

*   *   *

Ursula looked at her watch again: 9.30 a.m. They had to leave in half an hour. She wished time would slow down.

'That'll do, Lisa,' she shouted over the noise of the vacuum. 'Just put it away and make sure you're ready to go. I'm going to get changed.'

Lisa waved in acknowledgement but kept vacuuming around Tony's and Jim's feet. They both sat on the couch staring at the television. Ursula went back through to the kitchen.

A pile of sandwiches was stacked on a plate, and Wendy was buttering more bread. Ursula approached her and put her hand on her arm. 'Wendy, don't worry, we've got enough sandwiches now. Go and sit down.'

Wendy looked up. She wore Ursula's apron over her black dress. 'I've made all this egg, I'll just finish up this batch.'

'Honestly, just leave it – put some cling wrap on the egg and we can make more later. We're running out of time.'

'It won't take me long.' Wendy kept buttering.

Ursula knew what would happen: no one would be ready when the cars came, then the house would be a tip when everyone came back after the service. 'Did you find the curry powder?'

'Oh. I just made plain egg, with some mayonnaise . . .'

'People like curried egg.'

'I thought this was safer. I can —'

'No.' Ursula could feel her face reddening. 'It's fine.'

She walked away, slamming her bedroom door closed. Not that anyone would hear it over the din of the vacuum and the TV.

When she had changed, put on her make-up and sprayed her hair, there was still ten minutes to go. She emptied out her handbag on the bed, put everything back in again and then walked out to the lounge room.

Lisa was sitting on the couch with Tony and Jim, and they all seemed to be hypnotised by some loud music video. Tony drummed his fingers on the arm of the leather couch. Like his dad, he wore the same suit he had worn to his wedding, but today his tie was black. Ursula switched off the television as she heard the thrum of car engines outside.

'Ready?'

Lisa jumped up and held out her hand to Tony, who stood up with some effort. He was pale, unsteady for a moment, as if he'd forgotten how to walk.

'Come on, Tony,' Lisa said quietly, as she linked her arm in her brother's, then steered him towards the door. Tony was silent. Jim opened the front door and held it there for them.

Outside, she watched Wendy throw her cigarette butt to the ground and grind it into the garden bed with her black heel. She took a deep breath in and forced a smile. 'Come on, Wendy, it's time to go.'

They walked, single file, to the waiting black cars, Jim taking up the rear and locking the door behind him.

No one spoke as they began the grim drive to the church.

*   *   *

Tony couldn't understand how they had arrived so quickly. As they drove in, he saw some stragglers finish their cigarettes and hurry into the church. The droning of the organ inside grew louder as the driver opened the car door.

Somehow he managed to stand and get out of the car. He concentrated on putting one foot in front of the other. He just had to get through the day, had to hold it together a little while longer. Someone had their hand on his back and he began to move towards the church doors where two official-looking men waited with sad smiles on their faces. They didn't look him in the eye.

And now, as one set of wooden doors closed behind him and another set swung open, the organ music was deafening. He heard the pews creak as mourners turned round to watch them come in, the echoing of Lisa's heels walking behind him, and a cough reverberate around the church. Or was it a cry? Then it was as if someone pressed a button and he was watching everything in fast forward. He couldn't understand how he managed to walk down the aisle to this processional of sobs. He couldn't understand a word of what the minister was saying. Wendy clutched his hand, but she might as well have been holding the sleeve of his jacket: he couldn't feel it. Somehow he managed to walk to the front of the church and speak. What had he said? Everyone kept looking at him. What did they expect? Did they want him to break down, to scream, to weep? He wanted to do all of those things, but his body and mind were no longer connected.

He couldn't understand how he could be at his son's, at Jack's funeral. And, most of all, he couldn't understand what the hell Anna had done.

*   *   *

Outside, everything went back to normal speed. He stood to the left of the church doors, flanked by his mum and dad. So many people were spilling out, heads bowed, heaving and gasping for the fresh air, as if they were escaping a burning building. They hovered around him, hugged him and said they were sorry before darting off again, blowing their noses with soggy tissues, relieved to have done what was expected of them. Now they could chat about how beautiful the flowers were, what a tragedy it was, then go home and watch the news. A woman of about his mum's age clasped both his hands in hers and pumped them up and down. She leaned close to him and he breathed shallowly to avoid inhaling her cloying perfume. He wanted to take a step back but he was against the wall. She moaned and sniffed, and the sound of her phlegmy nose made him want to gag.

'Oh, Anthony,' she said. 'Well done.'

Well done? Who was this woman? What was she to him, to Jack? One of his mother's friends, no doubt, here to gawp. He could see the grey roots of her dyed red hair and her garish pink lipstick. She was still holding on to him, she was crying now, sniffing again. He pulled his hands away from her and sidestepped before she could hug him. His body was rigid; his face ached from clenching his jaw to keep his anger and his sorrow held tightly inside. He hadn't cried.

He hadn't done well at all.

Across the crowd he saw Sean and Emily standing with a group of their friends. He pushed his way towards them, noticing how the crowds parted to let him through. Emily looked up as he neared them and smiled, though her eyes were bloodshot and swollen. Her normally unruly blonde curls were tied back in a bun, and her freckles were faded behind her make-up. She stepped away from the group, and hugged him, hard.

'I'm so sorry,' she whispered. 'I don't know what to say.'

He hugged her back. He knew Emily was sincere, and appreciated that she didn't blurt out some cliché about heaven or Jack being at peace, or how it would get easier. As he let her go, Sean was waiting to hug him too. Sean sniffed, then gave a sad laugh. 'Bloody hell. That was horrible in there.'

He nodded.

'You OK?' Emily asked.

'I'm glad it's over. Well, that part anyway.'

'Me too.' She wiped her eyes again. 'Shit, I can't stop crying. Still got the wake to get through. We could all jump in a cab and go to the pub instead!' She tried to laugh, but it snagged; she sobbed, then reached into her bag for a tissue.

'Have you spoken to Anna today?' Sean asked, looking down at his shoes.

Tony gritted his teeth. 'Not yet. I'm going to go now, get it over with. Can I borrow your car?'

Sean put his hand in his pocket and took out the keys. 'Of course. It's parked just over there. Are you OK to drive though? I can take you . . .'

He wrapped his hand around the keys. 'No, I'm fine.'

'Let me come, Tony – you shouldn't be alone,' Emily took a step towards him. 'I'd like to see her too.'

'No – thanks, Em, but I need to do this on my own.'

Emily and Sean didn't ask anything of him; they let him go. He wanted to hug them again. They still believed in Anna.

'I'll see you at Mum and Dad's. And thanks. I mean it.' Tony walked away from the church, towards Sean's car.

*   *   *

He knocked on Anna's door and waited. He heard her clear her throat, then say 'Yes?' in such a small voice that he wondered if he'd imagined it. He opened the door and walked in.

She was lying on her side with her knees curled up, on top of the sheets, facing him. Her eyes widened when she saw Tony, taking in his black suit, and she propped herself up with her arm and began to sit up. She ran her fingers through her hair. 'Hi. Tony . . . ?'

He realised how he must look. Did she remember that he wore this to their wedding? Looking at her, he couldn't believe she was the same person he had stood next to at the altar. Then she'd been the most beautiful woman in the world. Now, she wore baggy black leggings and a grey singlet. Her hair was tied back, and her face was blotchy and bloated, with pimples on her chin. He could see from the working of her jaw that she was biting the inside of her cheek. He couldn't believe this was the same person he'd said his vows to, believing with absolute conviction that nothing could ever destroy them.

He tried to smile. 'Hi.' Closing the door behind him, he sat on the chair on the far side of the bed, near the window. 'How are you feeling?'

'OK. My head's sore.'

'Your mum said you were having more ECT this morning.'

Anna nodded, and tears filled her eyes. Neither of them spoke. There had been a time when they could sit in contented silence, but this was different: now the space was filled with tension. He saw her look at the plastic bag that he gripped in his hand. He lifted it onto his lap and put his hand inside.

'Did you . . . ?' she said. 'Have you . . . ?'

He leaned his head back and looked at the ceiling. They both knew what she was talking about. 'Yes. I've just come from the church.'

She brought her fingers to her mouth as if trying to stop herself from saying anything.

The bag rustled as he pulled out the photo frame. It was a picture of Jack, lying on their bed wrapped in a fluffy white towel, just out of the bath. His eyes were wide open and bright. Tony looked at it for a few seconds, then handed it to Anna. She held the photo in both hands and stared at it, unblinking. She bit her cheek again. He waited for her to say something, do something. But she remained silent.

He cleared his throat. He hadn't wanted to say this to her now, the day was hard enough, but he couldn't stand this blankness any more: he needed her to react. He needed to know what had happened. His voice trembled and he stared straight at her. 'I spoke to the coroner on Monday, about the autopsy.'

Anna kept looking at Jack's photo, as if Tony hadn't said a thing. He started to doubt if he had actually spoken out loud. 'Anna?'

'Hmmm?' She didn't look up from the photo.

He shouted now. 'Are you interested in how he died? In what actually happened to Jack? Or maybe you don't need me to tell you, because you know? Do you know?'

He covered his face with his hands, pressing his eyes with his fingertips until it hurt. He put his hands back in his lap and screwed up the plastic bag. She was still staring at the damn photo.

'It was a head injury,' he said. 'The police thought maybe you had shaken him at home and panicked, but the coroner said no. It was from the fall. He was still . . . alive, when you got to the beach.'

Had she heard him?

'Jesus, Anna.' He felt his heart beating faster and fought the urge to stand up and flee. He tried to breathe slowly; he had promised himself he wouldn't do this, not today. She was smiling now, a tense fixed smile that looked as if it was causing her pain. She was still staring at the picture. Tony needed to move, to stand up, to get out of here. His hands shook as he shoved the balled plastic bag in the pocket of his suit trousers.

'Right, well, I'm going now, Anna. Anything you want to say?' He waited. She didn't look up. 'Fine. If you decide you want to talk to me, I'll be at our son's wake.'

Anna didn't move; she just smiled stupidly at the photo. At that moment, Tony felt such an intense hatred for his wife that he practically ran out of the room. He slammed the door behind him.

*   *   *

Wendy stood in Ursula's kitchen and watched her and her friends rushing around with plates of sandwiches, sausage rolls and vol-au-vents. Wendy had tried to help, but Ursula had shooed her away. When she went to put dirty dishes in the dishwasher, Ursula told her they needed to be washed by hand; when she started to fill the sink with water, Ursula told her they would do it later.

She looked around the room. She didn't know any of these people. This was Anna's life, not hers. No one else from Western Australia had come over. Pam had offered, but Wendy had asked her to go and stay with their dad: he was too frail to travel and she worried about what this was doing to his heart. At the thought of her family back home, Wendy wished for a moment that she was back in her own house. She felt useless here.

Someone tapped her on the shoulder; she jumped, then smiled as Emily leaned in to hug her.

'You OK, Wendy?'

'Oh, Emily, not really. You know . . .'

Emily nodded, and both women took a moment to compose themselves.

'Have you got a drink? Wine?' Wendy said.

'No, but I'd love one, thanks.'

Wendy busied herself with pouring two big glasses of white wine.

'Is everything all right with the flat?' Emily said as she took one of the glasses.

Wendy put her hand on Emily's arm. 'Oh yes, it's great. It's so beautiful, thanks. I'm just sorry that I've taken over – I feel like I've kicked you out.'

'No, not at all, don't be silly. I spend most of the time at Jamie's anyway, so it's no hassle at all. I really should get rid of it, it's silly to be paying rent on two places, but I'm holding out for the ring . . .' She smiled and pointed to her left ring finger.

'Good for you,' Wendy said, then sipped her drink. She swallowed a mouthful then lowered her voice. 'Have you seen Tony?'

Emily shook her head. 'Not since the church. I think he went to see Anna.'

Wendy was pleased. She had hoped he would go and see Anna today; she needed him. 'I saw her this morning – they let me visit early.'

'How was she?'

'She's getting there, you know, slowly. I tried to talk to her about today, just to make sure she knew what was happening. All she said was that she wanted a photo of Jack. That's got to be progress, right? It's got to mean that she's coming to terms with what's happened. Do you think?'

'Yeah, Wendy, of course it is. She'll be better soon, I'm sure of it. We just have to get through each day at the moment, stay strong.'

'Definitely.' She looked at Emily again, and saw the little girl who used to play in the backyard with Anna, and have sleepovers at her house. When did they grow up into women? Anna was still her child, still too young to have to go through this. She should be standing here with Emily, a glass of wine in her hand and complaining about the cost of rent. Wendy put her glass down on the kitchen bench and leaned in to hug Emily. 'I'm so glad you're here.'

Emily hugged her back. 'It'll be OK, Wendy.'

'I know. I'm just going to pop out for a cigarette. You go and find that boyfriend of yours.' She smiled at Emily, picked up her glass and walked towards the back door.

*   *   *

Tony stood outside his parents' house and listened to the voices and laughter coming from inside. He wiped sweat from his forehead with his hand; he'd had to park Sean's car in the next street and walk. Cars rested with an air of abandonment at odd angles on the verges. He loosened his tie and started to take off his suit jacket, then stopped. Was that disrespectful to Jack? He left it on.

He opened the door. The house was full: even the hallway was crammed with people, holding glasses of wine and fingers of sandwiches. A hush swept through the crowd like a Mexican wave as one person after another spotted him. He allowed himself to be hugged and kissed and glanced at and patted like a child, then walked down the hallway to the living room, which was filled with more people sitting on white plastic seats and green deckchairs. He felt the corners of his mouth curl up and wanted to laugh at the absurdity of it all. He saw Sean perched on the arm of the sofa eating a sausage roll while talking to his mum's next door neighbour. What was the point of all this? He went over and handed Sean his keys, took off his jacket then walked out of the room. He forced himself to speak briefly with some more people, as was expected of him, avoided his mum, then went out the back door.

His dad loved this garden. Winter or summer, he was out here planting or pruning, or mulching the garden beds that framed the lawn. White roses reached up the brick wall at the rear of the garden, while yellow pansies bobbed their heads underneath. Jim's little piece of England, even though he hadn't lived there since he was a kid.

Wendy was sitting on the bottom step of the wooden deck with her feet on the lawn. An empty wine glass stood at an angle on the grass. Winston, his parents' boxer dog, lay on his side while Wendy stroked his ears with her left hand. Her right hand shook as she brought a cigarette to her lips. He pulled the screen door closed behind him; Wendy jumped and dropped her right hand down out of view. Walking down the steps, he shooed Winston out of the way then sat down next to her.

'You got another one of those?' he asked.

'A smoke? Didn't think you did that any more.' Wendy took a packet out of her handbag by her feet and held it out to Tony.

'No, I don't.' *Anna made me stop when we were trying for a baby*, he wanted to say. Didn't matter any more. Now, he wanted a cigarette.

He put the cigarette between his lips, then bent down to the lighter Wendy held out to him. He inhaled, coughed, then did it again. They both watched a lone willy wagtail parading on the lawn.

'Anna should have been there,' Wendy said softly, looking at her cigarette.

He said nothing, but nodded slightly.

'She'll be heartbroken, you know, when she's well . . .'

'We didn't have a choice.'

'I know, but maybe we should have tried harder, seen if they could let her out for a couple of hours.'

He pictured Anna's face, that smile as she looked at the photograph. Would she be heartbroken? He wasn't so sure. 'I don't think that would have been a good idea.'

'Why not? It's her own child's funeral – if they were ever going to let her out, it would be for that! I don't know, Tony, sometimes I wonder if people are just forgetting about her.' She turned to look at him.

He stared down at his shoes, away from her gaze. 'Wendy, it would have just caused a lot of problems, made it hard for everyone . . .'

'Everyone? Or you? It sounds like you didn't want her there!'

'What, I'm not allowed to try and make things a little easier for myself? After all . . . all this?' He swept out his arm as if everything he'd been going through was scattered around him. His arm dropped to his side; he had no energy left to fight. 'Maybe I didn't, OK? Maybe I didn't want her there. Maybe I didn't want to have to worry about her, while everyone whispered and stared. Can't I have a day when I don't have to think about Anna? A day just for Jack?'

Wendy's face burned. 'He was her baby too. She is part of this, you can't just forget about her.'

'I'm not forgetting about her! But just for today, I am going to try. I'm going to go in there and get a drink and be with my friends and family and people who cared about Jack, and who care about me. You are welcome to join us, but today is about Jack, not Anna. Nobody wants to hear her name right now.'

He stood up and stamped on his cigarette, then threw open the screen door. He wrenched at the handle of the back door, and heard the satisfying metallic clash as it closed behind him. He paused for a second, waiting for Wendy to follow him, but she stayed where she was, sitting on her own with the dog.

CHAPTER TWENTY-ONE

Two weeks before
Friday, 28 August 2009

Tony stared out of the window of his office, watching the rain run down the glass. It wasn't even four o'clock yet, but it was dark. He could see the blurred lights from the ferries crossing the harbour below him, but otherwise it was like being in the middle of a cloud. He liked the way the battering sound of the rain soaked up the noise around him. He leaned back in his chair and put his hands behind his head. The warmth of the room made him drowsy. He hadn't been able to sleep much last night; every time he had turned over or stirred, Anna had been awake. He didn't know why: Jack had slept quite well, only waking twice during the night, but Anna had been restless and tense, which in turn had meant that he couldn't relax.

He yawned, then sat up straight and reached for the phone on his desk. He picked up the receiver, then hesitated. When he called her just before lunch, Anna had said she was fine. She was going to lie down if she got a chance; she might be sleeping now. He put the receiver down. She needed her rest; he wouldn't disturb her. He'd leave soon, and they could go out for dinner tonight.

There was a knock at his door, and he looked up to see Neesha, one of the secretaries. She smiled. 'You coming for a drink? We're going to have it in the boardroom tonight, too wet out there.'

Tony looked at his watch. It would be awful on the roads now, in that weather. He smiled back. 'Yeah, OK, just one. I'll be there soon.'

By the time he drove out of the underground car park, the rain had slowed to a drizzle. The six o'clock news came on the radio. 'Shit.' He hadn't meant to stay so long; Anna would be angry. He took some chewing gum out of the glove box to hide the beer on his breath. Looking up at the endless stream of red tail-lights ahead of him he groaned: the traffic seemed to be conspiring against him.

When he finally walked into the house, Anna was on the couch in her pyjamas and her old pink fluffy dressing-gown watching the news. Jack was asleep in his bassinette on the floor. Anna's face was blotchy and wet; she didn't even glance at him as he walked in.

'Anna, what is it?' He dropped his bag and hurried over to her.

She didn't move her eyes from the television. She smiled as she wiped her nose with the back of her hand, and then the damp sleeve of her gown. 'Nothing,' she said. 'It's just the news. It's so sad.'

'Babe, the news is always sad.' Tony walked over to the couch and massaged her shoulders as he stood behind her.

'There was an accident on the M5. A whole family killed, just the grandma survived.' Her voice quivered and her eyes filled with tears. 'I was worried, you were late . . .'

'Oh no.' Tony walked around the couch to sit next to her. He shouldn't have stayed for that drink. 'I'm sorry I was late. I should have called you.'

'No, I'm just being silly. It's fine.'

'Why don't you go and have a shower? I'll look after the little man. Take your time. Then we'll go to Roma for some pasta.'

Anna smiled wearily, pushed herself up off the couch and walked out of the room. Tony took a beer out of the fridge and unscrewed the top, then sighed as he sank onto the couch. He looked at Jack, fast asleep with his eyes flittering behind his eyelids. Anna seemed all right. They'd have a quiet dinner, a glass of wine, and an early night, and then maybe they'd both have a good sleep. They needed it.

When Anna came back, she was wearing jeans and a silk blouse. The blouse stuck to her shoulders where her wet hair dripped onto it, but Tony didn't say anything. He was relieved to see her looking more like her old self. He missed their life before Jack; the past four weeks had been hard, but he knew it was just an adjustment. Soon, they'd have their life back: a different life, but a happy one.

He picked Jack up from the bassinette, then ushered Anna out of the house.

*   *   *

He cradled Jack in one arm and sipped at his glass of pinot while they waited for their main course to arrive. He'd thought that Anna was OK but here, in the restaurant, he could see there was something not quite right about her: she was talking and smiling, but Tony wasn't convinced. She tore small pieces off her garlic bread and rolled it into tiny balls while she listened to him. When her pasta arrived, she pushed it around her plate with her fork, but barely ate anything.

'You're not hungry? You usually love carbonara!'

She twirled her spaghetti. 'I had a big lunch.'

He raised his eyebrows. He hadn't seen Anna eat a proper meal in days. Why was she lying to him? Was she worried about her weight? Jack was asleep; Tony put him in the pram next to their table. 'Don't get upset with me, but there's something I need to say.' He paused. 'I'm worried about you, babe.'

She didn't look up; she kept twisting her fork. 'There's nothing to be worried about. I'm just tired.'

'Jack's sleeping a bit better now, though. He was up, what, twice last night?'

She dropped her fork and pushed her plate away. 'You're not the one who has to wake up, get out of bed, feed him, change his nappy, resettle him. You hear him twice and then you roll over and go back to sleep! I end up fully awake, then I have to try and wind down again.' She narrowed her eyes. 'Don't you dare tell me this is easy!'

Tony reached for her hand across the table, shocked at her outburst. Anna rarely got angry; she tended to cry or worry, but she had never before looked at him with such contempt. He didn't think he'd said anything to make her that agitated. 'Sorry, babe. I'm just worried. I know you haven't been sleeping well.'

'I'm fine.'

'Why don't you get your mum to come over and help out? You know she's desperate to meet Jack. She'd love to come, I'm sure. Or my mum could come over during the day.'

Anna glared at him. 'I don't want anyone! That will make it worse. It'll be more work for me, someone to entertain and talk to. There's nothing they can do – there's nothing anyone can do.'

'They could help with cooking and go to the shops for you . . .'

'You can do that, Tony.' Anna's anger seemed to drain away and her eyes filled with tears. 'Please, I don't want anyone to see me like this. I'm fine. Please don't tell them.' Her voice shook.

He sighed. 'All right. Well, I want you to rest this weekend, yes? You need to let me help you. Promise me you'll do nothing: no tidying, no cooking, no cleaning. Just sleep when you can and feed him when you need to. Don't even get out of bed.'

'But there are things that need to be done, Tony! We need clean clothes —'

'Anna, stop! I'll do it.' Tony took another deep breath. He had to bring it up. 'You don't think you might be depressed, do you?'

'No!' she said, tears welling up again. 'Don't try to turn this into an illness, a problem with me. I'm not depressed, I'm just exhausted! You try surviving on one or two hours' sleep for weeks on end!'

'OK, OK . . .' He raised his hands. He had expected Anna to react like that, but he'd needed to say it, to make her consider it. 'I'm sorry, babe. I'm just worried. I have one condition then, and there's no arguing: I want you to go to the doctor and get checked out. Just tell her how you're feeling and see what she says. She'll probably say everything's normal, but I want to make sure. Will you do that?'

Anna didn't look at him; she dabbed at her eyes with her napkin, 'Fine.'

'Thank you.' He smiled at her and took her hand again. 'I just want you to be OK. Let's get some gelato takeaway and go home, eh?'

She nodded. Letting go of her hand, he poured himself the last of the wine and took a big gulp. He was relieved that she'd agreed to see her doctor, someone who would see new mums all

the time and would know what was normal. And Anna was right;
this probably *was* normal. She would be fine.

*   *   *

Anna had to drive home from the restaurant. Tony seemed to enjoy
the fact that he was always the one who was allowed to drink. First
it had been the pregnancy, now the breastfeeding. He assumed he
could drink as much as he wanted and she would drive. And she
did, of course. She opened the window, hoping the fresh air would
wake her up a bit and blow away the smell of alcohol from Tony.
Jack was fast asleep in his capsule in the back; if Tony had been
sober, she'd have made him drive around the block all night with
him and give her a break.

Back at home, she tiptoed down the hallway carrying the baby
capsule, then put it gently on the floor of Jack's bedroom. It wasn't
worth risking waking him to transfer him into his bassinette. She
left the door ajar and went into her bedroom to get undressed, then
walked through to the bathroom in her underwear. For a moment
she looked at herself in the mirror. She looked so bloated, and her
breasts bulged out of the huge maternity bra. Her skin was terrible,
and her eyes were circled by dark shadows. She turned away and
started to brush her teeth; it was better not to look.

The bathroom door opened; Tony came in and put his arms
around her from behind. She froze. He didn't seem to notice her
discomfort as he kissed the back of her neck. She could feel his
rough stubble and smell the stale red wine and garlic on his hot
breath. She spat the toothpaste in the sink, then wriggled out of
his embrace and turned to face him. 'Tony . . .'

'You look beautiful,' he murmured as he leaned in to kiss her.

She moved her head to the side, 'No, I don't.'

'You do. I love your new figure.' His hand wandered towards
her breasts.

'Tony!' She pushed him away as he bent down to kiss her chest.
'Please, the doctor said six weeks.'

'We can just —'

'No, Tony, no. Please . . .' She saw the hurt in his eyes. Couldn't he understand that all she wanted was some peace? Some time alone? 'I'm sorry, I'm just so tired.'

'It's OK.' he said. He grabbed his toothbrush, squeezed paste onto it and started brushing his teeth.

Anna watched him until he was finished, then put her hand on his arm. 'I'll just be a few minutes. You get into bed.'

He walked out, and she closed the bathroom door behind him. She listened to his footsteps moving down the hall towards their bedroom, turned the shower on full and sat down on the cold floor tiles, letting herself sob. It felt as if Tony was just one more person putting demands on her. Her body was no longer her own: her breasts were for feeding, and her skin and hair and nails were all weakened by her hormones. Everyone seemed to want something from her, and she gave everything she had. Where was *her* time? All she did was wait: wait for Jack to wake up, wait for Tony to come home, wait for the weekend. There was nothing to look forward to, no end in sight.

This was her life now.

She let her nose run; the tears streamed until her face hurt. Would Tony be asleep yet? She stood up and turned off the shower, then splashed her face with cold water from the sink. She brushed her hair, put on her pyjamas, and walked along the hall.

To her relief, Tony was snoring softly. She switched off the light and got into bed. Maybe he was right about her being depressed. Was it normal to feel like this? She was sure it would pass; it had to get easier. The first six weeks were the hardest, that's what she had read. A part of her didn't want to go to the doctor and give Tony the satisfaction of being right; she didn't want this to be her problem. It was like when they were trying to get pregnant: Tony was so happy to know that it wasn't his fault. If she was depressed, it let him off the hook. The truth was that if he was at home more, if he helped her, then she wouldn't be in this situation. Other dads took weeks off work, but not Tony: work was too busy. Anna wanted to let him know just how hard it was, that he couldn't expect to go to work drinks and out to dinner and still have the same life as he did before. Everything had changed.

Tony was snoring louder now. She picked up her pillow and the baby monitor and went to sleep in the spare room.

*   *   *

The rest of the weekend passed in the same mindless fatigue and Anna felt her energy continue to drain away. On Monday morning, Tony brought her breakfast in bed while she fed Jack. She thanked him, then forced herself to eat, aware that he was pretending not to watch. She washed each mouthful of stodgy cold toast down with tea, trying not to gag. When Tony was out of the room, she fed the crusts to Jessie, who sat on the floor next to the bed looking up at her hopefully.

If she didn't do it now, she never would. She reached for her mobile on the bedside table and called the general practice. Dr Fraser was very busy, the receptionist said. There were no appointments until Wednesday. Was it urgent?

'No,' Anna replied. 'It's not urgent.'

CHAPTER TWENTY-TWO

Two weeks after

Monday, 28 September 2009

Anna fumbled for the white cord next to her bed, and followed it with her fingers until she found the panel of buttons. Her eyes were too heavy to open. Anyway, the light would give her a headache, and she didn't want to see the yellowing bruises on her arms and legs again. From a distance, it looked like a child had touched her with mustard-coloured finger paint. She didn't know why she'd bothered fighting as they jabbed the needle into her thigh; if she'd known how the medication would make her feel, she'd have gladly consented. The medication let her sleep; sleep let her forget. This sensation, when the sedation wore off, was far more painful.

Her fingers found the large circular button and pressed it hard. She heard the click as it engaged, but nothing else. She tried again, and again. Finally, she heard footsteps outside her room, and she slumped back in the bed.

'Good morning, Anna.' It was Rachel's voice.

She swore under her breath; she'd hoped it would be someone she didn't know. Then she had more chance of getting what she wanted.

Rachel walked over to the window and pulled the curtains open. 'I think it's about time we got you up and out of bed, don't you?'

Anna opened her eyes slightly and squinted. 'I need another tablet.' Her voice was croaky.

'What for?'

'Sleep. I can't sleep . . .'

'You've been doing nothing but sleeping, Anna. Anyway, it's after nine, it's not time for sleeping now.' Rachel picked up the blanket that was crumpled at the bottom of the bed and began folding it. 'And those tablets are only to be used if you're anxious and agitated.' She draped the blanket over the chair, then walked to the end of the bed and picked up Anna's medication chart. She frowned.

'You've had the maximum dose anyway. The night nurses gave you plenty of medication. I want you to get up and have a shower and something to eat. It's no wonder you can't sleep at night if you sleep all day.'

'I *am* anxious and agitated. I feel horrible – please?' She began to cry.

'I know that it's tempting to keep yourself knocked out, but this is real life, and it'll still be here whenever you wake up, it's not going to go away.'

'I know!' Why did she keep stating the obvious? She wasn't in charge. Anna opened her eyes fully and yellow flashes bounced around her field of vision. The light made her head pound. 'I don't feel well.'

Rachel cupped her elbow in one hand and rested her chin in the other. 'You'll feel better if you get some food and fluids into you, and some fresh air.'

'I don't want to! Call Dr Morgan. You don't understand. Please, call her.' He chest tightened; she couldn't get enough air. She tried to sit up and breathe more deeply, but it felt as though someone was crushing her.

'Anna, calm down. Slow your breathing – Anna, breathe with me.' The nurse began counting in a monotonous, calm voice. Anna tried to concentrate, but the tears wouldn't stop falling, and her mouth was getting drier. The room began to spin.

She felt as though she was drifting, spiralling up, but Rachel put her hand on her arm, anchoring her, like someone grabbing the string of a balloon before it floated away. She didn't want anyone to pull her back.

She tried again. 'Please, can you call Dr Morgan? She'll give me something else.'

There was a timid tap at the door. Anna looked over and saw her mother peering round the doorframe. She was holding a plastic bag that Anna knew would be full of magazines, chocolates and energy drinks for her.

'Mum!' she started crying again. Her mum cared about her; she cared so much that Anna felt terrible and undeserving.

Wendy dropped the bag at the door and ran over. She sat next to Anna on the bed and hugged her. Anna breathed deeply, smelling the cheap perfume that Wendy had worn since Anna was a little girl. It was the most comforting smell she knew.

'Mum,' she sobbed. 'I feel horrible.'

'Shh.' Wendy stroked her hair. 'I know, I know darling . . .'

Rachel got up and muttered something to Wendy, who nodded, and then the nurse left them alone.

Anna waited until she could talk without gasping. 'I saw them.'

Wendy stroked the hair from Anna's forehead. 'Who, darling?'

'The police. They were outside, talking to Dr Morgan.'

'I'm sure they weren't —'

'They were!' Even though they weren't in uniform, Anna was certain they were policemen.

Wendy bit her lip and looked down.

'Mum, see, you know!'

'Oh Anna, I don't know anything.'

'Well, why were they here?'

'They still need to talk to you.'

'Why? I don't know anything, I don't remember anything.' Anna's voice was getting higher and higher. She didn't want to talk to the police; she thought that as long as she was in here, in a crazy ward, they'd leave her alone. Jack was gone; what good would it do to talk to her? What could she tell them that would bring him back?

Wendy pulled Anna towards her and hugged her. 'It doesn't matter if you don't remember anything. You'll just need to tell them what you can, just be honest.'

She pulled away. 'Honest? Not you too. I know what everyone else thinks, you know. Even Tony . . . He can't bear to see me.' She looked away from her mum, towards the picture of Jack.

'Tony's just upset, darling. Just give him some time.'

'Have they spoken to you?'

'Who?'

'The police!'

'Yes. Of course they have, and I told them that you could never do this, that it would never cross your mind —'

She swallowed, forcing herself to voice her worst fear. 'But what if it did, Mum? What if it did cross my mind and I can't remember? I must have done something. I'm locked up in here with all these crazy people, they're giving me electric shocks . . .' She suddenly felt the weight returning to her chest as the reality of it all set in. This was no dream, no story. This was her life, and her family. Jack was dead.

The room started to spin as an overwhelming wave of uncertainty swept over her. She would never hurt her boy. Her Jack. The police thought she'd killed her son.

Had she?

'Darling, you've been sick, so sick . . .'

She looked Wendy in the eye, then spoke quietly, trying to make sense of it all. 'How could you not tell me?'

'Tell you?'

'About Jack! Everyone knew, but no one told me, for days and days. I thought he was okay, I just thought he couldn't visit.'

Wendy's face went pale. 'You were too sick . . .'

'You and Tony just left me here, locked up, in this place! And I couldn't even go to his funeral. How could you, Mum?'

Wendy tried to take Anna's hands. 'Calm down. The doctors – I wanted you there, but —'

'Don't blame everyone else! You're my mum. Imagine if I died and you weren't allowed to come to my funeral!'

'Anna, I'm sorry!'

Wendy tried to take her hands again, but she turned on her side, pulled her legs up to her chest, and wept. Her fury dissipated, replaced by shame. Shame at what she might have done. Shame at what she was putting her family through. She could hear Wendy crying behind her. Anna wanted to tell her to be quiet, to leave her alone. But she said nothing, and Wendy waited there, as Anna knew she would. Gradually, the heaving in her chest settled and she turned onto her back and looked at her mum.

'What's wrong with me?'

'You've had postnatal psychosis, but Dr Morgan said —'

She shook her head. 'No, no, no. I mean . . . what's wrong with me? What kind of a mother . . . could do this?'

Wendy's eyes widened. She could only shake her head as the tears rolled down her face.

Anna stared up at the ceiling. Wendy leaned over and pulled her into a tight hug. Anna clutched onto her like a child, as though her mother had come to save her, to wake her from a nightmare. But she knew her mother was powerless to make this better, that she couldn't promise her that everything would be all right.

*   *   *

Tony saw the grey ball coming towards him; he had to move immediately to get out of its way. He clenched the racquet in his hand with his arm raised just above shoulder height, midway between response and surrender. Time sped up; he felt the sting as the ball hit him under his arm, hard, on his ribs. He dropped the racquet and clutched his chest, pain radiating across his torso.

'That was uncalled for!'

'Sorry, mate!' Sean tried not to laugh. 'You asked for that. You've got to be quick!'

He bent down and picked up his racquet. The pain was subsiding and in its place was the buzz of adrenalin; it felt good. He twirled the racquet around again in his hand then wiped his forehead with his wristband. 'OK, I'll get you this time . . .'

They lined up to face the peeling red tape on the wall. Sean lifted the ball in his left hand, preparing to serve, and Tony bounced from foot to foot, ready. Suddenly, his phone rang. Sean stopped. 'Do you need to get that?'

'Yeah. Sorry, hold on.' He ran to his bag at the back of the court and rummaged around for his phone. 'Yes, hello?' He was panting.

'Is that Tony?'

'Yes, it is.'

'Tony, it's Dr Morgan, from the hospital.'

Tony felt a now-familiar burst of anxiety mixed with resentment. 'Oh, hi, I've been meaning to call you . . .' He turned to Sean and pointed to the phone. Sean nodded, put down his racquet and ball, and picked up his water bottle.

'I'm sorry to interrupt your day. Is this a good time?'

'Yes, it's fine. What's wrong?'

'I wanted to give you a quick update. I've just spoken to the police. Wendy was just here, so I've let her know too, but I wanted to tell you myself . . .'

He closed his eyes. Every nerve in his body jumped to attention. His mouth was parched, filled with a taste of dry dust and stale sweat, so familiar from his memories of the school gym. It had been a few days since he'd heard from the police; he had hoped that maybe, just maybe, they would leave her alone. 'Yes?'

'Well, as you know, the police still need to interview Anna. I think she's well enough now.'

'Well enough? To be interviewed? You've got to be joking!'

'She's come a long way – I'm not saying she's back to normal, but I can't keep the police away from her any more. We've stopped the ECT, she's eating and drinking, and there's no sign she's still paranoid or hearing voices.'

He crouched down on his haunches. 'So what did the police say?'

'They want to take her to the station tomorrow morning to interview her.'

Tony thought of his own interview, the way the detectives had tried to manipulate him into giving them the answers they wanted, and he knew that Anna couldn't cope with that. She would never question authority; the way she was now, she would be so easily bullied into telling them what they wanted to hear. He felt dizzy; he ran his free hand across his forehead. 'Shit. Does Anna know?'

'Yes. I told her just before I called you. She asked me to contact you.'

'OK.' He didn't know what else to say.

Dr Morgan continued, 'Tony, it's not my place to say this, and she'll get someone from legal aid, but have you thought about getting her a lawyer?'

'No, I . . .' A lawyer? He rocked back and sat on the ground. Why hadn't he organised a lawyer? Jesus, what had he been thinking? That was something he could do for her, something practical, something helpful. 'I will, though, I will.'

'As I said, it's not my place, but I think that in the circumstances . . .'

'Yes.' He got to his feet. 'Yes, thanks. I'll get onto it now. Dr Morgan?'

'Yes?'

'Thank you.'

He put his phone back in his bag. It was too hot in here; he needed some fresh air. How could they be interviewing Anna already? Jesus, she'd be terrified. She wouldn't even walk on the grass if there was a sign telling her not to; this would be a nightmare for her.

Sean walked up to him. 'Is everything OK?'

'It's the police – they want to interview Anna. Shit.' Tony scraped his fingers through his damp hair. 'Look, sorry, I need to go, I've got to sort things out, a lawyer . . .'

'Of course. Let's get out of here.'

Tony zipped his racquet back into the plastic cover and picked up his bag, already thinking about who he could call. He hurried out of the sports centre to his car on the street outside, waved goodbye to Sean, and drove home. Why had he left it so late?

As he drove, his eyes were drawn again and again to the glove box. The letter was still in there. He didn't know what to do with it: it might help Anna, but it could also make things far worse for her. He wished he'd never seen it.

He pulled into the car park of a fast food restaurant. Before he could stop himself he leaned over to the glove box and retrieved the envelope, then unfastened his seatbelt and jumped out of the car. Walking over to a large grey wheelie bin, he lifted the lid, holding the envelope in his trembling hand. He looked at the cardboard burger cartons and paper packets full of old chips, then back at his hand. He couldn't do it. He let the lid of the bin fall closed again, went back to the car and put the letter back in the glove box.

*   *   *

The next morning, he and Wendy arrived at the hospital just after nine.

He was nervous. He told himself to trust Anna. As much as he had tried to disconnect himself from her, they were still inextricably bonded.

They walked in silence towards the car park exit, and out into the grounds of the hospital. Dry leaves swirled and crackled around their feet in the breeze. He could smell Wendy's hairspray and perfume and it made him feel a little sick.

The receptionist at the front desk of the mental health unit stood up as soon as she saw them and unlocked the security door without saying a word. Tony went through first then held the door open for Wendy; as it closed behind them, he saw the broad backs of the detectives who had interviewed him, Hill and Kaminsky. They stood inside the nurses' station, enclosed by glass and more security doors. Dr Morgan was there too, looking up at Detective Hill and nodding. He wished he could hear what they were saying.

Wendy put her hand on his arm; she was trembling. He looked at her and smiled reassuringly, despite not feeling reassured himself. Anna didn't need to see her mother looking so frightened; it would unnerve her even more. 'It's OK, Wendy. Come on.'

'Where's the lawyer?'

'Don't worry, he'll be here. We won't let them start without him.' Even so, Tony glanced at his watch. He'd said nine o'clock; where was he?

'Are you sure he knows where to come?'

'Yes, he'll be here. He's a good bloke.'

'It's been a while since you were at uni though; what if —'

'Wendy, stop worrying.'

'Sorry.'

As they approached the door to the nurses' station, Dr Morgan saw them and beckoned. Hill and Kaminsky turned around too, but didn't smile. Tony nodded at the psychiatrist, took a deep breath and walked slowly forward, as if the few extra seconds might allow him just that bit longer to work out what to say. He hoped his voice wouldn't shake when he spoke; he needed to appear confident. He had told the detectives what they needed to know, but was it enough to keep Anna safe? Did he even want to keep her safe? His face flushed; he had wondered all night if he'd done the right thing in organising a lawyer for her. Part of him wanted to leave her to work this situation out herself. But when the morning had arrived, he had realised that no matter how much he hated Anna at times, he couldn't leave her defenceless. He had to believe with all his heart that she had been ill. The alternative was unbearable.

Dr Morgan led them all to a small interview room. It was bare except for six grey plastic chairs arranged around the perimeter. There was no window, just a fluoro tube on the ceiling that gave off a sallow light. They all sat down: Tony and Wendy on one side of the room, the police on the other, and Dr Morgan along the wall between them, an empty chair beside her.

After some polite, pointless greetings, Tony cleared his throat and said, 'Detective Hill, I wanted to catch you before you interviewed Anna. I just want to ask, what is this leading to? I mean, what are you going to do?'

The detective leaned back in his chair. 'At this point, Tony, we will interview her at the station, and once we've done that we'll decide what to do next.'

'What do you mean? What are your options?'

'I'm sure you understand that we need to decide if there's enough evidence to charge her —'

'Charge her?' Wendy gasped at his words. 'I thought this was an interview – you know, just a talk. That's what I told her.'

Tony felt a surge of adrenalin go through him as he spoke. 'No, no, no, you can't . . . Surely the doctors have told you how ill she's been. You've seen her – she couldn't even talk, she didn't know what was going on! I know they say she's better, but obviously she's been ill, really ill, and she didn't know what she was doing. Dr Morgan, you've told them, haven't you?'

Dr Morgan nodded. 'Of course, and that will all be taken into account, but we still have to go through this process.'

Detective Hill puffed out his chest like a cane toad and sat with his legs open as if he were relaxing at home. Tony couldn't bear to look at him.

The detective spoke unhurriedly. 'Tony, our job is to gather evidence to see if we believe a crime has been committed. Then it's up to the courts to determine guilt or innocence.'

Tony turned to look at Wendy. Her chin was twitching, but she looked down at the floor, defeated. Had she given up on Anna already? Was he the only one still fighting for her? Yes, it had crossed his mind, how easy it would be for them to just take her, for her to just disappear out of his life so he never had to see her again. But now that could be a possibility, his body burned with guilt.

He looked at both the detectives: they watched him blankly. To them, this was just another case, a normal day's work. But this was his family, Anna's life. Jack's memory.

There was a knock at the door and someone entered. Tony stood and smiled in relief.

'Scotty!'

Scott Hardy had been in the year above him at university; they had both played in the rugby team and Scott's nose was still a bit crooked after breaking it in the final against Melbourne Uni. He had put on a few kilos, but Tony was relieved to see that otherwise, he was unchanged. Scott was a link to his life before this, to something familiar in the chaos around him.

Scott shook Tony's hand and smiled, but then his expression became serious. He nodded to the others in the room, and Tony let himself breathe out.

'Scott Hardy.' He shook everyone's hands. 'Sorry I'm a few minutes late.' He sat in the empty chair next to Dr Morgan, unzipped his leather satchel, then took out a black notebook and a shiny silver pen. He stretched out his right arm, exposing a gold cufflink from under the sleeve of his navy blue suit, then settled back into his chair, pen poised. Tony saw Wendy gazing at the lawyer with a smile on her face, and he could understand her awe. He had definitely done the right thing. Maybe now *someone* would be on Anna's side.

'I take it you haven't interviewed Anna yet?' Scott said to the detectives.

'Of course not,' Hill replied.

Scott nodded. 'Right. I met with her briefly this morning . . .'

That was why Scott was late: he'd been with Anna. Tony should have known he could trust him. Last night, when Tony had rung him, Scott hadn't hesitated to take on the case. He had said he'd be here, and he was. Tony suddenly felt lighter knowing that someone else would share the burden of protecting Anna; someone objective, free of internal conflict.

Scott continued, 'She knows that she's going to be interviewed today, and I assume you'll be doing that at the station?'

Kaminsky nodded.

'Is she allowed? To leave, I mean? To leave the hospital?' Wendy said to Dr Morgan, her eyes pleading.

'Yes, I'm happy for her to do that.'

'But —'

'Wendy, I'm not saying she's well, or ready for discharge, nowhere near it. But she is well enough to be interviewed.' Dr Morgan leaned towards Wendy and her voice softened. 'I wouldn't agree to release her if I didn't think she'd be safe, OK?'

Wendy nodded.

Tony looked around the room realising that the meeting was about to end and the police were about to get their hands on Anna. This wasn't OK at all. It was going too fast. He heard shoes scuffling on the ground as everyone shifted in their chairs to stand up.

'Wait!' he said, trying to slow everything down. He'd tried to convince the police already that someone else was to blame, but they hadn't listened. He had to turn their attention away from her. He thought of the letter, still in the glove box of his car, and felt the panic creep up into his throat. He had to convince them that she was sick, too sick to know what she was doing. That's what Dr Morgan and Wendy believed. Did he?

'Listen, I've been thinking, and there are some things I've remembered, that might help, you know.' He raked his fingers through his hair. 'There are a few things that make me even more sure that she's been really ill . . . confused, that she didn't know what was happening.'

'Tony . . .' Scott held his hand up in the air to try to stop Tony from saying any more.

Hill leaned forward. 'We've got your statements, Tony. Of course, if there's anything else you'd like to tell us, we can do that down at the station.'

But that would be later, wouldn't it? That would be after they interviewed Anna; that might be too late. 'If anyone's guilty here, it's me. I am – was – Jack's dad so I am just as responsible for anything that's happened. More so, even, because I wasn't sick. So I'll tell you everything, but only if you make sure that if anyone is charged or arrested or whatever, it's me, not her . . .' Tony talked quickly now, turning from one detective to the other, trying to read their faces, to find the point of weakness. There was always a good cop, wasn't there, always one who had some compassion? But as Tony looked back and forth between them, their faces didn't change.

'Tony,' Hill said. 'We do need you to tell us everything, but we can't make a deal with you. I understand —'

'You don't understand anything!' Tony clenched his hand into a fist and looked for something to hit, finding only his knee. He saw Kaminsky stiffen and shift forward in his chair, so he took a deep breath and lowered his voice. 'Listen. Take me. Hold me responsible. I'll do anything you want me to. But don't . . . don't blame Anna.' His head dropped and his voice wavered. He needed to convince them; they needed to listen to him. 'I don't know if Anna will survive this. It'll kill her if you charge her with . . . with this. It will just kill her. Please, please . . .' He looked up and held his hands out. 'It's my fault, all my fault. Arrest me.' He hated to beg, but what else could he do? He sniffed, then wiped angrily at his face.

'Tony.' Wendy dragged her chair closer to his and put her arm around him. 'We don't know what's going to happen – it's just an interview.' She was crying too.

Scott cleared his throat and leaned forward. 'Tony, listen to me. I'll look after her, I promise.'

He looked at Scott's face. The past weeks had seemed unreal, like a terrible dream, like someone else's life, but the enormity of what was about to happen hit him hard, right in the guts.

Jack was gone forever, and Tony was about to lose his wife too.

* * *

Anna heard footsteps approaching her door, and closed her eyes. She took a deep breath and willed herself not to cry. Everything was still so confusing. Her head was clearing, but every so often she began to think of terrible things, so terrible that she shut them out immediately. She looked back down at the tattered magazine she'd been flicking through, not sure who she was trying to fool. She could hear murmurs outside the door. Actual voices, she knew that now. Not those others; they had faded away, although in some ways it had been easier when she wasn't certain that what she heard was real or imagined.

The door opened and Dr Morgan came into her room.

'Anna, the police are ready for you now,' Dr Morgan said quietly. She sounded almost apologetic.

'I'm ready.'

She stood up and smoothed down her jade silk dress. She had asked her mum to bring it in for her yesterday. The last time she'd worn this dress was on her final day of work, but then the silk had billowed down over her pregnant belly. It hung limply now. There was still a tiny grease spot above the waistband, a drop of oil that had dripped from an olive at her farewell afternoon tea. She tucked her hair behind her ears; she had blow-dried it this morning, and put on some make-up. She thought that maybe if she looked more like a professional than a patient, then maybe the police would see that she was a normal woman. This – the hospital, the police – wasn't her world.

She had been surprised to see Scott this morning. He had looked familiar, but it was only when he introduced himself that she remembered him from uni. He'd given her hope: not only because she knew he was a good lawyer, but also because if Tony had organised this, he must still care about her. Scott had explained what was going to happen and insisted that all she had to do was tell the truth. That was easy: she couldn't remember what had happened. But would the police believe her?

She picked up her cardigan, and walked towards Dr Morgan. Just outside the doorway, she saw the two policemen who had been hovering around before, as well as Scott, her mum, and Tony.

'Tony!' Anna's breathing quickened. It had only been a week or so since she'd seen him last, but his face was somehow thinner, older. 'You came! I didn't think I'd see you.'

He nodded and gazed at her. For a moment, Anna felt as though it was just the two of them there, the way it had been before. The way it was when they met, when they said their vows, when they read the Sunday papers in bed, and when they held their little boy. She blinked; already the moment had passed. She was walking now, away from him, away from her mum, towards the door. She turned her head so she could see him for just a moment longer. He stood there, watching. Anna wanted to run back and grab him, but she had to keep up with Scott and the police. She kept moving forward, away from Tony, and left him behind.

* * *

As the heavy security door of the unit slammed closed, Tony's legs began trembling. Wendy clutched his hand and her fingernails dug into him. He took his hand away; he didn't want anyone clinging to him now. It should be Anna's hand he was holding, her he was supporting. What was he doing? That was his wife they were taking away, and he was standing here like an idiot. Why didn't he go with her? She had looked so small as she walked out. Tony thought he heard an engine start; Anna would be in the car by now.

Dr Morgan put her hand on Tony's arm; he jumped. 'She'll be OK,' she said. 'Your lawyer seemed good.'

Tony nodded.

'They could be a few hours, but you're welcome to wait here until they bring her back.'

'Tony,' Wendy said. 'Do you want to wait?'

He shook his head. 'No. Do you?'

'I don't mind, but I suppose she could be a while . . .'

'Let's go then.'

He regretted not saying anything to Anna, but he'd been scared that if he did, she would cry or ask more of him and, for now, this was all he could manage. She needed to hold it together; even with Scott there she would need all her strength to cope with the police interview. And part of him was relieved when she'd walked out. He could never say it out loud, but he wanted the police to take Anna away and question her; maybe she would tell them what she refused to tell him. As much as he pitied her and worried about her, he couldn't close his eyes without seeing Jack. And when he pictured his lifeless child lying still, so still, he didn't care if Anna was scared in an interview room. Jack was dead, and only she knew what had happened.

His face burned and the room around him blurred and swirled.

'Tony? Tony? Are you all right?'

He opened his eyes and blinked hard, seeing Wendy's and Dr Morgan's faces come into focus. 'Yeah, I'm OK.'

'Do you want to sit down in my office for a while?' Dr Morgan asked. 'I'll get you some water —'

'No. I'm fine, I just need to get out of here.'

'Let's go then,' Wendy said, and he felt her hand on his arm, propelling him towards the door.

'Just give me a second . . .' He took a few deep breaths as if he needed to catch his breath, but really he wanted to wait a moment before he went out into the car park to make sure that Anna had definitely gone.

CHAPTER TWENTY-THREE

Two weeks after

Monday, 28 September 2009

Tony gasped when the cold waves slapped his legs, but he kept moving. He needed to take his mind off what was happening to Anna at the police station. What were they asking her? What was she saying? He had taken Wendy home, promising to call her as soon as he heard anything. But waiting was torture.

He ignored the chill of the water and ran through the breakers, then leapt onto his board and paddled furiously. The sea was a sharky grey, and the surface simmered with froth. Tony had been big on surfing when he was a kid, and used to love his dad taking him down to nippers on a Saturday morning. He'd always thought he'd do the same for Jack.

He watched as a big set came in, then turned around and paddled to catch it. The force of the first wave propelled him forward; he was weightless, powerless. He grinned as the wave closed out around him, even as he was thrown from his board. The pounding of the ocean drowned out his whoops and screams, and he was still yelling when his head went under.

He closed his mouth and the noise around him faded away into the gurgling wash. He stopped kicking and let his burning muscles relax. The currents shifted his floating limbs in a freefall dance and he imagined himself going deeper and deeper. He opened his eyes and watched the silver-white bubbles rise up to the turquoise light. Below him was dark weed. The salt water stung his eyes and his chest was red-hot, needing air. The ocean forced itself to the back of his nose and throat and pushed into his sinuses. He kicked for the surface.

Gasping, then coughing as he inhaled the spray, his chest heaved and his arms and legs trembled, but it felt good. He pulled his board towards him and clambered on, panting. He surrendered and caught a broken wave into shore.

He lay down on his back on the beach. He was exhausted from his exertion, but just for a minute, he had been able to forget.

The sun was lower in the sky now. He looked at his watch – almost four o'clock. Anna had been gone all day. He didn't want to think about whether that was good or bad. He wrapped his beach towel around his shoulders.

His phone rang.

'Hello?'

'Tony, it's Scotty.'

He held his breath.

'Sorry it's taken so long —'

'What's happening?'

'Mate, it's been a long day. Are you sitting down?'

'Just tell me!' His heart was thumping.

'They've decided they have enough to charge her.'

'Charge her? Oh, shit . . .'

'They've charged her with something called infanticide.'

'Infanticide?'

'Look, Tony, it's probably the best outcome. It's a charge used for women who've been mentally ill after having a baby, and who've done this sort of thing. It means they're not contesting the fact that Anna's been ill, they're agreeing she had diminished responsibility.'

He closed his eyes. He couldn't think, couldn't take this in.

Scott continued, 'It's what I expected really. And the good news is that they've agreed to grant her conditional bail.'

Bail? The word made Tony think of police cells and courts and prison. That was what Scott was talking about now; Tony's body reeled as the implications hit him.

He couldn't keep the panic out of his voice. 'Where is she?'

'She's still here at the station – the police are doing the paper-work. She'll go back to the hospital soon and stay there on bail as long as she keeps getting treatment.'

'How is she?'

'She's as good as she can be, under the circumstances.'

Tony thanked him and hung up. He gripped the phone and let Scott's words reverberate around his head. Infanticide. Anna – his wife – had been charged with killing his son. He began to shiver all over, and his teeth chattered. It had been different when it was something that everyone speculated about. Now it was real. Anna would have to go to court, maybe even prison.

The worst thing was that he wasn't sure whether he should be relieved or devastated.

*   *   *

Anna stared out the window of the police car as they drove back to the hospital. The roads were busy as people hurried home to make dinner, or to help with their kids' homework, or to watch television. These ordinary people stared at her through their tinted windows, no doubt wondering what she'd done, then they went back to their own lives. She'd have done the same – before.

She'd told the police again and again that she didn't know what had happened, but they kept trying to make her say something wrong. They had confused her, and now she wasn't sure what she'd actually told them.

They'd left her alone in that terrible room for ages. Then they'd come back in, but they didn't look her in the eye. Detective Hill had put his hand on her shoulder, cleared his throat, and told her that she was under arrest. They marched her through to another room, and he said that he was charging her. He hesitated, just before he said Jack's name, as if he couldn't quite remember it. She stared at them, then at Scott. She might have gasped, maybe even laughed. That would have really made them think she was mad.

Now they were driving her back to the hospital. The concrete building loomed ahead, but it looked different from how it had this morning.

Everything was different now.

The police led Anna back into the building. Through the small glass window of the security door, she saw her mum and Tony standing outside the nurses' station. She raised her hand in a small wave, but neither of them waved back. She was flanked by the detectives and had no choice but to keep walking through the door. She looked straight across the room into Tony's eyes, and heard the slam of the door closing behind her. She jumped and her legs started to buckle under her. Nausea crept up into the back of her throat and saliva seeped into her mouth; she was going to throw up. They turned right into the passageway towards her tiny room. Tony was still there behind her. She stumbled, looking back at him.

'Tony.' She was at the entrance to her room now, but she couldn't take her eyes off him. She held out her hands, but he stood there, watching her, motionless. He was crying; Tony never cried. It was almost more than she could bear. 'Tony, I didn't do anything, please . . .'

He shook his head and turned away from her.

'Do you believe me? Tony?' she shouted. 'I would never . . .'

He was walking now, but in the wrong direction, away from her. For a moment, Wendy looked as if she was going to follow him, but instead she hurried towards her. Anna didn't want her mum. All she had ever wanted was gone.

She put her hands over her face and screamed.

CHAPTER TWENTY-FOUR

Twelve days before

Wednesday, 2 September 2009

Anna stood in the doorway to the bedroom and watched Tony playing with Jack on the bed. He was tickling him, trying to get him to smile.

'He's too young,' she said.

He didn't stop. He talked in a stupid high-pitched voice. 'My little boy is so clever, he'll smile for Daddy!'

She clenched her jaw. He was going to get Jack all excited, then go off to work and leave her to deal with him when he was agitated and overtired. Then Jack would cry and cry; that's when Anna got frightened.

She started to walk towards them, then stopped. She didn't have the energy. Taking a step back, she left them to it.

She went to the kitchen, poured a glass of water and sipped it while she sat on the couch. She wished she could cancel the doctor's appointment this morning. But Tony knew it was today, and she had promised him she'd go.

After he went to work, she held Jack to her breast without saying a word, avoiding his accusing eyes. Her breasts felt empty. She wasn't even sure he was getting any milk.

When he had finished feeding, she put him on a play mat on the living room floor, walked into the bathroom and closed the door. She showered and washed her hair for the first time in days. Back in her bedroom, she held up her black yoga pants, then dropped them on the floor and pulled out a clean pair of maternity jeans instead. They were loose around her hips and she had a moment of satisfaction as she thought about the weight she must have lost, but then that warm feeling was sucked away again. She went back to the bathroom, took her make-up bag out of the vanity drawer then wiped the condensation off the mirror. When she'd put on some foundation and mascara she looked like her old self, almost. But she knew it was only a veneer.

*   *   *

They arrived at the doctors' practice ten minutes early. As soon as Anna sat down in the waiting room, Jack started to cry. *Just give me a break*, she wanted to shout. *Just shut up for five minutes. I can't do this*. But, of course, she didn't shout. She stood up and pushed the pram back and forward, back and forward. The lady sitting across from her was trying to catch her eye; Anna felt obliged to meet it.

'Aww, he's so little! How old is he?' The woman leaned over to see into the pram.

'He's four weeks,' she said with a slight smile, then turned away.

'He's so beautiful.' Now the woman's head was right inside the pram. 'Hello, gorgeous boy. What's the matter with you? Are you hungry?'

'No he's not,' she said. 'He's just crying. That's what babies do.'

The stranger raised her eyebrows and went back to her magazine.

'Sorry,' Anna mumbled. Her face burned. She didn't want to cry, not here, in front of everyone. She sat down and took a deep breath, but she couldn't get enough air. Her lips and fingers tingled. That woman was staring at her, but her face was blurred around the edges and white flashes exploded in front of Anna's eyes. Was the woman laughing at her? She gripped the arms of her chair with her numb fingers and hoped she was smiling. Her ears rang, but she could still hear Jack crying.

Somehow, she managed not to collapse, not to break down in tears, not to pass out. The room started to come back into focus. The woman across from her wasn't staring; she was reading her magazine. Anna stood up again, and picked up Jack. He stopped crying. She forced herself to smile in case anyone was watching her. Everything was OK; she was still in control.

'Anna?' Dr Fraser popped her head out of her room as an old lady shuffled out, holding a prescription.

'Yes!' Anna said. She cleared her throat, smiled at the doctor, then put Jack back into the pram. She bent down to pick up her bag then manoeuvred the pram with her free hand. It clattered into the coffee table. Her face began to burn again and she felt the flush of red across her cheeks; she couldn't work out how to get around the table. Everyone was looking at her. 'Oops,' she said, and giggled, knowing she must look ridiculous.

'No rush,' Dr Fraser said as she handed something to the receptionist, still watching Anna. The lady who had talked to her earlier moved a chair out of the way; she mumbled her thanks, then followed Dr Fraser into the consulting room.

Anna had been in this room many times over the years. On her right there was a cluttered desk with piles of papers and notes leaning against the wall, and on her left was an examination couch. Dr Fraser closed the door behind her, indicating that Anna should sit down, then sat in the black leather swivel chair nearest to the desk. She looked at her GP. Dr Fraser was in her fifties, she guessed, with short hair that could be either grey or bleached blonde. Today, Anna couldn't stop looking at the string of brightly coloured glass beads around the doctor's neck. She had seen a necklace like that when she and Tony went to Murano, an island just off Venice. They had watched a man hand-blowing glass, then looked at some similar beads; Anna had liked them but thought they were too expensive. Tony had proposed on that trip. Her eyes started to water; she had really wanted those beads. She should have bought them; she might never get another chance.

Anna arranged the pram behind her in the cramped room and sat on the edge of the chair at the corner of the desk. Her knees almost touched Dr Fraser's.

'How are you, Anna?' Dr Fraser asked.

'I'm fine, thanks. How are you?' Anna blushed as she spoke. The doctor wasn't just being polite; she was trying to get Anna to talk about why she was here.

'I'm very well, thanks, and I've been looking forward to meeting this little one! I heard from the hospital that he'd been born. What's his name?'

'Jack.' Anna took a deep breath. That was her opening; she needed to get this over with. 'That's kind of why I'm here. Well, Jack's OK, I think . . .' She paused, flustered. She had practised over and over what she would say, but now she couldn't remember any of it. Dr Fraser sat back and waited. 'I'm not sleeping very well. Tony – my husband – wanted me to come to see you. I'm not sure there's anything you can do. I mean, it's all part of being a mum, I suppose. I just thought I should check it out with you . . .'

Dr Fraser frowned, put down her pen, then sat back in her chair. 'Tell me a bit more, Anna.'

'I'm just so tired . . .' Anna's voice died away. Then the tears started. She pulled some tissues out of a box on the desk, then began to talk. She faltered and trembled through her story – Jack's crying, how much it hurt when he fed. 'It's just not how I thought it would be!'

'How's your sleep, Anna?'

'I don't think anyone with a baby sleeps well,' Anna said, smiling through her tears, but Dr Fraser didn't smile back. 'Not good. I can't even sleep when he does.'

'And your appetite?'

She shook her head. 'Not good either. I'm trying . . . I know my milk is going to dry up, I need to eat more, but I just can't. It makes me feel sick.' The tears started again.

'Anna, having a newborn is hard work, you've got to give yourself a break. We'll have a look at Jack, all right?'

'OK.'

Dr Fraser undressed Jack, looked him over, then put him on the scales. She looked back at the notes. Anna stared at him: his tummy looked so swollen, his limbs so scrawny, his skin so loose. Poor little baby, he deserved better than her.

'He's doing fine, Anna. He's put on about four hundred grams since he left hospital. That's not bad, but I'd like to see him putting on a bit more. It might be useful to top him up after his feeds with some formula.'

She knew it. Because of her failings, Jack was starving. 'I really wanted to breastfed him!'

'You are breastfeeding him, and you still can. You're doing everything right – you're doing your best.'

'But my best isn't good enough, is it? I can't even feed my own child properly.'

'Anna, listen to me. You're doing a brilliant job. All I'm suggesting is that after each breastfeed you offer him some formula. If he's still hungry he'll drink it, but if he's not, he won't. It's not forever, just until we can get your appetite sorted out. It might help him to sleep a bit longer as well. You must be exhausted.'

Dr Fraser dressed Jack again and put him back in the pram. She sat in her chair, her hands clasped in front of her as if in prayer. 'How do you think your mood is?'

Anna shrugged.

'Does anything make you happy at the moment? Is there anything you enjoy?'

She shook her head, tears running down her face. It was such a relief to hear someone articulate the way she'd been feeling.

'Anna, I'm worried about you. I'm worried that you've become quite depressed. Can I ask . . . Do you feel that you're bonding with Jack?'

Finally, someone had asked. Everyone had assumed – *she* had assumed – that it would be easy, that she'd love her baby straightaway, but sometimes . . . She couldn't finish the thought. 'I don't . . . don't feel anything for him. Oh, I do, I mean, sometimes. But he doesn't seem . . . like I thought. I thought I'd feel more.'

'I need to ask you something that I ask everyone who feels down or depressed. Have you ever had any thoughts of hurting yourself, of trying to end your life?'

'No, no, I haven't.' She dabbed at her eyes with a tissue, which had disintegrated into damp flakes.

'And what about Jack? Have you ever had any thoughts of hurting him?'

Anna gasped. 'No! I'd never do that!'

'Sorry, it's just something I needed to ask. Look, there are a few things we need to do. First, I'm going to prescribe some tablets for you – antidepressants. I want you to start taking them today. It'll take a couple of weeks before they start to work, so keep taking one every day, even if you don't feel like they're helping. I know you're breastfeeding, but these are safe. Some will get into the breast milk but the risks of that are far less than if you don't take them.'

Anna nodded. She felt safer knowing that someone was telling her what she needed to do. It was so hard these days to make any decisions; she almost wept with relief that someone else was taking charge.

'I'm also going to refer you to a psychologist. I think you need someone to talk to, to help you deal with some of the feelings that you are having. OK?'

'Yes.'

'And you need some help at home. Is there anyone who can help you?'

'Tony's mum's offered. And my mum, she's in Western Australia but she could come . . .'

'Good. I'd like to speak to Tony too, just to let him know what we're doing. Have you got his —'

Anna sat up straighter. Tony didn't need to be involved. 'He's at work, in meetings all day.'

'I can leave a message on his mobile.'

'No, don't disturb him. It's fine, I'll talk to him.'

Dr Fraser hesitated, then nodded. 'All right. Make sure he knows to call me if he has any questions or is worried about anything. That goes for you too. Otherwise, make an appointment for early next week so we can see how the tablets are going.'

While Dr Fraser made some notes, Anna splashed her face with cold water from the small sink in the corner of the room. She pulled two paper towels from the dispenser on the wall and patted her face.

'Thank you,' she said quietly. She took the prescription and some printed information about the medication, dragged the pram backwards out of the room, and paid her bill. She told the receptionist that she'd call later to make the follow-up appointment.

Anna went straight to the chemist before she could think about it too much, and handed in her prescription. While she waited, she picked up a tin of formula and some bottles. She wanted to hide them, to tell the sales assistant that she wasn't really bottle-feeding, it was just temporary, doctor's orders. But the sales assistant didn't seem to care. She paid with her credit card then shoved the carrier bag in the basket of the pram and walked out.

When she got back to her car, she strapped Jack into his capsule, put the pram in the boot then swallowed one of her tablets without water, straightaway. If she waited until she got home she knew that she might talk herself out of it. The pill stuck in her throat and she gagged. It tasted foul.

* * *

That evening, Tony made sure he left work on time. When he walked in, he smelled spices wafting from the kitchen. Anna was standing at the stove, stirring something in a pot. Music was playing from the television. Jack was asleep in his bouncy chair on top of the kitchen counter. Tony felt himself breathe out; Anna looked more like her old self. She loved cooking; she must have had a better day.

He smiled. 'I thought I said no housework?' He walked over to her and kissed her head. 'How did it go at the doctor's? You look happier.'

She shrugged. 'It was OK.'

'What did she say?'

'She said I was normal.' Anna didn't look him in the eye. 'She said I'm tired, just adjusting, you know.'

'That's great, babe.' It was fantastic news; it was all he had wanted, someone else – a professional – to check Anna out and make sure this really was just fatigue or baby blues or something. She'd be better in no time.

Anna added salt to the pan. 'She gave me some tablets.'

She had spoken so quietly, so casually, that Tony barely heard her. His stomach flipped. If she was OK, why did she need medication? 'What for?'

'Oh, just to help me sleep a bit. They're over there, in my bag.'

He took the box out of Anna's bag and looked at it. He opened the box and unfolded the thin paper information sheet. 'Anna, it says these are for depression and anxiety.'

She kept stirring. 'Yeah, they are, but she's not using them for depression. They help you sleep too, and while I'm breastfeeding they're safer than sleeping tablets.'

'Oh.' There was something in Anna's voice that unnerved Tony, but he told himself he had no reason not to trust her. Anyway, as long as she was taking the tablets, what difference did it make what they were meant for? He wondered if maybe Dr Fraser had told Anna they were to help her sleep to make sure she took them. 'Did she say anything about Jack?'

Anna cleared her throat. 'She had a look at him. He's fine, no problems.'

Tony put the tablets down and smiled. 'I'm so pleased that you went. Things will get easier, I promise.' He put his arms around her from behind and kissed the back of her head. Her hand didn't stop stirring the wooden spoon round and round in the pot. Chunks of brown meat bobbed on the surface of the curry sauce then sank into the thick folds and disappeared.

He rested his chin on the top of her head and relaxed for the first time in weeks; things were going to be fine.

*   *   *

Anna took another tablet the next morning, but she didn't feel better. By lunchtime, she felt much worse: she couldn't keep still, every part of her body urged her to move, to scratch, to pace. She tried to lie down when Jack fell asleep in the afternoon, but her legs itched and tingled. She couldn't eat; she felt sick. It was unbearable.

Giving up on trying to nap, she typed the name of her medication into her computer and started to read about the terrible side effects. These tablets weren't going to help at all. Her hands shook as she picked up the box of pills from the kitchen bench and stared at them. What good could they do? She felt worse now than before she started them. And Dr Fraser had told her that the chemicals went into her breast milk – what were they doing to Jack? What about his brain?

She walked through to the bedroom, opened the drawer of her bedside table and put the box in there. She put a book on top of them, closed the drawer and walked out of the room, slamming the door behind her.

CHAPTER TWENTY-FIVE

Three weeks after
Monday, 5 October 2009

Anna pushed away her half-eaten cereal. The milk was too thick and warm; it tasted like it was about to go off. She stared at the melamine plate and tried to ignore the other patients around her. Rachel wouldn't let Anna eat her meals in her room any more; she wanted her to socialise. But Anna had nothing to say to the other patients. Initially, she had convinced herself that she was different, but now she stayed away because she knew that she was exactly like them.

She sipped her weak coffee, then grimaced. Caffeine was a drug that some people abused, Rachel said, so the nurses kept the jar locked in their office and spooned out daily rations of a few granules of cheap, bitter, instant coffee floating in tepid water. It wasn't worth drinking.

She smelled Dr Morgan's perfume wafting toward her, competing with the odour of burnt toast and rubbery sausages. She looked around and saw that Dr Morgan had cut her hair: the ends looked sharp.

'Hi, Anna. Are you finished eating?'

'Yeah.'

'Great. I wanted to have a chat with you. Is that all right?'

Anna was glad for an excuse to get away from the other patients. She took her plate and cup over to the tray near the sink, then followed Dr Morgan towards one of the interview rooms off the main corridor. Her eyes darted around the room: she did trust Dr Morgan, but she still always expected a policeman to be waiting for her. The room was empty.

Dr Morgan sat opposite her and smiled. 'How are you?'

Anna shrugged.

'How was breakfast?'

'Not good.'

Dr Morgan gave a small laugh. 'No, it's not very good at all, is it? The nurses tell me you're eating a bit better now, though. What do you think your appetite's like?'

'It's OK.'

'Are you sleeping?'

'Too much. I can't keep my eyes open . . .' As if to prove the point, she stifled a yawn.

'I'm sorry about that, it's a side effect of the medications.'

'I don't care.' Anna looked at her, defiant. 'I'd rather be sleeping.'

'I can imagine.'

'Can you? I'm sick of the sympathy.' Her eyes stung but she blinked back the tears.

'I'm sorry. That was insensitive of me. You're right: I can't imagine how you feel. Anna, what do you remember about when you came into hospital?'

Always the same questions, and she gave the same answer. 'Nothing.'

'Nothing at all?'

She shook her head.

'What's the last thing you remember?'

'I don't know!' Sometimes, at night, she could recall fragments of sounds, images that she knew must be memories of that day, but she chased them away. She didn't want to remember.

'Do you know why you were at the cliffs?'

She didn't want to talk about this; she'd rather talk about her physical symptoms, or her childhood, as they often did. Going back to that day wasn't going to help.

Dr Morgan spoke slowly. 'Anna, when you came into hospital, you were psychotic – do you know what that means?'

'Crazy.' She knew what it meant; most of the patients in here were psychotic.

'Well, I suppose some people might still say that, but when I say someone is psychotic, I mean that their thinking becomes disorganised – they lose touch with reality. Some people believe things that aren't true, others have unusual sensations like hearing voices.'

She could hear what Dr Morgan was saying, could understand it, but couldn't think of it as anything other than a lecture, something from a book that had nothing to do with her.

'Does any of that sound familiar to you? Does it sound like what you were experiencing?'

It was impossible to imagine herself – a sensible, married schoolteacher – being like that. 'It's like you're talking about a different person.'

'I know it's hard to hear. When you came into hospital, you could barely speak, and when you did, it didn't make much sense. You seemed scared, you thought you were in danger.'

She remembered the fear. But it wasn't she who had been in danger. The fear she'd had was for Tony and Jack – her husband and son. It wasn't clear in her mind, but she had known that she was the dangerous one, and there was only one way to save them. The memory faded and she recalled the terror of being held down by countless heavy hands, having a policeman at her door, having no idea where she was. Those memories were clear, tangible, and she clutched at them. Her heart began to pound. 'I *was* scared. I was locked up! How do you think you'd feel if you woke up in a place like this and no one told you what was going on? Not even your family.'

Dr Morgan nodded in that way she did when she wanted to look sympathetic. 'But knowing what you know now, can you understand why Tony would find it difficult to talk to you?'

Always this, always skirting around the real issue. She glared at Dr Morgan. 'Why can't you say it? No one will even say his name any more. I know Jack died, and I know that it was my fault!' She rubbed her hands up and down her face. 'That's what you wanted to hear, wasn't it? That's what the police wanted me to say. They didn't want to hear that I couldn't remember, they wanted all the gory details, for me to tell them everything and make their job easier.'

'Anna, you don't have to remember, or say anything. I'm not the police; I'm your doctor. I'm here to try to get you better.' Dr Morgan sat back in the chair, crossing her legs. 'It will take time – a long time – to come to terms with this. You may never remember. It's quite common not to be able to recall things that happened when you were psychotic, but trauma itself can make us block out memories. Sometimes our minds do what they can to protect us.'

Anna bowed her head and folded her hands in her lap; she could say no more.

'Let's leave it there for today then. I just need to ask you one more thing before we finish. Do you have any thoughts at the moment about hurting yourself?'

Dr Morgan asked her this every day. 'No.'

'Because it wouldn't be unusual – in fact, I think it would be quite normal in your situation.'

But how many people had been in her situation? Really, were there studies on people *like her*? She bit her lip. 'No, I don't.'

She stood up and followed Dr Morgan back down the corridor. The nurses had locked her room, so she had no choice but to go to the morning meditation class. Just before she entered the room, she paused and took in the patients lying on the floor. They looked unkempt. They had bad skin, bad haircuts, their fingers were stained with nicotine. But more than that, even as they lay stretched out on the floor, breathing deeply, they looked lonely. Lonely and sad.

She tiptoed in and lay down on the floor next to the nurse who was running the group. She tried to hold her body still, but her chest heaved. Her mind couldn't rest either. Pieces of thoughts and memories flew past her and she scrabbled to grasp them, but she couldn't. She didn't have the strength.

*   *   *

Tony hesitated outside the doctors' practice. It was on the fourth floor of a huge shiny shopping mall, opposite a gym. He supposed it was meant to make people think that going to see the doctor was just like buying a pair of shoes. He hadn't expected that the shopping centre would be this busy on a weekday morning: there were mums pushing prams everywhere. He couldn't look at them; they reminded him too much of Anna and Jack. Maybe he should have encouraged Anna to spend more time out of the house, to walk around the shops, have a coffee with these other mums – maybe that would have helped. He cut off his train of thought: what was the point of thinking about it? It was all too late now.

He pushed open the glass door. He walked up the stairs to the waiting room, then marched towards reception. Behind the desk, one receptionist processed an elderly man's payment; the other rummaged under the desk. He walked to her side of the counter.

'I need to see Dr Fraser,' he said over the top of her head.

She stood up straight. 'Your name?'

'Tony Patton.'

She pointed at her computer screen with a long nail sparkling with tiny stars. 'What time was your appointment?'

'I don't have one.'

'If you don't have an appointment, you can't see her. All of our doctors are fully booked. If it's an emergency —'

'Just tell her I'm here, and it's about my wife.' He turned around and pointed to the chairs in the waiting area. 'I'm going to sit here until she sees me. I'm not in a hurry. Just tell her I'm here.'

The receptionist started to argue, but he ignored her and sat in the chair nearest to the desk, so he had a good view of the doors to the consulting rooms. He heard the receptionists mumbling to each other. He waited. He would wait as long as it took. The more he had thought about it, the angrier he had become at Dr Fraser. He had done the right thing in insisting Anna see the doctor; Anna had done the right thing by seeking help here. So why was Anna the one to blame when the doctor had told her there was nothing wrong with her?

Ten minutes later, Dr Fraser came out of her room with a patient and walked over to reception. Her long string of brown beads clacked and bounced on the desk. The receptionist raised her thin, over-plucked eyebrows and nodded at Tony as she whispered to the doctor. The GP nodded, fixed a smile on her face then pulled her shoulders back. 'Tony Patton?'

'Yes.' He stood up slowly, straightened his t-shirt and followed her into her room. He was going to stay calm.

Dr Fraser closed the door behind her, then pulled her chair out from behind the desk so that she sat between him and the door. She smiled at him again, and gestured to a chair. 'Please sit down. What can I do for you today?'

Tony heard the slight quiver in her voice and knew she was worried. He had been right to come here; she knew she'd done something wrong.

He sat down. 'I'm here about my wife, Anna Patton. Do you know who I mean?'

Dr Fraser's eyes dropped. 'Yes, of course, I heard. The hospital contacted me. Mr Patton, I'm so sorry about your loss, it really is a tragedy.'

'That's one way of looking at it,' he said evenly. He waited. Dr Fraser looked at him, waiting too. Tony knew he had the upper hand here. 'So, what I need to know is, what did Anna say to you when she was here?'

'I'm so sorry but I can't discuss that with you, I'm bound by doctor–patient confidentiality —'

'Doctor–patient confidentiality? You've got to be joking. My wife is locked up in a mental ward after killing my baby, and you can't discuss her with me? She has to go to court and probably jail, it's all over the papers and half of Sydney knows about it, but you can't tell me, her husband, what she said when she came here right before she did it?' He realised it was the first time he had said out loud that she had done it, that Anna had killed Jack.

Dr Fraser shook her head. 'I'm sorry, I can't. I can assure you, Mr Patton, that there was absolutely no indication that something like this would happen. My notes will probably be subpoenaed by the court, but there is a process and I'm afraid I can't tell you the details of that consultation. But I'm happy to hear what you've got to say, to talk to you about your experiences . . .'

He sat forward. She was so bloody patronising. 'What *experiences* would you like me to talk about? Identifying my son's body? Watching my wife being led away by police, or maybe seeing her screaming, being held down and having a needle stabbed into her? You think I'm here to talk to you about that?' His voice shook and tears began to fall. He wiped his eyes; he didn't want to look weak, he needed her to admit that she was partly to blame. It wasn't all Anna's fault. He swallowed, composed himself, then pointed his finger at Dr Fraser. 'Anna came to see you for help. I knew there was something wrong – even she knew. You were meant to help her!'

Dr Fraser pushed her chair back slightly and held her hands out in front of her. 'Please, Mr Patton, I need you to calm down. I know how terrible and confusing this is for you, and I know that you must want answers.' Her voice was trembling. 'But I can't talk to you when you're like this.'

Suddenly the phone on her desk rang. She kept her hands up in front of her. 'I'm going to have to answer that.' She slowly moved her left hand towards the receiver.

He gripped the arms of his chair, trying to stop the shaking in his hands. He no longer knew if the trembling was from anger or grief.

'Yes,' Dr Fraser said. 'Thank you, I'll be right out.' She gently replaced the receiver and kept her voice soft. 'I'm just going to step out of the office for a second, OK?'

Tony knew that Dr Fraser had organised for the receptionist to call if she heard shouting, or after a few minutes to give her an excuse to get away. What was he doing? He wasn't trying to intimidate her, that wasn't him. But he had such a rage inside him at times, a sense of injustice, a need for someone to blame. He needed Dr Fraser to understand her role in this, to understand what his family was going through.

He tried to talk without his voice faltering. 'Are you frightened of me? I'm not here to . . .' He shook his head, then looked her straight in the eye. 'Just imagine that fear you're feeling now, but multiplied a million times. Imagine how I felt when I couldn't find them. Imagine how Jack felt when . . .' He couldn't breathe properly; standing up he pointed his finger at her. 'Anna asked for help and you gave her nothing.'

Before Dr Fraser could reply, he wrenched open the door. He didn't care when it slammed into the wall, or that everyone in the waiting room stared. He looked straight ahead and stormed out into the mall. He ran down the escalators, past a group of chatting teenagers who didn't seem to understand the concept of keeping to the left with their oversized bags of crap. His face was burning and his eyes were wet, but he made it back to the car. He managed to unlock it and clamber inside, then he pulled his arm back and slammed his fist into the windscreen. He yelled from the pain, then looked at the blood that seeped from a cut between his knuckles. He shook his hand, and the throbbing intensified. The scary thing was that it felt good. It was something real; there would be a bruise there later, something that he, and everyone else, could see. People could understand physical pain; they knew what to say and do. But no one could understand the agony of his situation, and no one could say or do anything to help.

CHAPTER TWENTY-SIX

Three weeks after

Monday, 5 October 2009

Ursula heard the front door open just as she finished putting on her lipstick. She opened the bathroom door. 'Jim! That'll be Tony. I'll be right out.' She sprayed on some perfume, then switched off the light and went into the living room. Jim and Tony were each holding a bottle of beer.

'I'm driving, I suppose?' she said, nodding towards the drinks.

'You never have more than one glass of wine, Mum.'

'Well, maybe I wanted to tonight.' Ursula gave Tony a surreptitious once-over; his t-shirt was crumpled, and he hadn't shaved. He had a defiant look in his eye, the look of a rebellious teenager. At least Jim had showered and put on a shirt.

Jim walked over to Ursula and put his arm around her. 'You're the best taxi driver we know. Unless you want some of my beer?' He winked at Ursula and held up his bottle.

She wrinkled her nose. She knew she shouldn't be angry at him for trying to break the tension; he'd been trying so hard recently to cheer her up, but it only made her more irritated. She was sick of playing games, of pretending to be calm and understanding. It would be easier if they could all scream and brand each other with blame. She knew she was angry: angry at Anna for bringing this on her family, angry at Tony for not confiding in her, angry at Jim for not supporting her. He always let her look like the bad one, the critical one, while he behaved more like a mate than a father. She sighed; maybe, after all, that's what Tony needed right now, a mate. Anyway, Jim had been like that for thirty years, why would he change now? They'd always had a tacit understanding that she managed the family while Jim stood back and let her. But sometimes she wished she had married someone more like herself.

Tony raised his bottle to his mouth and Ursula gasped. 'Anthony! Your hand!' Tony looked at his right hand as if he'd only just noticed that his knuckles were swollen and red. She rushed over, took his beer from him and put it on the floor, then opened out his fingers.

'Mum! Let go!' He pulled his hand away, glaring at her.

'Don't tell me you've been in a fight? For God's sake.'

'It's nothing.' He picked up the bottle again and took a step back.

'Jim, have you seen Tony's hand?'

'Yes, I've seen Tony's hand. He said it's OK, love. Just leave it.'

She opened her mouth, then closed her lips tightly. As usual, they were ganging up on her, and she didn't have the energy to fight back right now. She picked up her bag from the couch and slung it over her shoulder. 'We're late. Lisa and Wendy will be waiting – I said seven.'

*   *   *

Ursula scanned the packed restaurant, then waved when she saw Lisa sitting at a table at the back of the dining room with a glass of wine in her hand. Wendy was opposite her, with her back to the door. The perfume of chilli and coriander drifted around the room; waiters darted and danced between the tables. The customers' chatter reverberated around the room, bouncing off the high ceilings and the crimson and gold canvases hanging on the walls. Her mouth watered as a waiter sashayed past with a plate of glistening noodles and steaming pink prawns. It was nice to feel hungry again; ever since that day she had been forcing herself to eat out of habit. She exhaled, trying to leave the tension behind in the car, then made her way towards Lisa. Tony trudged along behind her, shepherded by Jim.

Lisa and Wendy both stood up as the three of them approached the table. Ursula hugged her daughter, then turned to kiss Wendy's pale cheek. 'Hi, Wendy. How are you?'

'I'm all right, thanks. You?' Wendy had that sad, pitiful look on her face already. Ursula smiled and looked away without answering. She didn't want to hear a sob story right now; it was just a greeting. She walked around to the back of the table and sat next to Lisa, patting the seat of the chair next to her and beckoning to Jim. Tony sat opposite her, next to Wendy.

'I got a bottle of wine,' Lisa said. 'And a lemonade for you, Mum.'

Ursula smiled. 'Thanks, love. How are you?'

'Good, thanks. I was just telling Wendy, the shop's been really busy.' Lisa glanced at Tony; he was staring at the menu. She looked back at Ursula, who nodded her encouragement. Lisa smiled back and kept talking about the shop.

Ursula turned in her chair so she could look at Lisa, and listened with pleasure to her daughter's latest news and gossip. It was so nice to hear some normal conversation, something other than misery. But she couldn't kid herself that this wasn't all for Tony's benefit. She watched as Wendy sipped her wine, listening to Lisa too. She hadn't seen Wendy for a few days. Emily was spending more time with her, and Ursula was glad to be relieved of that duty. Wendy only seemed to be able to talk about Anna; Ursula wanted to talk about anything but her.

'Did you hear that, love?' Ursula reached across the table and touched Tony's hand. 'Lisa's got some designs in a fashion show in Melbourne next month.'

Tony put down the menu and smiled. 'That's great. Nice city.'

Lisa blushed. 'Yeah, well, it's hardly New York, but there's so much art and fashion there, it'll be great to get some contacts, you know? Wendy, have you ever been to Melbourne?'

'No, I haven't,' said Wendy. 'I'd like to though – I'd love to see a footy game at the MCG. Western Australia's just so far away, it takes so long to get anywhere, and it's a bit expensive.' Her face went red.

'Should we order?' Ursula said. She didn't want Wendy to start talking about her guilt at not flying over to see Jack when she'd had the chance.

'Good idea, and Tony and I need a beer,' Jim said. 'Wendy, is there anything in particular that you like, or don't like?'

Wendy shook her head. 'No, I'm happy with whatever you want.'

Ursula nodded, called over a waiter, and ordered food for everyone.

As they waited, Ursula thought again what a delightful young woman her daughter was. She led the conversation and was so polite and inclusive. She'd make a wonderful wife and mother one day. Ursula felt the creep of old age in her bones, the sense of achievement in having raised the next generation coupled with the sadness in knowing that her own children were adults and didn't need her any more. She blinked hard and turned her attention back to the table. Jim was laughing loudly as he told his usual yarns about work and fishing, but Tony was quiet despite everyone's attempts to include him. Ursula was glad when the food arrived; they were running out of things to say and now at least they could eat and talk about the merits of their meal.

But Tony didn't eat. She watched him moving the food round and round on his plate. She tried to ignore it, but the screech of the metal cutlery on the plate got louder and louder until she couldn't bear it any more. 'Anthony! Stop it!' she said. 'That noise is driving me crazy —' She tried to stop herself halfway through the word 'crazy' but it was too late. She paused for just a second too long.

Tony held his fork upright for a moment, then let it fall with a clatter. He stared at Ursula. The others had stopped talking.

Lisa looked at her mother and brother, then sighed and put her own cutlery down. 'Well, let's stop ignoring the elephant in the room. How are you, Tony?'

Ursula glared at Lisa, who avoided her eyes and looked directly at Tony. Wendy looked at her plate.

'You calling me an elephant, sis?' Tony tried to joke.

'Hardly, you're too skinny,' she said.

Ursula held her breath. Tony looked down at his plate, then pushed it away.

Lisa did the same. 'How's Anna?'

'Lisa!' Ursula said.

'What?'

She glared at her children. She hated it when they did this. They'd always done it, even as kids. They'd fight and scream at each other, but as soon as she tried to intervene they would act like she was the one causing the problem. She shook her head. 'Nothing.'

Lisa looked at Tony again. 'What's happening with the trial?'

'There's a committal hearing next week.'

'What?' Ursula looked at Jim, and was pleased to see that he also seemed shocked. Why hadn't Tony told her about this?

Wendy shrank into her chair. She put her fork down, wiped her face with her paper napkin, then cleared her throat. 'The charge – it'll have to be heard in the Supreme Court, it's too serious for the magistrates court, so this hearing is just a formality to organise that. Sorry, I thought you knew . . .' She looked at Tony, as did Ursula.

'It doesn't matter. Tony must have forgotten,' Jim said. 'The Supreme Court. Wow.' He shook his head.

'Oh, don't act so surprised, Jim – this is a pretty serious case, don't you think?' Ursula said.

He ignored her and spoke gently to Wendy. 'When will the trial be?'

Wendy finished her wine, then smiled as Lisa started to pour her some more. 'Mr Hardy, the lawyer, he's not sure. It'll probably be in a couple of months.'

Lisa put the wine bottle back in the bucket and screwed it into the ice. 'It'll go so quickly. It's weird, I can't really believe she'll have to go through that. I bet you'll be glad when it's all over.'

'Of course. Though in some ways it's easier not to know what will happen. If, if she . . .' Wendy closed her eyes for a second, then continued, 'If she has to go to jail, it'll be . . .' She put her hand to her face. 'Sorry.'

Lisa reached over and put her hand on Wendy's, then looked at Tony. 'How's she doing?'

Tony gulped down some beer. 'Fine. I haven't been in for a while.'

Ursula frowned. 'Why —'

'She's doing well.' Wendy glanced at Tony. 'The voices and things are better, but she's . . .' Her eyes filled with tears and her voice trembled. 'She's sad, very sad. She's scared . . . Sorry, I promised myself I wasn't going to do this.' She bent down to search in her bag for a tissue.

Ursula pulled a few napkins from the metal dispenser on the table and flung them towards Wendy. This wasn't the place to make a scene.

'Has the lawyer said what her chances are?' Lisa asked. 'I mean —'

She couldn't just sit and listen to this any longer. 'Lisa, that's enough! We didn't come out to talk about Anna.'

'Ursula.' Jim put his hand on hers, but she shook him off.

'Well, we can't really sit here and play happy families, Mum, can we?' Tony said.

Ursula narrowed her eyes. 'I just don't think we need to talk about this now.'

Tony set his jaw and turned back to Lisa. 'We don't know. Because she was mentally ill at the time, hopefully she won't have to go to jail. After this committal hearing, there's another one when she'll enter a plea, and then a trial or sentencing or whatever. It's all pretty confusing, but Scott knows what he's doing.'

Ursula couldn't believe that all this was coming out now, and she hadn't heard a word of it before from Tony. She realised that she hadn't really asked; she'd been quite happy not to hear about Anna. She hung her head a little, then brushed away the guilt. 'I didn't even know she had a lawyer.'

Tony looked straight at her. 'I called my mate Scotty, and he agreed to take it on. He's a criminal lawyer now.'

'I remember him,' Jim said. 'The guy you played rugby with? You remember him, Ursula? Black hair, big fella.'

Ursula glanced around them at the other tables, then lowered her voice. 'A criminal lawyer sounds expensive. How is Anna going to pay for that?'

'I've spoken to the bank,' Tony said. 'We're using the money that we've paid into the house.'

'But that's your future.' She clasped her hand over her mouth as she realised what she'd said.

Tony looked at her with a clenched jaw. 'What future do I have at the moment, Mum? And Anna – her future could be spent in prison. What do you expect me to do? Just walk away from her?'

Ursula felt her cheeks burn. In fact, that was exactly what she expected. She wanted Tony to stay away from Anna, to let her face the consequences of what she had done and deal with it on her own. But she couldn't say that out loud; she was ashamed to even think it. Instead, she picked up her cutlery and shovelled food into her mouth. Jim started talking about the weather or something ridiculous, and Wendy nodded and smiled and looked up at him with wide eyes. Lisa filled up the wine glasses again, and this time Ursula turned her own glass the right way up; she needed a drink.

As soon as their eating and fake conviviality started to slow down, Ursula nudged Jim. 'Get the bill.'

He nodded, then went up to the counter to pay while the others gathered their things and walked outside. Lisa hugged everyone, and insisted on driving Wendy back to the flat. Ursula drove Jim and Tony home in silence.

*   *   *

Back at home that night, she sat on the couch next to Jim and stared at the fishing show that he was watching. She couldn't sit still, but she hoped that by fixing her eyes on the set, the rest of her body would be grounded. She traced the gold cross that hung from a chain around her neck in a figure of eight pattern on her chest. Jim glanced at her a couple of times.

'What is it, Jim?'

He cleared his throat and turned to face her. 'What's going on, love?'

She didn't shift her gaze from the television. 'Nothing. What do you mean?'

But of course she knew exactly what he meant. After thirty years of marriage, they could always tell what the other was thinking, yet they had to play this ridiculous game and draw it out of each other.

'You're so angry . . .'

Ursula's face burned, but she forced herself to speak clearly and slowly, determined that he wouldn't be right. 'I'm not angry.'

'Yes, you are. Look at the way you acted tonight! It's not making it any easier for the rest of us.'

She sat up straight, perched on the edge of the couch and glared at him. 'The way I acted? Do you think this is an act? It's the rest of you who are acting! Being nice, polite, smiling over cups of tea, talking about the weather over a bottle of wine. At least I'm being honest!'

'Now, come on. I don't think that's fair. We're all devastated!'

'Well, you don't show it! It's as if nothing's happened. Everyone's so worried about Anna, and her treatment, and her lawyers, and her trial, and what she's going to do . . . I don't give a shit what happens to her!' Tears simmered up and boiled over, scalding her eyes and cheeks. *Breathe*, she told herself. *Calm down*. If she lost control, he'd win.

Jim put his hand on her knee. 'Ursula. This isn't the same, you know.'

She narrowed her eyes. 'The same? The same as what?'

'You know what I mean.'

'No I don't, Jim! You think this is about something I did – *we* did? This is completely different! She was just a kid, I've never regretted that, never!' She swatted at the tears. 'You're wrong. This is about Anna and what she did. This has nothing to do with us. I can't believe you'd even bring that up!'

'Ursula . . .'

'No, I'm not having this conversation. Thanks for spoiling another lovely evening!' She stood up. 'Why won't you just let me be?'

She ran out of the room before he had time to grab her hand. In the hallway, she hesitated for just a second, wondering if he would come after her. She heard him sigh, then the squeak of the sofa as he sat back down. She looked down the hallway at the closed bedroom doors. She had raised her family here, and now Tony's and Lisa's rooms were used to store junk. She had always assumed that grandchildren would fill that space, but now . . . Would Tony ever be able to have another child? Would Lisa?

She looked at the photos on the hallway table: graduation photos; Tony's wedding; Jack's beautiful plump face. She covered her mouth with her hand to catch the sobs; she didn't want Jim to hear her. She walked into the bathroom and started to run a bath, then turned the radio on and closed the door while she cried.

*   *   *

The next morning, she crept out of bed while Jim was still snoring like a purring cat. She dressed quietly and left the house. Her stomach churned; it had been a long time since she'd been to church. Her mother used to make her go to mass every Sunday without fail, and sent her to a Catholic school to be taught by the nuns. She had kept it up for years as a grown woman. Why? Had she really believed the stories? She was an intelligent woman, but it had taken a long time to see the hypocrisy, to realise that the tenets of the church couldn't tell you what was right for your own family. She still wore the gold crucifix around her neck that her mother had given her on her confirmation. But for the past few weeks, that cross had been rubbing at her skin, making her itch.

She pushed open the heavy wooden door of the church. It was cool inside, almost cold. There was no service on. The door creaked closed behind her and she began to walk down the central aisle, her heels thudding on the wooden floor. Without thinking about it she walked to the front of the church on her tiptoes, then slid into a pew on her right. Churches all smelled the same, of musty wood, candle wax, and musky incense. She could taste the memory of the bitter metallic tang on her fingers from passing round the offering plate.

Eleven years. That's how long it had been since she was last here.

She had last come for strength, for guidance, but instead she'd realised that she could not do what the church demanded of her. The church's teachings had always propped her up, kept her on a straight knowable path, but when she had most needed help, she had realised how rigid they were.

She stared at the iconic paintings on the wall, the motes floating in the red light shining through the stained glass, then turned away again, looking at the altar. She muttered the Lord's Prayer, her whispers echoing around the building. She felt nothing. What did she expect to achieve by coming here? To erase what had been done in the past? To find out if she was being punished?

The door creaked open behind her. She turned to see an old lady labouring down the aisle. Ursula nodded at her, then turned around to face the front again. She wiped her cheeks and smoothed down her hair. Picking up her bag she walked back up the aisle, smiling at the elderly woman as she passed her.

There was nothing for her here.

CHAPTER TWENTY-SEVEN

Four weeks after
Tuesday, 13 October 2009

Anna stared at the back of the driver's seat headrest as Scott drove towards the magistrates court. She clasped her hands together to try to stop them shaking; it didn't help so she unclasped them again and laid them flat on her knees, pressing down to blot the sweat onto her stockings. Her hair was tied back in a low ponytail, and she wore pale pink lip gloss. She had agonised over her outfit: did she want to look nice and respectable? Or was it better to look crazy?

She inhaled, closed her eyes and let her head loll back onto the soft black leather of the seat. The new-car smell blended with Scott's expensive aftershave. When she was pregnant, even a trace of Tony's aftershave had made her retch. She opened her eyes again, swallowed, then pushed the button to open the window and let in some of the cool morning air.

'Feeling OK?' Scott asked from the front.

She cleared her throat. 'Just a bit hot.'

'Don't worry, today's just a formality. You don't have to say anything – I'll do all the talking.'

She nodded. But she was still shaking.

* * *

Anna had never been in a court before. She must have walked past this building a hundred times, but had never noticed what it was or thought about what went on inside. And now hundreds of other Sydneysiders were doing the same things that she used to do: hurrying to work, talking on their phones, sipping coffees. If they looked up above them, as she did now, they would see the five-storey Georgian building, the colour of sand, with gold detail and pointed turrets on top. Anna had never noticed how beautiful the building was – how beautiful most of the city was – until she thought she'd never see it again.

Walking along the pavement next to Scott, buses spluttered and roared, taxi horns blared and pedestrian crossings beeped all around them. Such ordinary sounds. Her eyes widened as they approached the front steps to the court. There were news crews there with video cameras and microphones. Were they waiting for her?

She looked down at her feet and concentrated on each step, but what she really wanted to do was turn around and run. Scott must have sensed her hesitation: he placed his hand in the small of her back until they were inside the court building.

In the courtroom, she didn't dare look around in case her instincts took over and she fled. She was sure everyone seated behind her in the public gallery could see her whole body trembling. The magistrate sat at the head of the courtroom behind a desk diagonally in front of Anna, on her right. His complexion was ruddy. He read some papers while they all waited. When he began to speak, she realised that her ears were ringing and the sounds around her were muffled. Her stomach churned. She focused on Scott, who was sitting at a table opposite the magistrate, and didn't take her eyes off him, in case the room spun away and she fell from her seat. He stood up and said something to the magistrate about witnesses.

Witnesses? What witnesses? Had someone seen what had happened?

He sat down again. He nodded at Anna and smiled, but her face felt frozen.

She jumped as the magistrate's voice boomed around the room. She managed to turn her head slowly to face him without falling over, and concentrated hard so she could understand what he was saying.

'The matter before me is committed to the Supreme Court of New South Wales, on a future date, yet to be decided.'

He had barely finished his statement when the legal teams stood up, and the people behind her began muttering and moving from their seats. Was that it? While she was relieved it was over, she was terrified at now being one step closer to prison or – worse – release.

*   *   *

Scott ushered her out of the court into a corridor, then into a small room. She sat down, legs shaking. He sat down opposite her. 'How are you doing?'

She nodded, not trusting herself to speak.

'As I said, it was nothing to worry about. The prosecution are happy with the charge of infanticide, which is good: they're accepting that you were mentally ill at the time. We just need to wait for the date now, then we can enter your plea.'

'How long?' Her voice caught; her throat was dry.

'At least a couple of months. Plenty of time.'

She nodded again. Plenty of time for what? To wait for her life to be decided for her? To prepare herself for prison? To waste away in a psychiatric hospital?

Scott put his hand on her shoulder. 'Anna, it'll be OK. I don't think anyone wants to punish you.'

But what he didn't understand was that Anna wanted to be punished.

'Can you take me back now?' Her head was buzzing and her body was so heavy now, so tired. 'I want to go back.'

He stood up. 'Of course. Come on.'

Outside on the street, the cameras were still there. She clenched her fists, but kept her eyes down and ignored the shouts and questions from the reporters. As she and Scott walked along the pavement towards the car, her eyes were drawn to the left, towards a figure standing against the wall of the building. Before even registering his face, she knew it was Tony. She hadn't seen him since the day she'd been charged. She tilted her head a little and a smile started to spread across her face. Her body pulled towards him like a car left to drift through traffic.

'Tony!' she called.

He was leaning against the wall. His eyes were red.

'You came!' She stopped. Scott stopped too and took a step back to give them space.

Tony looked up briefly, then dropped his eyes again. He nodded.

'I . . . You haven't been . . .'

He shook his head. 'Anna, not here.'

She looked around her; heat radiated from her face. 'Can you come and see me, then? Please – I need to see you.'

'I'll try . . .'

She knew that he didn't mean it: he wouldn't try. He wanted to stop her making a scene, to make her go away. She knew him too well; had he forgotten that? As she stared at him, the sounds around her faded away until it was just the two of them. Just like on their wedding day. Then, too, the crowds, the noise, the frenzy had all disappeared and it was just them.

'Tony,' she whispered. 'Please. I'm sorry.'

'Don't . . .'

'I am, I'm sorry!' She could barely stop herself from shrieking.

He looked away from her with tears in his eyes, then she found herself walking forward again, or maybe he was walking away. It didn't really matter.

*　　*　　*

Back at the hospital, she crawled into bed fully dressed. For once, the nurses had let her go back to her room after lunch rather than forcing her to endure group therapy. And they'd given her some extra medication. The room was bright; she thought about getting up again to close the curtains. Instead, she pulled the blankets over her head and closed her eyes. It was stuffy under the sheet; she enjoyed the feeling of being smothered and running out of oxygen. Her warm breath filled the pockets of space around her face and she felt herself start to drift away.

There was a knock at the door.

She jolted awake, and it was all she could do not to cry. She just wanted some time to herself.

'Anna!' It was one of the male nurses. 'There's someone to see you. Are you awake?'

As if she could sleep with someone yelling two metres away from her.

'Anna. Visitor. Do you want to see them or not?'

She opened her eyes. A visitor? Tony had come after all. She sat up quickly and swung her legs over the side of the bed. Her head spun; she cleared her throat. 'Yes, please. Coming. I'm coming.'

'In the common room.'

Anna felt her eyes close again, weighed down by the medication, but she raised her eyebrows, hoping that the muscles of her forehead could help lift her eyelids. She stood up and shuffled towards the door.

*   *   *

Ursula sat on the edge of a saggy brown chair and tried not to breathe too deeply. The unmistakable smell of stale sweat and smoke had soaked into the walls and furniture. She looked at her fingernails to avoid catching anyone's eye. Even the nurse who had shown her to this room looked suspect. What kind of professional had pierced eyebrows? She glanced around her. In the centre of the room was a circle of mismatched chairs, with a space where the two seats that the nurse had dragged over to the window had been. The walls were covered in poster paper with vividly coloured drawings, collages and poems. It was more like a junior school classroom than an adult hospital. There was an old pool table in the far corner with shiny felt and one leg resting on some folded-up napkins. There were no cues or balls; at least that was something. She didn't like the idea of dangerous patients having easy access to potential weapons. She wasn't quite sure that it was safe in here: she had already been approached by a man who asked her some frankly rude and personal questions before he was escorted away by a nurse. She uncrossed her legs, crossed them the other way, then looked through her handbag.

She heard the creak of the door handle, and the door swung open. She looked up and stared as Anna staggered into the room. Anna's arms were stiff by her sides; she was walking like an old woman. Her black dress was crumpled: was that what she wore to court this morning? Her loose hair was lank and tangled, her face was puffy. She didn't look like the beautiful young woman who had married her son. Ursula swallowed and thought about just saying hello and leaving again. No, there was something she had to say. She realised she was still staring, so she fixed a smile on her face that didn't quite reach her eyes.

Anna walked towards her. She didn't look surprised, or happy, as Ursula had expected; she looked disappointed. Ursula waited until Anna sat down opposite her and the nurse walked away before she spoke.

'How are you, Anna?'

Anna didn't move. Her voice was quiet, slurred. 'Fine. How are you?'

Ursula gave a businesslike nod. 'I'm not doing too well, really. As you can imagine.' She watched Anna's face, saw her look down, saw her bite her lip. Ursula sat up straighter, and spoke louder. 'This won't take long. I just have a few things to say, then I'll go.' She hoped Anna couldn't hear the trembling in her voice. She needed to keep calm, do this, then leave.

'Is Tony here?' Anna said in a small, hopeful voice.

'Tony? No. Look, Anna . . .' Ursula took a deep breath. 'I think it's best if you don't see Tony for now.'

'What?' Anna looked straight at her, her eyes wide, confused.

Ursula looked away. She felt terrible saying it out loud, but she had thought about nothing else for days. She needed to protect her own family, and herself. They needed to deal with their grief, and that couldn't happen while everyone was so caught up with Anna's drama. 'I'm sorry,' she mumbled, 'but I think it's best if you don't see our family any more.'

Anna opened her mouth as if to speak, but said nothing. She slumped back in the chair and stared at her.

Ursula couldn't meet Anna's eyes. If she did, she might relent, might apologise for saying such a terrible thing to the woman she had once thought of as her daughter. But she knew that this was the only way she could look after her own children.

She leaned down and picked up her leather bag from the floor. The shoulder strap slipped through her sweaty hand, so she bent down again, then looked up, tears threatening to give her away. Anna was still just sitting there, staring. Couldn't she even think of something to say? Why didn't she argue, plead, beg? Was Anna really that cold?

She shook her head. 'How could you? Dear God, what kind of mother could kill her own child?' Her voice broke and tears began to fall. She stood up and stared at Anna, whose face had begun to quiver. Ursula's face hardened.

'Goodbye, Anna.'

She walked out without looking back.

*   *   *

Anna didn't call out to Ursula, didn't say anything. She just sat there, looking at the indent on the pilled brown chair where her mother-in-law had sat only moments ago. She rubbed her hands over her face, pinching her cheeks, unable to believe what she had just heard. Tears streamed down her face but she didn't make a sound.

Rachel appeared and sat in the empty seat. 'Anna? What is it?'

She couldn't form any thoughts, let alone speak them.

'Do you want to tell me what she said?' Rachel asked.

Anna shook her head, then somehow found the words. 'Nothing I don't deserve.'

As she said it, she knew it was true. What did she expect? That people would tell her it was OK, that they forgave her? That she could go back to her normal life as if nothing had changed? Of course that couldn't happen.

This was exactly what she deserved.

*   *   *

For the next few days, Anna did as she was asked: she took her medication, she answered Dr Morgan's questions, and she ate what they put in front of her. But she was thinking all the time. It wasn't like before: her thoughts weren't rushing around in panic, nor were they slow and sluggish. Her thoughts were clear, and they were calm.

Dr Morgan was right: she was better now. The ECT, the tablets, the therapy; it had all done its job. She couldn't really remember being ill, but when she looked back she knew that she had been in a terrible way. The old Anna, her true self, was coming back. But that didn't change the fact that she had killed Jack.

Whenever she was alone, she thought about her future. The idea of going to prison didn't bother her now; it was preferable to going home. She knew what prisoners thought of child killers, but threats and beatings would be better than whispers and gossip. However, Scott had told her that even if she was sent to jail, the maximum sentence she would get was twenty-five years. Not life. One day she'd have to walk out, and what would she do then? She'd be over fifty. She'd have no friends, no job, no relationships. No children. Tony didn't want her; he wouldn't wait for her. No one would ever trust a woman who'd gone crazy and killed her child.

All she wanted was to have her family back, Tony and Jack.

That was impossible.

She knew, deep down, what she'd been doing at the top of that cliff. The only option was to succeed this time. Everyone would be better off: Tony wouldn't have to be tortured by his sense of obligation to stick by her; Ursula would be relieved; no one would have to worry about the safety of their children around her. Her mum; well, she would be sad. She'd be devastated. She pushed those thoughts away, and began to make a mental list of her options. As she did so, she felt better than she had for weeks.

Every day, Anna took the little plastic cup from the nurses at medication time and poured her tablets into her mouth. She used her tongue to push them down into the space between her gum and her cheek, then funnelled a mouthful of water straight down her throat. As soon as the nurse left, Anna spat the tablets into a pouch made from a piece of paper, then slipped it into the corner of her pillowcase.

She would know when she had enough.

CHAPTER TWENTY-EIGHT

Four weeks after
Saturday, 17 October 2009

Tony stepped out of a taxi then nodded to the doorman shuffling around outside the pub. Sean had insisted that he come out for a few drinks, said it would do him good to get out of the house. He hadn't had the energy to say no, but now he wished he had.

The bouncer pulled open the heavy door and the thump of the music spilled out into the dark Paddington street. He took a deep breath, ducked his head, then stepped into the thick air inside the pub. The door closed behind him. He stood at the edge of the room trying to see Sean's red hair among the hundreds of bodies bunched together. He stumbled as a girl pushed past him, too busy shrieking at someone to notice that she had spilled her neon pink drink on his jeans. He glared at her, then his eyes filled with tears; he blinked them away. Anna would know how to get the stain out. But he couldn't ask her things like that any more.

He headed towards the bar. He'd stay for an hour, then go home. His house was empty and sad, but that suited him at the moment.

'Tony, mate! Over here!'

He craned his neck and saw Sean's hand waving above the canopy of bodies. Tony turned back to the bar, ordered two beers, then pushed his way towards his friend, holding the schooners high as if he was wading through a river.

Standing with a group of four other guys, Sean grabbed one of the beers and took a big gulp. 'You made it – brilliant! These are the guys from work I was telling you about: Dave, Phil, Macca, Paolo . . .'

Tony could see the euphoria in Sean's flushed cheeks and wide eyes, and envied him: Tony didn't think he'd ever laugh again. He sighed; he had to stop thinking like this. He forced himself to smile then shook Sean's workmates' hands. They said hello, then returned to their conversation. Did they know? Of course they knew: Sean was bound to have told them. Tony could always tell when people knew; they did anything they could to avoid mentioning babies, or wives, or death. Which meant there was very little to talk about, and instead they didn't say anything at all.

He realised that Sean was shouting something to him above the noise, and he bent down so that his ear was close to Sean's mouth.

'We're going to the Cross later, you should come. Macca can get our names on the door, there's a new club open . . .'

He nodded and sculled his beer. His fingers tingled and his limbs relaxed as the alcohol coursed through him. He pointed to the bar and his empty glass, and headed off for another round.

*   *   *

A few hours later, the group staggered out of the pub onto Oxford Street and started to walk towards Kings Cross, each holding their left arm out to try to flag a taxi. The cold air jolted Tony back to reality. 'Sean, mate, I think I should go home . . .' He was surprised at how slurred his voice was.

Sean stopped in surprise, then reached up and put his arm around Tony. 'What? Nah, mate, you haven't been out with me for ages. Come on, it'll do you good to have a night out.'

Tony was still walking the wrong way. Home was the other direction; he was getting further and further away. He knew he could turn around, but what else did he have to do? There was no one waiting for him except the dog. He looked behind him and pictured it: the street would be quiet, dark, full of houses with people sleeping after watching a movie at home. He looked forward again, towards Darlinghurst. He felt himself being pulled towards the sound of cars revving, swaying people screaming and laughing, and he wanted to be amongst it, just for a few hours, to feel part of life again. He knew he would regret it later, but he patted Sean on the back. 'All right, maybe just one.'

Sean hugged Tony, and they stumbled forward, just as a taxi pulled up and emptied its load of passengers at their feet. They hopped in, and Sean shouted to his mates further down the street, 'Meet you there!'

The club, when they got there, was even darker, even louder, even busier than the pub had been. Tony followed Sean to the bathrooms. Inside, Sean knocked on a cubicle door, and Macca opened it and let them in. Someone was bending over the cistern, snorting a line of coke through a rolled up twenty-dollar note.

Tony started giggling. 'It's like a fucking tardis.'

They all laughed.

'Shh.' Sean waved his hand at them as he leaned down and moved his head in circles around the toilet lid to snort up any stray coke. He sniffed loudly, licked the end of the rolled-up note, and handed it to Tony.

Tony hadn't done this for years; Anna was never into it. But it felt so familiar. This was who he used to be, before he met Anna. He used to have fun, he had nothing to worry about, just did what he wanted. Right now, this was what he wanted to do. He put the rolled-up note into his left nostril, held the right nostril closed with his finger, crouched down and inhaled.

*　　*　　*

Tony felt alive. He was on the dance floor, moving with the crowd. Sean was next to him, his fist pumping into the air along with the dance music. Opposite Tony, a girl with shiny lips swayed in slow motion. He moved towards her. Her short dress swung over her thighs, and with each flick of her hips it seemed to lift just a little bit higher. She wore a long string of beads that fell between her breasts. Tossing her hair back she looked up at Tony through dark eyelashes. She turned around so that her back was to him and raised her hands, throwing her head back again and writhing her hips towards him. He put his hands on the girl's waist and felt the thin strap of her underwear beneath her dress. She stepped back, fitting perfectly into his groin, then spun around to face him. He still held her waist, and moved his hands a little lower as she put her hands on his chest and gripped his shirt. She stared up at him, biting her lip.

The room began to spin. Letting go of the girl, Tony staggered back to the table and slumped into a seat. The girl was on the edge of the dance floor near him, dancing, staring at him. He rubbed his face then glanced back at her. Shit, she looked like she was still at school. Tony could see the sweat stains on her dress under her arms, and the black smudges of mascara around her eyes. What was he doing? He was married; he had fathered a child. He shook his head and looked away. He needed some water, some food, and he needed to get out of here. He looked for Sean and saw him leaning against a pillar, talking to some other young girl.

Tony walked over. 'I'm off.'

'Really?' Sean stood up straighter and brushed the girl away. 'All right, mate, I'll come too.'

'You don't have to.'

'I've had enough. Come on, let's get out of here. Let's go get a burger.'

Tony nodded and walked towards the door.

More than anything, he wished he was going home to Anna.

CHAPTER TWENTY-NINE

One week before

Monday, 7 September 2009

Tony woke up to the sound of Jack crying. He looked at the digital clock next to the bed: almost six. He turned over in bed; the other side was empty. Jack was wailing. Where was Anna? He rubbed his eyes, got out of bed, went through to the baby's room and picked him up, then stumbled along the hall. He could hear music coming from the living room.

When he walked in the smell of vinegar was overpowering. Anna was in her pyjamas, kneeling on the floor and rubbing at the glass doors with a tea towel. There was a pile of used rags in the corner, next to a bucket of soapy water. The rug from under the coffee table was rolled up, and the kitchen stools were stacked upside down on the bench. Anna turned towards him; strands of her hair had escaped her ponytail and were stuck to her face with sweat. Tony's pulse quickened.

'Anna, what are you doing?'

She grinned. 'Morning! Oh, Jack's up, I didn't hear him. Just hold him for a bit longer, will you? Now that you're both up I can vacuum.' She stood up, wiped her forehead with the back of her hand, then started to walk towards the hallway cupboard.

Tony put out his arm as she passed him. 'Don't be silly. When did you get up?'

'I don't know, a while ago. It won't take long.'

Jack squirmed and fussed, mouthing at Tony's bare shoulder. 'He's hungry, babe. Just sit down, I'll make you some tea. You don't need to be doing the cleaning —'

'Hungry, hungry, he's always hungry . . . Come here, you hungry hippo.' She held her arms out to Jack, and Tony passed him to her. Anna lifted her pyjama top and latched Jack onto her breast, then sat on the edge of the sofa, gesticulating with her free hand. 'I just feel so much better today, normal again – well, better than normal, really. I don't feel tired, I have energy. I woke up starving! There's nothing in the cupboards, so I'm going to go shopping today to restock the fridge. What have we been eating? This has gone on long enough, I need to be more organised. Go and get ready for work, I'll make you breakfast – what do you want, eggs? I'll make you eggs and toast.'

Tony scanned her face, confused. This was a complete turna-round. How could she have changed so much overnight? 'Anna, slow down. You're talking too fast. I'm glad that you feel better, but you'll wear yourself out. You need to go back to bed.'

'No, I'm fine! When I've fed him, I'm going to go for a big walk to the park, show Jack the ducks. I need to get fit again, I haven't been looking after myself. Then we'll go to the shops – I want to get back into cooking.'

'Anna, stop for a second.' His mouth was dry; something wasn't right. 'Are you OK?'

'Yes!' Anna frowned. 'You ask if I'm OK when I feel sad, now I feel great and you're still going on at me!'

Her voice rose and Tony thought she was about to cry. She was right: he should be thankful, it was good to see her bright and active again. He stepped forward, ready to hug her, but she smiled again and waved him away with her free hand.

'I'm fine! Go and have your shower. I've ironed your shirt, it's hanging in the laundry – that's one less thing for you to do!'

He hesitated, not sure how to react. She was saying all the right things, but why had her mood changed so suddenly? Maybe the tablets were working after all. He looked at her again: she was talking to Jack as she fed him. He turned around, glanced back at her one more time, then went into the bedroom to get ready for work.

*   *   *

Anna pushed the pram out of the front gate and smiled. It was a beautiful day. The warm breeze tickled her face and the sun had tinted everything lemon. She took a big breath in; even the air smelled fresh, like citrus. She straightened her back and stood tall, pushing the pram with her arms straight out in front of her. This was life, not her pathetic tears about not getting enough sleep. This was the world at work: smartly dressed women waiting for the bus to their glamorous jobs in the city; beautiful children chattering on their way to school; cars waiting impatiently at the traffic lights.

Anna walked faster. There were so many other mothers out pushing strollers, she'd never realised before. They were all so thin, so well dressed. She looked down at her clothes. She should have worn shorts, rather than these faded jeans. And she needed some fancy new trainers, not these old thongs that were already rubbing the tops of her feet. She touched her hair, still wet from the shower, and wished she'd worn her contacts instead of squinting through her thick glasses, the lenses dotted with dried tears. How had she got to this state?

'Morning!'

Anna jumped. A woman in tight black lycra pants and a clingy turquoise singlet smiled at her. Her baby, maybe a month or two older than Jack, was fast asleep in the stroller. Anna looked up again, ready to chat, but already they were too far past each other. She bit her lip. She should have said hello, stopped to ask about the baby, and asked the woman if she wanted to go for a coffee. If she had been brave enough, she could have asked her how she coped, how she slept, how she managed to look so good and not lose herself in the monotony of caring for a newborn. But by the time she had thought of all this, it was too late.

Jack was still asleep. Anna picked up her pace again, determined to leave her negativity behind. With each step, her breath became more laboured but her mood lifted futher. She went into a cafe on the beachfront and bought a takeaway coffee, then went to the park.

Once she'd put the brakes on the stroller and draped a muslin cloth over the hood to keep the sun off Jack, she sat down on a bench and sipped her coffee through the little hole in the plastic lid. It tasted amazing. She removed the lid and licked off the chocolate powder stuck to the inside. Next to the bench, gulls pecked at the rubbish bin and the discarded fish and chip containers strewn around it. She looked over towards the green oval. Two toddlers screeched and chased a ball while their mothers sat talking on the grass beside them. A man wearing industrial headphones drove a lawnmower up and down the pitch.

Jack stirred. Anna lifted the muslin cloth, peered into his pram and smiled at him. He smiled back.

It was his first smile.

She unstrapped him and cradled him in her left arm, squeezing his warm little body tight. His eyes were open and he gazed up at her. She didn't want to put him down; she wanted to snuggle into him and cuddle him and protect him. This was the feeling she'd expected from the start, the one she'd waited for. She almost cried with the joy of it; everything was going to be OK. She had known that she didn't really need medication, and she had been right.

It was time to go; she had things to do. She put Jack back in the stroller, tucking the muslin wrap around his legs. 'We're going to go to the shops and buy Daddy something nice for dinner. What will we cook?' She sprung up, pushing the pram ahead of her as though she was in a race, then sprinted across the road. She would cook some Thai curry.

In the supermarket, she picked up a jar of curry paste, read the ingredients, then put it back again. These sauces were full of nasty additives; it would be much nicer to make it from scratch. Tony deserved it; she'd been so horrible to him lately. She rushed up and down the aisles looking for the ingredients: ginger, garlic, chilli, vegetables, chicken. Damn it, she needed galangal. The recipe definitely had galangal in it. She searched among the pile of ginger, in case some was hiding in there. None. She raced round to the spices aisle looking for some in a jar but there wasn't any. She'd have to walk home, get the car, and drive to Chinatown, or out to Cabramatta; they'd definitely have some there. Come to think of it, the vegetables were much nicer there. She'd just buy the chicken from here. And some rice, just in case.

Anna bounded up to the express aisle and hummed as she waited, leaning on one leg, then the other. She paid, then rushed out of the shop, no longer feeling her thongs rubbing. It was hotter now. She turned her face up to the sun and closed her eyes, then giggled as she tripped over an uneven kerb. Jack's arms shot forward as if to stop himself falling into a hole.

'Oops, sorry, little one!'

His arms relaxed by his side and he fell asleep again with his feet stretched out in the warm sun. Anna looked at his tiny toes. She needed to buy some baby sunscreen, especially now that she was going to do lots of walking. And a water bottle to keep in the pram, one of those metallic ones to keep the water cool. And some new running shoes, a nice pair. She would do that after she found the galangal.

*　*　*

Tony opened the front door slowly, unsure of what to expect. He had been worried about Anna all day; he was glad that she felt better, but something about it made him uneasy. He could hear the television blaring from the lounge room as he closed the door behind him and put his laptop bag on the floor.

'Anna?'

She rushed down the hall to the door and flung her arms around him.

'Wow! This is a nice welcome home.' Tony hugged her then held her arms with his hands and took a step back. She wore an apron, smudged with food. She was smiling. 'Are you wearing lipstick?'

'Yes. I've had enough of being fat and frumpy.' Anna extricated herself from his grip and walked towards the kitchen, beckoning him to follow.

'Babe, you're not —'

'We've had a great day. I've realised that I've just got to keep going. I'm not the only one who's not getting any sleep. I have a new plan: every day I'm going to go walking in the morning after Jack's feed, and I've joined the gym – I'll just put him in the creche. And we're going to the movies tomorrow; they have a special session where you can take your baby – how good is that? Now, come in and sit down, I've made you a green curry, fresh!'

Tony looked at her and smiled. He shouldn't have been worried. It was just that he'd become so used to seeing her miserable that he'd forgotten how lively and vivacious she really was.

She pulled a cold bottle of riesling out of the fridge. 'One won't hurt.' She took two glasses from the cupboard and poured generously, then licked the foot of the glass where she had spilled some. 'Yum.'

Tony took his glass and tasted the wine. It trickled down his throat, cold and sweet. He let out a deep breath. Thank God. Anna seemed her old self again. He had missed her.

He walked over to the bassinette, next to the couch. Jack was inside, fast asleep. 'What a handsome little fella,' Tony whispered.

Anna came over and leaned her head against him, and he put his arm around her. This was what he had imagined it would be like; the three of them, happy and content. At that moment, he knew that everything was going to be fine.

CHAPTER THIRTY

Six weeks after

Monday, 26 October 2009

Anna reclined on her hospital bed, reading a tattered old romance novel that she'd found in the ward bookshelf. Not so long ago, she could barely concentrate on a column in a gossip magazine, but she was enjoying this book. Reading took her back to life before this, when she used to spend hours with a book in the garden chair with Jessie asleep beside her. She missed that.

Anna looked forward to this time of day, after lunch and group therapy, when she could rest. She had become used to the order and routine. It meant that she didn't have to think too hard, and that meant she could forget. Prison would be the same. The fact that she liked being institutionalised scared her. But whatever happened, it wouldn't last forever. At some stage she would have to leave and rejoin the world.

There was a knock at her door. Rachel looked into the room. 'Anna, Mr Hardy is here to see you.'

Anna nodded, and put her book facedown on the bed. She ran her fingers through her hair to smooth it.

Scott walked in, his shoes clicking on the floor. He wore a crisp white shirt with thin threads of blue and red woven through it, and chunky silver cufflinks on the French cuffs. Tony had a shirt like that.

'Hi, Anna. I've got some news.'

Her heart began to beat faster. She didn't want news; she wanted to stay in this state of uncertainty. News meant change. 'Yes?'

He sat down next to the bed, unzipped his leather document wallet, and took out a thick sheaf of papers held together with a bulldog clip. He reached into an inside pocket of his suit jacket, flashing the blue silk lining, and took out a silver pen. Anna held her breath.

He spoke softly, almost apologetically. 'We've got a date.'

She breathed out. 'A date? For the trial?'

'It's not a trial, it's a hearing. We're pleading guilty, remember? The infanticide charge fits your case exactly. There's no question that you were mentally ill, and no doubt it was a direct result of birth or breastfeeding, the way it's defined in the law.' He stabbed his pen on the paper. 'It's our best chance of avoiding a custodial sentence. We enter your plea, the judge will read the submissions from me and from the prosecution, then he'll set a date for sentencing. It's quite straightforward.'

Anna clenched her jaw as she nodded. She hated people talking to her as though she was a child. Of course she remembered; it was all she had been able to think about. And *we're* pleading guilty? *Our* best chance? Scott didn't have to stand up and admit that he'd killed his child, he didn't have to face going to jail or returning to a life that was completely destroyed. But she didn't bother pointing this out to him. It didn't matter.

'But there's no guarantee, is there? I mean, anything could happen. I could still go to prison.'

Scott twirled the pen round with his thumb and forefinger. 'Well, I'm really hopeful we'll get a community order. You're pleading guilty, the prosecution have accepted the charge, you've never been in trouble before and we can easily prove you're of good character.'

She looked out of the window. 'I don't care anyway.'

'Anna, please don't worry —'

'It's OK.'

'What's OK?'

She turned and looked him in the eye. 'Tell them I'll go to prison.'

'What?' He stopped twirling his pen.

'It's the best place for me.'

Scott leaned forward. 'Anna, I'm here to provide you with the best legal representation that I can, and I wouldn't be doing my job if I didn't try to keep you *out* of prison.'

She shook her head and looked away. There was no point discussing it with him; she'd already made up her mind what she had to do. 'So when is it, then?'

He glanced down at the papers on his lap. 'Nineteenth of November.'

'November,' she said. 'Next month.' Her hands began to shake.

Scott put his hand on hers. 'We'll be ready.'

She blinked back tears. 'Thanks . . . Thanks for trying to help me . . .'

'My pleasure.' Scott shook her hand, gathered up his things and walked out.

The door opened again almost immediately. She quickly wiped her eyes, thinking he must have forgotten something.

'Only me,' said Dr Morgan as she walked in and closed the door. 'I heard that your lawyer was here, and I wanted to see how you were feeling.'

Anna raised her eyebrows. She wanted to find out the gossip, more like. Dr Morgan looked tired today and there was a run in her stockings. Anna knew that sometimes she worked all night in the hospital. Looking after crazy people like her must be tiring. How many other patients did she have? Anna had realised that she'd been naive to think Dr Morgan really cared about her; she was just another patient to her, just more work before she headed home to her undoubtedly perfect family. She turned her head away from the psychiatrist.

'Anna?'

She spun around and spat the words out. 'It's on the nineteenth of November. The hearing.' But her voice broke as she said it. She laid her head back on the pillow and looked up at the ceiling, trying to blink away her tears.

Dr Morgan sat down. 'Are you OK?'

She shrugged.

'I suppose it's good in a way to have a date, to know what's happening, but on the other hand, it makes it all very real, doesn't it?'

Anna didn't want to talk about her feelings right now; she had no idea how she felt. 'It's fine, I'm fine,' she said impatiently. 'Had to happen.'

'Do you want me to call your mum?'

She shook her head. She was a grown woman, not a child. 'I'll do it.'

Dr Morgan leaned back and clasped her hands around one knee. 'I've been waiting to find out when the hearing is before we make plans about your treatment from here on.'

'What do you mean?'

'Well, we need to decide when you'll leave hospital – whether you stay until the hearing, or the sentencing, or whether you go home before that.'

She sat up, her eyes wide. What did she mean? Go home before the hearing? 'But the police said . . . My bail . . . I have to stay here!'

'No, no, you just have to comply with your treatment; that doesn't mean you have to stay in hospital.'

She couldn't do this; it wasn't in Anna's plan. She'd thought she had more time. 'I'm not ready!'

Dr Morgan held a hand out towards her. 'Anna, calm down. I'm not discharging you today, I'm just saying that it may happen before you go to court, but you'd still have all the support you need from us. There's a long way to go before we get to that point. I'm sorry for bringing it up, I thought you understood that . . .'

Anna grabbed the box of tissues from her bedside table, whipped out a few, then wiped her eyes. She looked away from Dr Morgan. No one was ever honest with her. No one trusted her any more, and that was how it would always be from now on: people tiptoeing around her, worried about how she'd react, worried that she'd become insane if they upset her. She couldn't live like that. Her breath came in shallow gasps. It felt as though she'd been dumped by a wave at the beach, and now she was flailing around trying to work out which way was up. She wasn't strong enough to right herself.

The time had come; she needed to act soon.

*   *   *

It was dark. Anna had spent the rest of the afternoon tidying up her room and thinking about tonight. She was calm, content even. She had called her mum, thanked her and told her she loved her. Wendy would be all right, she knew. She had thought about contacting Emily, but worried that she would know something was wrong. There was no one else to call; Tony wouldn't answer anyway.

The nurse had switched the ward lights out over an hour ago, but a dim light crept in under her door. She heard the faint tinny sounds of a television coming from the nurses' station. There were three night nurses on, as usual. They had just done their rounds, checking everyone was where they should be. They wouldn't be back for another four hours; she had plenty of time.

Anna rolled over and sighed loudly, listening for a reaction from outside her room. She coughed. Nothing.

Slipping her hand into her pillowcase she found the little paper parcel of tablets in the corner. She moved her hand as if fluffing up her pillow. Still no one came. Some of the pills had stuck to the paper; she peeled them off. She slowly raised her hand and slipped about half of the tablets into her mouth, then reached for the glass of water by her bed. She gulped down the water then did the same with the rest of the tablets. She hoped it would be enough.

Turning onto her side she pulled the blankets up to her chin. She pictured the tablets being washed down by the cool water, hissing and fizzing as they dissolved into her bloodstream. She closed her eyes, breathed deeply, and willed sleep to take her.

CHAPTER THIRTY-ONE

Six weeks after
Monday, 26 October 2009

'Anna, can you hear me? Wake up! Call Dr Morgan, quick!'

Her head was pounding with pain. She was tired, so heavy, sinking down into the deep, into the dark. She heard a groan, and knew it was her own.

'Anna, can you hear me? Open your eyes.'

Someone was shaking her. She wanted to tell them to stop, to leave her alone, but no words came out. Suddenly, her limbs jerked involuntarily as her sternum burned in agony. Someone was grinding the bone with their knuckles. She heard herself cry out.

'Get the trolley, let's get her over to Emergency.'

And then she was rattling along, her shoulder blades, her heels, the back of her head banging and bumping on cold metal. She was sure she was going to fall off, but she couldn't move, couldn't speak. Her left arm bounced to the edge of the trolley then hung off with her elbow locked out straight. Her hand whacked into something hard, and the pain shot up her arm.

She was still alive.

She had failed again.

*   *   *

Tony watched Anna sleeping. He had been just about to get into bed for another night of fitful sleep when the hospital called. He had driven to the Emergency department again, shaking and crying. He knew it was partly his fault: he'd broken his word. He hadn't

246

been to see her. When he'd reached the hospital, they'd led him straight to Anna. She was even in the same small room she'd been in that day. The nurse told him that they kept it free for the *psych patients*. The doctors told him that she would be fine. Apparently it was difficult to kill yourself with the tablets she had taken. But Anna hadn't known that. She was lucky, according to the doctor. It was as if they were talking about putting the wrong petrol in the car.

Tony didn't think she was lucky at all.

It was after midnight now. There were leads on her chest monitoring her heart, plastic tubes in her nostrils blowing oxygen into her lungs and a clip on her finger to make sure it was getting into her blood. The beep of the heart monitor was hypnotic. Tony rested two fingers on his own pulse and compared it to Anna's. His was faster.

He stroked the back of her hand, avoiding the tape that secured the plastic cannula. Asleep, she looked like his wife again. His eyes filled with tears. When would this end? He bit his lip as he allowed himself to think about what it would be like if she had succeeded. Back then, at the cliffs, or now. It wasn't like he hadn't thought it before, but that had been in anger. Now it was out of compassion. Or was it selfishness?

Anna's eyes fluttered open and she licked her lips. She took a while to focus on him, then gasped.

'Tony?' Her voice was a croak.

He nodded, smiled. 'I'm here.'

Anna looked away, but he could see her bottom lip quivering. He put his fingers on her forehead and brushed the hair out of her eyes. She turned back towards him with a hint of a sad smile.

'I've missed you,' she said.

Tony stiffened, took his hand away. Was that why she had done this? Did she think it would make him come back? That because he was here, everything would return to normal?

'Is that all you've got to say? You missed me?' He felt a wave of anger go through him again.

She reached her arm out towards him. 'Tony —'

'How could you? Haven't we been through enough? How could you do this to me? To your mum?'

'I —'

He clenched his fists, shook his head. All his worry now turned to fury. 'I can't believe you'd be so . . . so selfish!' he shouted. 'You must know what I've been through, and now you'd leave me to deal with this too? Did you even think about me? Jesus, your mum is frantic, she's given up her life to be here with you, to help you, the doctors have done everything they can, you've got a brilliant lawyer, and still you'd leave me to pick up the pieces?'

She shook her head, crying, 'I'm sorry!'

'Did you think I wouldn't care? You're my wife: what did you think this would do to me?' He thumped his fist down on the arm of the chair. His face burned.

'But you haven't been to see me. I thought —'

'And that's why? That's your reason? It's my fault?' He couldn't believe what she'd just said. She was blaming him? As if he hadn't already tortured himself with what he could have done differently. He knew he wasn't faultless, but he wasn't solely responsible either. And he certainly wasn't responsible for Anna deciding she'd be better off dead. That was her choice.

He pointed his index finger at her. 'Don't you dare put this on me. It's not my fault, OK? I did . . . I've been doing the best I can!'

He had run out of energy. He leaned back in the chair, out of breath, and stared into the corner of the room, not trusting himself to look at her.

'I didn't mean . . .' Anna began, in a timid voice. 'Of course it's not your fault. It's all mine. I just mean . . . what's the point? How can I live after this? Everything is gone now . . .'

Tony heard her sob quietly, and he sighed. He wished he could stay angry and just walk away, but time after time he was pulled back towards her. 'The point, Anna, is that it's not all about you. There's more than just you to think about. I have to live with this too.'

Her voice was clearer now. 'But you didn't do it, did you? It was me.'

The room was silent except for the beeping of the monitors.

He cleared his throat, but his voice still quivered as he spoke. 'Just promise me something. Promise me you won't try to hurt yourself again.' He couldn't look at her.

'Do you hate me?'

'Hate you? God, of course I don't hate you.'

Anna hugged herself with her arms. 'I would if I was you. I hate myself.'

He looked at her. She looked so small. 'I hate what you've done, I hate that this has happened to you, to us. It's not you I hate.'

'OK. I promise . . .'

Tony leaned towards the bed and wrapped his arms around her; it felt so natural to have his wife in his arms, and suddenly he missed her so much and realised how lonely he'd been. They both sobbed. He forced himself to pull away and hold her at arm's length.

'I love you, Tony.'

He nodded. He couldn't bring himself to say it back to her; he no longer knew if it was true. And he couldn't let her think she could get what she wanted by trying to end her life. He wasn't convinced yet that he wasn't still being lied to; he hated to think that she might be manipulating him, but his sense of love and loyalty and family was completely shattered.

He looked into her eyes. 'We'll get through this, all right?' he said.

That was the best he could do.

*　*　*

Ursula walked along the pavement to Lisa's shop clutching a paper bag from the French patisserie at the end of the street. She didn't come to this area very often; there was little else here to interest her. There were a couple of cafes, full of university students, a second hand bookshop, and a few other clothes shops run by young designers like Lisa. She needed to talk to her daughter in person. Tony had called that morning and told her what Anna had done. He'd been at the hospital for hours with Wendy, waiting to see if she'd recover. Ursula hated the thought of Tony having to deal with this; he'd been through enough. It's not that she couldn't understand how distraught Anna was, but this was a selfish act, unforgiveable.

She walked in through the open door of Lisa's shop. Long racks stuffed with clothes stretched down either wall, and in the middle of the room was an old, faded wooden table stacked with belts and jewellery.

Lisa was standing behind another wooden table at the back of the shop. Beside the cash register was a jumbled pile of clothes that she was putting back on hangers. She looked up, smiled, then tilted her head and frowned. 'Mum, hi . . . What are you doing here?'

'Oh, I was just passing by. I thought you might want a treat.' She held out the white paper bag.

Lisa raised her eyebrows. 'Long way to come to bring me a snack . . . Not that I'll say no, of course.'

Ursula knew that Lisa was suspicious and understood why. It had been a long time since she had visited the shop. Ursula felt a twinge of shame, but she shouldn't need a reason to visit her daughter. She missed Lisa; they used to be so close. As she walked towards the back of the room, she looked at the clothes all around her. She was proud of her daughter for building up this business. She and Jim had promised to help her do this if she made the right choices in life. Lisa hadn't let them down.

She put the bag down on the counter, and began to rip it open. Her stomach started churning. 'I suppose I did have something I wanted to talk to you about. Have you heard about Anna?'

Lisa slid out the cardboard tray and picked up a purple macaron; she paused and looked at her mum. 'No. What's happened?'

'Tony hasn't called you? Maybe I shouldn't . . .'

'Mum! What is it?'

'Everything's OK.' She took a deep breath. She didn't want to upset Lisa, but she needed to know. And Ursula admitted to a strange sense of vindication in sharing the news; it confirmed that Anna was unstable, and made Ursula more convinced that she was right to distance herself from her. 'Look, she's all right now, but she tried to kill herself last night.'

Lisa dropped the macaron and clasped her hand to her mouth. 'Oh my God! What happened?'

Ursula put her hand on Lisa's arm. 'Don't worry, she's fine. Apparently she took an overdose. She saved up her tablets and took them all at once, so she must have been planning it for a while.' She thought about her own visit to Anna, a couple of weeks ago, but pushed away the guilt. She had no way of knowing how long Anna had been thinking of this. She looked back at Lisa, who was pale. 'Sorry, I didn't mean to shock you, sweetheart.'

Lisa shook her head. 'It's OK. I'm OK. It's all just so . . . so horrible. Poor Tony.'

'I know. He got the call late last night and spent most of the night at the hospital. Wendy's there now, and he's gone home to try to sleep. It's just one thing after another.'

'Maybe it would help if I go and see her. I suppose we've just gone back to normal, you know, while she's still waiting in hospital.' Lisa shook her head. 'I've been a bit torn, Mum. Sometimes I just don't know what I'd say to her. I don't want to take sides, but I feel so sorry for Tony. This is all so . . . so unbelievable, and I don't know whether to hug her or scream at her. Then I wonder if I'm being selfish —'

'Lisa, don't you go feeling guilty! We're all doing our best. Let's wait and see what Tony says.'

'How is he?' Lisa leaned against the counter. 'And Wendy?'

'Wendy's all right, she'll be OK. She's still at the hospital. And Tony, well, he's as good as can be expected, given what he's been through.'

'Excuse me a minute. I'll go and make us a coffee.' Lisa disappeared into the back of the shop.

Lisa had always been like that, never one to let anyone see her upset, and Ursula had always respected that. But all this business had made her think that maybe some things did need to be out in the open. She chewed slowly on a macaron until Lisa came back carrying two mugs of coffee; her eyes were red and her mascara was smudged.

'Lisa, while I'm here, there's something else I wanted to talk to you about.' She picked up her mug, took a big gulp of coffee, then put it down. She told herself that her hand shook from the caffeine, not nerves.

Lisa didn't look up; she picked at a macaron.

'I've been thinking a lot, you know, with all this . . .'

Lisa shook her head. 'Don't. Don't Mum, it's all in the past.'

'Love, we've never talked about it, it's important . . .'

'No, it's not. I don't even think about it. I don't want to talk about it. Just leave it alone.' Lisa scrunched up the paper bag and wiped the crumbs off the counter with her hand, then walked out to the back room again.

Ursula thought back to those months: the tears, the screaming, the silences. Lisa walking off, just like now. She felt sick. The macarons hadn't been a good idea, all that sugar was bound to make her nauseous.

A few moments later Lisa came back, her face redder than before. Ursula held her arms open and took a step towards her. 'I'm sorry, love, I shouldn't have . . .'

'It's fine, Mum.' Lisa picked up a dress from a cardboard box on the floor, ignoring her mother's invitation for a hug. 'Sorry, but I have to get back to work now.'

Ursula looked around the shop, which was empty except for the two of them, then sighed and nodded. She picked up her bag and walked back out onto the street, towards her car. As she approached, she saw a white piece of paper curled around her windscreen wiper. Her heart began to race. She leaned over the bonnet and snatched it. She had to use both hands to flatten it out. Of course. A bloody ticket.

She screwed it up in one hand and threw it in the gutter, then fumbled in her bag for the keys. She managed to clamber into the car just before she began to cry. Her breath came in gasps; she rested her head on the steering wheel and sobbed. All she had wanted to do was take her daughter a treat, make her happy.

Was nothing ever going to go right for her?

CHAPTER THIRTY-TWO

Six weeks after
Tuesday, 27 October 2009

Tony wrapped a beach towel around his damp board shorts just as the doorbell rang. He picked up his t-shirt from the bedroom floor, put it on, then went to answer the door.

Wendy stood on the front step, pale and wrung out. She looked up at Tony, shook her head, then walked into the house. He closed the door behind her, then hugged her.

'They've moved her back to the psychiatry ward now,' Wendy said. 'The medical doctors are happy with her.'

Tony sighed. 'Thank God. Come through.' They walked down the hallway into the kitchen. Used plates and cups covered the kitchen bench. 'Sorry about the mess.'

Wendy waved her hand at him. She sat on a stool with her back hunched. 'I can't believe it. Just when I thought she was getting there, you know, starting to get better, this happens . . .'

'I know.' Tony heard his voice thicken. He cleared his throat and turned towards the coffee machine. 'Do you want a coffee?'

She nodded.

He scooped ground beans into the metal filter then twisted it into the machine. 'I thought a surf might help. I tried to sleep when I got home from the hospital, but I couldn't stop thinking . . .'

He opened the cupboard and took out two mugs. One was Anna's favourite. He was about to put it back, but there were no others that were clean. He swallowed. It was only a cup; it didn't mean anything. He sighed, then filled a metal jug with milk and began to steam it. When the coffees were poured, he handed one to Wendy, kept Anna's mug for himself, and pulled up a stool to the kitchen bench.

'I'm sorry,' he said, sipping his drink.

'What for?'

'I feel like it's my fault. She said . . . she said she did it because she thought I hated her, because I hadn't been to see her.'

'God, Tony, she doesn't mean it, she's just —'

He shook his head. 'No, it's true, I haven't been to see her. I just couldn't.'

Wendy stared at her coffee. 'I understand.'

'I just keep thinking . . .'

She turned to him and leaned her head to the side. 'Thinking what?'

'That I should have been there.'

'Tony, you were —'

'No, I should have been at home with them, not rushing off to work and leaving it to Mum. I should have seen this coming, you know.' He reached for the sugar jar and stirred a teaspoonful into his drink. 'I knew she wasn't well. I should never have just accepted —'

Wendy put her hand on his arm. 'Don't, Tony. You could never have known this would happen.'

'You don't understand. I *did* know there was something wrong, I was just too busy . . . She wasn't sleeping, she was crying all the time, then one day she was really happy – too happy – over the top, you know. And then that morning, she was mumbling, behaving really strangely. What kind of husband am I? What kind of dad?' He looked away from Wendy and blinked back tears. It was true. He had known that something was seriously wrong with her, but he had convinced himself she was fine, just so he could have a break from the baby, and from her. He had used work as an excuse, an escape.

'Tony, this isn't your fault.' Wendy looked down, staring at her coffee. 'We've all had a part to play. I'm her mother, I know her better than anyone, maybe even better than you, and I never imagined . . . I should have got on that plane as soon as the baby was born, I should never have listened to her when she said she was OK.' She sighed, then looked to her right, out the window. Tony could tell she was imagining what might have happened if she'd done something differently, the same way that he had gone over and over different scenarios in his mind, each one leading to a better outcome.

She started to speak again, quietly. 'I should have known she was at risk. I should have warned her this could happen.' She reached for the box of tissues on the bench and handed some to Tony, then blew her nose.

Tony didn't ask her to explain; he was Anna's husband, Jack's father. 'I was meant to be looking after them . . .' His voice was thick.

Wendy slammed her coffee down, and he jumped. 'Stop, Tony! This isn't helping, this competition over who's to blame. No one is! It just happened.' She combed her fingers through her hair. 'I've spent years looking for someone to blame for everything that's gone wrong in my life, but I haven't found anyone yet. Life is just not fair and there's nothing we can do about it. And now, we have to be there for Anna. What else can we do?'

She stood up and walked towards the window. Tony looked at her back, and her ghostly reflection in the glass. She'd lost weight; she looked frail. From behind, you could almost mistake her for Anna. He bowed his head. Wendy was right: it didn't really matter what each of them could have done, because they didn't do enough and it was too late now. He walked over to her and put his hand on her shoulder. She clasped it, and they stood in silence.

'Can I ask you something?' he said.

'Of course.'

He took a big breath; he didn't want to say it, but it was time. He didn't know who else to ask. 'His room. I haven't been in it, since . . .' His voice broke. 'I just can't, I don't want to see it the way it was. It's still the same as it was when she left.'

Wendy nodded. 'Let me do it, Tony. You don't need to go in there.'

'Thanks.' He rubbed his face, then turned and hugged her. In a way, he thought, they had both lost their children. 'Come on, let's get out of here. We can go down to the beach for lunch.'

'OK.' Wendy sniffed and tried to smile.

'I'll just jump in the shower.'

Tony padded through to the bathroom and turned on the shower. The hot water stung his salty skin, and sand fell off him in clumps. He washed his hair in Anna's shampoo and inhaled, then rinsed and lathered it on again. That was the scent that was missing, from the pillows, the sofa, his clothes. For the first time in a long while, he thought about the possibility of her coming home, how nice it would be to just go back to their life, the way it used to be. But as he switched off the shower, the scent faded and that possibility disappeared.

*   *   *

There was someone sitting by Anna's bed. She didn't think she could move her head to see who it was without throwing up. She managed to look down at her chest. Who had taken her pyjamas off? The hospital gown that she now wore was stained with something black and sticky. She could smell vomit. She gagged.

'Anna, just breathe slowly. It's me, Dr Morgan. You're back on the ward now. Would you like some water?'

Anna attempted to nod, and someone put a straw in her mouth. She sipped, swilled the water round her mouth and swallowed. She could feel the liquid trickle down her throat into her stomach. She opened her mouth, like a child, and sipped from the straw again.

She managed to turn her head to the left. Dr Morgan sat on the chair, holding the glass of water. Her head was cocked to the side and she was frowning.

Anna quickly turned again. She wanted to jump out of bed and run away, or at least pull the covers over her head and pretend the doctor wasn't here. They'd moved her back to the ward, which meant they must think she was stable again. She thought of the looks on Tony's and her mother's faces this morning, and shame scorched her cheeks.

'Anna, it's OK.'

Anna shook her head. She couldn't look at Dr Morgan. She couldn't bear to see the disappointment in her eyes.

'I'm sorry,' she whispered.

Dr Morgan sighed. 'It's all right.'

'It's not. I'm sorry . . .'

'You don't need to say sorry to me, Anna. Can you look at me?'

'No.' *Go away*, she wanted to say. *Please go away.* She heard the creak of Dr Morgan's chair as she sat back.

'I need to tell you what's happening now. I'm worried about you. There will be someone watching you for now, and I'll review that every day, OK?'

'I won't do it again.' Anna turned her head towards the doctor just for a second. Dr Morgan wasn't frowning any more. She didn't look angry. 'I'm sorry I lied to you.'

'Lied?'

'You asked me if I had thoughts of hurting myself, and I said no.'

'Oh, I don't care about that. I'm just glad you're OK. Anna, this doesn't surprise me, you know. I can understand why you wanted to end your life. I don't think it means that you're necessarily ill again, or back to square one. I think it's a sign that you're starting to process everything, starting to understand what's happened and what it means for you. I think in your situation, it's entirely normal to feel like this.'

Anna raised her eyebrows. It had been easier when Tony shouted at her this morning, it fitted the way she felt about herself. Now, she didn't know what to do or say in response to the doctor's words, so she said nothing.

'That's not to say I'm not really worried. But I do understand. I hope you can talk to me about this, when you feel up to it.'

Anna nodded. She breathed out, and managed a slight smile. She closed her eyes again, and heard Dr Morgan walk out quietly. It was hard to think clearly. She hadn't expected understanding; she wasn't sure that she wanted it.

CHAPTER THIRTY-THREE

Six weeks after
Wednesday, 28 October 2009

Anna jumped as someone touched her hand. She had been sleeping, dreamlessly, the type of sleep you don't want to be woken from.

'Mum,' she said, sitting up. 'You scared me.' The corner of her mouth was wet with saliva; she wiped at it, then rearranged her night-gown, which had twisted as she slept. It was clean; she didn't remember changing it. 'How long have you been there? What time is it?'

'Not long, sweetheart. It's just after nine. How did you sleep?'

Anna blinked hard. 'In the morning?'

'Yes. I came in yesterday afternoon with Emily but you were asleep and we didn't want to wake you. Emily left you those.' Wendy pointed to a bunch of lilies in a plastic vase on the windowsill, obscuring the view of that horrible brown courtyard. Anna almost cried at the sight of them. Emily knew they were her favourites. 'She said she'll call you today, and she brought you chocolates and magazines too. I put them in your bedside cabinet.'

Anna smiled. Her dry lips cracked and stung. 'Can I have some water?'

Wendy passed her the tumbler. She noticed that her mother's eyes were swollen, bruised-looking. She glanced away, knowing that she was the cause, and sipped the water.

'Mum, are you OK? I —'

'I'm fine. I'm just a bit tired.'

She clutched at the glass of water with both hands. She needed to explain this to her mother. 'I'm sorry, it's my —'

Wendy shook her head. 'Shh. It doesn't matter. The important thing is that you're safe, you're OK, thank God.'

'I didn't want —'

Wendy sat up straighter. 'Anna. We went through this yesterday. No more apologies. You don't need to say anything, please.'

She had rarely heard her mother raise her voice. She nodded, then lay back down on the bed and pulled the blanket up, but it didn't reach her shoulders. She tugged at it, trying to pull the edges out from where they had been tucked tight under the mattress. Beginning to cry, she grabbed her pillow and pulled it further down the bed, shuffled her body down and gathered the sheets around her chin, then curled up on her side.

Wendy waited until she was still again. 'I wanted to say something.'

Anna closed her eyes.

'It's important. I've been thinking about it for weeks, months, years really. And now . . . I've already told Dr Morgan, because I thought it might help with your treatment. She asked, you know, if there was anyone in the family who had been ill. And I —'

'Don't, Mum.'

'But —'

'I know, OK?'

'I don't know what you think you know, but I need to explain.'

Anna threw back the covers and sat up again. Why was her mother bringing this up now? Didn't she have enough to deal with without listening to some confession? 'God, Mum, it's always about you! Do you think I didn't know? That you'd barely spoken to me for months, and nothing I did or said made you smile? That I didn't hear you crying all the time, see you getting thinner and thinner and growing more distant every day? That – that you dumped me on Pam, just disappeared for weeks. Did you think I didn't notice?'

'Anna —' Wendy's eyes were wide, her face scarlet.

'No! I've always had to look after you, to pretend that everything's OK. It's my turn now, my turn to be looked after! Even after what I've done, it's still a competition – you still have to be the martyr!'

Anna got out of bed and stormed to the door. She thumped her fists on it and looked down at the floor, breathing heavily.

'Anna,' Wendy said, whimpering. 'I just wanted —'

She spun around. 'What? To help me? Or to stop yourself feeling guilty? Maybe to get some sympathy? I told you, I don't want to know. It doesn't matter any more!'

Wendy crumpled in the chair, then reached for her bag and zipped it closed. 'I'm sorry.' She could barely speak for gasping.

Anna's fury dissipated. She understood now, of course. Why her mum had left her with Pam, where she had gone. It all made sense – the tears, the secrets, the silence. She knew that her mum had been ill, had needed treatment, just as she herself had. It wasn't fair to stay angry with her. Her bottom lip began to quiver and she took a step towards Wendy. 'Mum . . . I'm sorry. Don't go.'

Wendy stood up and hugged her tight, then put her bag down again. 'Oh darling, *I'm* sorry. I am here to look after you, I promise. I'll always look after you.'

She clutched onto her mother. 'I know.'

And as she said it, she knew it was true. She crawled back into bed and cried. Wendy was quiet, and stroked her forehead until she fell asleep.

*   *   *

Anna had been fourteen, that summer. It was almost the end of term. She sat cross-legged on her bed, leaning over a textbook, trying to finish her final assignments before school broke up. Nirvana blared from her ghetto blaster; she had bought the tape with the money she'd saved up by skipping lunches. In between the songs, the cicadas outside chirped an interlude.

There was a quiet knock at the door. Anna looked up, and frowned. Mum never bothered her after dinner; she rarely bothered her at all. She tried, Anna knew. She asked how school was, she pretended to listen to her response, but for months now, it had felt like they were each standing on opposite sides of a glass window. 'What?'

The door opened a little, and Wendy took a step into the room, her head bowed. She looked up and smiled, but only her mouth moved; the rest of her face was still. Her eyes looked bloodshot. 'You all right, Anna?'

'Yeah . . .' She cocked her head to the side, and waited.

Wendy walked into the room and turned down the music, then took a deep breath. 'Anna, next week, when school's finished, we're going to go and stay at Aunty Pam's.'

'In Perth?'

'Yes.'

Anna closed her book and sat up straight. 'Why?'

Wendy cleared her throat and looked past her. 'I need to have a procedure. It's nothing serious, but they can't do it here. I won't be away long, just a week or two in hospital.'

'Why can't I stay at Grandpa's?'

'He's too old to look after you. It'll be fun, OK?'

'Fun? No it won't.' Anna saw that her mum wasn't listening. She still had that stupid smile on her face but she was backing into the doorway. The skin on Anna's face started to tingle around her jaw. She was going to cry. She pressed her lips together to stop herself, then nodded. 'OK.'

Wendy nodded too, then closed the door. Anna heard her mother's footsteps recede along the hall, and the click of her door closing. She turned her music up to full volume, then turned out the lights.

A week later, Anna loaded her bag in the boot of the car next to Wendy's. They drove north with the windows open, singing along to the radio most of the way. When they weren't singing, Anna told stories about the kids at school. She laughed loudly, hoping her mum would join in.

Pam and her husband, Charlie, lived in a posh house by the river, all white with big balconies. It was huge compared to their own fibro cottage. Anna and Wendy had stayed there last Christmas for a few days. This time, Anna had the spare room all to herself, while Wendy slept on the couch so she didn't disturb her when she left early the next morning. That night, she lay diagonally across the double bed with her fingers in her ears so she couldn't hear her mum crying or Pam trying to calm her down. Eventually, it went quiet.

The next noise Anna heard was a car idling outside. She looked at the clock by the bed: 7 a.m. She hurried over to the window and held back one of the thick cream curtains, then squinted against the sun outside. There was a taxi waiting.

Someone was walking towards her door. Anna let the curtain fall and leapt back into bed. She turned away from the door and curled up under the sheet with her eyes closed, trying to breathe slowly, evenly. The door opened. Anna heard quiet footsteps. She smelled her mum's hairspray as she approached the bed. Anna didn't move, even as her mum kissed her on the forehead and whispered, 'I love you.' Wendy tiptoed away and the door closed. Anna didn't open her eyes until she heard the slam of the car door, and the taxi driving away. She allowed herself ten minutes to cry, then dried her eyes and went down to breakfast with Pam and Charlie as if it was the most normal thing in the world.

No one mentioned Wendy.

After breakfast, she sat out on the balcony on a wicker chair. She picked at the sharp ends of the frayed wood and looked out at the river. Last year, she had sat in this same chair and watched three brown baby swans desperately paddling as they tried to keep up with their graceful black mother. They weren't here today. She opened her book, and concentrated on the words on the page.

*   *   *

Three weeks later, Anna was reading in the shade of a sprawling fig tree on the banks of the Swan River opposite Pam's house. She heard a car stop across the road, then her mum's voice.

She shaded her eyes with her hand and peered back towards Pam's house. Her mum was heaving a bag out of the boot of the taxi. She looked different, even from a distance: puffy, bigger. She hadn't done her hair; it hung limp and flat, and her roots needed to be bleached. Anna looked away, then shifted so that she was hidden from the road by the vast, thick trunk of the tree. She dug her nails into the dry crumbly sand until there was a little trench on either side of her.

There was no point going back yet. There would be too many tears and questions. She looked out across the water, towards the spit.

Then she heard frantic calls behind her and a golden shaggy dog bounded towards her. She smiled and half stood, ready to brace herself, but the dog ran past her towards a beautiful black swan and her two gangly young strutting around on the shore. The mother swan raced into the water with her wings fanned out, but the cygnets hung back. They stood their ground until the very last minute, then darted into the water behind their mother, hissing over their shoulders. The dog stopped at the edge of the water, panting, its tail wagging.

Anna went back to the house eventually. Her mother was smiling, and pulled her into a hug. It felt warm, real, but Anna no longer wanted to hold onto her. Something had changed in Anna that summer. She knew her mother had something wrong with her, something shameful and secret, something she couldn't trust her own daughter with. When Wendy had driven off in that taxi a few weeks ago, she'd broken off a piece of the bond that had held them together. Anna gently pulled away from the embrace and went inside.

The next day, they loaded up the car again and drove back down south with the windows wide open. As soon as she opened her mouth, the wind stole the words that started to form on Anna's tongue. This time, neither of them sang.

CHAPTER THIRTY-FOUR

Eleven weeks after
Tuesday, 1 December 2009

Tony leaned back in his office chair, watching the ferries chug in and out of Circular Quay. The harbour sparkled. It was one of those summer afternoons that drew people down to the Quay to drink cold beer and white wine in the waterside bars.

He looked back at his computer. He had been back at work for two weeks now. He'd waited until Anna had entered her plea – Guilty. It seemed like a milestone and he knew he couldn't sit around at home waiting for her sentencing. When he first returned to the office, people had avoided him, stopped their conversations when he walked in, and blushed when they mentioned their children. But they were treating him more normally now. Tony wasn't sure who felt most relieved. Most of the time it was good being back at work. It felt nice to be part of something again, and to be useful.

He stood up and closed his office door, then picked up his mobile. Ursula answered on the first ring.

'Hi, Mum.'

'Anthony, hi. How are you, love?'

Tony sighed. 'Tired. OK. You?'

'We're fine. Your dad and I were thinking of going out for something to eat tonight – do you want to come?'

'No, thanks.' He paused, then forced himself to bring up the question he'd been dreading. He hated to raise it. 'Actually, there's something I wanted to ask you. I wondered if it would be OK if I moved back into yours for a little while, just until I find something else.' He could picture Ursula frowning as she tried to work out what was going on.

'Move in? Of course. But why?'

He took a deep breath. 'Wendy called. They're discharging Anna next week. I thought it would be better if she and Wendy stayed at the house, until . . .' His mouth went dry. 'Until January.'

'Oh. Well, yes, of course you can. But is she ready to be discharged? Is she safe?'

'Mum . . .' He shook his head; it had been too much to hope that his mother would accept the decision, just keep quiet for once. 'Of course she's safe. Don't you think the hospital and courts would have thought of that? There's only six weeks until the sentencing – don't you think she deserves a bit of time at home?' He bit his lip as he realised what he was saying. He actually thought that Anna would go to jail. His face flushed. He listened to Ursula drumming her fingers on the table and gritted his teeth, waiting for her to react.

'Anthony, are you sure you want to move out? Once you do that, you'll lose any right to that house. Maybe Anna and Wendy can —'

Tony forced himself to speak slowly. 'Anna's got enough to deal with at the moment without having to find a new place. And we don't know what's going to happen.' Was he trying to convince his mother, or himself?

'Does Anna even want to move back there? I mean, it might be too much for her, the memories . . .'

He gripped the phone tight. 'I won't stay with you long, Mum, just until we see what happens.'

'Oh Anthony, I don't mean that. We'd love you to stay. I'll get Dad to clear his junk out of your room.'

'Don't go to any trouble, I can do it. I thought I'd bring my stuff over this weekend.'

They said their goodbyes, then Tony put the phone down. He raked his fingers through his hair, scratched at his chin. Part of the reason he found it so hard to talk to his mum recently was that she always seemed to say out loud the things he hated to admit to himself. But he knew he was doing the right thing for Anna, and it was just a temporary move. There was plenty of time to make decisions about the future.

But the real question in his mind was one Ursula hadn't asked. It was a question he didn't know the answer to: why was he moving out because Anna was coming home?

*   *   *

Anna woke early, before the nurses switched on the lights. She rubbed her eyes; she'd barely slept. It had been her last night in hospital; she was going home today.

It was almost three months since she'd been home, since she'd slept anywhere other than in this terrible, uncomfortable bed. In the past couple of weeks she'd had some days out of the hospital with her mum, and with Emily, but this was different. When Dr Morgan had confirmed to her last week that she didn't need to be an inpatient any more, Anna had opened her mouth to argue, to beg to stay another month until the sentencing. But she closed it again and said nothing: if she stayed, it could be another twenty-five years until she slept in her own bed, cooked herself a meal or walked in the park. There were other things that she needed to do, too.

She showered then dressed in the new clothes that Emily had brought in for her: a pair of jeans and a navy and white striped T-shirt. Anna looked at herself in the mirror; she didn't look like a patient any more. Then again, she didn't look like a murderer either. But she was.

In the bathroom, she dried her bottles of shampoo and conditioner with the threadbare hospital towel and wrapped them in a plastic carrier bag. She left out her toothbrush and toothpaste until after she had eaten breakfast. She made the bed, even though she knew they would strip it for the next patient in the queue, then rechecked the cupboards for anything she had missed. Tony always left things behind when they went on holiday; it had been Anna's job to check the cupboards. She stopped herself; there was no point thinking of the past.

She sat on the bed to wait. It wasn't cold, but she started to shiver, and soon her body shook all over.

Footsteps approached her room; she tried to settle her breathing. The door opened and Dr Morgan walked in with Wendy behind her. Dr Morgan looked pretty today in a cream flowery dress and strappy tan sandals; she looked as though she was going out to lunch. Maybe she was celebrating, happy to see Anna go.

Wendy sat on the bed next to Anna; she let her mother clutch her hands for a moment, then withdrew them. She felt like a little girl being collected from school camp. Were the other patients picked up by their mothers? Perhaps parents were the only people left who loved you after you spent time in a place like this.

Dr Morgan handed Wendy some paperwork and talked about Anna's follow-up appointment and medication. Anna curled one leg underneath her and started twirling her hair in her fingers.

'Anna, how do you feel now the day has arrived?' Dr Morgan asked.

She looked up, then turned to her mother, who was grinning. 'Well, a bit anxious, but it's good – of course it's good to be leaving a psychiatric hospital.' She looked straight at the psychiatrist, nodding to indicate that she had said enough. Thankfully, Dr Morgan took the hint and didn't ask anything else.

Her hands started to shake again. It was really going to happen; she was really going to walk out of here and go home. She linked her fingers together and squeezed them. Her wedding ring ground into the middle and little fingers of her left hand. For better or for worse, that's what Tony had sworn. Obviously those vows didn't cover something like this. She wondered if her ring would buckle if she squeezed hard enough.

Wendy and Dr Morgan were both watching her, but she couldn't look at them. She knew she would cry if she did.

'Do either of you have any other questions?' Dr Morgan said.

Anna looked at her mum, then they both shook their heads.

Somehow she stood up, picked up her bag and followed Dr Morgan down the corridor to the security doors at the front of the ward. Wendy walked behind her. Dr Morgan unlocked the door and held it open.

'Good luck, Anna,' she said.

She looked through the doorway and out through the glass of the external doors. The path wavered in front of her like a mirage. She blinked away her tears and the image sharpened. She took a deep breath, then turned to Dr Morgan and shook her hand. Although she'd promised herself she wouldn't, Anna started to cry again. She wanted to close the door and run back to her room. She realised that she was still grabbing onto Dr Morgan's hand, but instead of letting go, she reached out with her other arm and hugged the doctor.

After a moment, she managed to stand back, take her mother's hand and walk out into the bright sunshine.

*   *   *

Anna sat on the edge of the couch and looked around her lounge room. In the kitchen Wendy unpacked a bag of groceries. Anna felt like a visitor in her own home. She couldn't shake the feeling that someone was going to knock on the door and tell her that they'd made a terrible mistake in letting her go.

She bit her lip. She looked around the room; everything was in the same place. Their wedding photo was still on top of the dresser under the window. It would be easier if Tony had smashed the glass and ripped up the photo, or burned all of her things in a bonfire in the garden. If everything was trashed, it would reflect what had happened to her life. It seemed cruel that the house was so familiar, teasing her with memories of her old life. But everything had changed; her old life no longer existed.

She stared out of the French doors to the backyard, where brazen dandelions were dotted all over the overgrown lawn. She stood up suddenly, ran over to the doors, unlocked them and slid one open.

'Mum!' She looked over her shoulder. 'Mum!'

Wendy hurried over, holding a plastic carton of milk. 'What is it? What's wrong?'

Anna scanned the garden, tears falling. 'Jessie, where's Jessie?'

'Oh, love. Tony took her to his mum's house, he wasn't sure —'

'What? If I could look after her?'

'Oh no, love, not that, just —'

She slammed the glass door closed and spun around. 'No one asked me! It was all I wanted, to see my dog, and he took her!'

Wendy put the milk down on the floor and stepped towards Anna with her arms held out. 'I don't think it was like that, love. He just thought maybe you didn't need the extra stress of walking her.'

She leaned into her mum and cried. Tony didn't even trust her to look after a dog. 'Jessie's *my* dog, Mum. I was the one who took her for walks, who fed her. Tony didn't even like her!'

Wendy rubbed her back as they embraced. 'Shh, it's OK. We'll get her back, Anna. Come on. Come and sit down.'

Anna walked back to the couch, then sat down and curled her legs under her. She hugged one of the cushions and rested her chin on it. They shouldn't have let her out of hospital. What was she doing here?

She felt Wendy touch her shoulder. 'Anna? What about a cuppa?'

She nodded, and looked up at her mother. She tried to smile. 'Thanks, Mum. I'm sorry . . . I'm OK. I think I'll go and have a shower now, all right?'

'Of course, love. Go ahead – I'll bring you a clean towel.'

Anna walked into the bathroom and locked the door behind her.

*   *   *

For the next week, Anna planned each day to the minute. Shower, breakfast, take tablets, go for a walk, lunch, nap, dinner, television, bed. But she couldn't plan her nights. When she went to bed, she lay on her back with her eyes closed, imagining conversations with Tony in which she asked him what he had done at work that day, what they would do on the weekend. In her mind, he'd reply, just as he always used to, and they'd be a couple again.

Jack never featured in those dreams. Anna didn't want to think about what she'd say to Jack; she didn't want to think about him at all.

*   *   *

Wendy didn't talk about Jack either. She, too, pretended that everything was normal. She tried not to watch Anna, but she was terrified that she might do something to hurt herself again. Wendy kept Anna's medication in her handbag and didn't let it out of her sight, day or night.

In the evenings, she sat beside Anna and pretended to be interested in the news, or some TV show.

She pretended that she was able to sleep.

She pretended that this might not be the last month she would spend with her daughter. If Anna was imprisoned for twenty-five years, Wendy might not live to see her set free.

CHAPTER THIRTY-FIVE

Three months after
Christmas Day 2009

Tony woke to the cackle of kookaburras just as the sun rose. He stretched out in the single bed and looked at the yellowing plastic stars and planets still stuck on the ceiling from when he was a kid. His skin was clammy already; it was going to be a hot day.

He looked around the room in the dim light, half expecting to see a pillowcase stuffed with presents at the bottom of the bed next to an empty glass and a saucerful of crumbs. But he was a grown-up now, and all he saw was his open suitcase, clothes spilling out of it.

He sighed, sat up, and rubbed his face. He picked up his board shorts and a T-shirt from the floor, put them on, and walked out into the kitchen.

'Dad. You're up early.'

Jim was sitting at the kitchen table reading yesterday's newspaper. His grey hair was sticking up at the crown and he hadn't shaved yet. An empty mug lined with tidemarks of frothed milk sat next to the paper. He looked up and smiled at Tony. 'I wanted to get the turkey in the Weber soon; it'll take a while.'

Tony leaned against the kitchen bench. 'What time are people coming?'

'Oh, not till twelve, but you know what your mother's like.' They both smiled.

'I thought I'd go down for a swim. Fancy it?'

Jim raised his eyebrows and his eyes twinkled. 'Me?'

He smiled at his dad. It was nice to be spending more time with him now. When Tony had last lived at home, as a teenager, he had been self-absorbed, unable to see his parents as people with their own hopes and independent history. When he thought of his relationship with his mum and dad, it was the volatility of Ursula that dominated, but being at home had made him realise that Jim, with his quiet reliability, deserved as much space in his mind and his life. 'Come on, you're not that old!'

Jim chuckled. 'Yeah. All right then, maybe I will. Let me grab my stuff.' He leaned towards Tony and whispered, 'Your mother will have a heart attack!'

*   *   *

By mid-morning, the house was in chaos. Ursula was mixing and chopping and blending and whisking. Tony offered to help, but after slicing the strawberries too small, he had been banished to the backyard with Jim to fill the eskies.

'Dad, I'm just going to the servo to get some more ice.'

Jim was crouched over a huge esky, ripping the cardboard off six-packs of beer and stacking them inside. He raised his hand to wave Tony goodbye.

He went round the side of the house to his car, and drove towards the service station. Midway along the main street he sighed, then pulled over and switched off the engine. He took out his phone, hesitated for a moment, then called Anna.

She answered on the first ring. 'Tony!'

He closed his eyes; it was nice to hear her voice. He hadn't had a Christmas without her for years. 'Hi. What are you doing?'

'Nothing much. Emily's coming over soon for a coffee, then Mum and I are just going to have a quiet day.' Her voice quivered. 'What about you?'

Tony laid his head against the headrest. 'Just getting some ice. Mum's doing the full Christmas as usual.'

He could picture Anna's sad smile.

'It's always fun though, isn't it?'

He wondered if he should have made an effort to spend today with Anna, in case it was her last Christmas, for a while anyway. Maybe he should have tried to make it more special for her. 'Did you want to . . . I'm sure it would be —'

'No. Thanks, but I don't feel very Christmassy.'

He nodded, relieved. He was sure she was just saying no to make him feel better, and he appreciated the gesture. 'I know. Me neither.'

'How are you, Tony?'

His eyes filled with tears. 'I'm OK. I've got a couple of weeks off work now. But work . . . helps. How about you?'

'Oh, you know . . . I can't – I can't think of anything else, I just want to get these next few weeks over with. I feel . . . stuck. And I can't think of . . . him. It's too much.'

Tony bit his lip. 'It'll get easier. Or so everyone keeps telling me.'

'Will you come, Tony? In January?'

Did she really think he would stay away? 'Of course I will.'

'Thanks.' He could barely hear her.

There was a pause. 'I better get this ice.'

'OK. Thanks for phoning . . . Tony?'

He leaned his head to the side, as if cradling the phone between his face and shoulder could somehow substitute for her. 'Yes?'

'Merry Christmas.'

His bottom lip quivered. He cleared his throat and managed to say it back. 'Merry Christmas, Anna.'

* * *

Anna and Wendy sat on the couch with dinner plates on cushions on their laps. Anna looked down at the meal her mother had made, and smiled. Ham, roast potatoes, carrot, little chipolatas rolled in bacon, gravy. Just like they'd always had when she was a kid. She cut a potato in half and lifted the fork to her mouth, actually looking forward to eating for the first time since she got home. *It's a Wonderful Life* was showing on the television in the background. She thought about turning it off, but didn't. It was just a movie title; she had to realise that the world was going to go on regardless of whether or not she was in prison.

She put her plate down on the coffee table, went into the kitchen and came back with two glasses clinking in one hand and a bottle of shiraz in the other. Putting the glasses on the coffee table in front of them, she unscrewed the lid of the bottle and filled them up. She handed one to her mum. 'May as well drink this.'

Wendy nodded, smiled, and took a sip. 'Thanks, sweetheart.'

She sat back down and sipped her wine. It was bold, strong, spicy. She licked her lips and took another sip. She put it down again and picked up her food. 'Thanks for making this, Mum. I'm glad you did.'

Wendy raised her glass into the air. 'Merry Christmas.'

They ate the rest of their meal in silence, and finished the bottle of wine. They found some ice cream and frozen raspberries in the freezer and made dessert. When Anna went to bed, she fell asleep straight away for the first time since being home.

*　*　*

She woke a few hours later with her heart thumping. Her mouth was dry and her tongue felt rough. She lay still, listening, but heard nothing other than the high-pitched purring of the cicadas outside. It must have been a dream.

She reached for the glass of water by the bed and gulped it down. It was lukewarm. Even though she wanted to finish it all she made herself leave a little in the bottom of the glass so that she wouldn't need to get out of bed if she woke up again.

Her skin was clammy. She kicked off the cotton blanket, then took off her pyjama pants and lay in her underwear and singlet on the edge of the bed where the sheets were still cool. She took a few deep breaths and tried to ease herself back into sleep, but she couldn't. The dream stayed with her.

A lopsided fake Christmas tree on top of a glass coffee table; red paper wrapped around a plastic stem; presents arranged to hide the tripod stand. Tinny laughter from the TV in the corner. The sweet, sickly smell of bourbon, then the dark liquid oozing across the floor like lava running over the rocks of the shattered bottle. A tall man, dishevelled, with blond hair, yelling. Mum yelling back. Crying, crashing. A sharp, stinging pain on her forehead, her eye warm and sticky.

She should never have drunk that wine tonight.

Or perhaps she should have drunk more.

*   *   *

The next morning, she asked her mum for two paracetamol tablets, and forced down the scrambled eggs on toast that Wendy had made. She picked up her cup of tea and walked over to the kitchen, where Wendy was filling the sink with water to wash the frying pan.

'Mum?' She took a deep breath. 'I was wondering if you would take me . . . to Jack.'

Wendy dropped the pan into the sink. Water and bubbles slopped out onto her top. She turned around and stared at Anna. 'Oh . . . Are you sure?'

She nodded. 'I should have gone before.'

'Have you talked about it with Dr Morgan? Did she say it would be all right?'

'It's not up to her. I . . . I need to go. Please.' She didn't want to argue; she'd been putting this off for too long. Now that she had decided to go, she didn't want anything to change her mind.

Wendy bit the inside of her cheek. 'OK. When do you want to go?'

'Now.'

'Now?'

She nodded.

'OK, I suppose . . . But Anna, promise me something. Promise me that you're all right, that you're going to be all right. If it's too hard, please tell me and let me call the doctor. Please . . .' Wendy's eyes filled with tears.

Anna stepped forward and took her mum's hands, still wet from the dishes. 'I'm OK, I promise. It's just something I need to do before . . . It's just something I need to do. Please don't worry.'

'I'm your mum, I worry about you all the time.'

'I know.' She dropped her mum's hands. 'Thank you.'

Wendy smiled. 'Go and get ready, I'll finish up here then we can go.'

Anna gulped the rest of her tea and practically ran to the bathroom to have a shower before she changed her mind. As she passed the door to Jack's room, still closed, she hesitated and allowed herself to remember what was behind it. She moved her hand towards the handle, then let it drop back down by her side.

*   *   *

Wendy leaned against the car and smoked another cigarette. She craned her neck again to see if Anna was coming back yet – she had insisted on going alone. They had been silent on the drive here; there was nothing to say. It was so bloody unfair. Anna never had a chance to say goodbye, and now here she was, walking on her own to find the plot. Wendy threw her cigarette butt down on the concrete and stamped on it, then looked at her watch. She should have gone with Anna, she shouldn't have assumed she'd be OK. There was so much going on for her, with Christmas, Anna returning home, the sentencing in a few weeks. Wendy's breathing sped up. She reached down into her bag for her phone. Would Dr Morgan answer on Boxing Day?

She looked at the phone, then put it back in her bag. Dr Morgan would be with her family. There was no need to call her yet. Catastrophising, that's what her therapist used to call it. Forty-five minutes wasn't that long really. She should have brought a magazine or something, to occupy her mind.

Looking up again she saw Anna in the distance, walking towards her, hunched over. She exhaled, wiped her nose and eyes, then walked around the car, bent down and pretended to examine a bright red grevillea flower.

When Anna was close, Wendy turned around quickly as if startled. Anna's face was red and blotchy, her eyes swollen and bloodshot. Wendy moved towards her daughter and put her arms around her, but Anna was limp; she had nothing left. Wendy swallowed her own tears down. This was not the time for her to fall to pieces, too.

She put her arm around Anna and guided her to the passenger side of the car, opened the door, and helped her in. Anna stared out of the windscreen while Wendy fastened her seatbelt, closed the door, and drove them both home.

Anna managed to get out of the car herself. She walked into the house, went straight to her room, and closed the door behind her.

Wendy let her be.

CHAPTER THIRTY-SIX

Four months after
Thursday, 14 January 2010

Anna stared at her meal. Fresh pasta, homemade pesto, sun-dried tomatoes and green olives. Emily had made it all, then brought it over to Anna's house with a bottle of Tasmanian pinot. Her last supper.

She twirled a piece of fettuccine around her fork and put it in her mouth, but it didn't taste of anything. It seemed to take forever to chew; she took a mouthful of wine to wash down the rubbery ball of pasta. She wanted to keep drinking the alcohol, get drunk and pass out until the morning. But she couldn't risk losing control tomorrow. She was teetering on the edge as it was.

Wendy and Emily were talking about the neighbours, the gossip magazines and the weather. Anything but tomorrow. She tried to follow the conversation and nod at appropriate times but she didn't want to talk about which Hollywood star was in rehab. They were trying so hard that Anna felt like weeping.

She watched her mum laugh at something Emily said. It was too loud to fool anyone. Wendy hadn't touched her pasta either. How would her mum cope tomorrow?

As soon as she thought it was polite to do so, Anna gathered up the plates.

'I brought chocolate cake,' Emily said. 'I'll just —'

She shook her head. 'Not for me. I'm tired.' She put the plates on the kitchen bench and walked over to hug Emily. 'Thanks for coming, Em. I really appreciate it. And thanks for dinner – I'm sorry I couldn't eat much.'

'Don't be silly.' Emily had tears in her eyes. 'Try to get some sleep. I'll be there tomorrow, and we'll be able to have a proper dinner very soon. It'll be OK, I know it will.'

She tried to smile, then turned to Wendy. ''Night, Mum.' Her voice started to break; she cleared her throat.

Wendy reached out her hand. 'Goodnight.'

She squeezed her mum's hand. She wanted to hug her, but didn't trust herself to be able to let go. She looked again at her best friend, and her mum, then ran out of the room.

* * *

The next morning, Anna was wide awake when Wendy knocked on her door and brought in a bowl of porridge and a glass of orange juice. Even though she hadn't slept at all, Anna was calm. There was nothing she could do now. She forced herself to eat, wishing that her mum had made this kind of breakfast when Anna was at school instead of leaving her money to get something from the bakery on the way. There must have been times when she cooked for her, or at least sat with her while they ate cereal together, but Anna didn't remember those days. Most of her memories were of Wendy being too depressed to get out of bed. She scolded herself; her mum was here for her now.

Everyone else in Sydney was having breakfast. They'd be getting ready for work, or for school, or to take their toddlers to swimming lessons. Anna was going to the Supreme Court to be sentenced for infanticide.

She managed to finish her breakfast and take her tablet, then went to have a shower, just as she always did. She dried herself with a big clean white towel, and started to dress. From her wardrobe she took out her pale blue shirt, still in the plastic sleeve from the drycleaner. Anna held the hanger in one hand and tried to remove the plastic, but it stuck to her fingers. She shook her arm until it fluttered to the floor, then stamped on it with her stockinged feet. Her breathing quickened and became shallow; she was hot, itchy. She scratched at her arms and stomach, unable to stop, and started to cry.

'Anna!' Wendy opened the door and rushed in. 'What's going on?'

She shook her head, wiped her eyes. 'I can't get the bloody shirt out.'

Wendy put her hand on Anna's shoulder and gently guided her back towards the bed, then sat her down. She picked up the shirt and folded it over her arm. 'We've got plenty of time. You take as long as you need – I'll go and iron this again for you.'

Anna looked up, tears spilling down her face. 'Thanks. I'll be all right in a minute.'

Wendy walked out, closing the door behind her. Anna let herself cry. She cried because she felt sorry for herself and she didn't want to go to jail. She cried because she was scared and lonely. She cried for how much she had hurt her family. She cried for everything she had lost: her past, her dreams, her future.

Her baby.

Then she walked back into the bathroom, blew her nose and washed her face. She took a deep breath and started to put on her make-up. And, just for a moment, she saw herself in the mirror – not a patient, not a prisoner, just Anna.

But the make-up would wash off. She had no idea what was left underneath.

*   *   *

Tony sat on the back steps sipping a cup of coffee. He knew he shouldn't: he already felt shaky and sick, but he hadn't slept at all and he wasn't sure he could make it through a day in court without some caffeine. Jessie ran up to him with her ball in her mouth, dropped it at his feet and looked up at him with a doggy grin. Winston, his parents' dog, hung back. He kicked the tennis ball and the dogs chased after it.

He went back inside. Jim was reading the paper in the kitchen, already in his suit pants and shirt. He looked up at Tony and nodded. 'You OK?'

He shrugged. 'Yep.'

'Your mother's in there ironing your shirt.'

Why did she always interfere? 'I told her I'd do it.'

He walked through to the laundry. Ursula stood at the ironing board in her dressing-gown. Her hair and make-up were done. She barely looked up. 'This material is so bloody hard to get the creases out of; by the time I do one side, the other side's all crushed again.'

'It's fine, Mum, just leave it.'

'I'm almost done . . .'

'Mum, leave it!' He stepped towards her.

Ursula picked up the iron, turned it upright and slammed it down on the board. 'I'm just trying to help, Anthony!'

'I know you are, Mum. Sorry . . .' He picked up the shirt. 'Thanks for doing this.'

Ursula spoke softly. 'You'd better get dressed, we have to go soon.'

He tried to smile. 'Are you going like that?'

She looked down and seemed surprised at the sight of her dressing-gown. 'Oh, I'll just get changed. I bet your father's dillydallying —'

'He's ready, Mum.' Tony walked out of the laundry. 'I'll be five minutes.'

In his old bedroom, he put his suit on. He looked at himself in the full-length mirror on the back of the door and swayed at the memory of the last time he wore it. He should have bought a new one, should have thrown this one out after the funeral. He could just wear work pants, and the shirt, but it seemed too casual for a day like today. This would be the last time he would wear this suit, he decided. When he came home from court, it was going in the bin.

He wondered what Anna was doing now, whether she was dressed, whether she had managed to sleep, or eat anything. She would be so scared, so alone. He closed his eyes as his hands began to shake. He clenched and unclenched his fists but the tremor was still there. His stomach churned; he shouldn't have had that coffee. He looked away from the mirror, took a deep breath, then opened the door.

It was time to go.

CHAPTER THIRTY-SEVEN

That day

Monday, 14 September 2009

Tony woke up with his pulse racing, and knew immediately that something was wrong. He held his breath, but couldn't hear anything. Jack wasn't crying. What had woken him?

He turned his head towards the other side of the bed where Anna should be. It was empty, cold. He turned back and checked the time: 4 a.m.

Clenching his fist he thumped it hard on the mattress. He switched on the lamp beside the bed, blinked until his eyes adjusted to the light, then gulped down some water from the glass on the bedside cabinet. This wasn't what he'd imagined parenthood would be like. He wished he could just switch off the light again, pretend he hadn't noticed Anna was gone, and go back to sleep. But he was wide awake now and knew it would be yet another day of worry and exhaustion on top of being flat out at work. He waited for a moment, hoping Anna would come back, then threw off the cotton blanket and stormed out of the bedroom.

He walked down the corridor towards the living area. There were no lights on, though the darkness was washed with a faint pink tinge that told him sunrise wasn't too far away. He switched on the light; Anna wasn't in the kitchen or living room. He switched it off again, then walked back towards Jack's room. The door was ajar and a faint glow from the night-light trickled out into the hallway. He tiptoed towards it and then paused, just outside.

He could hear Anna whispering, 'I'm so sorry, Jack, you don't deserve this, I'm so sorry . . .'

His eyes widened. What the hell was she talking about?

He pushed the door open. Anna was sitting cross-legged on the floor next to the cot, tears falling down her face. Jack was asleep on his back with his head turned away from her, towards the wall. His arms were raised next to his head, bent at the elbows, palms up in surrender. His brow was furrowed, his eyes tight in concentration and his little mouth slightly open.

Tony took a deep breath to try to calm himself. 'Anna,' he whispered. 'Anna, come back to bed . . .'

She glanced up at him, shook her head, then turned back to look at Jack.

He walked in and crouched down next to her, then took her hands. She looked at him, then stood up as if she was hypnotised. Tony kept hold of one of her hands as he led her out, closed Jack's door, and took her back to the bedroom.

He sat her on the bed and rubbed her back. He felt sick now. His anger had been replaced by something far more malevolent: fear. 'Anna, what's wrong?'

She looked at him with wide eyes, pupils dilated, then bit her lip and shook her head quickly.

'Please, tell me what's going on,' he begged.

'Don't, Tony.'

'Don't what? You're scaring me!'

'I'm sorry,' she whispered. 'I'm so sorry.'

'Don't be stupid, don't apologise!' Acid surged up his throat. What was going on? Was she sleepwalking?

'I'm sorry, Tony. I love you. You deserve better. It's all my fault.'

'What's your fault, Anna? What are you talking about? You haven't done anything wrong . . .' His voice faltered and tears welled up in his eyes.

Anna looked at him, then reeled back. 'See, look what I've done now. You're sad, and it's all my —'

He grabbed her hands again as if to prevent her from retreating further into herself. 'Stop this! You haven't done anything!'

She looked away. 'You're wrong, Tony,' she said in a flat voice. 'It's all my fault.'

'It's not, Anna. You haven't done anything wrong. Oh babe, come here.' He tried to pull her towards him but she was immovable. He didn't take his eyes off her; she was still, and she stared at the window, even though the blinds were closed.

Suddenly she whipped her head to the side and stared into the corner of the room with her mouth open and her eyes wide. Tony heard her breath quicken, and he turned his head too, to see what she was looking at. There was nothing there. Anna mumbled something.

'I didn't hear you, Anna. What did you say?'

She looked at him, shook her head, then looked at the corner again.

'What are you staring at?' he said. His mouth was dry. Something was very wrong. 'Talk to me.'

She turned to him. He had never seen her look so frightened. 'I'm just so sorry . . .'

He pulled her towards him and this time she leaned into him. He held her until her breathing had slowed, then managed to get her to lie down on the bed. Her eyes closed. He kissed her cheek, smoothed back her hair and got into bed beside her, holding her hand while her breathing deepened. He didn't dare close his eyes.

At six-thirty, the alarm shrieked. Anna was still, lying on her side, but Tony knew she wasn't asleep. He turned off the alarm then rolled towards her and put his hand on her shoulder. Her back went rigid, so he took it away again. He thought about moving over in the bed towards her, wrapping his arms around her and just holding her, but he could tell she didn't want him to. Her hair was tangled at the back of her head, damp with sweat. He leaned over and kissed it, then got up and quietly left the room.

After he had eaten and showered, Tony called his mum. He had one meeting at work that morning that he had to go to, and then he'd come straight back. He'd call Dr Fraser as soon as the practice opened and make an appointment. This time he'd take Anna there himself.

Jack was grizzling. He picked him up, changed his nappy, then walked into the bedroom. Anna was fast asleep. He took Jack through to the kitchen, defrosted the last bag of frozen breast milk in the microwave and fed him. He laid Jack down in his cot again while he got ready for work, then went back to the bedroom with some breakfast for Anna.

'Anna?' he whispered.

She moved her head reluctantly. 'Mmm?'

'I've got to go into work, just for an hour or two. I've fed Jack – he's back in bed, he'll be fine there. Mum's coming over soon.'

Anna sat up. 'No! Tell her not to come, please. It's OK, I'm OK!'

He swallowed, then spoke calmly. 'Anna. You're not well. I'm worried about you. The tablets aren't working; we'll go and see Dr Fraser later, all right?'

Anna was silent. She looked at him, opened her mouth as if to say something, then lay back down on her back and closed her eyes. Tony went to walk towards her, but stopped himself. He wasn't sure he could hold his ground if she begged him.

'Bye, Anna,' he said. 'It'll be OK, I promise.'

She didn't reply. He looked at his watch; his mum would be here soon. He left the door ajar, went back into Jack's room and kissed him goodbye.

And then he walked out.

CHAPTER THIRTY-EIGHT

Four months after
Friday, 15 January 2010

Anna looked at the ground and concentrated on putting one foot in front of the other without falling while the crowd buffeted her. On her left-hand side, Scott gripped her elbow. Chloe, a younger lawyer, scurried behind them, pulling a black bag on wheels, like a suitcase. She glanced up at Scott's face: his head was held high and he had the confident look of a celebrity on a red carpet. Someone shoved a fluffy grey microphone in her face and Anna instinctively ducked, but she managed to stop herself from screaming in fright. A man ran alongside them with a video camera on his shoulder. She wished she'd brought something to cover her face with, like she'd seen other people do on the news. Or at least worn her hair loose so she could bow her head and hide.

'Anna! Anna!'

Without thinking she looked up, assuming it was someone she knew. But it was just another reporter. Anger surged through her. How dare they use her first name? Who were these people?

She could see doors in front of her now, and walked quicker until she was almost running. Someone held them open and she stumbled inside. She was shaking. The frenzy faded as the doors closed softly behind them. Inside it was cool, almost cold; she had goosebumps. They were in a large lobby with high ceilings and muted cream walls. It was quiet, like a library, the sort of place where you whisper and walk on tiptoes.

'Well done,' Scott said, and Chloe smiled at her.

Two security guards loomed in front of her; she froze. Was this what her life was going to be like now? She looked at Scott, unsure of what was happening: he greeted the guards, then turned to Anna. 'After you.'

She realised she was supposed to put her bag on the conveyor belt in front of her and walk through the metal detector, just like she was catching a flight. Did she need to take her shoes off? She looked up at one of the guards and started to bend down.

He smiled at her, avuncular. 'No, love, that's OK.'

She walked through with her pulse racing. Did they know who she was, what she'd done? No alarms sounded. At the other end she held her arms out as another guard swept a handheld metal detector around her body. In front of her was a big television screen on the wall with a list of the day's cases.

There it was. *Court 2: Crown v Patton.*

*   *   *

Anna was led into the dock on the left-hand side of the courtroom. She focused only on staying upright, fearful that her legs would collapse, but she could tell that the room was full and everyone was looking at her. She felt herself blushing; she didn't know what to do with her face. Should she smile? Look straight ahead as if she hadn't seen them? Or would that make her look more guilty? Anna almost laughed at herself: in a case like hers, were there degrees of guilt? She had pleaded guilty; that was that. Whether she *looked* more or less guilty didn't change the fact that in the law, it was one or the other. Not guilty. Guilty.

She sat down and looked straight ahead at a blue leather chair behind a large desk. It must be where the judge would sit. In front of it, an elderly woman held her fingers poised above some kind of typewriter, ready to transcribe what was said. Scott and Chloe sat near Anna, at one end of a long table.

She kept her head still but turned her eyes as far as she could to see who was in the court. There were reporters: young men and women who leaned back in their chairs holding notebooks with pens pushed through the rings at the top. One guy had his pen balanced behind his ear and was chewing gum; he looked completely relaxed, even bored. It was clearly just another day at work for him. She was determined not to cry. It wasn't his fault she was here; it was her own.

On the other side of the centre aisle, in the seats at the back right-hand corner of the room, were some more familiar faces. Emily gave her a tense smile and a wave. Wendy sat next to Emily, a wad of tissues clenched in her hand. Anna moved her head a fraction more to the right, so she could see the rows behind Emily and Wendy, and she couldn't help but smile in relief. Tony was there. Ursula sat next to him with her arms folded. Next to her was Jim, then Lisa. For just a brief moment, she thought that her mother-in-law was smiling at her, but she wasn't: it was a grimace of disgust. Anna swallowed then looked back at Tony. He sat forward in his chair with his back very straight and stared at the wall behind the judge's desk. She knew he'd be bouncing his leg up and down, the way he always did when he was stressed. She held her gaze on him. His eyes flickered towards her, then he smiled, just a little. Anna couldn't look away; she wanted to saturate herself with this picture of him. But his attention had moved now back to the front of the room. A hush had fallen over the court. Anna turned around again and watched the judge walk in, carrying a sheaf of papers in which her future had already been written.

* * *

Tony put his hands flat on his knees to steady them. In his peripheral vision, he saw the side of Anna's pale face; he could tell she was biting the inside of her cheek. He wished he could hold her hand and tell her to be strong; he knew she could get through this. In a couple of hours, this would be over; there was no way she'd go to prison. Surely anyone could see that she'd been punished enough.

The judge looked exactly as he'd expected: thick-necked, grey-haired, stern. His voice was quiet and low, but there was no doubt that every single person in the court was listening to every word. Tony began to feel strangely disconnected: his ears were filled with a hypnotic buzzing and the judge's voice sounded as though it was coming from underwater.

'Anna Margaret Patton has pleaded guilty before me to one count of infanticide, an offence under section 22A of the Crimes Act 1900, punishable by a maximum of twenty-five years' imprisonment.'

Tony held his breath and watched Anna. She didn't move at all, didn't even blink. He wiped his upper lip and forced himself to exhale as the judge continued.

'The Crown has accepted the plea on the basis that at the time of the act, Mrs Patton was suffering from a severe mental illness as a result of childbirth.'

Tony tapped his knuckles on his teeth as the judge kept talking. The legal jargon couldn't make him forget they were talking about his son and his wife. Jack and Anna. He bit the knuckle of his middle finger to keep himself focused.

The judge looked up from his notes and straight at Anna. 'Today I am to sentence her for the crime of infanticide.'

*   *   *

Anna felt as if the room was spinning around her. She reminded herself to breathe. There was a pain in the back of her head as though someone was twisting a screwdriver into it. Her whole body was rigid. She shifted her weight a little, then heard the flap of someone turning over a page in their notebook. Her face flushed. What were they doing, watching every move and writing it down? Did they think she was reacting appropriately? She turned her head further towards the front of the room so the reporters couldn't see her face, then leaned back into the chair, wishing her body could disappear into it.

The judge was reading aloud from the pages of statements and submissions in front of him, every one about her. Her entire life and future were condensed into those papers. She looked down at her hands in her lap.

'At 12.20 p.m. on 14 September 2009, Anna's husband, Anthony Patton, called Rose Bay police station to report that she and their six-week-old baby, Jack, were missing. He was concerned about her mental state. At approximately 1.30 p.m., police received a call from Mr Mark Stone, a local surfer, who, after hearing screams, had found Mrs Patton lying on some rocks just over the edge of a cliff.'

Anna covered her face with her hands. She didn't want to hear this; she couldn't hear this. She tried to think of something else, another sound to drown out the story. The flapping of Jessie's ears when she shook herself dry after a walk at the beach, or the rhythmic clicking of her claws on the floors at home. The chatter of the children at school, or Tony laughing. Her favourite songs.

She could still hear the judge in the background as his deep voice droned on about Anna's life. Every so often she let herself listen for a few moments, but then blocked him out again. She didn't want to hear everyone's theories about why she had done what she had done, and she certainly didn't want to hear the details of what had happened. There was a reason she couldn't remember that day, and being forced to relive it might make her insane – if she wasn't already.

The judge's voice had softened a little, and she sensed the fear in the room. She heard Jack's name and immediately turned up the internal volume of her thoughts. When the judge stopped reading that page the room was in silence, broken only by a strangled sob behind her.

Anna's neck ached. She held the back of her hand to her cheek, then her forehead. It was too hot in here, stuffy. How long had the judge been talking for? Minutes or hours? The air was thick and cloying. She looked around, hoping to see a window. There were none. A tear dropped onto her arm. All she wanted was to breathe some fresh air, some air that had blown in from somewhere far away, somewhere she had never been.

There wouldn't be any windows in prison either.

She shifted in her chair. Her legs burned with agitation; she needed to move them, to walk. She circled her ankles, uncrossed

her legs, then crossed them the other way. She closed her eyes.
The judge's voice had slipped into the background now, and Anna
could hear the whoosh of her blood as it pulsed around her head.
It sounded like the wind, or maybe a shell held up to her ear. And
she could hear other things too.

She could hear the slap of her thongs hitting the path; the roar
and hiss of waves breaking; seagulls screeching. She could feel the
cold ocean spray misting over her, and smell tangy saline and sour
rotting seaweed. Sharp stones stabbing the soles of her feet; the
chill of soaked slippery rocks. Jack crying. Then silence.

Anna gasped, or maybe she screamed. The judge stared at her;
the court was silent. She forced herself to breathe. Her face burned,
and her chin began to tremble. She gripped onto the arms of her
chair. Everyone was looking at her; she couldn't get away. A glass of
water appeared in front of her and she gulped it down, grateful for
something to focus on. The memories were fading now, receding
like the tide, further and further away.

CHAPTER THIRTY-NINE

That day

Monday, 14 September 2009

She had been lying still, awake, long before the alarm clock shrieked through the room. She heard Tony sigh. She tried to slow her breathing, but surely he knew she was awake? She wanted him to pull her into the warm hollow of his shoulder and tell her she would be all right, but he didn't. His hand brushed her back; she flinched. She felt him hesitate, and her heart quickened, but then he took his hand away again. He sighed and kissed the back of her head. She stayed silent, still.

She listened as Tony crept out of the room and closed the door behind him. She heard him turn on the radio. She could hear people whispering in the corner, but when she looked, there was no one there. Were they outside? The patio doors squeaked, and Jessie's dog biscuits rattled as Tony poured them into her bowl. Someone laughed; a cruel, cold sound. She pulled the blanket tighter around her and screwed her eyes shut. She jumped as the door opened. Tony tiptoed into the room and opened the wardrobe. She didn't move. He walked out. Then she heard him talking on the phone.

Anna knew it was time. She sat up, opened her bedside cabinet and took out the envelope. Tony's bag was propped against the wall; she jumped out of bed and put the letter inside, praying he wouldn't find it too soon. He was still talking on the phone. She got back into bed and closed her eyes. Jack cried, but Tony didn't bring him to her.

Later again. Had she fallen asleep? Tony was talking to her. He was sending his mum to babysit her.

She sat up; she couldn't breathe. Didn't he understand? Couldn't he see? 'No! Tell her not to come, please. It's OK, I'm OK!'

Tony stared at her as if she was nothing to him, as if she disgusted him. He wasn't going to listen to her. Everything the voices had been telling her was true.

She said nothing.

She wished she could say goodbye.

*   *   *

Anna heard the bells on the front door jingle as it closed, then waited until Tony's car had driven away. She didn't have much time before Ursula got here; she needed to hurry. Tears stabbed her eyes; she let them fall. She breathed deeply, slowly got out of bed, and went to the door of Jack's room. From the doorway she watched him sleep for a minute, then turned around and walked into the bathroom. She closed the door, turned the shower on and stepped in. When she looked up the water slapped her face. She turned up the hot tap and stood there until her skin burned.

Turning off the water, she stepped unsteadily onto the cold, damp towel on the floor. The heat from the scorching shower quickly disappeared as the water dripped off her. She breathed in the humid air, wiped the condensation off the mirror, and stared at herself. She lifted one thin arm up towards her tired neck and held it there. Her damp hair clung to her face as the water dripped over her craggy collarbone. The hairs on her arm stood on end as her skin cooled.

Anna moved her head until the ugly crack in the corner of the mirror appeared over her forehead and distorted the outline of her face. She moved so it was over her eyes, her lips, her chin, then settled it back on her brow. Like a fracture: cracked and broken.

She looked into her own eyes. They were more tired than she remembered, the sleepless nights written in the lines around them. She closed them and breathed in slowly, then opened them quickly and watched the dark pupils instantly constrict. The light that they once gave out had vanished; they looked back at her flatly, like something dead. She barely recognised the image that the mirror threw back at her. When she frowned, she saw her mother's face. She would never know what facets of herself had been bestowed by her father.

Turning her back on her reflection, she looked down at the crumpled towel under her feet, soaked now. She reached for another from the rail on the back of the door and wrapped it around her. It smelled musty.

She opened the door to the hallway. The house was quiet. She found her dressing-gown in the laundry basket, took it out and put it back on. She walked through to the living room and collapsed on the couch. Closing her eyes, she wished she could fall asleep again. She couldn't hear the whispers any more. But she knew they were there, waiting. There wasn't much time.

She sat up with a faint smile and her strained shoulders slackened. She went back into the bedroom and dressed for the first time in days. She found a belt. She combed her hair and tied it back. She made the bed, then went back into the bathroom, picked the wet towel up off the floor and hung it on the rail.

In the kitchen, she read the instructions on the tin of formula and made up four bottles with boiling water. She put them in the fridge, then quickly tidied the dishes away and switched on the dishwasher. She walked quietly into Jack's room. He was awake, but silent. She didn't look at him as she went to his drawer and took out a sleep suit and some clean clothes for the next day. She folded them and stacked them at the end of the change table.

Going to the window, she separated the blinds with her fingers and glanced outside, but there was no sign of Ursula yet. She looked at Jack again, then walked out.

She stood at the front door with her car keys in one hand. She heard Jack whimper. Was she doing the right thing? Her hands began to shake as someone laughed, and her eyes filled with tears. Were they in the house? Would they hurt Jack if she left him here alone until Ursula arrived? She shook her head; they'd follow her. She was the problem, not Jack, and once she was gone, he'd be

safe. Jack whimpered again. Where was Ursula? What if she was
held up, and Jack was here by himself for hours? The thought of
him crying, alone, was unbearable.

Before she could change her mind she ran back to the baby's
room, stuffed some nappies, wipes and clothes in his nappy bag,
and picked him up. Jack folded into her and she covered his head
with kisses. She wanted to have every inch of his warm, soft skin
touching her, to keep him so close to her that he'd be safe. But
there was no way to protect him. She had to stay strong and follow
through; there was no other choice.

She slung the bag over her shoulder and, with Jack in her arms,
went to the front door. This time she didn't hesitate. She opened the
door, stepped outside, and closed it behind her without looking back.

*   *   *

Anna drove slowly. Jack was quiet, strapped into his baby capsule
in the back. She tried to watch the road in front of her, as well as
look out for Ursula's car driving past. Which way would she come?

She was close to Jim and Ursula's place, but hadn't passed her
mother-in-law. She indicated, turned into their street and drove
towards their house. She was too late: Ursula's car was gone. She
stopped the car and let it idle. Her thoughts were all tangled, and
that burning panic started to build up in her stomach again. Her
thoughts were going so fast now, so fast that she couldn't catch
them before they disappeared, and she couldn't work out what to
do. She couldn't leave him here. Should she go back?

Jack made a sound from the back, like a growl. She gripped the
steering wheel to stop her hands shaking. She needed to drive on
before he started crying. If he cried, she didn't know if she could
go through with it. He'd be hungry soon. There wasn't enough
time. She released the handbrake, indicated and drove off again.

She thought it would have taken longer to get there, but the
traffic was all going the other way and she arrived in twenty minutes.
She turned off the main road and followed the track to the small
car park above the beach. There were a couple of other cars there,

but she couldn't see anyone. This was the only place she could think of where she wouldn't risk seeing someone she knew. She could still hear the mumbling, somewhere behind her. She picked up Jack and closed the car door.

She walked down the uneven wooden stairs, holding onto the handrail with one hand and carrying Jack in the other arm. The soft sand at the beginning of the beach seemed to pull her back with every step, but soon she reached the hard, cold sand at the edge of the ocean. She looked out to the horizon: there were people out there surfing. This wouldn't do.

Her breathing was laboured now and she heard herself wheezing as she ran back up the steps to the car park and started to walk quickly along the path to her right. Her entire body was shaking now. She looked straight in front of her. Jack didn't make a sound. The path inclined upwards; she stumbled as her foot slipped on a flat rock covered with powdery sand. Her arms were wrapped tightly around Jack, and even as she fell to her knees she didn't let go of him. They were coming; she had to think of a way to keep him safe. Her knees stung as the gravel scraped her skin, and she cried out. She clutched Jack to her and heard herself scream. He started to wail against her chest. She stayed on her knees and rocked back and forth to try to calm him.

She had to get up. Somehow she struggled to her feet, but Jack was still crying. He was nodding his little head all over her chest looking for her breast. She blinked to try to clear her vision and kept going.

When she had gone far enough she stood at the edge of the cliff and looked down at the heavy waves smashing into the rocks. It was as she remembered it, as wild and beautiful and desolate as when she and Tony had come here, years ago, before they were married, before Jack. Spray exploded upward then crashed down to be sucked back out to sea. Even high up here, the air was wet and salty, and the rocks were slick.

Jack had stopped crying now. So had Anna.

She looked out to the sun and then she stepped forward.

CHAPTER FORTY

Four months after
Friday, 15 January 2010

The court was silent; even the air seemed to have stilled, waiting for the judge's sentence. The stenographer's hands hovered above her typewriter. Anna held her breath, and stared into her lap. She closed her eyes and concentrated on taking oxygen in through her nose, down into her lungs and through her body, then out again, again and again until the judge began to talk. She opened her eyes; he was looking straight at her.

'In summary, I accept the psychiatric evidence that has been submitted to me, which is that at the time of the act you were suffering from a severe psychiatric illness characterised by delusions and hallucinations.'

Anna nodded slightly. She didn't blink.

'As such, you are not to be held responsible for your actions.'

Anna stared at him, not comprehending.

'I will now pass sentence.'

The judge put his papers down on the table. Anna could barely breathe: this was it. The room in front of her was blurred with her tears and she gripped the edges of the dock.

'I do not think that a custodial sentence would serve any purpose here. You will be punished enough by having to live for the rest of your life knowing what has happened to your child. There is no suggestion that you are a danger to the community.' The judge paused and looked around the courtroom. 'Under section nine of the Crimes Act 1999, I am sentencing you to a bond for a period of four years.'

A collective gasp went around the room; silence was replaced with sniffing and crying and rustling and murmuring. Anna had heard the judge but couldn't understand what he'd said. What did it mean, a bond? She turned to Scott: he was grinning, as was Chloe next to him. Anna looked back to the judge.

'Ultimately, this is a tragedy that no one could have foreseen. You and your family have suffered enough.' He took his glasses off and looked at Anna. 'Mrs Patton,' he said. 'I wish you the best for the future, and please do remember what has been said here in this courtroom.'

Anna tried to smile in acknowledgement of his words but felt her face contort. She began to shake and tears streamed down her cheeks. People were standing up now, talking, shaking hands. She heard sobbing and turned around; Emily and Wendy were clutching onto each other, bobbing up and down and crying. Wendy saw her looking and grinned, then blew her kisses. It was so surreal, she didn't know what to do. She looked for Tony; how was he feeling? He wasn't hard to find: he was still seated, with his hands over his face as his shoulders shook. She wanted desperately to go to him, to hold him and cry together, and to find out if he was crying with relief or fury. Anna didn't know if she was allowed to leave the dock; everyone seemed to have forgotten about her. The sobs she'd been holding back started to escape and she slumped forward, holding her head in her hands.

Finally, it was over.

*   *   *

Once the courtroom had been cleared, Scott helped Anna walk towards the exit while Chloe lingered behind, tidying up their paperwork. Anna couldn't stop crying and shaking; she just wanted to collapse and give in to the exhaustion, all that was left now the adrenalin had drained away. She felt like an old woman: every part of her ached and stooped.

'You OK, Anna?' Scott said, putting his arm around her shoulder to support her.

She could only talk in gasps. 'I don't know. Confused. Exhausted.'
She shook her head as another sob bubbled up in her chest.

'I know. It's a lot to take in; you've been through so much. Some
of that stuff was pretty hard to hear.'

Anna nodded. Hard for her to hear? Or for him?

'So do you understand what the judge said?'

'No!' They had reached the exit of the courtroom now. Anna
stopped at the door. Was this what she wanted? To walk out a free
woman instead of being transported to jail as a prisoner? She didn't
think she could take the next step.

Scott stopped too and turned her towards him, putting a hand
on each of her shoulders. 'You've been given a bond for four
years, a good behaviour bond if you like: you have to stay out of
trouble, keep seeing your psychiatrist and do what she recommends.
That's it.'

'No prison?' Anna croaked.

'No prison.' Scott smiled. 'You can start getting your life back
together now.'

She shook her head, staring at the door in front of her. 'You
make it sound so easy.'

'Anna, this is the best outcome we could have hoped for,' Scott
said firmly. 'And it's what *should* have happened. You didn't deserve
to go to jail.'

She nodded slowly, looking away as her mind raced. She had
no idea what to do now. She was terrified.

Scott reached forward to push the door open. Anna grabbed
his arm. 'Wait!'

He paused, then linked his free arm in Anna's. She brushed at
the tears on her cheeks, then nodded slightly, and Scott opened
the door.

The first person she saw was her mum. She let go of Scott and
ran towards her. 'Mum!'

'Anna! Thank God, thank God . . .' Wendy sobbed and clutched
her. Anna felt another pair of arms around her and looked up to
see Emily.

'I knew it, Anna! I knew it'd be OK!'

'I can't believe it,' Anna said through her sobs.

'Do you know what we need? A drink! A big one!' Emily laughed, wiping her eyes.

Anna managed to smile, and for the first time in months she even felt a tiny sliver of hope. Not happiness, but a sense of the possibility of a future.

Wendy took her hand. 'Come on, let's get as far away from here as possible.'

She began to walk with her mum and Emily, then turned around to look at Scott. He was watching them with a smile on his face. Anna dropped her mum's hand and ran back to him. She hugged him. 'Thank you, Scott.'

He shook his head. 'Just doing my job.'

She looked at him for another moment, then spun around and joined Wendy and Emily, and the three of them walked towards the sunlight together.

*   *   *

Ursula shifted her weight from foot to foot just inside the doorway of the court building and watched Anna coming down the corridor. When Ursula had heard the verdict, she too had cried. She was glad it was over, glad for Tony's sake that there was a resolution to it all, but she couldn't help but wish that Anna had received more of a punishment. She didn't want her to be locked up for the rest of her life, but maybe a year or two would have taught her . . . What? Ursula knew that Anna must be hurting, but she thought that the judge was wrong: she *hadn't* suffered enough.

Tony had rushed outside as soon as the court was cleared, in a state. He hadn't even been able to speak. Jim had hurried out after him; now, Ursula and Lisa were waiting anxiously to hear from him. And while Tony was somewhere on the streets of Sydney, distraught, Anna was walking away from the courtroom, smiling and hugging that lawyer that Tony had paid for, then skipping over to Wendy and Emily.

Ursula nudged Lisa. 'Have you seen her?'

'I know, Mum,' Lisa said, looking up from her phone. 'We should go. We can head back to the car and just call Dad. If he's with Tony, they can get a taxi back later. They're probably in the pub.'

'Look at her! She's celebrating, like there's been some kind of victory. It's disgusting. It's like she's forgotten why she's here in the first place.'

'This isn't doing us any good. Let's get out of here,' Lisa pleaded. She tried to steer her mum outside but Ursula shook her off.

'Not yet.'

Anna was walking towards them now, a smile on her face. She hadn't seen them. Ursula stepped forward; Anna couldn't avoid her.

'Mum! Don't —'

'Just wait, Lisa! Anna,' Ursula said loudly, trying to keep her voice steady.

Anna stopped and looked up; her eyes widened. 'Oh, Ursula. I —'

'I suppose I should congratulate you.'

Anna shook her head and tears fell down her cheeks. Emily stepped forward so that she was standing just in front of her; Wendy gripped Anna's hand. But Anna just stood there, visibly trembling, like a tiny trapped animal. Ursula was sick of being made to feel like she was the bad one, being made to feel guilty for admitting that she didn't agree that Anna was a victim. It didn't help when Anna wouldn't argue back; it made Ursula look worse, as if she was a bully. But she wasn't a bully: she just wanted to make Anna understand that what she had done, ill or not, was unforgivable.

*　*　*

Anna stared at Ursula's tight lips and narrowed eyes, and the tiny glimpse of hope she'd felt for a fleeting moment vanished. She didn't have the energy, not today. She glanced at Lisa, hoping she would rescue her, lead Ursula away, but Lisa wouldn't look at her. Anna dropped her head; she wanted to whimper. Ursula had always made her feel inadequate, and now she felt like a small child being put in her place. No, it was more than that: she felt persecuted. She blinked back the tears and clenched her fists. She'd had enough of apologising for herself. She lifted her head and looked Ursula straight in the eye. She thought she saw her flinch.

'Ursula, we both know that there are no congratulations in order today. Is there something you want to say?'

Ursula seemed to inflate and her face contorted. 'Well, yes, I suppose there is. You may have got away with this, but I want you to leave Tony alone. He doesn't need you.'

Anna felt herself shrink back behind Emily, but forced herself to maintain eye contact and not let Ursula see how much she wanted to run away. She stepped in front of her friend, and let go of Wendy's hand. 'I understand how you feel, but that's not your decision. Tony is a grown man; I'm sure he'll make up his own mind.'

Ursula's mouth opened and she moved forward until she was right in front of Anna. Anna flinched, then prepared herself, expecting Ursula to slap her. That was fine; she was ready for it.

But Ursula didn't raise her hand. She leaned forward and Anna could see her dilated pupils and the tension in every muscle of her face. 'After what you did, you expect him to come back to you?' She was practically hissing.

Anna could feel the tension and rage ricocheting between them, but she wasn't going to be the one to lose control, not this time. She knew that Emily – and Wendy – were right beside her. She forced herself to breathe slowly. When she felt calm again, she spoke.

'You know I'd do anything, anything, to change what happened. You must know that.' She cleared her throat, hoping she could finish what she needed to say before her nerves overwhelmed her. Ursula looked as if she was going to choke. 'I don't expect you to forgive me, but I was ill, Ursula. I didn't know what I was doing.' Anna was amazed that she hadn't broken down yet.

Ursula was biting her lip. Her face was red. As Anna kept looking at her, Ursula looked away, then started to cry. Anna's eyes filled with tears too and she wanted to tell Ursula that she understood, that the hatred Ursula felt towards her was the same way she had been feeling towards herself this whole time. She took a step towards her and put a hand on her shoulder. 'I'm sorry.'

Ursula clasped her hand over her mouth, then shook her head and turned away. Lisa looked at Anna, but Anna couldn't tell whether she was trying to apologise for Ursula's behaviour or say goodbye. Lisa put her arm around Ursula's shoulder and they walked out onto the street.

Wendy hugged Anna. 'Well done, darling.'

She began to shake and her shoulders slumped, but she stayed standing. And when she was sure Ursula had gone, she walked out of the court onto the street on a normal Friday afternoon in Sydney.

CHAPTER FORTY-ONE

Four months after
Friday, 15 January 2010

After Anna had picked at her fish and chips and stared at the television for a polite length of time, she yawned loudly and stretched her arms above her head. The day had left her completely ragged; every joint, muscle, bone ached with fatigue. But it wasn't the judge's words that kept replaying in her mind; it was Ursula's.

She got up. 'Mum, thanks for today, and, you know, for everything.'

'You don't need to thank me.'

'Yes I do.' Anna went over to Wendy, hugged her and said goodnight.

In her bedroom, she changed into a pair of pyjamas, turned out the light and got into bed. This morning, she had expected that she'd be in a prison bunk by now, but instead she was free. She started to shake. Could she be trusted? What if they were wrong to say she was better, that she wasn't a danger to anyone?

As the minutes and hours passed, she heard her mum turn off the television, put the plates and cups in the dishwasher, then brush her teeth and go to bed. Anna had hoped that the silence would make it easier to sleep, but it only amplified her thoughts. Not so long ago, she would have done anything for a full night's sleep, but now she'd give anything to hear Jack cry for her. She wanted him to scream and she wanted to go to him and cuddle him until he was calm, and see his little face feeding from her breast and gazing at her with his half-closed eyes. She could hear him now, if she listened hard enough. His cries got louder. She pulled back the blanket and got out of bed, then made her way out into the hallway. She walked down to Jack's room, and opened the door.

In the dark, Anna could just make out the silhouette of the cot on her left, with the mobile above it swirling in the draught from the door. The change table was still against the wall on her right, along with the rocking chair with its bright blue and red cushions; the small chest of drawers was in front of her, under the window. The curtains were closed, but harsh yellow light from the streetlight squeezed through the gap between them and seared a sharp line across the room. She didn't turn on the lamp that sat on top of the drawers. Instead, she closed the door softly behind her and sat with her back against it, allowing her eyes to get used to the dimness.

She remembered a line she'd read once at university: *In every nursery there are ghosts.* Now that her eyes had adjusted to the gloom, she looked around the room. Was Jack still here? Could the faint movement of the mobile be caused by his breath? That small tickle on her bare foot – was it his touch? But as much as she willed Jack to come to her, she knew that he wouldn't. There were no ghosts here. Just a small room, the barest and emptiest room she'd ever seen.

She slowly stood up, braver now, and touched the wooden frame of the cot. The mattress was bare, with the flannelette sheets and blanket clean and neatly folded at one end. She leaned over the frame and inhaled. Nothing – only washing powder. She moved to the window and opened the top drawer of the chest. Some tiny blue bodysuits, and miniature socks, also blue. They were all folded neatly, but not in the way she folded them. Who had done this? She tried the bottom drawer – muslin wraps, spare blankets, towels, all folded up wrongly too. Quicker now, she touched everything in the room, searching for him. Her eyes blurred with tears as she looked under the drawers, then under the cot for something that might have fallen unnoticed, something that hadn't been washed clean of memories. But there was nothing. He was gone.

The grief hit her hard, punched her and kicked her and held her down. Her whole body was under attack, and she lay there on the floor and surrendered to it, with no strength left to fight it. It felt as though her bones were breaking, not just her heart.

Anna had no idea how long she lay there, sobbing quietly for her son. At some point she heaved herself up onto all fours. Her head pounded, her eyes smarted, her chest burned. With one last effort, she held onto the cot and pulled herself up, first to her knees, and then onto her feet, and clambered over the rail. She curled herself up like the first ultrasound pictures of Jack and rested her head on the soft fleecy blankets. With her knees up against her chest, her head bowed, she fitted perfectly within the small space. She closed her eyes, and she dreamed.

*   *   *

When she woke, Wendy opened the blinds of the spare room and was surprised to see that it was bright outside. She had slept so well; it was one of those nights when she was sure that she had barely moved once she fell asleep. She rubbed at her face and looked at her watch; it was almost 9 a.m. She felt rested for the first time in months. The current of dread that had been drifting around in her belly was gone. Anna was home for good.

She hadn't heard Anna get up, but hoped she'd had a good sleep too; she deserved some rest. She tiptoed past Anna's room and went to the front door to get the paper, then went into the kitchen. She took a bottle of orange juice out of the fridge and poured two glasses. Leaving her own glass on the bench top, she went back down the hall.

Anna's bedroom door was ajar. She inched it open and peered in, then stared in shock. The bed was empty. Wendy's heart pounded. She should never have let her sleep alone; what had she been thinking? After everything Anna had been through yesterday, what if . . . ? But if she'd gone off in the car, Wendy would have woken up, surely? Her hands were shaking, she put the glass down on Anna's chest of drawers before she spilled it, and looked around the room. The bed linen was pulled back, so Anna must have slept in it at some point. Her clothes from yesterday were draped over the chair. Wendy put her hand on the mattress; it was cold.

'No, no, no . . .' she whispered. Her eyes filled with tears. When would this be over?

She ran along the hall to check the bathroom, then the living area, but they were empty. Rushing outside, she saw the car was still in the driveway, so she came back and stood in the hall. She didn't know where else Anna could be. She hesitated outside Jack's door, which was still closed. No one went in there any more. She swallowed, then grabbed the handle and opened the door. Her eyes widened: Anna was curled up in the cot. She didn't know whether to laugh or cry.

'Anna, what are you doing?'

Anna jumped at the sound of her mother's voice and struggled to sit up. She moved her neck slowly as if in pain. 'Mum. I . . .'

Wendy took a step back across the threshold of the door. 'I was worried – your door was open when I got up but you weren't there. I . . . I was looking for you. I'm sorry, I didn't mean to disturb you.'

'No, Mum, it's fine. I couldn't sleep.'

Wendy looked at her, and nodded. Even though her behaviour was bizarre, Anna didn't look unwell. She wanted to call Dr Morgan, but she knew she had to trust Anna; there were no rules for grieving, and she had so much to grieve for.

Anna brushed her hair off her face and smoothed down her pyjama top, then smiled. 'I think I'll go and have a shower now. I'd love a cup of tea if you're making once.'

Wendy didn't smile back. She spoke softly. 'OK, love. I'll make you some tea and toast.' She glanced again at the cot, then turned around, walked out and closed the door behind her.

Wendy hummed loudly in the kitchen while she listened out for Anna. She heard her go into the bathroom and turn on the shower, then go into her bedroom. Wendy put two slices of bread in the toaster and poured hot water into the teapot. As Anna walked in, she was spreading the toast with butter and Vegemite.

'Here you go,' she said, and smiled.

Anna took the plate, then sat on the couch and put her breakfast on the coffee table. She stood up again and unrolled the newspaper from the cling wrap. Wendy opened her mouth to speak – after bringing it in this morning she had forgotten to hide it – but it was too late. She took a deep breath, then got the milk out of the fridge to finish making the tea.

She walked over to Anna with her mug and one of her tablets. Anna held the paper open and stared at a page. As Wendy approached, she quickly closed the paper, folded it in half and threw it on the couch beside her. She turned and took the pill and the tea. Wendy watched while she put it in her mouth and washed it down.

She put her hand on Anna's shoulder. 'You OK, love?'

Anna bit into a piece of toast. 'Yeah.'

'Are you sure? We need to go and see Dr Morgan on Monday anyway; do you want me to check if she'll see you today?'

'No, Mum, I'm fine.'

Wendy sighed.

Anna looked up at her and put her hand on top of Wendy's. 'I promise I'm OK, Mum.'

Wendy wasn't convinced. She sounded OK, she sounded good actually. But the cot . . .

'So, what have you got planned for today, Mum?'

She moved around to sit on the armchair. 'Nothing, love. Did you want to do anything?'

Anna shrugged. 'I don't know. I can't remember what I used to do, before . . . It's different now. I kept thinking that I might, you know, not be here very long. What did I do before?'

'Well, I suppose you used to go to work during the week, and catch up on things on the weekends. Then your day was filled up with looking after . . . the baby.' Wendy's cheeks reddened. 'Sorry . . .'

Anna looked down. 'Mum, it's all right. You can say his name.'

'Sorry, love. I can't seem to say anything that doesn't relate to – doesn't remind me of – Jack.' Wendy forced herself to smile. 'You should just take it easy for a while anyway, you've been through a lot.'

Anna nodded, and gazed out towards the back garden. Wendy waited, but Anna just kept staring.

'Anna?'

'I'm just thinking, Mum, I've got so much to sort out. I don't know what's happening with the house, with work. I don't think the school will want me to teach again.' She blinked hard and Wendy knew she was barely holding back her tears. 'Tony . . .'

Wendy pressed her lips together to stop herself from crying. She gave herself a moment, then took a deep breath and stood up. 'Well, you need to eat. Come on, finish your breakfast.'

Anna nodded and took another bite of her toast. Wendy busied herself in the kitchen. It was the only way she knew how to help right now.

CHAPTER FORTY-TWO

Four months after
Saturday, 16 January 2010

Tony stretched out his arms when he woke, then rotated his wrists until the ache in his neck and shoulders had eased. His throat was raw from crying after the sentencing, but he also had a sense of calm: this nightmare was almost over.

He linked his hands and put them behind his head on the pillow. He wondered if Anna had managed to sleep, and whether she was awake yet. He should have called her yesterday. Lisa had already told him about his mum having a go at her, so he'd spent the evening with Sean, going home only when he knew his parents would be in bed so he wouldn't have to deal with his mum. And then he'd convinced himself it was too late to call her.

He sighed and reached for the glass of water on the floor beside the bed. The house was quiet; his parents must have gone out. He eased himself out of bed, then opened his bedroom door. He called out, but there was no answer. He dressed quickly. There was something he needed to do, and he needed to do it alone.

*　　*　　*

He didn't want to think about where he was driving to, so he just drove. He left the bright suburban streets behind for the shady, winding roads to the cliffs. He could hear the wind rushing to keep up with him, and felt it rocking the car as though it was trying to force its way in and stop him, turn him back. But soon enough, he was there. The car crunched to a stop in the empty dirt car park.

He put his hands in the pockets of his jeans and looked out over the ocean. It was rough out there today; there was no one surfing. The waves below him pounded and clapped, dragging anything they could reach back out to sea with them. He hesitated slightly, then put his head down and took off along the path to his left. He stumbled on the tree roots stretching through the sandy scrub but kept going until he reached the place he was looking for. He stopped, and stood still. This was where they had found her. He looked down the cliff to the craggy outcrop of rocks.

That was where they had found him.

He sat down on a flat rock ledge at the top of the cliff. The cold spray seeped through his jeans. He brought his knees up to his chest and circled them with his arms. What was he going to do now? He had thought – no, hoped – that some sort of catharsis would happen here, that something would release him. But he felt nothing.

He hadn't brought anything with him; he should have some flowers or something. He stretched his legs out and patted his pockets, then took out his wallet and looked through it. He didn't even have a picture of Jack in there. His vision blurred with tears. He should have paid the damn money for the photographer in the maternity ward. Anna had said it was too expensive, and he had thought they'd have all the time in the world to take photos of Jack.

Tony wiped away a tear, then took out an old photo of Anna that he'd kept in his wallet for years. The colours had faded, but it didn't matter. He remembered the light in her eyes as she smiled and laughed. She was so happy then: that was the Anna that he had married.

He tried to imagine what she had been thinking and feeling when she came here four months ago. Yesterday he'd listened to the judge detail every event of that day, and every theory about what had happened, but it was too far removed from the Anna he knew. The facts didn't help him to understand what had really made his Anna so sad, so desperate.

Suddenly, he slammed his fist down on the rock, glad to feel the crunch of pain. He put his head in his hands and clutched his damp hair with his fingers. 'Fuck!' he yelled. 'Fuck!'

What had *he* been thinking? He'd known something wasn't right, but he just kept going to work as though it was all normal, assuming she would cope like she always had, as if work was more important than his wife and baby. And it was too late now. He was too late. He shook his head. What was the point of being here now? He should have been here with Anna and Jack when it mattered; maybe then he could have helped them.

He shivered, despite the sun. His clothes were damp from the saltwater mist that showered over him as the waves broke below. His hands and feet were numb, as was he. The small photo of Anna was still clutched in his hand. He looked at it again, then laid it on the rock next to him. He stood up slowly and walked away, leaving the photograph behind. He didn't believe in God, but he did believe that among the memories that swirled around these ancient cliffs in the ocean winds were those of a tiny baby, and that Jack knew, somehow, that his mother loved him.

CHAPTER FORTY-THREE

Four months after

Saturday, 16 January 2010

Anna put two cups and saucers down next to the teapot and milk jug on the wooden garden table. Emily came out behind her with a lemon madeira slice that she'd bought on the way over, two plates and a knife. She set them down in the shade and they both sat. Anna poured the tea.

The garden was overgrown. Insects buzzed as they flew between the long blades of grass and the pink hydrangea mopheads. It had drizzled overnight but now the summer sun shone and the damp garden glistened. Anna had always kept the garden so neat in the past, but she liked the wildness of it today. Perhaps she'd let it ramble from now on. She found herself thinking of the things she needed to do now that she was back home, and realised that it was the first time in months she'd thought about her future.

'So, did you manage to get any sleep last night?' Emily said, wiping a crumb of sponge from her chin.

Anna shrugged. 'A little.' There was no point worrying Emily by telling her about the night in the nursery.

'Your mum looks a bit more relaxed today.'

'I suppose she is. She won't stop watching me though. The only reason she's gone out now is because you're here to babysit me.' She heard the bitter tone in her voice and blushed. 'Sorry, I shouldn't have said that.'

'Don't worry – you're right, I've got my orders not to let you out of my sight.'

Anna looked at her best friend and raised her eyebrows. Of course she couldn't blame her mum for being worried. She'd put her through so much. 'I know it's horrible, but I wish in some ways she'd go home. A part of me just wants to be on my own now. I need to be a grown-up again.'

'There's plenty of time, Anna. It was only yesterday you were in court!'

'I know.' She shouldn't have said anything. It would hurt Wendy so much to hear that she wanted her to leave. 'I just feel like I need to see if I can cope on my own. I don't know, maybe it's not that. Maybe it's just guilt that she's had to give up so much to be here all this time. God, when I think of what I've put everyone through . . .' Her cheeks flamed with shame.

'Have you heard from Tony?'

Anna looked down and shook her head. 'Not yet.'

'You will.'

'Do you think I should call him?'

Emily stretched her bare legs out into the sun. 'I don't know. Maybe.'

'I don't know what I'd say to him. What can I say?' Anna looked up at the sky. 'I'm worried that when I see him, I'll just . . . freak out, lose it.'

'But what would be so wrong with that? It'd be a normal reaction. You don't have to pretend to be something you're not.' Emily tilted her head. 'You'll be fine, Anna. You will be able to cope. You've been through probably the worst thing that anyone could ever experience, and it can only get easier.'

Anna smiled through her tears. 'I didn't cope before,' she said in a small voice.

Emily frowned. 'You've got to stop this! You need to stop torturing yourself. You were *ill*. It's no different from someone who gets cancer – you wouldn't blame them for that, would you?'

Anna felt herself tense. 'But what if you're wrong? What if the doctors and the lawyers and the judge were wrong?' She knew then what she was terrified of. 'What if this happens again, Em? What if I do something like this again?' She covered her face with her hands.

She could never have another child. Never.

Emily was silent while Anna cried. She waited until Anna's sobs began to quieten before she spoke again. 'Anna, it wasn't your fault.'

Anna waited a few minutes to compose herself and then she looked at her best friend. She had to believe Emily. She had to stop feeling sorry for herself. How else was she going to move on? 'I just wish I could go back. I'd do anything . . .'

'But you can't. You can't. It's happened.'

Anna's voice was hoarse. 'I know.'

And she did know. She couldn't change what had happened that day. She had to let it go.

*　　*　　*

Once Wendy had returned and Emily had gone home, Anna knew what she had to do. While her mum was unpacking the shopping, Anna looked in the fridge, then the pantry, then the bread bin, knowing she needed an excuse to leave the house without Wendy.

'Mum, I really fancy sushi for lunch. I think I'll just walk round to the Japanese down the road. Do you want some?'

Wendy paused and looked up. 'I'll come —'

'No, it's OK,' Anna said and smiled. 'What would you like?'

'Do you think —'

'It's only round the corner. I'm fine.'

She could see that Wendy was struggling with the idea of letting her go out on her own. She felt a surge of irritation, then guilt. She lowered her voice. 'Sorry, Mum. I'd just like to have a bit of a walk on my own. I promise I'll be fine.'

'OK. Just get me whatever you're having.'

Anna nodded. She saw her mum's pale face and leaned forward to kiss her on the cheek. Then she picked up her bag and walked out.

As soon as she was out of view of the house, she opened her bag and took out her mobile phone. She scrolled through her contacts until she found Tony's name; her finger hovered over it and she paused, tapping her foot. God, what was she going to say? Maybe he wouldn't answer; then she could leave a message. That would be easier. She took a few deep breaths, then quickly touched the screen before she could change her mind.

He answered. 'Hi.'

'Hi. It's me. Anna.' She shook her head. Of course he knew it was her.

'I was going to call you today, sorry,' he said quickly. 'I meant to call you yesterday . . .'

She didn't know whether to believe him or not. She wanted to. *Don't cry, don't cry*, she told herself silently. 'I need to talk to you.' Her voice shook. 'Tony, I'm so sorry. Can I see you? I really need to see you . . .'

His voice shook too. 'Hold on, let me just go outside.'

Anna pictured Ursula hovering in the background, trying to work out who he was on the phone to. Did Tony know about what had happened between her and Ursula at the courthouse? In a way, she hoped he did know, and that he'd be proud of her for standing up for herself. But what if he sided with his mum? What if he agreed with Ursula, and didn't want to see Anna again? She swallowed; her avoiding Tony wouldn't change that. If he didn't want to see her again, it was better to know. It was the only way she could move forward.

His voice returned. 'Sorry. I'm outside now.'

Anna could hear a car driving past and some birds cheeping. 'Are you at home?'

'Yeah. Should we go out for dinner or something, talk properly?'

Dinner? Anna gasped. Dinner was a couple of hours together, more than she'd dared hope that he would give her. She closed her eyes and smiled, wishing she could hug him. She knew he was struggling to keep control of his emotions, and felt such fondness and love for him. 'Yes, yes, it sounds great. When?'

'Tonight? Why don't I pick you up about seven?'

Anna let the tears roll down her face, but tried to keep her voice even so as not to give herself away. 'Great. That sounds great. Yes, I'll see you then.'

She replayed the conversation in her head as she sauntered towards the Japanese restaurant. He had said he was going to call her; he wanted to go for dinner. Could she dare to hope that maybe there was some chance for them after all?

Tonight, she would know for sure.

*   *   *

Anna sat on the couch next to her mum as the six o'clock news started. Wendy was sitting with her legs tucked under her, frowning at the crossword in the paper. The French doors were open to the back garden to let in some air, and the room was filled with the heady scent of jasmine. Anna couldn't concentrate on the news. She had spent the rest of the day trying not to think about tonight. It seemed ironic that after so many imagined conversations with Tony, she now had no idea what she would say to him. But first she had to tell Wendy. She took a deep breath, kept her eyes facing forward, and spoke as casually as she could.

'I'm going out for dinner tonight, Mum.'

Wendy lifted her pen into the air and turned to her, peering over her reading glasses. 'Oh?'

'With Tony.'

Wendy smiled. Anna relaxed a little. She felt like a teenager telling her parents about a first date, hoping for approval. And her mother approved. 'When did you talk to him?'

'I called him earlier, when I went to the shops.'

'Are you OK?'

Anna forced herself to sound nonchalant. 'Yes, fine; it has to happen sooner or later. I need to talk to him properly.' She got up and yawned. 'I suppose I should go and get ready.' Before Wendy could say anything else, she walked out of the room.

After showering, she stood in the steamy bathroom and blow-dried her hair. She opened her make-up bag and put on some foundation and mascara, then added some blusher and just a touch of eyeliner. She looked in the mirror: too obvious. She picked up her phone from the vanity and swore: she was running out of time. The make-up would have to do. She found a hairband under the sink and tied her hair back in a ponytail. That was better. She looked nice but not like she was trying too hard.

She hurried through to her bedroom and put on some jeans and a sheer pink floral blouse that Tony had always liked. Some tan wedges and she was ready. She glanced in the full-length mirror on the back of her door and paused. She looked normal; she looked like herself. If someone didn't know, they'd never guess to look at her.

She went back into the living room to say goodbye. Wendy was outside, pacing around the garden smoking. Anna slid open the glass door. 'I'm off, Mum. Do you want me to order you some takeaway?'

Wendy dropped her cigarette and scrunched her foot on it, then took a step back towards the house. 'No. I can drive you if you want, then you can have a drink. I can get some food on the way back, then pick you up later?'

'No thanks, Mum, Tony's picking me up. I'll wait out the front. There are some delivery menus in the bottom drawer in the kitchen, so order yourself something nice.'

Wendy looked down, and Anna sensed her disappointment. It must be hard for her mother to let her go again, just like when she left home for the first time, off to university in another city, no longer in need of her mother. Now, like then, Anna needed to step away. And now, like then, she was overwhelmed with guilt at leaving her mother alone. But they both needed to learn how to be themselves again. She looked at her phone: almost seven. 'I've got to go, Mum. Thanks. I love you.'

Wendy raised a hand to wave goodbye and blew Anna a kiss. Anna walked through the house to the front door and then closed it behind her.

*   *   *

Tony turned the taps on full to rinse the shaving cream and dark stubble from the sink, then patted his face dry with a hand towel.

Glancing up at himself in the mirror, he could see he'd lost weight. He looked pale too, and his dark eyes were dull. He sighed and hung the towel back on the towel ring.

He knew that this conversation with Anna had to happen. While he knew what he ultimately wanted to say to her, he was scared that when he actually saw her, he'd change his mind. Part of him wanted Anna to convince him that he was making the wrong decision.

Once he had dressed in jeans and a short-sleeved checked shirt, Tony hesitated outside the lounge room. The door was ajar, and he could hear the television. He pushed the door open and leaned around it. Jim and Ursula both looked up.

'I'm off,' he said, hoping they wouldn't ask questions.

'Anywhere nice?' Ursula said, smiling.

Tony took a deep breath; they'd find out anyway. 'Yeah. Just into Bondi for dinner . . . with Anna.'

Ursula's eyes widened and she said nothing. Jim looked at her, then smiled at Tony. 'You OK?'

He nodded and tried to make his voice sound casual. 'Yeah, of course.' He could see that the colour had drained from his mother's face and she was floundering. He felt a pang of tenderness for her. She was trying her best, he knew that, and she was just doing what she thought was right. He let go of the door and walked over to the couch, then crouched down next to her. Seeing that she was trying not to cry, he put his hand on her shoulder. She clasped her hand over his.

'Mum, don't worry. I know what I'm doing.'

Ursula nodded and tried to smile.

'Well, have a good time,' Jim said.

Tony smiled in gratitude at his quiet old dad, with his grey stubble and dirt under his fingernails from a day's gardening. Jim had always trusted Tony to make the right decision – even if it turned out that he'd chosen badly, Jim still trusted him to fix it. He was just the kind of father that Tony hoped he would be one day, if he had another chance.

'I won't be late,' he said softly, and then he stood up again and walked out.

*   *   *

Ursula sat motionless as Tony walked away from her. She listened to the front door open and close, and heard his car engine start up then fade as he drove away. Her bottom lip began to tremble. Jim turned off the television, moved closer to her and put his arm around her. She bowed her head.

'He's gone, Jim.'

'He'll be back.'

She shook her head. 'Tony's gone. He'll go back to her.' She managed to lift her face up to look at her husband. 'We've lost him . . .'

Jim sighed. 'Don't be silly, love.'

'I knew this would happen. Everything I've done in my life has been for my kids, and they just throw it back at me!'

'Don't cry.' Jim squeezed her towards him. 'He's not throwing anything back at you. It's only dinner with Anna. It's something he needs to do – he can't avoid her forever.'

She felt herself crumple up in his arms and her shoulders heaved with sobs. 'I can't help but feel this is all my fault.'

'Oh love, not this again. Don't be silly, it's —'

'Silly?' She shrugged him off and stood up. 'Silly? I didn't see you trying to help! You just sat back and let me make all the hard decisions, and now you blame me —'

He looked up at her. 'I'm not blaming you, Ursula. You're blaming yourself. Come on, sit down.'

She wiped away her tears, furious with herself for getting so upset. She wanted to scream at someone, but she knew it wasn't Jim's fault. Over the last few months she'd focused all her anger on Anna, but maybe the person she held the most vitriol for was herself.

'What am I meant to think? First Lisa's baby, now Tony's. What have I done to deserve this?' She put her hands over her face and sobbed. Jim stood up and embraced her, then drew her down onto the couch again.

'Oh Ursula,' he whispered. 'Lisa was so young – you know we made the right decision. Look at how well she's doing now. Anyway, this has nothing to do with that.'

Ursula could remember that conversation with Lisa as though it had happened only minutes ago. Lisa was only fifteen then; just a child. It was some older boy's baby, of course, some monster who took advantage of a young girl at a party after she'd had a few drinks. Lisa wouldn't tell Ursula who he was, and had begged her not to tell Jim, but she'd had to. It wasn't the kind of decision she could make alone. That day had been terrible. They'd sat here, in this very room, and cried and shouted at each other. Ursula had tried to listen to Lisa, tried to be supportive, but she couldn't show anything but fury. In reality, she had been frightened. Lisa was so naive, thinking she could have the baby then put it up for adoption. She couldn't have hidden the preganacy – what would they tell people? Besides, Ursula knew that once a mother held her newborn in her arms, they were bonded forever. Lisa – at fifteen – couldn't understand the pain and endless longing she would suffer if she didn't keep the baby.

Exhausted, Ursula had gone to church the next day. She lit a candle; she fingered her rosary beads; she prayed. Why had she gone there? She knew its stance on abortion – it was the same as her own. It was wrong. Until it involved your own child. Perhaps she had gone there hoping that something would change her mind. A sign, a message, to renew her faith. But there was nothing in that church that could counter the image of her own child being teased and ostracised and judged. Nothing that could overpower the image of her own child sobbing when she realised that she had to say goodbye to her baby. There was no choice: she couldn't let Lisa ruin her life. She had walked out of the church, and as the heavy door swung closed, left part of herself behind. She called the clinic, made an appointment for the next day, then told Lisa what was going to happen. Lisa screamed and cried, but Ursula stood firm. She knew what was best for her children.

But now, years later, she wasn't so sure she'd made the right decision. She looked up at Jim. 'We shouldn't have done it. It's come back on us, full circle.'

Jim held her until eventually she stopped crying. Then he said, 'Ursula, I love you, and the kids love you. This is not your fault.'

Ursula nodded brokenly. She wished she still believed in God, so she could accept that there was some warped, divine reason for this. But she knew there wasn't. She curled up under Jim's arm. As her breathing settled and her mind calmed, Ursula felt safe for the first time since that morning in September when she had called Tony to say Anna and Jack weren't at home.

Ursula had done her best; she had always done her best to look after her family. It just felt like it wasn't good enough.

CHAPTER FORTY-FOUR

Four months after
Saturday, 16 January 2010

Anna watched Tony's car drive towards the house. When he pulled up she opened the passenger door and got in.

'Have you been waiting long?' he said, without looking at her, as he drove off.

She shook her head. 'No. Just wanted to get away from Mum, though I'm sure she's been watching through the window.'

She saw Tony smile slightly and then they drove for the rest of the five-minute journey in silence. She tried to keep her legs still, though her limbs crawled with anxiety. She clenched and unclenched her hands, then smoothed down imaginary strands of her hair, wishing they could get there faster. As soon as Tony slowed down near an empty parking spot on a side street, she knew he was taking her to the little trattoria nearby. Before they had Jack they used to eat here at least once a week.

Tony reversed into the space, then switched off the engine. He looked at Anna; she wanted to reach over and touch him, but instead unbuckled her seatbelt.

'Do you want to go and get a table?' he said.

'OK, see you in there.' She got out of the car and closed the door. It was just like before: she would go and get a table, and Tony would go to the bottle shop next door and buy a bottle of red. What did he mean by bringing her here? In one way, she was thrilled: perhaps he was telling her that they could recover some of the life they used to have. But she was also incredibly sad as it reminded her what she had lost.

The restaurant was cramped and noisy, and strong smells of garlic and oregano spilled from the kitchen. Anna was shown to a small table near the window; she squeezed past the couple huddled at the next table and sat down. The waitress left a bottle of water; Anna poured two glasses. As she tried not to listen to the couple's conversation, she realised that Tony must have chosen this place for practical, not emotional reasons: it was so public, they would have to be civil to each other, and it prevented them both from talking about the real issues. She stared at the menu, trying to distract herself from the impulse to cry and run out of the restaurant.

When Tony walked in she sat up straighter, waving to him as he looked around for her. He smiled, then made his way over and sat down. He took a bottle of pinot – one of their favourites – out of the brown paper bag and unscrewed it. She pushed the wine glasses towards him and he poured them both a large drink.

She took a sip of her wine, hoping the alcohol would relax her quickly. Tony took a big gulp of his, then topped up his glass and leaned back. She watched him over her glass, wishing that this was just a normal meal out together. She had missed him so much.

He picked up the laminated menu, frowned as he looked at it, then put it down again. 'The usual?' he said.

She nodded, and smiled. 'Sounds good.'

Tony raised his hand to attract the attention of a waitress. Anna wanted to put her hand on his and tell him to slow down. She wanted to spend every minute she could with him, but he seemed intent on getting this over with as quickly as possible. The waitress came over with her notepad, and Tony ordered: one bruschetta, one caprese salad, and one large ham, olive and artichoke pizza. When the waitress left, Anna watched Tony fiddle with his napkin, then his glass.

'I'm glad it's cooled down a bit,' he said.

Oh Tony, she wanted to say, *let's not talk about the weather*. He looked so sad, so lost. She wanted to reach over and grab him and never let him go. He hadn't deserved any of this. Her stomach wrenched with pity and regret.

She tried to keep her voice steady. 'Me too, after such a humid day.'

He nodded, then twirled the wine bottle towards him and started reading the label.

'So, how are you, Tony?' She cringed: her attempt at conversation was no better than his.

'I'm OK,' he said. 'Well, I've been better.'

She nodded, looked down at her place setting, then straightened the napkin.

'How about you?' he asked.

She tried to smile. 'Same, been better . . .'

'Is everything OK with, well, the illness? Your tablets?'

'Yes. I'm "normal" now, apparently. I'm seeing Dr Morgan again on Monday, and I'm still on the antidepressants, of course. I just have to keep seeing her every week and take it as it comes.'

'That's good to hear. I'm glad.'

She looked up at him and frowned. 'Are you? Sometimes I think it would be easier for everyone if I'd stayed crazy, or if they'd locked me up. People could forget I ever existed.' She shook her head and bit her lip at the bitterness in her voice. 'Sorry.' She picked up her wine and took a sip. 'I suppose what I mean is that it would be easier for me to be a coward and be locked away so I could avoid dealing with life.'

'Don't say that, Anna. You'd never survive in prison. That's not where you should be.' His voice quivered; he reached for his wine glass.

Anna blinked a few times, trying not to cry. So he didn't want her jailed; did he forgive her? She spoke quietly. 'Do you hate me, Tony?'

He closed his eyes and didn't answer straightaway. She wished she hadn't asked him: what if it wasn't the answer she hoped for? She was still playing games with him, trying to get him to say what she needed to hear.

'Sorry, forget I said that. I just keep feeling so bloody sorry for myself and I hate myself for it.' She grabbed her glass again and took a gulp of wine.

Tony sighed. 'I did hate you, Anna. Shit, I didn't know how to feel. I still don't. I've gone through every emotion you can imagine, emotions I didn't even know existed. I just couldn't understand how . . .' He looked around him, then spoke quietly. 'I'm still trying to get my head around it. I know, logically, that you were ill, really ill. But I can't help it – when I look at you, I just don't know how you could have done it.' His eyes glistened with tears.

She looked away and dabbed at her own eyes with her napkin. 'I don't know either.' She rubbed her hands over her face then looked up at him. 'All I can say is that I'm so sorry. So sorry.'

Tony shook his head. 'Don't say sorry again.' He looked up at the ceiling. 'I still keep picturing him —'

Anna put her hand up in front of her. 'Don't, please, I don't want to talk about Jack.'

He glared at her. His eyes were dry now, and he looked at her accusingly. Anna's heart pounded as she waited for him to speak. She knew that he was preparing himself for something, and that she needed to let him say it, no matter what it was. This was why she was here. But what he did say shocked her.

'I got your letter.'

Her eyes widened. 'What? What letter?'

He shook his head, eyes narrowed. 'Your letter, the letter you left for me to find.'

'Tony, I —'

'Do you have any idea what that did to me? There I was, assuming that something terrible had happened to you, that someone had raped you or tried to kill you and Jack, and then, just like that, out of my bag falls an envelope with my name on it in your handwriting! I defended you, Anna, trusted you completely. I told them to look for some other explanation: there was no way that my wife, Jack's mother, could have done something like this!'

Acid and thick red wine churned in Anna's stomach and rose up her throat; she felt sick. She didn't know what he was talking about. 'Tony, I don't —'

'Do you want me to show you your suicide note? It's still in the glove box of my car. I had to hide it there so the police didn't arrest you immediately or use it against you. I had to lie to everyone: my family, your family, the police! I told myself that maybe I'd misread it, misunderstood what you meant, that maybe you were just going to leave me, that you didn't intend to actually kill yourself —'

'Please, Tony! I don't know what you mean!' The room spun around her and she wanted to run, but she couldn't move. All she could do was stare at Tony in horror.

He lowered his voice and practically spat his words at her. 'I'll remind you. I know it off by heart – I've read it hundreds, maybe thousands of times. *Tony, I'm sorry to do this to you, but I've got no choice. This is the only way to save you and Jack. He deserves better than me, you both do. I'm sorry, I've got no choice.*' Tony gritted his teeth and Anna could see that his eyes were wet again. As she stared at him, her mind blank, he spoke more gently.

'But you *did* have a choice, Anna. That's what I can't bear.'

She shook her head, unable to take any of this in. Did she write a letter like that? Had she even known what she was doing? *Had* she had a choice?

'At first, I thought maybe the letter meant you were leaving me, leaving us, just going away somewhere, and there'd been an accident. You'd left Jack's clothes, his milk. But then you would have taken your clothes, your phone. You knew you wouldn't need them, didn't you? God, there was less than an hour between me leaving and Mum arriving at the house – how long had you been planning this?'

Anna's mouth was bone dry. 'I don't know,' she rasped.

He pointed his finger at her. His face was red. 'You wanted to top yourself, but why the hell did you have to take the baby? Why the hell didn't you wait for Mum like I told you to, or just leave Jack behind in his cot? Then he'd have been OK.'

His chin shook and he collapsed back in his chair. Anna watched him take deep breaths and wipe his eyes with his trembling hands. She opened her mouth to speak, but had nothing to say. She just shook her head, shocked. Leaning over the table she reached for his hand.

'Don't! Don't you dare!' Tony glared at her, then scraped his chair back and stood up. 'Excuse me.' He walked towards the restaurant toilets.

She reeled back in her chair as if she'd been shot. She had vague images in her mind of scribbling something on a piece of paper and finding an envelope in the kitchen drawer, but the memories were too hazy. Tony wouldn't lie, though; she must have written those things.

The waitress sauntered over to the table and put the bruschetta and two side plates down, politely pretending not to notice Anna's tears. Anna didn't move.

When Tony came back, he picked up a piece of the bread and chewed furiously. Anna made herself take a piece too. They were both silent. She wished that they were having a normal argument about money, infidelity even. She wished she could tell everyone here that none of that mattered, not really. She slumped in her chair. She still didn't know what to do. Any hope that Tony would tell her he forgave her and wanted to come home was gone.

As they continued to eat in silence, she sensed the tension fade. Each of them let the past slip away, replaced by sorrow and regret. Anna ate automatically, and was surprised and sad when she realised that the meal was almost over. Tony insisted that she eat the last piece of pizza, and smiled at her almost apologetically; she could have wept.

'Do you want to go for a walk?' he said.

She nodded. 'Yes, that would be nice.'

'I'll go and pay. Meet you outside.'

*   *   *

Anna and Tony walked along the street until they reached the park. It wasn't quite dark yet, but the floodlights shone on the rugby pitch, where some teenagers were throwing themselves into tackles. They sat on a bench at the edge of the grass, both with their hands in their laps, and watched.

'What are you going to do now?' he asked.

Anna noticed that he had said 'you', not 'we'. She sighed. 'I don't know. Mum's asked me to go back to Western Australia with her, but I don't want to. Maybe I'll go there for a break, but ultimately I want to stay here.'

Tony nodded.

She bit her lip, then glanced at him. 'How about you?'

He didn't return her gaze; he focused on the kids, now sprinting up and down the pitch between cones. 'Well, I'm just doing what I always do. Going to work, that's about all. Had enough of living with Mum, though,' he said, smiling.

Anna paused. She spoke quietly. 'I can move out if you want. Or . . . you could come back home.'

Tony immediately shook his head. 'Sean's offered me his spare room. I think I'll go there for a while.'

Anna's lip started to tremble. She should never have asked him like that; now, she had no hope left. He'd told her where she stood. She nodded, kicked at a tuft of grass at her feet. 'That's a good idea.' She had to ask, even though she didn't really want to hear the answer. 'What about us?'

Tony stretched his neck back to stare at the sky. He ran his fingers through his hair. 'I don't know, Anna.' He was crying now, she realised. 'I miss you . . . but I just can't . . . I just can't be with you.'

'Ever?' she whispered, her heart thumping.

'I don't know. I hope it gets easier . . . with time. But it just hurts me too much. It wouldn't be any good for either of us. I'm sorry.'

Anna nodded slowly. 'It's OK. I knew you'd say that.'

Tony moved his hand across the endless space between them and put it on her knee. 'I'm sorry.'

She longed to grab him and bury her head in his chest, but instead she put her hand on top of his and squeezed tightly. A few moments later, they stood up without saying anything and headed back to the car.

They both had tears in their eyes.

*   *   *

That night, Anna lay alone on her half of the soft king-sized bed. She had never found the gold wristwatch that Tony had given her for their anniversary, and her wedding ring was still loose on her finger. She curled her left hand into a fist and felt the ring slip towards her knuckle. She hadn't noticed if Tony had been wearing his. She had been too afraid to look.

ACKNOWLEDGEMENTS

This book may never have evolved past the earliest drafts without the support of the Queensland Writers Centre/Hachette Australia Manuscript Development Program, which gave me the confidence to think of myself as a writer. Thanks to all at the QWC who took part, in particular Kim Wilkins, who helped to shape this book from the first paragraph.

Thanks also to my agent, Benython Oldfield, and my publisher, Vanessa Radnidge, for believing in *Fractured* from the beginning and encouraging me to keep going with it.

For reading endless early drafts and supporting me the whole way, thanks to David Thornby and Vicky Dawes. For giving me insights into police and court procedures, thanks to Ray Sieber and Laura Spence.

The book would not be what it is today without the entire Hachette team, especially Kate Ballard and her sharp pencil, Roberta Ivers, Clara Finlay, Fiona Hazard, Matt Richell, Marie Isaacson, Anna Hayward and all those behind the scenes.

Thank you most of all to my family near and far, especially those nearest: Will, Isobel, Isla and Olivia.

If you or anyone you know is experiencing emotional difficulties, there are people who can help you. Here are some suggestions:

- Your local GP or health-care professional.
- Lifeline, which provides 24-hour telephone crisis support. Call 13 11 14.
- SANE Australia can advise on how to access assistance in your area. Visit www.sane.org or call 1800 18 SANE (7263).
- beyondblue, the national depression initiative, has an information line. Call 1300 22 4636.
- The Family Crisis Service (*after hours only*) can be accessed on 02 9622 0522 or 02 9622 0313.

If you need urgent help, you can call 000 or visit your local hospital emergency department.

Fractured

DAWN BARKER

READING GROUP NOTES

A READER'S INTRODUCTION
TO THE BOOK

Fractured is the intensely powerful story of a family torn apart by a tragedy that pivots on the events of one day, all the pieces of the jigsaw gradually fitting together as the story builds to its devastating and inevitable conclusion.

ABOUT THE AUTHOR

Dr Dawn Barker (*pictured left*) is a child psychiatrist. She grew up in Scotland, and studied Medicine at Aberdeen University. In 2001 she moved to Australia, completed her psychiatric training and began writing.

Fractured is her first novel, although she has written many non-fiction articles on parenting and psychiatry for websites and magazines. She has also published academic articles on mental health and writing.

Dawn lives in Perth, Western Australia, with her husband and three young children.

www.authordawnbarker.com
Follow Dawn on Twitter: @drdawnbarker

THE BACKGROUND TO
FRACTURED

I had thought about writing *Fractured* for a long time – years in fact. I started it dozens of times, but never got further than a page or two before I declared that I couldn't write and was wasting my time. While working full time as a doctor, I didn't really have the time or emotional space to tackle such a big project. However, when I had my first baby, I found myself at home on maternity leave with only a newborn for company, and I knew that if I was ever going to write a novel, then that was the time. I signed up for an online novel-writing course through Queensland Writers Centre and I wrote 500 words each day while my baby napped until it was finished. After a couple of redrafts, I entered the manuscript into the 2010 Hachette/Queensland Writers Centre Manuscript Development Program and was lucky enough to be chosen to participate. The program gave me invaluable insights into the world of publishing, but more importantly, confidence in myself and the book.

QUESTIONS AND ANSWERS
WITH DAWN BARKER

What inspired you to write this novel? Did you have any particular influences?

In my study and work as a psychiatrist, I had seen many women affected by mental illness in the perinatal period. While I must stress that this book is fiction, and in no way based on any real cases, I had always wondered how a family could ever cope with a tragedy like that dealt with in *Fractured*. I thought that a novel would be the ideal medium in which to explore this, but I worried that it was too confronting a subject, and so never pursued it until I read *We Need To Talk About Kevin* by Lionel Shriver. That was the turning point for me: I realised that you could write about horrific situations sensitively, and that many people do want to read about uncomfortable issues.

Most readers will find the plot of *Fractured* disturbing. Did such a confronting theme make it difficult to write at times?

The idea of this happening to a family had always distressed me, and in some ways writing this novel was a cathartic experience for me. That's not to say it wasn't difficult to write at times, particularly by the end of the book when I felt quite engaged with the characters. I certainly shed a few tears while writing some of the final scenes.

What kind of response do you hope readers will have to *Fractured*?
I hope that readers are engaged with the story and the characters, even
if it's difficult to read at times. Most of all, I hope that it makes people
think and that it promotes awareness of postnatal mental health
issues. While this is a novel, we all know that the central tragedy
in *Fractured* does actually happen to some families, and perhaps by
encouraging discussion it will help a woman to ask for help.

**What research did you do for the book? Does the story draw from
your experience as a clinical psychiatrist?**
Fractured is complete fiction and is not in any way based on any real
clinical cases. However, I have spent many years studying mental
illness and working in psychiatric clinics, so inevitably my experiences as a doctor have influenced my writing. I also don't think
I could have written this if I hadn't had my own children, as my
experiences as a mother of a newborn also shaped the story. I was
lucky enough never to experience mental health problems myself,
but I think that many emotional difficulties in the early weeks after
having a baby are universal.

Because of my own experiences, I didn't have to do much
formal research for the book. I read media stories of real cases,
court transcripts, and I picked the brains of a police officer and a
lawyer to clarify some facts.

**The way in which you move back and forth between narrators and
in time, bringing us ever closer to the events of that fateful day and
then beyond, is a brilliant way of gripping your readers from the very
first page. Was this structure important to you in telling the story?**
The structure of the book was something that I struggled with
initially. In my first draft, I wrote Anna's point of view, then Tony's,
then tried to weave them together. It was still a linear story though,
and it didn't quite work. Over subsequent drafts I started to flit
around in time, adding in other characters' points of view, and it
was then that I knew it would work. I think the structure reflects
the nature of memory after a trauma, where things in the past only

take on relevance in retrospect. As a psychiatrist, I often have to piece together patients' stories to make sense of a situation, and I wanted the reader to be part of this process too. It also mirrored most closely the fragmented mental state of the characters.

Each of your protagonists feels partly culpable for the tragedy at the heart of the story. Did you deliberately try to ensure readers could relate to aspects of each of their personalities?
Initially I tried to think in terms of a protagonist and antagonist in the story, but it quickly became apparent to me that it wasn't realistic and life isn't that black and white. Ultimately I wanted to write about a family – and characters – that we could all relate to, and people are complex with many conflicting emotions. So it wasn't a deliberate decision; the development of each character became almost unconscious.

The feelings of guilt and bewilderment experienced by each member of the Patton family (and Wendy) are inextricably linked to their individual secrets, and forgiveness and understanding necessarily don't come easily for any of them. Was the complex nature of mother–child and sibling relationships something that you consciously chose to explore?
Not consciously, no. But I work with families in crisis and know that a family is a complex system where the actions of one member affect everyone. So, for me, it felt natural to explore the nature of these relationships.

Who are some of your favourite authors?
This is a hard one! I read widely, and make time to read every day. Some of my favourite 'big name' authors– those whose books I would rush out to buy – include Tim Winton, Kate Grenville, Isabel Allende, J.M. Coetzee and Margaret Atwood. But there are so many other wonderful writers whose books I have recently read and loved: David Vann, Chris Womersley, Jon Bauer, Tony Birch . . . It's hard to pick a few!

SUGGESTED POINTS FOR DISCUSSION

1. The structure of the novel – with its flipping back and forth in time and perspective – is key to its success as a gripping tale. What role did the shifting point of view play in your reading experience? To what extent do you feel the narrators' authority as storyteller, and ultimate source of truth for the novel, is undermined by this role being shared by four characters, the reliability of whom is sometimes difficult to establish? How did any such undermining affect your reading of the novel?

2. The complex nature of husband-wife, mother-son, sibling and in-law relationships is explored in some depth alongside the conflicting emotions inspired by immeasurable grief. Discuss the ways in which different characters deal with their emotions.

3. Anna and Wendy share not only their mother-daughter bond, but also experiences with clinical depression. To what extent do you think Anna's denial about her postnatal depression can be attributed to her mother's shame about her own depression during Anna's childhood?

4. It is through the individual stories of the main characters and the complex tangle of emotions inspired in them as they react to the unfolding events in very different ways that we appreciate

postnatal depression's sometimes devastating consequences. In what ways do you think the tragedy impacts differently upon Wendy and Emily from members of Tony's family? Whose life do you think is most affected by it (after Anna and Tony) and how is this shown?

5. Having witnessed first-hand the ease with which Anna's emotional well-being so rapidly descends into crippling hatred and self-doubt, do you feel this book is a sympathetic portrayal of a woman suffering from a debilitating and often misunderstood psychiatric illness and what can happen when it is left untreated? And, if so, to what extent do you think she could be held responsible for the events of that fateful day?

6. Discuss the linked themes of grief, blame and forgiveness, and the parallels that can be drawn between the main characters in their handling of each.

7. There is an almost palpable tension throughout the novel – how do you think the author achieves this and builds upon it?

8. Discuss Ursula's reaction to the central incident. Do you think her response and almost immediate cooling towards her daughter-in-law are justified? How do you think you would react in her situation?

9. Anna's despair and subsequent suicide attempt following the realisation she may be released from the psychiatry ward before the court hearing is utterly shattering. Which other aspects of the novel made you feel uncomfortable and why? Did they lead to a new understanding or awareness of some aspect of your life that you'd not previously considered?

10. Do you think Dr Fraser, Anna's GP, should have been more insistent about contacting Tony herself when she diagnosed

Anna with postnatal depression? Do you think Tony being aware of this diagnosis would have made a difference to Anna's subsequent actions?

a. What is your experience of, and views about, the postnatal care provided by hospitals and child-health clinics?

b. Postnatal depression is far more common than we realise. Do you think it is acknowledged as much as it should be? Is there an unhelpful stigma attached that inhibits women from sharing their experiences?

11. Do you think Tony should bear any of the responsibility for what happens in the novel?

12. A mother's feelings of inadequacy lie at the core of this novel but such feelings are also experienced by Tony, Wendy and Ursula. To what degree do you think they each feel partly responsible for the tragic outcome? What impact do you feel their individual feelings of guilt have on the story?

13. Discuss the self-destructive and almost catastrophic way in which Anna deals with her emotional turmoil and the reasons why she felt so unable to carry on.

14. To what degree do you feel the prospect of freedom following the Supreme Court ruling liberates Anna and enables her to finally address the events of that day? What do you think the future might hold for her?

SUGGESTED FURTHER READING

Still Waters – Camilla Noli
I Came to Say Goodbye – Caroline Overington
We Need to Talk About Kevin – Lionel Shriver